SINFUL

RESURRECTION

CSA Case Files, Book Two

Kennedy Layne

SINFUL RESURRECTION

Copyright © 2013 by Kennedy Layne
Print Edition
ISBN: 978-0-9899739-4-6

Cover art by Sloan Winters

Dedication

To my fellow indie authors—I am thankful for each and every one of you.

Cole...you are the reason I started this journey. Always remember, you can be whatever you want to be. I am so proud to be your mother.

Jeffrey. My husband. You bring me happiness with every smile and touch you bestow on me. I love you.

Prologue

Crest heard the telltale vibration of his phone and remembered that he'd left it on the other nightstand. Reaching carefully over the woman sleeping beside him, his fingers captured the familiar glass rectangle. He settled back on the pillow, grateful that tonight's blonde didn't stir and pressed a button on top of his cell. The screen lit up to reveal an incoming text alert. He didn't need to read it to know that the time had come to initiate a case that he wanted no involvement in, but unfortunately he needed the details. Owing favors was part of the job, but that didn't mean he had to relish the idea.

Easing the sheet off of his body, Crest leaned up on his elbow. It was rare for someone to notice he had to enter eight digits into his phone keypad rather than four. After inputting the correct sequence, he placed his right thumb in the square that appeared in the middle of the screen. On the rare occasion someone did remark, he simply commented that it was a new model.

Crest carefully read the entire message and crafted his succinct reply. He didn't want his words to be misconstrued, so he kept his response as brief as possible. That was something he'd learned as a junior staff noncommissioned officer, when his executive officer would email him another copy of the *Manual for Naval Letter Format.* The damned thing had been so big it filled up his mailbox and prevented him from receiving any other mail. The executive officer's message had always accompanied a voluminous amount of corrections and a not so subtle reference to read the fucking thing. Crest had learned early on that clear, concise messages tended to be terse but effective in conveying what his executive officer wanted to say.

This current situation was going to affect one of his team and he took that to heart, as he knew Jax Christensen would as well. Crest ran through several scenarios as to how he could contain the situation and lessen the damage it would cause, but knew it was an exercise in futility. The past, like the Phoenix, had a way of resurrecting itself.

"Leaving?"

Crest had just sat up, his feet touching the cold hardwood floor of the bedroom when she'd spoken. He held back a sigh, wishing he'd been able to find his clothes and leave before she had awakened. They'd enjoyed a few cocktails and indulged in one of his favorite proclivities, which was displayed nicely on her slightly flushed curved bottom. Both knew that this would go no further.

"Yes, I've got to head out," Crest replied softly as he reached down for his black gabardine dress pants.

After exchanging light conversation over drinks, she'd invited him back to her place. She lived in an upscale apartment building within the city of Minneapolis. It hadn't been closer than his penthouse downtown, but it did give him the luxury of leaving when the time came. It had crossed his mind when he'd accepted her invitation that she looked nothing like

Jessie, but he'd quickly discarded that thought. Jessie was nothing more than his personal assistant—very young personal assistant—and he would do well to remember that. He banished her image from his thoughts once more. There was enough moonlight streaming in the window to afford him a view of the other articles of clothing that were strewn on the floor. His shirt lay on top of her dress.

"What time is it?"

Gavin shot a quick look over his shoulder at the green neon display of the clock sitting on her bedside table. If he remembered correctly, she'd mentioned that she was an attending physician and was working a twelve-hour shift at the hospital emergency room starting at seven in the morning.

"It's only four, so you have a while before you need to get up," Crest said as he finished getting dressed. The last two pieces of clothing he picked up were his Armani suit jacket and his Galco holster rig, which he swung over his shoulder before turning to face her. "I enjoyed last night."

"As did I." They hadn't exchanged more than first names as there was no need and he was relieved to see that only gratitude and fondness shone in her green eyes. She had turned slightly, making no pretense of covering herself with the sheet. There was no need. She was a beautiful woman and she knew it, although she didn't need to use it to her advantage. "Feel free to stop by anytime."

"I'll keep that in mind," Crest replied, a small smile of appreciation on his lips.

With a nod of gratitude, he turned and walked out of her bedroom. The small lamp near the couch lit a path to the door. He made his way down to the parking garage and bypassed the attendant to where his car waited in the guest parking slot, adjacent to one of the building security posts. He heard last night's game being rebroadcast on the radio from within and didn't fail to notice the attentive pair of eyes that tracked him to his vehicle.

Crest was thankful that spring was arriving, but that didn't take away the hint of chill in the night air that stole its way into his clothes and clung to his skin at the precise moment. The icy wind outside would be brutal. Old habits died hard, so Crest took in his surroundings as he walked across the cold cement. It didn't surprise him to see Schultz Jessalyn leaning up against his vehicle.

"I thought you might make an appearance," Crest said, coming to a stop in front of his old friend. Schultz was currently a Special Assistant to the National Security Advisor to the President of the United States. He was far away from home, but the mission that he wanted Crest and his team to take was not. He had to wonder how far this friendship extended. "I guess it's futile to ask how you located me. My GPS *is* encrypted."

Schultz laughed and extended his arm. They shook hands and then Crest used the opportunity of silence to shrug into his shoulder holster and suit coat. He continued to scan the area, knowing full well that Schultz would never arrive here on his own. The question was how many agents were now in the immediate area.

"Don't worry," Schultz said with a smile, "they're around."

"I wouldn't want you to scratch your knee on my watch, Schultzy," Crest replied, using his friend's old nickname. "The President and his cronies might take issue with that. Speaking of protection, where's the witness?"

"Safe," Schultz replied, the condensation of his one word drifting in the air and then disappearing. He gave no outward appearance that the cold affected him in any way. "We'll make the transfer in five hours. Your team checks out, but I am still concerned about Jax Christensen. Do you think he'll be a problem?"

"What about your witness?"

"No. She only agreed to protection if it was under your firm and that of Mr. Christensen"

"Then you have your answer," Crest said, crossing his arms and shifting his stance. "Who will be accompanying you?"

"It will just be me and the witness." Schultz looked around, as if assuring himself that he had enough protection even though Crest knew of his background and was confident he could take on an opponent or two without additional support. Lifting one side of his long black dress coat, Schultz pulled out a manila folder. "This is everything we deemed necessary for your need to know with regards to her protection. The Attorney General is in the process of verifying the evidence that our witness provided."

Crest took the folder but didn't glance at it. He'd take his time before their nine o'clock morning meeting to ensure he had all of the facts pertaining to this mission. There was one thing that bothered him about the scenario that Schultz was presenting.

"You mean this folder contains what I'm cleared to know, not necessarily the truth." Crest had made sure upon retirement that he kept certain clearances active. It had only helped his firm. The government contracts that his business was allotted paid him and his team a handsome salary. The assignment that Schultz was giving him superseded most clearances due to the involvement of the United Nations. "How do you know her?"

"I'm not sure I know what you're talking about," Schultz replied with a tilt of his head.

"Don't bullshit me, Schultzy." Crest held up the folder. "You told me that she has evidence that Grigori Alekseev, the United Nation's Secretary-General, has his finger in the sale of WMDs to mid-eastern countries. You also revealed that the former Secretary-General was murdered, leaving pertinent facts out. I'm assuming they're tied together, but your information is scarce. How is it that she knew she could go to you, let alone trust you?"

"Because I'm that kind of guy?" Schultz asked, raising an eyebrow. With a small salute, he stepped away from the car. "Review the file and have your men triple check the location you'll be transporting our witness to. And as I stated previously, trust no one that you wouldn't trust with your life."

Crest despised that gut feeling he got when things were about to become some half-assed cluster fuck. He was feeling it now and didn't like being kept in the dark. His 'need to know' for compartmentalized information required advancing a notch or two and he knew just the person to make that happen. Unfortunately, Crest didn't hold all the power here and had no choice but to see this assignment through. As much as he would like to prevent it, Jax was about to come face to face with his past.

Chapter One

J ax poured himself a steaming hot cup of coffee, leaving it
black just the way he liked it. Doing the same for Kevin
who looked like hell after a long night on the streets, Jax
shoved the pot back onto the burner. Picking up the beverages,
he made his way back to their cubicles and placed Kevin's
battered ceramic Vikings mug next to his keyboard.

"Any luck finding the bastard?" Jax asked as he continued
to walk to his desk on the other side of the partition. The
question regarding Kevin's case was more out of courtesy than
anything. He didn't feel up to chitchat this morning and
wanted to avert Kevin from asking about Connor. Jax was sick
and tired of being reminded of how happy the new couple was,
regardless of the fact that he'd had a helping hand in bringing
the two together. "Your perp has raped two victims, right?"

Kevin was one of the six member team who worked for
Crest Security Agency. It used to be five before the new guy
showed up. Jax still wasn't too sure of him, but then again, he
was suspicious of any newcomer. Lach Evans was too quiet,
although he more than proved himself by putting it all on the
line during their last big case.

Each colleague had been hand picked by Gavin Crest himself. Military backgrounds were a prerequisite, along with whatever-the-hell special trait Crest saw in each of them. Jax didn't really care as long as he was kept busy, it was legal, and money was deposited in his account every week. Their cases ran from simple divorce investigations to complex international government contracts. He was thankful he was about to catch a flight to Kandahar for an extradition case, needing the time away. Kevin's chair squeaked as he leaned back with an audible sigh. Hopefully that wasn't a sign that this conversation would drag on.

"Yeah, two," Kevin replied. "I think he's going to escalate though. Call it a gut feeling. This guy is truly a fucking scumbag. I have Taryn running similar patterns through the computer in hopes that maybe we can finally get a trace on this perp. He started out with rape, but the second victim suffered from severe physical injuries. If he's just beginning it'll be like finding a needle in a haystack, but something is telling me that he's working his way up to murder."

Jax took a drink of his coffee and then set it down beside the folder he wanted to review one more time before leaving the country. He'd done the socializing bit, but now it was time to get to work. Thankfully Taryn joined in on the conversation, adding her opinion on the case and letting him off the hook to partake in any further words. If Jax tilted back in his chair, he'd be able to see the fiery blonde at her computer workstation. Hell, it was more like a console for NASA, multiple screens and all that jazz. She was Crest's resident IT guru, the only member their boss didn't scrimp on when it came to the latest computer technology.

"Have you heard from the lovebirds?" Taryn asked over the clicking of her keyboard keys.

Fuck. Jax took off his favorite skullcap and ran a hand through his messed up hair. Connor Ortega, the man who always had his back and claimed the title of best mate, had taken the love of his life, Lauren Bailey, to meet Connor's father in Jersey. Jax wished them nothing but happiness, but knowing they had what he could not was like a dagger to his side. Why everyone had to keep bringing it up was beyond him.

"I told him I'd cut off his nuts if he so much as called me or the office," Jax replied, knowing he had to answer. Taryn could be a pit bull when she sank her teeth into a juicy steak. For some reason Connor's love life had her attention or maybe it was because he was the first one in the office to fall victim to a serious relationship. It wouldn't surprise any of them if an engagement announcement was on the horizon. He needed to change the course of this conversation or he'd be here forever. "Is Crest in yet? I haven't seen him or Jessie."

"Jessie had a dentist appointment," Ethan answered, coming around the corner. The youngest member of the team, not counting Jessie, came bearing donuts. The unspoken rule was that if you were going to be late, arrive with donuts in hand or there would be hell to pay. He set the box down on Connor's desk, which was situated behind Jax as they shared a cubicle. Jax finally conceded the last hour he had wasn't going to be spent going over his assignment. He'd have to do it on the plane. "I don't know about Crest."

"I saw Crest come out of his office about thirty minutes ago to grab some coffee," Taryn said. She pushed up her black-rimmed glasses as she walked around Ethan and opened the box. Her blonde spikey hair fit her buoyant personality. "He's here, although I saw Lach leaving around an hour ago. Ethan, I can't believe you didn't get my butternut cream-filled donut with chopped nuts. What's going on in that head of yours?"

"Stop whining, squid," Ethan said, shoving a white bag in front of her. The nickname had Jax cracking a smile, as squid was in reference to her Navy background. She was the only one on the team whom Crest had recruited from that particular service. "Or next time you'll do without."

"Like that'll happen." Kevin shoved his way into the small square space. He snatched up a jelly donut, not bothering with a napkin. He waved it toward Ethan. "Squid's got you wrapped around one of her tiny tentacles."

"Fuck you," Taryn replied, laughing. She squeezed around Ethan, who was still standing in the doorway, and made her way back to her cubicle. "Ethan knows who's got his back at the base."

"That would be me," Kevin mumbled around the food in his mouth. "I can count three times where I've saved his ass on a mission."

Jax waited for his space to clear before getting up and walking towards Crest's office. He really did love his team members, but there were times when he liked his space. Now was one of those stints and he looked forward to going on assignment out of the country. Glancing down at his watch, he saw that it was a little after ten-thirty in the morning. His flight was at one o'clock, so he'd check in with Crest and then hit the road.

Feeling his cell phone vibrate in the front pocket of his jeans, Jax removed it to see that it was Elle. She was his new manager over at Masters, a club that he and Connor had bought at a reasonable price when its previous owner had gone to jail for running a prostitution ring. He'd taken over the reins early on, Connor being more of a silent partner.

"Elle, everything okay?"

"Just wanted to check in with you before you left for your trip."

Elle was a tall, long-legged, raven-haired beauty who deserved a break from a past that no woman should ever have had to experience. Unfortunately her attractiveness had been the anchor that kept her in the trenches of the streets, as the crime element wouldn't allow her a way out. It was Kevin who gave her this opportunity and she'd grabbed it with both hands. Jax had just gone along with it.

"Not much to say," Jax replied, stepping into the conference room that was located on his left. "You can reach Connor if anything goes wrong, but we hired you since we're busy here at the agency. You're in charge."

"Just the way I like it," Elle quipped, then gave a light laugh. She kept her cards close to her chest, not revealing much about what she was truly thinking or feeling. It had quite a few of them worried, Kevin more so since he seemed to have taken a vested interest in her. Jax noticed that she didn't seem to appreciate Kevin's attention. "Have a safe trip."

"Will do."

Jax disconnected the call and shoved his phone back in his front pocket. Stepping back into the hallway, he walked a few steps down the hall. Everyone knew that if Crest's door was shut he was not to be disturbed. Seeing as it was cracked, Jax didn't hesitate to swing the heavy wood access open.

That familiar fragrance was like a hammer blow to his soul, instantly taking him back two years ago. Images of *her* face appeared as if no time had passed, but Jax was well aware that he was in the present. It was only upon looking in front of him did he see a woman standing before Crest's desk.

"Jax—"

Crest's voice faded as Jax's chest tightened and he struggled to draw air. It felt as if he were right back in New York City, the place where she'd been gunned down in a convenience store robbery. One week was all they'd had before she'd been taken from him and he'd lived in hell ever since. Seven days had changed his life forever, but held him back from actually living.

Her hair was different but the shape of her figure, the scent of her perfume, and the angle of her stance told him all he needed to know. Emily Weiss was alive, well, and standing in front of him. It didn't take him but a few seconds to process everything.

"Get out." Jax ordered everyone else out of the room. His hearing was finally finding its way back and he wanted the office cleared for what was about to take place. It didn't take a fucking genius to figure out that she'd returned to the land of the living. But he deserved to know why. "Now."

He'd cataloged three people in the room. Crest was behind his desk, Emily was standing in front of him, and one other person was to his right. Jax didn't give the man a second glance. He didn't give a shit who the tight ass suit was. He only cared about the woman standing in front of him. Emily slowly turned and faced him, her blue eyes filled with regret and something else he couldn't name. Whatever it was couldn't hold a candle to the rage that was simmering in his veins. He changed his mind. There was no reason fucking good enough for what she'd put him through, only to turn up two years later as if nothing had happened.

"Jax, you need to listen to me," Crest said, coming into his line of vision.

Jax turned and within seconds had Crest shoved up against the wall with his forearm against his boss's throat. He was breathing hard, waiting for an excuse to be able to physically take out his frustration on another human being. Finally clearing the haze from his eyes, it dawned on him that Crest had known all along who Emily was and what her connection was to Jax. What else did Crest know? He pulled his arm back, with every intention of getting retribution.

"Jax, please don't."

Emily's voice cut through the miasma that had surrounded him. He was trained better and knew that the slightest hesitation gave the other person the advantage, but it was too late. Before Jax could blink Crest brought up his hands, breaking the hold. Jax found himself up against the wall, Crest in total control.

"I'm going to release you and you're going to listen, because Emily's life depends on it." Crest's voice never wavered, instead remaining calm and cool like his demeanor. That caused Jax to feel even more rage, but he bottled it quickly, knowing Crest had the upper hand at the moment. Jax relaxed his muscles, leaning his weight on the wall. He could play this game with the best of them. Crest continued to speak. "I know this looks bad, Jax, but she had good reason for what she did."

"Just like you had good reason to keep it from me?" Jax asked, unable to keep all of his fury contained. He remained as still as Crest, relaxed in his hold, and waited until the man took a step back. Jax wiped the back of his hand over his mouth, unable to believe this was really happening. Disloyalty was something he couldn't tolerate. He thought Crest held the same morals, but apparently not. "Nothing will ever make that right, Top."

Jax had purposefully used the nickname that grunts used in reference to Master Sergeants in the Marines. He wanted—no, needed—to drill into Crest what an intimate betrayal this was.

He personally had never called Gavin Crest by the nickname that Connor seemed to use like a minion did to a god. He understood his friend's need to be grateful to Crest for giving them a chance to live their lives as a normal civilian, but Jax felt like he'd repaid his debt tenfold. He did his job and he did it well. No one could ask for more.

Connor had repeatedly said that Jax had changed on their last combat tour. Emily's absence from his life had done that to him and made him realize what a person went through when people were ripped away. Switching his gaze to the woman he would have laid his life down for made him understand that her death would have been easier to accept. Her perfidy and deceit was just too much.

"Jax, I didn't know until a month ago," Crest explained. He took another step back, as if unsure how Jax would react, before slowly moving to stand in front of his desk. He loosened his tie and then made sure his cuff links were still in place. Jax couldn't bring himself to look Emily in the eye and instead concentrated on Crest. She disgusted him and the only way he was going to get through this was if he listened to what Crest had to say and then left for his flight out of the country. He wanted to be anywhere but here. Crest motioned to the other man. "This is Schultz Jessalyn, Special Assistant to the National Security Advisor."

Jax ignored the man who still stood on the other side of the room. There was no need for introductions, regardless of this man's position. He could be the fucking Pope and Jax wouldn't have cared. Not wanting to appear anything else but bored with this conversation, Jax stepped forward and crossed his arms. The faster he dealt with this the sooner he could leave.

"I have a flight to catch," Jax said, keeping his tone even. He thought about quitting, handing in his resignation right here and now, but the assignment that would take him around the world and away from the duplicity that was filling up this room sounded even better. "Don't worry, Crest. I'll do my job."

"Jessie is on her way in," Crest said, as if Jax hadn't spoken. His dark green eyes zeroed in on Jax. "She's going to change your flight information over to Lach. He's taking the overseas assignment. I need you here. Emily needs you here."

Jax ground his teeth together to prevent himself from saying they could all go fuck themselves, but something held him back. Even though it felt like he was roasting his entire body over excruciatingly hot flames, he forced himself to really look at Emily. She'd dyed her dark brown hair to a light blonde, although she had left the length that he used to love to play with and still dreamed about. She was slightly thinner than he remembered, but he could find no sympathy that she might have stressed over the choices that she'd made. Her athletic build was still there, although slightly less obvious. There were shadows underneath her blue eyes and her skin had taken on a pale pallor, yet still he could feel their enduring connection. A mental barrier shifted into place, blocking out any emotion that may have lingered. Emily had no idea the hell she was putting him through but he immediately had closure that he hadn't before. She was deader to him now more than ever. That switch was thrown.

"She made her choice." Jax turned on the heel of his boot and walked to the door. He changed his mind on quitting. "You'll have my resignation on your desk by the end of the day."

Chapter Two

"**D**on't you fucking walk out that door, Jax Christensen."

Emily was exhausted, disgusted, and downright fed-up with life. Worse, the man she loved more than anything was walking out without hearing the reason she'd returned to the land of the living. He needed to understand that it was for her protection, as well as his, and that of thousands of innocent people. She'd done what her country had asked of her, only to end up being targeted for murder. Jax had been everything to her—still was really, and there was no way in hell she was allowing him to leave her to fend for herself. She'd protected him for two years, not that he knew that. Now it was his turn to protect her.

His lean, muscular body stopped in midstride. His shoulders were tense. As he stood stock still, she was sure he was questioning if he'd heard her right. The last time they were together, Jax had given her an interesting introduction to the lifestyle in which he'd indulged. What she remembered distinctly was that although she might have surrendered her mind and body to him in the bedroom, day-to-day reality was something entirely different. She was about to remind him of that.

"Gentlemen, would you please excuse us for a moment?"

"Emily—" Schultz started to try to reason with her, but she cut him off with a look. She'd called him a gentleman to keep things formal, but if she had to use the personal knowledge she was privy to in order to get her way, she would. He was also well aware of that. "Fine. We'll be out in the hallway. Just to point out, you've been out in the open for far too long. They need to get you to a safe house immediately."

"I'm aware of that," Emily replied, her attention back on Jax. He needed a haircut, although he still looked as handsome as when she'd first set eyes on him. The long sleeved black turtleneck didn't cover up the contour of his upper body and the jeans only emphasized his thick legs and tight ass. She wasn't dead yet and she needed his help to keep her that way. "I need to speak with Jax privately first though. Please."

Jax was still far enough away from the door that the two men could easily slip past him, although Mr. Crest paused long enough to murmur something to Jax. Emily didn't catch the words, but whatever was said didn't appear to affect Jax at all. Once the door clicked shut, it seemed to bottle up the tension until she was afraid the air would combust. Her hands started to perspire and she ran her palms down the sides of her jeans. She'd asked for this moment, but she wasn't prepared for it.

"Jax—"

"There is nothing you can say to me that will make what you did right," Jax said in a low voice, not bothering to turn around.

Emily would have felt better had he yelled and screamed at her. She wanted him to face her and relieve himself of all the anger and hurt he felt, not shut down and walk away. A slight twinge of panic swept over her at knowing this was her one and only shot at making him understand. She mentally tried to put everything into words and nothing she came up with was good enough. All at once, she realized what an epic failure this could be.

"Maybe not," Emily replied, trying to explain things anyway. It wasn't in her to give up. "But I still chose to protect you. I would do it again."

Jax took a step toward the door and terror shot through her that she'd never see him again. She instinctively moved forward as if she could physically stop him, but brought herself up short. Emily knew she had to start talking, hoping against hope that he'd stay until she told her story, although there was a slight issue with the fact that the office was probably bugged. Schultz covered his own ass and he had the means to do it. Jax had to know that, too, and she prayed he would take her lead and read between the lines.

"I worked for the United Nations in their administration offices. You know that. I was nothing more than a paper-pusher. The day before you were to fly out for your last combat tour, we were supposed to spend it together. Remember?" When his head turned a little more, Emily knew he was following along. "I stopped by the offices first to finish up some paperwork. I came across something that I shouldn't have seen. When I put two and two together, I wasn't sure who I should go to."

"Really?" Jax asked, his tone mocking. At least her words had gotten a reaction. He didn't turn his body, but did shift his head to the side. His chiseled jaw seemed set in stone. "And what would that be?"

"You're going to find out soon enough, but I found evidence that the Secretary-General, Grigori Alekseev, was selling

WMDs to other countries," Emily said, rushing her words together, although grateful that he was taking her hint. She had no doubt they were being listened to by Schultz's men. "By the time I had figured out what the papers were in my hand, two men had appeared at my desk that I had never seen before. I knew if they were able to get me away from the grounds, my life would be over. So I started talking to another administrative assistant and told her I needed help in the ladies room. One near miss after another and I was barely able to get out of the building without being followed. That's when I called Schultz."

Emily realized her mistake a little too late and closed her eyes, berating herself. She chalked it up to exhaustion. There were things that he couldn't know for his own safety. Schultz had made that perfectly clear. She couldn't change the course this incident had taken. When she raised her lashes, Jax had turned around to face her. The brown flecks of his hazel eyes seemed to shine brightly in knowledge that she wasn't being as truthful as she let on.

"A lowly administrative assistant has someone that high up in government on speed dial?" Jax took a step closer, his hands fisted at his side. He studied her in a manner similar to how he studied her during their first chance meeting. It was disconcerting. "It seems to me that you knew exactly who you would turn to. Which part of this fucking charade do you expect me to buy?"

"He's my cousin, Jax," Emily said, the lie now coming more easily to her. After being on the run, she'd become accustomed to being deceitful in order to stay alive. "Why do you think he's taken such a vested interest in me? I wasn't sure how high up the chain this information went and was cautious about telling him but I knew I didn't have a choice. Within hours, he'd instructed me on how to set up a scenario where they thought I had died. It was the only way."

"The only way?" Jax stared at her as if she were a stranger. Emily felt the two halves of her heart being wrenched apart, but swore to mend what she'd damaged. "You stood back, letting your *cousin* help you stage your death, with no regard to how it would affect me. And now, after all this time, you're standing here without even an apology falling from those beautiful fucking lips that I once kissed?"

"Would you accept an apology?" Emily asked, already knowing what his answer would be.

"Fuck no." Jax closed the distance between them with one step. Emily stopped breathing, waiting for his touch. She would give anything to have him hold her and tell her everything was going to be all right. "You've sat back for two years, knowing I thought you were dead and not giving a damn. You can rot in hell, Emily Weiss."

Jax made it out of the office and down the hallway before Crest stood in his way, holding up a folder. Shouldering past him, Jax made his way to his cubicle not bothering to look at Taryn, Kevin, and Ethan. Lach had chosen that moment to appear and none too soon. Jax snatched the packet of information that was on his desk regarding the overseas assignment and shoved it against the man's chest.

"Here's your new assignment." Jax released the file, not caring if Lach had a hold of it, and then turned for his jacket and skullcap. The rest was just shit that could be boxed up and thrown out. "Crest, I'm sure you'll take a verbal resignation."

"No. I won't. You're not going anywhere," Crest replied, putting a finger into the knot of his already loosened tie and pulled some more. He seemed to be setting in for a long conversation that Jax wanted no part of. He held up the folder in the other hand. "I can guarantee you this—if you walk out that door, Emily will refuse our protection. You are the only one she trusts besides Schultz. If you bail on her, I have no doubt in my mind that the people after her will succeed in their task of eliminating her after an extended period of interrogation to determine their exposure. I understand how hard this is for you, but do you want her actual torture and death on your conscience?"

It took every ounce of strength he possessed not to destroy everything in sight, including the man speaking. Crest had no concept of the hell Jax had gone through or the agony that he was in now. It felt as if the air was compressing his chest to the point of suffocation and the anguish coursing through his veins seared his heart until he wanted to scream. In the end, he just threw his head back and laughed. So this was what insanity felt like.

"Good morning," Jessie called out, unaware that she was walking into the pits of hell. Crest's personal assistant smiled brightly, revealing her newly cleaned and obviously whitened teeth. The longhaired brunette with vibrant green eyes came to stand next to Lach, although she paused long enough to give her boss a onceover. Crest didn't notice and if he did, ignored it. She handed Lach a piece of paper. "This is your boarding pass. At last check, the plane is scheduled to leave on time. Um, did I interrupt something?"

"No," Jax said, knowing that Crest was right about one thing. He couldn't live with himself if something happened to Emily when he could have prevented it, but he was damn sure going to be the one to walk away when this was over. She didn't get to have that pleasure twice. Turning so that his back was to them, he closed his eyes to try and maintain some semblance of composure. He threw his jacket and skullcap back down on his chair. "Crest, you get your way for now. Let's go over this in the conference room."

Jax left his desk, ignoring the curious and concerned stares from his teammates. He stopped at only one desk and that was Taryn's. She would be able to access what he needed.

"I want everything you can find on Emily Weiss," Jax murmured. He'd leaned down and spoke close to her ear, making certain that no one overheard their conversation. "From the moment she was born to the minute she walked into our offices this morning, I want each minute of her life chronologically categorized. The file I'm about to be given by her benefactors will be overly brief and to *their* point. I also need this to stay off the grid. So work your magic."

"Got it," Taryn replied softly.

Jax knew that he was asking Taryn a lot by trying to keep her cyber fingerprints away from the people involved on such a federal level. But after his morning, he didn't trust anyone. Hell, since the moment of Emily's *death*, he hadn't had a lot of faith in humanity in general. He had no doubt that Taryn could get her hands on the information he needed. He did have to extend a little trust her way in that regard. Wasn't that a bitch?

He walked down the hallway and veered into the conference room. A glance at Crest's office showed the door closed and he knew that Jessalyn and Emily were still cooped up. They could stew in there, because he wasn't taking this case until he'd been properly briefed.

"Close the door," Crest said from his position across the heavy oak table. He had yet to take a seat. "It's important you know that I wasn't aware of any of this until four weeks ago. And I wasn't about to give one of my team members hope over something as tenuous as this unless I had verified the information myself."

"Just give me the folder."

Jax didn't want to waste words or time. What did Crest want? Admiration for the way he'd handled things? They both knew that nothing would ever make what happened acceptable. At the end of this case, Jax would walk.

"I'll give you a verbal SITREP first," Crest replied, not backing down. His words also indicating that the file contained nothing more than what Schultz Jessalyn wanted them to know. Jax wasn't surprised. He walked around the table to the small metal stand in the back. Someone had made coffee in the conference room and left it on the burner. He had no idea how long it'd been sitting here, but he didn't give a shit. He needed to keep busy while Crest gave the situation report. "I'll take a cup while you're at it."

Jax didn't reply, he just poured two Styrofoam cups full of the dark sludge. Ethan had made the coffee; of that there was no doubt. The man could burn water. Since he'd arrived late in the office this morning that meant this shit had been sitting overnight. Once the pot was back in place, he turned and placed Crest's cup on the table. Let him come and get it, Jax thought. He wasn't wasting the effort handing it to him.

"Facts first. Emily Weiss was an administrative assistant at the United Nations. She came across evidence that the Secretary-General, Grigori Alekseev, was dabbling in WMDs. It's also come to my attention that the *former* Secretary-General was murdered. The two are obviously related and I'm assuming that whatever evidence Emily found connects the two. Both she and Schultz are being vague in relation to that information."

"I'm aware of Amato Bianchi having died, but assassinated? Do we know how?" Jax walked to the far wall and looked out the window that faced the train tracks located in the warehouse district. He knew the former Secretary-General by name due to a previous mission. He'd been a good man.

"Neurotoxin. From the information I've been given, the General Assembly kept that information under wraps from the public. Why cause a panic? They ended up keeping the investigation internal and turned it over to the Security Council." Crest paused to take a drink of his coffee. Jax could see him wince in the reflection of the window as he swallowed the bitter muck. "As for Emily, she managed to get the evidence she had on Alekseev's weapons distribution out of the building and contact Schultz. Her death was staged and concealed for two years. They are trying to build a case with the evidence she'd discovered."

"So she's been working with Schultz for two years?" Jax asked, wording his question carefully.

"From my understanding, the Attorney General's office actually. It's taken this long to verify the information. Now it's just a matter of gathering the Security Council to hear the evidence."

"Why come out of hiding?"

"Someone discovered she didn't perish in that convenience store robbery." Crest threw the folder down on the table. "Schultz wanted to move Emily once again, but she refused. Emily wants you to protect her—and only you. It was convenient that I'm in debt to Schultz over something that happened long ago. He got two for one. Schultz wants her safeguarded until the hearing takes place."

"If the two are connected, one would assume that Grigori Alekseev murdered the man he replaced." Something was not quite setting right with the story being told. He turned to face Crest. "For power?"

"I'm not privy to that information," Crest replied, placing his coffee cup on the table. "From observing Schultz and piecing together the information he's giving us, I would agree with you. I don't have that kind of clearance and Schultz hasn't shared with me the information that Emily has in her possession."

"Bullshit." Jax stared at Crest until the man shrugged. "You have clearance."

"Not for this, but I'm working on it." Crest slipped his hands in his pockets in his usual manner. "I want answers just as badly as you do. Despite the loathing I see in your eyes and whatever disgusting thoughts you're thinking of me, you know that I have your best interests in mind. This team is my family…and that includes you."

Jax looked away and finally turned back toward the window. He hadn't expected Crest to stoop to the family speech. His boss knew all too well that Jax's parents had died in an automobile accident right after his entrance into boot camp. Connor had become his brother and Jax would have followed that man anywhere, even into this madness that Crest termed a *family*. But there was only so much a man could take and since Connor was off with the love of his life, maybe it wouldn't be so bad to find himself a new place to belong.

"What evidence did she find?" Jax asked, disregarding Crest's attempt at making this intimate brotherhood connection. He also didn't buy for a minute that Crest wasn't privy to what evidence Emily had in her possession.

"Classified," Crest said, reiterating his stance and not backing down.

"I find it hard to believe that a man like Jessalyn would let his *cousin* dictate to him how he should go about protecting a witness with regards to national security, especially one that is family." Jax shifted and then closed the distance to the table. Picking up the folder, he leafed through the pages. It was all formality, with nothing substantial although there was a picture of Emily when she'd had her natural hair color. It shifted something inside of him, but he quickly put it back in place. "All right. Those are the facts that Jessalyn wants us to know...what Emily wants us to know. What's the truth and what's your plan?"

"As I said, I'm still working on the first part," Crest replied, running his hand through his hair. "Look, everything I know will be on the table for you to see. Emily wanted you to protect her, but I also owe Schultz a favor from my time in the service. He called on that when I tried to dig further into this, asking that I trust him."

"Do you?" Jax asked, keeping a hold of the folder.

He would take the file with him and read it later. Although the information was superficial, it would still provide the holes he needed in order to question Emily later. Now that he'd given himself some time, his thought process was turning just a little. Jax would still walk away when this was over, but he deserved to know what made her choose to run instead of allowing him to protect her like he was about to do. What had changed her mind?

"I'd like to think I can trust him," Crest replied vaguely, not truly answering the question but giving Jax the response he needed. He reluctantly admitted that maybe they were more alike than he originally thought. "His intentions are good, but my responsibility is to my team. I have a few calls into some old contacts and I'm in the process of verifying information myself. The team is at your disposal, as usual."

"Jessalyn is just going to hand her over?" Jax asked, raising an eyebrow. He found that unlikely. "Two years of building a case against the illegal sale of WMDs, with a possible link to an assassination, and they're giving us carte blanche with their witness? He's as close to the President's National Security Advisor as one could get, for fuck's sake. This makes absolutely no sense."

"Agreed. Which is why Lach is not going on that government contract. As of two hours ago, I've put things in motion to have the entire team surrounding you every second of the day while Schultz and his secret service teams think that you are on your own. Let's face it. I'm sure once Emily gave your name to Schultz, his men have tagged everything you own with listening and GPS devices."

"Which means since you're talking so openly, you've already had the office scanned," Jax said, nodding his head in approval.

"Of course," Crest replied, shrugging his shoulders. "It's done routinely, but this is the only time that we've actually discovered anything. Not as many as I would have anticipated though. I suspect there might be some additional burst transmitters we won't find without specialized detection equipment. For now, assume they have tagged everything electronic you own, as well as voice and video in your house and car. I tend to stay away from cases such as these, but I didn't have a choice on this one."

"So not only will we be surrounded by CSA," Jax said, tactics and strategies running through his mind, "but the Secret Service will know our every move. Kind of making protection a moot point, don't you think? I don't understand why Schultz would bring us in at this juncture, regardless of Emily's demands. He can protect Emily better than we can. Which means they need to have a scapegoat for when she's eliminated. They'll be held harmless while we get the blame."

"Normally, I would agree with you." Crest averted his eyes to the window. "But I refuse to believe that Schultz would do that unless I'm given evidence to the contrary."

"Then you feel Jessalyn has lost control of this and really does want her protected," Jax said, wondering if maybe Emily hadn't lied about the family relation, but quickly banished that thought.

If Schultz Jessalyn were her cousin, she would have let that slip two years ago. Emily had folded her arms when she said it and he knew from before that it was her tell when it came to being untruthful. Maybe if Jax had been able to see her that *fatal* afternoon, he would have known something was wrong, but he wasn't going to play the *what-if* game.

"Yes, but he also wants to keep his fingers in the pie."

Jax nodded, accepting the opinion in good faith. He could never fault Crest on doing his job. He was the best there was in his field, especially after hand picking the team, which is why the government still used them for specific contracts. If he was right, then Jax had no doubt Crest had a handle on this situation and was using every resource at his disposal to ensure the safety of their witness as well as the team. Jax had to wonder exactly what information Crest would turn up. There were some things that weren't meant to be found.

"Have you set up a safe house?" Jax asked, ready to get this thing in motion. The sooner this was over, the sooner he'd have his life back. Maybe now that he had closure, he could finally move on. "Or are we hopping?"

"Safe house. I have several we can use for this, however, I think it would be best to remain in one location unless forced to move. See Taryn for the information. First, I'm escorting Schultz down to the lobby while Jessie and Emily exchange clothes. They seem to have the same body structure and I think we can pull off a switch with whoever might be watching. You'll be using Jessie as a decoy later this evening."

"If Jessalyn is keeping tabs on this, as you say, he'll have feeds into the security cameras in the garage," Jax said, trying to think of every scenario and blockade they might run into. "And along every route of the highway."

"Taryn is taking care of that as we speak." Crest walked around the table and then stopped before opening the door. "Jax, emotion has to be set aside for this if we are to keep Emily Weiss from being assassinated. Don't let anger and old wounds get in the way of doing your job."

"I'll always do my duty, Crest," Jax said, staying where he was. He needed a minute alone before his life was dragged through the gutter once again. "But know that this doesn't change anything. Once this mission is said and done, you'll have my resignation on your desk."

Chapter Three

"This isn't going to work," Emily said for the third time in the last ten minutes.

She and Jessie had exchanged clothes, but instead of leaving the office, lunch and dinner had been ordered in and they'd kept her secluded in the conference room. By the time dusk had fallen, Emily was antsy. She knew the longer they waited to transfer her to a safe house, the riskier the relocation became.

Finally the CSA team members put a plan into motion. Now Emily was being shuffled down the hallway to where the elevators were located. She glanced up at the security camera in the corner.

"Jax, are you listening to me? There are things that I haven't told you yet that affect how this is going to play out. Schultz isn't going to just allow you to hide me somewhere without his knowledge, regardless of how he's making this look."

"When I want your opinion, I'll ask for it."

Emily grit her teeth at the disgust that lay underneath his tone. She knew he was furious and hurt. She also understood that it would take time for him to come to terms with why she had to do what she did, but that didn't mean his rejection hadn't stung.

Jax and a man named Ethan had exchanged jackets, although what seemed to cause a bit of angst was the skullcap Ethan had finagled out of Jax's fist. It was now safely fitted over Ethan's dark brown hair. The tallest of the three men was walking ahead of them and Emily recalled that he had a Scottish name, Lach. Flanking her from behind was Kevin, who seemed to have taken Jax's lead in hostility. Every time she looked over her shoulder, he was staring at her with gray eyes that cut like a laser.

"When we hit the garage, keep your head low and your eyes downcast." Jax stopped behind Lach as the button for the elevator was pressed. "It's not underground, so there will be access for anyone wanting to take a shot at you. There will be three SUVs lined up in a row and waiting on the third floor, facing outward. You are to immediately enter the one on the left, using the back door on the right side to keep you protected from the open area. Do as I say and we'll get you to the safe house alive."

"Don't I always?" Emily said, unable to keep the sarcastic barb to herself.

The others would have no clue what she was talking about, but Jax would. And the more she could remind him of their past, the better she stood in gaining his forgiveness. She'd done what she did to protect him. What could she say to get him to understand that? Her reference to following his orders in the bedroom didn't fall short, as she saw his shoulders tighten even more. She would have thought that impossible, considering the tension radiating off of his body.

Kevin coughed behind her and when Ethan's head whipped around, Emily felt her face flush slightly as she was fairly convinced now that they did know what she was talking about. Fortunately, the doors to the elevator swooshed open and the men shuffled the women in first, with the exception of Lach. He veered off to the metal access door to the stairs. Her embarrassment eased as disbelief took hold once more. They really thought they could out maneuver the Secret Service. It was almost laughable, had it not been her life on the line.

"I have a better idea," Emily stated, trying to get Jax to see reason. He was standing in front of her and she found herself wishing he wasn't wearing a jacket so that she could find comfort in his heat. Two years was a long time to be running in fear. If she could just insinuate a little bit of sanity into this ludicrous strategy, maybe she'd get the chance to be in his arms again. "Schultz—"

"Emily, you asked for me." Jax hadn't bothered to turn around as he spoke. "Feel free to call *your cousin* and tell him you want another agency to protect you. If not, then let me do my job."

Emily could feel her blood start to boil. Yes, she had wanted Jax...had always wanted Jax, but that didn't negate the fact that she had a right to voice her opinion. She was starting to realize she might have overestimated his relief that she was back in his life. Yes, Emily had seen that particular emotion within those hazel eyes of his, but anger had wiped it out almost instantaneously. Her fatigued and anticipative heart had hoped for a much more memorable and treasured reunion than what reality had given her. Emily had forgotten how stubborn Jax could be, but the faded memories were starting to return in waves.

"Doors are about to open. Jessie, follow Ethan's lead." Jax reached into his jacket and pulled out his weapon. The doors slid open and everyone filed out. Sure enough, three large black SUVs were situated not six feet from them. "Back door, Emily."

She quickly did as instructed and within seconds was ensconced in the back of the vehicle. Sure enough, dusk had fallen and the only lighting afforded to her was that of the artificial rays coming from the ceiling in the garage. Jax took the front passenger seat, while Kevin opened the door to the driver's side and buckled in. Emily looked to her right and saw that the middle SUV remained still as their vehicle and that of Jessie's, with Ethan driving, pulled out. She wondered why the third vehicle, but decided now wasn't the time to ask.

"I'll keep an eye on Elle while you're dealing with this." Kevin drove the vehicle smoothly down the ramp. "I don't like how she still keeps herself involved with the girls on the street."

"She's a grown a woman."

"No offense, but so is the woman sitting in the back seat of this vehicle, but that didn't stop her from getting her ass in trouble." Kevin looked both ways as he pulled out in traffic. "Do you want me to call Connor?"

"Yes," Jax replied, ignoring the barb about her. Emily bristled but chose to remain quiet. It wasn't as if she'd asked for this to happen to her. She tilted her head so she could see what Jax was doing. He was paying close attention to the side mirror of the passenger door. She turned in her seat, seeing Ethan and Jessie going in the opposite direction. Jax's voice had her turning back around. "I'm going to need him."

"Sounds like you have other plans than what's on Crest's agenda," Kevin said, although somewhat nonchalantly. "Anything you want to share?"

"Nope," Jax responded. "I just want you to follow through with my instructions."

That was the end of the conversation, although the tension in the vehicle had reached high levels. Something was about to take place and Emily knew she'd have to go along with it. She'd been flushed out and placed back in danger. She had no doubt that Jax would go to the ends of the earth to keep her alive. Unfortunately, when he found out the whole truth, Emily wasn't so sure she could continue to count on that. Where had Lach gone with the third SUV? Ten minutes later, they were on the highway.

"I'm not trying to tell you boys how to do your job," Emily said, looking up through the window at the streetlights that had security cameras imbedded inside of them, "but I'm relatively sure the highway isn't the best way to travel right now."

"Did she just call us boys?" Kevin asked, finally a little humor lightening his voice.

"This is it," Jax said in a short tone, ignoring both of their comments. "Emily, do not get out until I open your door."

Emily's eyes met Kevin's in the rearview mirror and she knew her face showed her confusion. Jax had something planned. Was Kevin in on it?

Seeing as it was just her, without any belongings, following Jax's orders wouldn't be hard. Schultz was to see that she got her clothes at a later date, although she had no doubt there would be GPS devices inside the bags. She also knew that Crest, Jax, and the rest of the team would be well aware of that as well.

The SUV drove under the bridge at the same time another pulled out. Kevin slammed on the brakes and shut off the headlights. Somehow, Lach had beaten them to the punch and was now taking their position. Emily had noticed earlier that all three license plates were the same and fully understood why, although she wasn't sure this tactic would work. How did they plan on leaving this position without being detected? They didn't seem too concerned about the surveillance cameras watching their every move.

"As I said, contact Connor. He'll know how to reach me," Jax said to Kevin before opening his door and getting out of the vehicle. Quickly he ushered her out of the vehicle and then led her up the steep incline of the abutment, situating her between a crawlspace of the girder. Much to her surprise, two backpacks awaited them. "Emily, put the lighter pack on your back. We'll be walking out of here in sixty seconds."

Emily did as instructed, watching as Jax maneuvered back down the incline to speak with Kevin once more. It looked like he was going against Crest's original proposal to take her to a designated safe house. Whatever was being said, he'd waited until now, when she was out of earshot. Not liking being kept in the dark, she knew that right now she didn't have a choice. Sure enough, Jax had returned under the minute he'd given her and swung his pack over a shoulder.

"We're on our own. Follow my lead and stay close."

✧ ✧ ✧ ✧

Jax followed the walk up to the small porch, Emily trailing behind him. They'd finally made it to a location that was a couple hours north of the city. Far enough away to establish safety yet close enough to keep tabs on the situation. Crest had to have figured out by now that he'd taken Emily and run. The team was in the clear, as Crest had specifically told them to follow Jax's lead. They'd followed orders as directed. The problem at the moment was that he was on his own.

After leaving the overpass, Jax had guided Emily along a secondary road until they came upon a vehicle that one of Kevin's informants had stashed for him earlier in the day. He drove aimlessly until he felt it was safe enough to stop and check the vehicle for trackers. Satisfied that Kevin's man had done his job, Jax finally drove Emily to a safe house that only he and Connor knew about. He'd deal with the fallout from Crest at some point, but it was the only way he knew to keep Emily alive.

Jax didn't like working this kind of operation without Connor. He felt exposed without his partner and friend, but knew at the moment this was the best option. Connor would know how to touch base when he entered the picture. Looking around the area for holes in the security, Jax was pleased to see that the cameras covered every square inch of the property. It would have to do.

Emily had remained quiet since they'd set out on their own, for which he was grateful. Jax hadn't been ready to deal with her alone, especially while he was concentrating on his job to keep her safe. Now that they had arrived at their destination the gloves were about to come off, but he felt ready for the fight ahead. He waited until they were safely established inside to have his say, although not giving her a chance to get acquainted with the small house.

"What the hell do you think you're doing?" Jax growled, spinning on his heel as he tossed his bag on the floor. She had yet to even drop her backpack. "The reason I helped you stage your death in the first place was for you to have a life. Do you have any idea the fucking hell I went through to give you that?"

"I had no choice, Jax! I—"

"Bullshit," Jax barked, taking a step closer to her. "I gave you the ability to have a choice. You had a new name, a new start and money to keep you that way. Now I find out that you went to a government official? Do you want to get yourself killed?"

"Jax, I know who murdered Amato Bianchi. It was never just about Alekseev selling WMDs." Emily's bag slid to the floor and she leaned herself up against the dim yellow wall in the foyer. "It took me a while to put the pieces together, but when I realized who executed Bianchi's murder, I couldn't—"

"You *had* a fucking choice, Emily," Jax yelled, needing to get that through her head. He ran a hand through his hair in frustration and then shrugged out of Ethan's black coat, tossing it onto his bag. "You could have called me when you changed your mind about hiding. I gave you specific instructions on how to reach me should you ever run into trouble. Instead, you go and get yourself into the middle of some goddamned bureaucratic shit storm that—"

"I needed to protect you," Emily exclaimed, her hands closing into fists. "You'd already risked your life by helping me disappear."

"Protect me?" Jax couldn't believe what she was spouting. He spun and took a few steps away from her, needing to keep his distance before he did something stupid. He wanted to touch her, hold her...fuck her until she understood how hard it had been for him to walk away without her. He turned back to face her. "Do you realize what I just did? I went against the man who gave me a life after you. I obviously didn't realize it at the time, or I wouldn't have helped you like I did. I guarantee you that Crest knew I would take the steps that I did, but it's still a betrayal to him and my team. You didn't protect me,

Emily. You've just stripped me of everything that kept me sane for the last two years."

"Please, Jax," Emily whispered, her plea cutting into his heart as if she'd just slit it with a fresh razorblade, "please, just hold me. That's all want."

Jax's anger, fear, and desperation seemed to dissipate into thin air upon hearing the same old longings in her voice. He tilted his head back and looked at the ceiling, delaying the inevitable. He knew he would do as she asked, but was very conscious of the consequences.

"What have you done to my life, Emily?"

Jax couldn't resist her any longer and slowly closed the distance between them, grabbing her close. He buried his face into her hair, unable to believe that he really held her in his embrace at long last. Her arms wrapped around his waist as her fingers clung to him. If Emily thought he could ever let her go now, after being given this second chance, she was dead wrong. He had to believe she had a good reason for blowing her cover wide open. The toll of having been away from her turned to one of desperation. He needed to salvage what was left in the most basic animalistic way and deal with the consequences later.

Pulling away, he framed her heart-shaped face with his hands and looked into her blue eyes that were filled with regret and something else that he couldn't attach a name to. It would come to him later, but right now, his gut twisted at how much time they'd wasted. If Jax had known all along that she would throw herself to the wolves like this, he wouldn't have made the decisions he had. This time would be different.

"Kiss me, please," Emily whispered, leaving her pink lips parted.

Jax couldn't ignore her pleading, although any other time his dominant tendencies would have reared its head. As it was, he needed this as much as she did right now. Discarding the preliminaries, he claimed her lips with a hunger that hadn't diminished in any measurable way. He drank from her well, holding her firmly so that he could have his fill. It was as if he was a man wandering the desert, searching to quench a thirst which had no end. She gave him unlimited access. It wasn't nearly enough to call it even a drop.

He dragged his lips away from hers, sucking in oxygen while reaching between them. Jax managed to shed the borrowed jacket from Emily's body, letting it drop to the floor. He had her jeans unbuttoned and unzipped before spinning her to face the wall. Emily cried out in hunger and placed her hands on the yellow cracked paint for balance as he whipped her jeans and red panties down to her ankles.

"Don't move," Jax murmured, lucky he could get that out.

Before standing, he took this moment to grab onto whatever sanity he had left. Her tanned legs still had the toned muscle mass that always amazed him for one so feminine. Jax let his callused fingers caress her skin up until he reached the curvature of her perfectly shaped ass. Her flesh was so flushed with warmth for it having been so cold out. Leaning in, he placed a soft kiss on the small of her back, promising himself that he would go slow next time around. The heat seamed to sear his lips. He forced himself to pull back. The cleft that was formed just below her heart-shaped ass and before her legs began framed her sex. The thought of tasting her peach once again caused his manhood to grow. His dick was so hard the restrictive denim was starting to cut off his blood flow.

Standing, he reached into his back pocket, snagging his wallet. Jax removed the condom he knew would be there.

Holding the wrapper in his teeth, he released his cock and then quickly went to work covering his granite member with latex.

"Hurry," Emily whispered, looking over her shoulder. "I need you."

"Who do you belong to?" Jax asked as he leaned his body against hers. The guttural tone didn't even sound like him. This is what she'd resorted him to...a ravenous animal. His cock lay in the warmth of her crevice. "Say it."

"You, Sir," Emily cried, pushing back against him with her hips. The fact that she didn't hesitate fueled his need to claim her. "You."

"Fucking right you always have," Jax exclaimed, trying to diminish the desperation that laced his voice.

He wrapped his hands around her waist. Tilting her hips back, Jax claimed her with one thrust. He swore everything went red as the blood rushed through his ears. The heat of her pussy wrapped around his cock. He stayed buried there, not moving, soaking in the sensations that he'd been deprived of for so long. His chest tightened as all of the emotions that he'd bottled up inside of him seemed to explode. Letting out a throaty groan, Jax finally registered that Emily was back in his arms.

For the first time in two years, Emily felt alive. She knew this little scene in the foyer didn't assure her that Jax wouldn't walk away when this was over, but it did give her some slight sliver of hope to hold onto. It was as if her body remembered every nuance of his, from the roughness of his fingers to the heat that registered off of his body. She threw her head back, letting it rest against his shoulder. God, she missed him.

"Do you remember the first time you called me Sir?" Jax asked, his voice raspy as he spoke against her ear. "And how differently you used that title when we ended up in the bedroom?"

A rush of memories overcame Emily while his body filled the depths inside of her. Her pussy was rippling, keeping its grip tight on his cock as if he might pull away. Now that he was seated so deep within her, Jax let his hands roam up the sides of her, following the path of her arms to her hands. Lacing their fingers together, he then leaned down and traced her shoulder with his moist tongue.

Emily remembered Jax in his fatigues, enjoying a beer with Connor Ortega. His best friend had invited her to join them for drinks and at first she'd said no. But then Jax had flashed this smile so intriguing that she found herself seated between the both of them. It didn't take long for Connor to realize that she'd only had eyes for Jax. For seven days and six nights, they'd spent every minute they could together until she'd revealed her secret.

"The way your cream is leaking around my cock, I would say you do," Jax whispered, tightening his fingers on hers.

"Fuck me," Emily said, her voice coming out strangled. "I need you to take me."

"God, I'm going to love training you again."

Emily was grateful she'd taken a deep breath, for Jax didn't slowly pull out. He lunged back and plunged deep within her sheath. And he didn't stop there. Over and over, he pounded into her until that telltale nerve traveling up her inner right thigh alerted her of her impending orgasm. She felt herself floating as she allowed his pacing to send her right to that edge and with one more thrust, she screamed her release. It wasn't long before she recognized that he had joined her in ecstasy.

Jax's words reverberated in her mind though, and Emily found herself wondering if she could stay alive long enough to once again become his submissive in the bedroom. She had found peace there that she hadn't been able to find anywhere else. Unfortunately there were still things he didn't know, but now wasn't the time to disclose that information...at least not all of it. As reality started to creep in that they were in the foyer of a safe house that probably wasn't as safe as he thought, Emily felt the weight of her existence returning to diminish her afterglow. She might as well start with who she really was.

"My real name is Grace," Emily blurted out. She rested her forehead on the wall and winced when Jax's hands fell from hers. "Grace Emily Weisslich."

Chapter Four

J ax monitored the computer screens, which displayed every angle of the land that the house sat upon. The area was vast, although to the east and south the forests were thick with vegetation. The north and west were wide open, giving him a clear view of anyone or anything that might approach from either direction. A few deer had passed by this morning, looking for fresh greens as the grass had started to grow upon spring's return.

"Coffee?"

Jax had known the minute she'd awakened, surprised that she hadn't slept longer. Letting her take one of the bedrooms upstairs, he'd crashed on the couch for multiple reasons. He just wasn't sure which one outweighed the other.

Jax hadn't said a word after she basically threw his reality into a tailspin, although he'd managed to grab a couple hours of fitful sleep. *Grace?* She looked no more like a Grace than he did. Needing time to process the fact that she had indeed lied to him made him take a step back and reevaluate every word they'd exchanged. He didn't like what he was coming up with.

"I'll get it myself, *Grace.*"

"Jax, less than eight hours ago we made love."

They'd fucked, but he wasn't going to argue over the verbiage. A coffee cup filled to the brim appeared before him. Out of the corner of his eye, he saw that she'd piled her blonde hair on top of her head. She'd showered and changed into jeans and a blue sweater that looked a little worn.

"Just because I withheld my full name doesn't change anything. I'm still Emily and that's what I've always gone by."

"We had sex." Jax took the offered mug, still smarting from the betrayal. Until he had a handle on the situation, it was better if he maintained some distance. "It was my mistake to start something that can't be finished. It won't happen again."

Emily sighed as if she were dealing with a petulant child. He resisted the urge to show her different. He needed answers and dragging their personal life into this shit storm wouldn't help. She stepped around him and took a seat in the desk chair.

They were in a room off of the kitchen. The small square area consisted only of a long desk surface with several monitors and one black leather chair. It wasn't meant for comfort. What it did have was a trapdoor escape route leading under the hardwood floor in case of an emergency. The underground path would lead them a quarter mile north to an old shed, which contained a vehicle that he and Connor had specifically placed with the intention of flight.

"I want every detail of every second from the time we first met." Jax paused, tracking movement on the left screen as the software automatically highlighted the frame with a red box. It was a doe looking hesitantly across the open field. Flexing his jaw to relieve the tension in his muscles, he continued to look at the monitors. "Now."

"I spent that entire week with you," Emily replied, spinning the chair so that she faced him. "There is nothing to add."

"Nothing to add? You withheld your name from me, Emily, even back then. I want to know why. I deserve to know why."

"I've always been called Emily. As for my last name, I worked for the United Nations. I was always careful when I gave out personal information," Emily replied, situating herself a little more comfortably in the chair. "Back then was no exception. And by the time I got around to trusting you enough, all hell broke loose and you had given me a new identity anyway."

Jax noticed that she crossed one arm across her abdomen and knew that she'd just lied. He withheld calling her out on it, holding that tell to himself. He remained silent, wanting to see how much she would reveal and how much she wouldn't. He didn't like to view this as a test, but he wasn't sure he could call it anything else. She didn't seem to understand the sacrifice he went through to give her back her safety while he continued on, living an empty existence. It was obvious that he'd built those seven days into something more monumental than they actually were.

"That Friday, when I found the evidence regarding Amato's death, I called Schultz—"

"Which I can't figure out," Jax said, shaking his head in confusion. "You called me that morning, told me what had happened and begged me for my help. When I realized exactly how perilous the situation was, we handled it the only way we could. You were safe. Why would you call Jessalyn and then call me? And don't play that *cousin* crap with me. If you had such a strong connection to such a high ranking official who was willing to help you, all he needed to do was send someone to pick you up and place you in protective custody."

"I didn't trust him like I did you. After deciding that hiding for the rest of my life—while you got to live yours—wasn't going to work, I then had no choice but to hand the evidence over to Schultz. Unfortunately, the minute it leaked that he had something so monumental, Alekseev knew that I was still alive."

"Now I know you're bullshitting me. You couldn't even bring yourself to tell me your name. Your lies are starting to run off the tracks."

"After I was able to leave the building, I had realized that I'd left my purse, keys and cell phone at my desk." Emily lifted her mug and took a sip. Jax was relatively sure she was stalling and thinking of this shit as she went along. His fingers tightened on his cup in frustration, although he continued to play her game. "I walked to the parking lot and bided my time, waiting for someone to come out. Once I spotted an older gentleman, I told him that my car wouldn't start and asked for a ride to the bus stop."

"I already know this part, Emily. What's this got to do with Jessalyn?" Jax asked, wanting her to bypass these mundane details that probably weren't true anyway. "How do you know him? It's a simple question."

"I didn't." Emily peered up at him through her lashes and for the first time that morning, Jax met her gaze. Instead of the anticipated guilt he expected to see for the lies that she told, her blue eyes seemed to be lit within and full of agitation. It was almost as if she was afraid to lose track of her lies. "When this gentleman dropped me off, I stole his cell phone. As I went to call you to come pick me up, it rang."

"And you expect me to believe that Schultz Jessalyn happened to be calling at that precise time? On a phone you'd just stolen from a stranger?"

Jax had had enough of this shit. The woman sitting in front of him was not the Emily he once knew. Taking one more look at the monitors and then confirming that the perimeter alarms were still active, he turned and walked into the kitchen. Tossing his coffee into the sink, he then slammed his mug onto the counter. He knew he couldn't stomach one more lie right at the moment.

"It doesn't matter if you believe me," Emily said, determination evident in her voice as she followed him into the kitchen. "What matters is that instead of following his orders, I called you."

"Why did you?" Jax asked, unable to prevent the words from slipping out. He turned toward her and leaned up against the sink. It wasn't a big room, although it did contain a small kitchen table off to the side. She didn't bother to sit down, but instead came to stand directly in front of him. He didn't remember her being so self-assured. "If you were going to throw away the life that I gave you, why pretend?"

"You might have believed that, but I never thought about walking away from you forever." Emily must have left her coffee in the other room, for she slipped her hands into her back pockets and shrugged her shoulders. Vulnerability crossed her features and it was all he could do not to reach for her and pull her into his arms. He'd already made that mistake; he wouldn't do it again. "I just needed time to be able to prove who murdered Bianchi and then hand over the evidence to Schultz."

Jax suddenly felt the blood in his veins run cold. He had to have heard her wrong. She was a lowly administrative assistant, with little clearance at the UN. Wasn't she?

"What do you mean you needed time to prove it?" Jax reached back and grabbed the counter so he didn't reach for her. "Didn't you leave for Florida like we'd planned?"

"Not exactly," Emily hedged, shifting on the balls of her feet and giving a tiny shrug. "I stayed in New York, although kept mostly to the suburbs while I tried to find more evidence."

Jax struggled to breathe, picturing her out in the open and basically making herself a target while he'd been out of the country. All he'd gone through, calling in every favor ever owed him to create her a brand new existence and she'd thrown it away. He'd made the biggest sacrifice of his life and she'd dishonored that for a pipe dream.

"And what then, Emily?" Jax asked, trying to make her see reason. He tightened his hold on the granite behind him. "Did you think that whoever assassinated the former Secretary-General was going to allow you to go back to living your life? In case Schultz hasn't gone over what will happen once the Attorney General takes this to the United Nation's Security Council, let me enlighten you. You will testify, be taken to an undisclosed location, given a new identity and placed into witness protection where you will then live out the rest of your life in a tiny house with a white picket fence situated in a small town—never to be heard from again."

"Jax—"

"And that's if you're lucky," Jax said, continuing over her interruption. "What is most likely the case, the person actually responsible for making the hit on Amato Bianchi will use his resources to locate you and neutralize the threat you pose. If it's Alekseev like you're claiming, he'll be given diplomatic immunity and be sent back to his country, able to carry out your execution throughout numerous available contractors."

"Damn it, Jax," Emily said, her hands coming out of her pockets to sit on her waist. Her brows dipped down and a frown marred her lips. "I know what *could* happen, but Schultz guaranteed—"

"If it's Schultz who's spinning these tales of a happily ever after to get you to do what he wants, he succeeded. Not only has he placed a big fucking bullseye on your back, but you've just endangered the lives of my team." Jax pushed away, needing to speak with Connor, but knowing he had to wait until his friend contacted him. Patience had never been his thing. Jax brushed by her and crossed the threshold into the monitoring room. "I didn't take you as naïve, Emily."

Emily opened the refrigerator in frustration, giving herself something to do. They had to eat, so she might as well make something to occupy her time. She saw that there were a few perishable items that had just been purchased and couldn't help but wonder by whom. Crest, Kevin, and the rest of the team didn't even know where they were, so how had Jax managed to get a message to someone without anyone knowing?

A carton of milk, a dozen eggs, bacon, and a few condiments were situated on the top shelf. Peeking in the freezer, she saw various frozen meals. Looking to the side, she saw a pantry. Opening it to reveal the contents, she decided Jax could fend for himself. She was having a bowl of cereal.

Once situated at the small table, Emily thought over her options as she stabbed her spoon into the milk. As she slowly chewed the small squares of puffed wheat and sugar, her mind churned and comprehended that she would have to tell Jax the truth sooner or later. She'd prefer later, as it gave her a chance to contain a volatile situation, but she honestly didn't know if she'd be given the time. It was as if she could actually see the sand of time running through her fingers. There was one vital thing that she needed to do.

Finally finishing her breakfast, Emily walked her bowl over to the sink and rinsed it out. Leaving it to wash later and glancing at the dark wooden door to confirm that Jax was closed up in the other room, she made her way through the house and into the living room where Jax had left his back-pack. Unzipping the outside pocket, she found the extra prepaid burner phones that she knew he would have. Taking one and then making sure the bag appeared untouched, Emily quietly maneuvered her way upstairs to her bedroom.

Once concealed in the old-fashioned room decorated with aging roses and lace wallpaper, Emily used the flip phone to dial the number she knew by heart. Situating herself in front of the window to give her a better angle of the grounds, she waited for the other end to connect.

"Hello?"

"Aunt Beatrice, it's me," Emily said with a smile for the first time since she could remember. Hearing the older woman's voice always managed to lift her spirits. While she was in her mid-seventies, the woman was an eccentric artist who would always remain young at heart. "I don't have long, but I need you to do me a favor and catch the first flight to Paris. Tell your friends you're going there to study something, anything that will be believable."

"Oh, sweetheart, it's so good to hear your voice! You were beginning to worry me. I haven't received anything in the mail for a couple of months," Beatrice said, her worry evident with every word.

"I'm doing what I have to do to end this," Emily said, scanning the view. The area was desolate, although the trees to the south gave coverage that she and Jax needed. "But you make it very hard when you don't do as I say. So I need you to—"

"We've been over this, sweetheart," Beatrice replied. She could picture her aunt shaking her head in bewilderment at how senseless Emily was being. "I should have gotten an Oscar for the performance I put on in the gallery when the police came in with the news of your death. Thank God you gave me fair warning, or it would have been real."

"I'm dealing with professionals, Aunt Beatrice," Emily said, suddenly feeling a stress headache discharge sharp twinges in her temples. "They'd wait until the smoke cleared and then confirm the slightest contact we may have had."

"But you're smarter than them, my dear."

Emily sighed, reaching up and removing the hair tie, hoping it would relieve the pressure in her head. Turning, she went to throw the small ring on the comforter when she realized the door was open. Jax stood there with his arms crossed over the long-sleeved black T-shirt he wore, his brown leather shoulder holster firmly secured across his back, giving him easy access to his weapon. Her stomach sank as her heart rate accelerated, causing the throbbing in her temples to magnify. The expression on his face said it all and now she was about to face the consequences.

Chapter Five

"I need to go now," Emily replied into the phone, keeping up the pretense that everything was all right. Jax knew that she'd expected him to stay in the monitor room the rest of the morning, but it was obvious she'd forgotten a lot about him in the past two years. "Please consider my request. It makes it easier on me. I love you, Aunt Beatrice."

Jax held out his hand, waiting for her to cross the room and give him the cell phone. He would now have to destroy it, leaving them only two more phones for emergency contact. Having limited resources was bad enough, but the fact that she'd foolishly wasted one of them on a phone call that might potentially get her aunt killed was almost laughable, if the situation wasn't so dire.

"It's not what you think," Emily said, closing the distance between them.

She was smart enough to drop the phone into his hand, for even Jax didn't know if he'd grab her and flip her over his knee for the punishment she deserved. He would do well to remember that she'd been lying to him all along and that he truly didn't know who this woman was standing in front of him. She also wasn't his now.

"So I'm wrong in assuming that you went through my bag, stole a cell phone, and then snuck upstairs to call a family relative," Jax said mockingly, nodding his head as if he was in total agreement. He held up the phone in one hand. Her face flushed in what seemed like anger, but it wasn't her right. It was his. "A relative I had no idea you had, although that's not so surprising, is it? Just out of curiosity…are you trying to get us fucking killed?"

"You and I both know these people will go after my—"

"Now we're getting somewhere," Jax said, flashing a smile that he knew didn't quite meet his eyes. He leaned up against the doorframe, crossing his black boots. "Exactly *whom* are we speaking about?"

Emily sucked in a deep breath, but she seemed to know that this wasn't the time to continue the stalling of pertinent information. Releasing the air from her lungs, she backed up and sat on the bed. Her hair bounced with her, draping across her shoulders. He really liked her as a brunette, but that was something easily changed had he wanted her to. He didn't.

"Grigori Alekseev, the one who had Amato assassinated, has someone from the Security Council on his payroll." Emily looked up at him, her blue eyes scrutinizing him. Jax wasn't sure why, but decided to stay silent in hopes she'd continue. It worked. "His name is Vadim Batkin. I met him once and there wasn't an ounce of humanity left in that man's soul. The evidence I gave to Schultz is enough to send Batkin and Alekseev back to their country, where I'm sure the FSB will take them into custody to never be heard from again."

Jax waited and when she just sat there, looking up at him with not-so-innocent eyes and wasn't forthcoming with any more information, he knew he'd have to lead her to where he wanted this to go. It would have helped had he had some direction, but when had things ever been easy with Emily? It was obvious she wasn't willing to give him too much information and he could only blame Jessalyn. She hadn't been like this before…had she?

"So you expect me to believe this evidence inadvertently landed on your desk and you put two and two together, instantly jumping to this miraculous discovery that the new Secretary-General murdered the former one? And that he didn't act alone?" Jax shook his head when she remained silent and now knew he had no choice but to take a different route in obtaining the information he needed. The sooner this was over, the sooner they could both get on with their lives. She'd certainly wasted enough of his life. "Grab your jacket. You can help me set up some additional perimeter alarms around the house."

Jax pushed off the doorframe and then proceeded down the stairs. He had no doubt that she'd follow, probably to see if he was really going to destroy the cell phone. He snagged his backpack off of the floor as he walked through the sparse living room, through the kitchen, and into the monitor room. One swift glance told him everything was still safeguarded. Tossing his bag onto the chair, he quickly took apart the phone and destroyed the SIM card by simply snapping it in half.

"How have you been keeping in touch with your aunt?" Jax asked, knowing she would be right behind him.

"You told me how to do it," Emily replied. When he looked over his shoulder, he found that she was already dressed to go outside. Jessie's jacket fit her perfectly. She held gloves in her hand. "Take something that would seem absolutely normal and use it as a way to share messages.

Around every other month, I would send a piece of artwork to her address from various galleries around New York."

"And you stashed your messages on the inside of the frame," Jax said, finishing her description of an old tradecraft technique. He threw the remains of the cell phone device into the trash. "Well done. You did listen to me after all...at least some of it."

Jax adjusted his shoulder holster and then shrugged into Ethan's jacket. They were relatively the same size. He automatically reached inside the right pocket for his skullcap, realizing too late that he didn't have it. Damn, he missed that thing. Crossing in front of her, he grabbed what he needed and then maneuvered past Emily, making certain they didn't touch. He then opened the back door located in the kitchen. As long as he could keep his head on straight until Connor came into the picture to help alleviate the situation, Jax had a chance of getting out of this situation with his sanity intact...his heart had been lost and damaged a long time ago.

"Stay close."

❖   ❖   ❖   ❖

Emily warily watched Jax as they strolled along the edge of the forest seemingly looking over the area, but she was relatively sure he was waiting for her to speak. She wasn't sure what he wanted her to say, but she wasn't about to apologize for calling her aunt. It was only a matter of time before this situation escalated and she needed Aunt Beatrice to be safely shielded somewhere else when it did. Schultz should have had her in protective custody the minute he knew that Emily's cover had been blown.

Due to the sun being behind clouds, the chill in the air seemed concentrated. Even though she wore form-fitting wool gloves, Emily shoved her hands into the pockets of Jessie's jacket for added protection. Jax wasn't sporting anything on his hands, but even if he had the proper attire, the small square devices in his hands would have prevented him from wearing them.

"If you didn't leave New York, what did you do with your time?" Jax asked, still walking beside her but focused on the edge of the property, which seemed to carry on for several acres. He spoke very nonchalantly, as if they were talking about the weather. She tried to figure out what angle he was working, but she couldn't put her finger on it. "Trying to prove someone guilty of murder is harder when you don't have access to the information you need."

Emily sighed and curved her mouth into a half smile. She'd go with his line of questioning and alter her answers as needed. At least Jax wasn't coming at her with both guns loaded. This way she could formulate her responses without giving too much away. Schultz had given her fair warning of what could happen to Jax should he find out the truth.

"After I decided that it would be better for me to stay and prove what I knew to be true, I called Schultz back and he was able to give me some names of people who had admittance in specific areas." Emily looked up at the leaves that were starting to fill out the branches on the trees. The birds flew overhead, presumably either looking for places to nest over the spring and summer or for food. She was well aware of predators and the lengths they would go to in order to consume their prey. "Piece by piece, I basically built a case for the Attorney General."

"I see two issues with what you just said," Jax replied, although not in a combative voice.

He didn't even bother to look her way when he said it, but left her where she was to walk a few steps away and place one of the devices against a tree trunk covered in vines. He then stood up and walked back toward her. Instead of continuing the direction they had being going, he cut across the perimeter.

"And what are those?" Emily asked, referring to the issues he spoke of. She fell into step beside him.

"One, why would he give you those names? Jessalyn has the ability to launch a full-scale investigation on the piece of paper you found, which quite honestly isn't evidence that a murder was committed." Jax looked back over his shoulder, causing her to do the same. Emily wasn't sure what he was searching for, but she found herself wanting a weapon of her own. Schultz had made her enter the CSA offices without one, but she'd gotten used to having it nearby. "By the way, don't think I'm letting go the fact that you withheld this information when I assisted you to fake your death. If I remember correctly, you said you had solid evidence. But that's my bad for not confirming and blindly trusting you."

"It all links together, Jax," Emily said, trying to stress the importance on the information. "Were you aware that my apartment in New York had been ransacked or the fact that my vehicle has been missing since that day? They wanted to find the papers that I took with me."

"No, I wasn't aware of that," Jax said, for the first time turning his face toward her. The brown flecks of his eyes seemed to turn to gold as he showed the first signs of life since coming outside. "Maybe it had something to do with the fact that after I made sure you were set up for the rest of your life, my ass went to Iraq for my second combat tour. Let's face facts. You're withholding something vital regarding this evidence and Schultz's part in it. Like I said, he wouldn't allow a civilian to investigate the Secretary-General. You'll eventually tell me. You'll have to when your life is really on the line."

Emily could see this was going to get them nowhere, unless she told him the entire truth. She wasn't ready to do that and in an odd way he seemed to accept that. It would only further push him away, when all she wanted to do was mend this rift between them.

"What about you?" Emily wanted the peace back that she felt upon walking outside. Whether it was deception or not, Jax had rid himself of the tension within his muscles. It made her feel as if she didn't need to be on the defensive. "What did you do after you got back from Iraq?"

"Connor and I flew into Palm Springs en route to Twentynine Palms and stayed there for a few weeks. I debated on trying to track you down, but knew it would be better to let things lie." They had almost reached the other side of the large area when he stopped and looked back over his shoulder once more. That was when she realized he was going to place the other small device horizontally across from the other one. Sure enough, he walked over to where some brush was and positioned the electronic device to his satisfaction. "It was a couple months later that Crest asked us to join his firm."

"I'm surprised you took him up on it," Emily said, falling into step with him as he continued farther away from the house. The sun peeked through the clouds for a brief moment, but Emily took full advantage of it by tilting her head and enjoying the heat on her face. "I pictured you staying in until retirement."

"Things changed after my second tour...I'd changed." Jax didn't need to elaborate and Emily opened her eyes to see him watching her. She tried to put a name to the emotion she saw within them, but it stayed just out of her grasp. Before she could say anything, he continued. "Connor was tired and wanted a change. Crest's offer was hard to turn down, particularly when we knew he was keeping his fingers in the government contracts. We are able to do what we're trained to do, yet have the civilian life we desired. It was a win-win for everyone involved."

"You said Connor needed a change, but what about you?"

"Connor's the only family I have left. I wasn't about to lose that."

Jax quickened his pace as if he'd revealed too much. But he hadn't. In the week that they'd had, they'd used every moment and shared intimate details about their lives. Sometimes she swore the only reason she'd lasted this long in hiding were the memories that he'd shared with her. Along with the hope for a future that he now seemed unwilling to renew with her. They'd had a lot in common. Emily was well aware that he'd lost his parents before entering the service and that he thought of Connor like a brother. He valued loyalty above all else. She knew that and was now terrified that her actions had pushed him too far away.

"What is the second issue you have with what I've told you?" Emily asked, taking the conversation back to the beginning. If she could erase one doubt or question he had for her one at a time, then maybe there was still a chance to get back what they had. "You said there were two."

"It's the Attorney General's place to investigate your claims." Jax stopped walking and faced her. It was the first time that he really just looked at her and it caused her breath to hitch. The intensity that was in his gaze seemed to consume her and she would have given anything for him to take her back to the house and make love to her for the rest of the afternoon, but she knew that wouldn't happen. She'd lost his trust, but the question was, could she regain it? His hand slowly lifted and he laid his warm palm against her cold cheek. "You're a civilian who got caught up in something way bigger than all of us, Emily. This is partly my fault. I should have insisted you take this to the highest authority and had them place you in witness protection while they investigated. Instead, I allowed our fear to cloud my judgment and went along with faking your death."

"Jax, it wasn't baseless fear," Emily said, needing him to understand they'd made the right decision. She took her hand out of her pocket and wrapped her gloved fingers around his wrist. "I would have been dead within the week had I done what you're suggesting. But I want back what we had. Is that what you need to hear? I want a chance to see what would have happened to us had we been given the time to cultivate our relationship."

"It's not what I want to hear, Emily." Jax dropped his hand, forcing her to do the same. "I want the fucking truth."

Emily opened her mouth to tell him that she was afraid that if she did that, she'd lose him forever. It didn't help that Schulz had basically forbid her to do so, not that she worked for him. Instead, she remained silent as Jax walked away and continued his path across the growing grass beneath their feet. Couldn't he see how torturous this was for her? She was so afraid that he would walk away and leave her alone.

"The truth is this," Emily called out, grateful when he stopped. Jax didn't turn around, but at least she had his attention. "I did what I had to do to be with you again. Now I'm in a situation where not even Schultz can keep me safe, but I have no doubt that you will. That's how much I trust you."

Jax turned his head to the side, although he still didn't face her. As if nature was trying to tell her that he was her sole reason for being there, the clouds parted and permitted a lone ray of sun to shine down upon him. The birds squawked overhead, heedless of the tremulous situation below. The wind had picked up, blowing the fresh green leaves on the trees and carried his words back to her. They were like tiny darts hitting their target as her heart was struck with each one.

"Trust is just an illusion, Emily."

Chapter Six

"It's taken you long enough," Jax said, speaking into the encrypted mobile that he and Connor kept for emergencies. He'd finally been able to get a full charge on it and would no longer need the burner phones. Walking through the living room where Emily was sitting on the couch, he didn't bother to look her way as he made his way into the monitor room before shutting the door. He wished it were that easy to close out the emotions that she was stirring up. "It's been two days. I need intel on whether I need to move her again."

"What the hell, man," Connor replied in anger. The echo surrounding his voice meant that he was in a stairwell. Was it that of the building where their offices were located or was Connor someplace else? Jax could picture his Cuban friend pacing back and forth, rubbing a hand down his face in frustration. "Crest gave me the SITREP. Emily Weiss? I leave for one week to take Lauren to meet my father and you get yourself involved in a fucking 'back from the dead' soap opera. She's a zombie. You can't continue to date them after they become zombies."

"Fuck you. This wasn't what I had planned either." Jax ignored Connor's barb at trying to lighten up the situation and pulled the rolling desk chair over with his foot, sinking into the worn black leather. He rested an elbow on the matching arm and ran a hand through his hair. "Connor, there's more to the story than what any of us are being told."

"No shit, jackass. I should have realized what was going on back then, but you can spill your guts when we meet up. Right now, you need to tighten your shit up and take notes."

Jax leaned forward, placing his elbows on his knees. The tenor of Connor's voice indicated that they would be seeing each other soon, putting him on high alert. It had taken almost a year to put backup plans in place for their safety. Working the government contract jobs that they did, enemies were easily made. This house and land were purchased with cash and deeded to a corporation that had long ago gone defunct. It sat on the outskirts of Cloquet, where no one really noticed it, as it was set so far back off of a lone back road. Maintenance was taken care of on a cash basis where no names were exchanged. Jax had a feeling his safety net was about to be yanked out from under him.

"What's the radius looking like?" Jax asked, referring to the search that was undoubtedly taking place.

"There is none," Connor replied in a low voice, setting off that alarm Jax had been waiting for. "Crest has quietly backed off the search for you and Emily. He knows you're keeping her safe. The team is looking toward me for guidance, as they know Crest was placed in a bad situation in returning some favor to Jessalyn. Speaking of which, that guy left for DC, although he's under the assumption that all is flowing true like the fucking Mississippi River."

"If we're in the clear right now," Jax said, looking up at the monitors to view the area, "why am I getting the feeling that you're about to tell me to hightail it out of here?"

"Because you'd be right," Connor replied, his tone as serious as Jax has ever heard it. "The Attorney General was killed in a car accident this morning. It's just now hitting the news outlets."

"Fuck me."

"I figure you have a few days window before whoever would go to these lengths picks up whatever measly thread we may have left when we bought that safe house."

"Alekseev," Jax responded, knowing Connor wouldn't let that bit of information faze him. They'd faced worse men in their past...this was just one of many, regardless that he was involved with the United Nations. "The Secretary-General is covering his tracks and from what Emily's told me, so is a member of the Security Council. A man by the name of Vadim Batkin. If either one gets wind that Jessalyn is the one who was aiding Emily all along, he'll be next...followed by Emily."

"Which is why I'm waiting for Crest to gather more intelligence before taking action on our part. It's obvious the minute the Attorney General started confirming the evidence Emily handed over, it alerted Alekseev that she was still alive. He's now eliminating the threats and will be coming after her. Either that or this flunky you're talking about. We both know that he won't get his hands dirty, which means he'll hire an independent contractor."

"Give me time to get things together on my end," Jax said, "before you clear out."

✧ ✧ ✧ ✧

Emily placed her empty bowl in the sink. They'd warmed up canned soup for dinner, although Jax hadn't joined her at the table. He'd stood at the kitchen counter, eating his meal and looking over several maps that were now spread over the granite. It was as if she didn't exist and that cut her to the bone. She wanted…needed…to be a part of his life again. Or else this was all for naught.

"Who is Elle?"

The question obviously startled him, although whether it was because the silence was disturbed or the subject matter, she wasn't sure. Emily tried not to feel the sting of jealousy that whipped through her, knowing that she had no right to experience it. But the name had weighed on her since Kevin had mentioned the woman.

"She's the manager of a club that Connor and I own."

The spoon clanked against the ceramic bowl. Emily leaned her hip against the small island that he was using as a desk. Jax shifted and placed the empty dish on the counter behind him. He then returned to studying the maps, as if his answer was good enough. It should have been, but it only fueled her to ask more.

"What kind of club?" Emily asked, already suspecting the answer, but wanting to hear it from him.

Jax sighed in resignation as he stepped back and leaned against the sink. He crossed his arms in the usual manner and the white shirt that he was wearing stretched across his broad chest. As usual, his shoulder holster cut into the material on either side of his thickly muscled chest.

"That's a pretty naïve question, considering you know the lifestyle I enjoy." Jax let his gaze roam over her body and Emily instantly felt the slack taken up on the trigger that only he could pull. A low hum seemed to originate from deep within her. "It's a kink club revolving around BDSM. A case that we were working on caused the owner to go belly-up, so I figure since I play there most weekends anyway, why not salvage what's left and keep a sane, safe, and consensual place for fellow lifestyle friends to enjoy."

Emily couldn't prevent her hands from fisting and crossed her arms to hide them from his view. She didn't want him to know how much it bothered her that while she had been sacrificing everything these last two years, he'd been surrounding himself with submissive women. He was making it more than obvious that her *death* hadn't affected his life. Their reunion had not been what she'd hoped it would be. He seemed angry more than anything else that she'd come out of hiding and inconvenienced his life. She needed to change the subject before she revealed too much. What was the old adage? Never ask a question when you're not prepared for the answer.

"I heard at the office the other day that Connor had met someone," Emily said, hoping to take advantage of the fact that he was talking. She didn't want to know anymore about his club, but didn't want to sever this connection. "I never thought he would settle down."

"Lauren's good for him," Jax replied. He was now studying her, as if he knew exactly what she was doing. Emily glanced toward the door, thinking maybe she better retreat when he continued, keeping her glued to his story. "She was involved in the same case that allowed us to purchase the club. Lauren modifies BDSM implements by adorning them with precious gems. Her occupation had her in the wrong place and wrong time, setting her in the sights of an unbalanced man who was intent on killing her. Connor fell for her pretty hard."

"I take it you brought down this unbalanced man?" Emily asked, wanting to know the outcome.

"As a matter of fact, I did indeed. Connor had the kill shot. He's dead." Jax seemed too relaxed, which should have alerted her that this conversation was about to take a turn. As it was, he caught her off guard. "Why don't you just ask the question, Emily? Unlike what you have done, I'll give you an honest answer."

Emily refused to believe that he could read her so well after all these years apart, but the heat in his hazel eyes was telling her a different story. She scrambled to think of a question that had nothing to do with his private life, but was coming up blank. It was time to seek refuge in the living room and leave him to his maps. As she uncrossed her arms and took a step forward, Jax closed the distance and blocked her way. His heat enveloped her and the capacity of her lungs seemed nonexistent. It didn't surprise her that her body still responded to his, but she hadn't expected it to be so hard in hiding it…or that she'd even have to.

"Go ahead, Emily," Jax murmured, the golden streaks of his eyes practically sparking. "Ask me."

"Who you scene with or have sex with is obviously not my concern anymore. You've made that more than plain. Just so we're on the record, I didn't expect you to wait for me…something you thought would never happen." Emily swallowed and knew that he'd seen the nervous gesture. Too bad, because technically he was well aware that jealousy was raging through her veins. It was the hurt in her heart she was most afraid to reveal. At this juncture, she couldn't allow herself to be vulnerable. "But I don't need to stand here and listen to how many women you've fucked. I'll leave you to looking over your maps. Should you like to enlighten me on Connor's earlier call and whatever information he might have had, I'll be in the living room."

Emily managed to slip by him without touching, which was a feat considering the small amount of space between him and the sink. Her hands were trembling and she almost wished she hadn't spoken at all. These past two days had passed by in relative silence, but at least the tension hadn't been so taut. Now it felt as if they were back in Crest's office, when Jax first discovered she'd come out of hiding.

Walking across the room to the window, she pulled the curtains back. Dusk had fallen and cast shadows on the front lawn. Emily didn't know what else to call it, but the large open area in the front was surrounded by trees, with the exception of the gravel drive. Again it made her wonder who kept up the maintenance of the grounds.

"Don't stand in front of the window. You're backlit by the kitchen light."

Emily turned to see Jax standing in the doorway, his fingers looped on the front pockets of his jeans. There still seemed to be an aura of excitement surrounding him, making her wary. It was as if she'd given him a glimpse inside of herself that he didn't want to return. Trying to ignore it and concentrate on the conversation, she hoped that their tremulous rapport would continue on until she formulated her next step. She refused to give up on what they had.

"Why?" Emily asked, doing what he said and letting the curtain drop. "We went outside a couple of days ago."

"Things have changed," Jax said with a shrug, seemingly unwilling to reveal information.

"I take it Connor did share something with you," Emily said, taking a few steps toward the plaid couch, which was now in between them. "Don't you think I should know what's going on? Maybe I can shed some insight."

"I think we've established that until I feel you've come clean with me, I'm running this as a solo operation."

Jax's words slammed into her, although he probably had no idea how hard. This was her life and she had the right to know every nuance of this operation. Emily knew that he was baiting for her, probably thinking if he kept taunting her that she would eventually cave and give him all the facts. She couldn't.

"Fine," Emily stated, calling his bluff. She tried to ignore the fact that she was being a hypocrite. "But don't expect me to feel bad if whatever it is that you're keeping from me results in collateral damage."

"I will find out what it is that *you* are withholding from me," Jax warned, flashing the smile that she remembered, though it wasn't good-natured. Déjà vu reared its ugly head and she was taken back to that week they'd spent together. "God help you if it's something that I can forgive, because if it is, you'll be too close at hand to avoid your punishment. Maybe it's best for both of us if I never find out."

Chapter Seven

R yland knew how to blend in amongst the wealthy and elite crowd. Looking in the mirror above the bar area of the ballroom, he confirmed that his tie sat just so in the collar of his perfectly starched white shirt. His tuxedo was hand tailored by a reclusive yet cutting edge Italian designer, the wing tipped shoes were from same exclusive collection, and his cufflinks were designed by Atelier Yozu. His black hair was cropped close, giving him the classic handsome quality he required.

It helped that Ryland carried himself with a refinement that appealed to women of a certain station, although he only used that to his advantage when absolutely needed. He had no close relationships and he preferred it that way. The job required the type of discipline that only a master craftsman could possess. If the women he encountered could only see the black marks that his soul had collected, they would know to stay clear of the devil within.

Resting an elbow on the bar, he caught the bartender's attention. Ordering his usual Crown Royal XR, he patiently waited turning his body just so in order to observe the room.

The man he was meeting was situated at his three o'clock, speaking with his wife and another couple whom he knew to be just static in the scheme of things.

"Sir, your drink."

"Did you mean to ruin my whiskey with ice or did the word neat escape your training syllabus?" Ryland pushed it back towards the bartender. "Again, please."

Upon being served a proper two fingers of the LaSalle distillery's finest blend, he finally nodded his appreciation. Ryland picked up the crystal tumbler and took a sip of the smooth full-bodied whiskey. He let the warmth infuse his body, although he wasn't using the alcohol to take the edge off. It was purely for his enjoyment. He was actually rather relaxed, as he'd gone over the list of people in attendance and had several exit strategies should anything unexpected happen.

"It's a beautiful evening."

Ryland lifted one side of his mouth in a wry smile. He'd seen the brunette eyeing him for the last five minutes and had wondered how long it would take her to make her way over and attempt to beguile him. She might have that sparkle in her eye of worldly experience, but she'd never played with a man like him. As a freelance contractor for whoever paid the highest, his social circles were vast. He wasn't picky about which government either and figured he had more fake passports than she did jewelry. He contemplated his time wisely as he studied her, but decided against enjoying her company for the evening. She truly was a beauty, but unfortunately, tonight was all about business.

"Yes, it is." Ryland finished his drink and set his glass on the counter. "Enjoy the rest of your night, Miss."

With a curt nod of his head, he blended into the crowd and let the flow of the people direct him to where he needed to be.

Everything was going as planned, not that he thought it would go differently. One could never be too sure.

"It's turning out to be a nice event," Ryland said in a low voice, repeating the phrase that he'd been given. He'd waited to approach his objective until the other couple had meandered off. The trophy wife was already walking away towards her next social target, leaving her husband to his own devices. Ryland knew that this man worked security detail for Alekseev and in fact, made sure he knew every nuance of this man's life should the need to take him out of the game arose. "It's nice to see you, Mr. Batkin."

"And you," Vadim said, a false smile crossing a face that had seen too many bouts in the ring.

He held out his hand in offer, which Ryland took, knowing that cupped in the man's palm would be a small USB device which contained his target's information. Technically, this type of drop was bad tradecraft; however, that was why Ryland had studied the guest list so scrupulously. Batkin was an amateur by comparison and he could not be expected to practice proper protocol in such matters. The device was encrypted with a one-time cypher key and protected by an anti-tamper apparatus that would shred the files and thus erase all data. All he needed was a name and he would take it from there.

"Make sure to try the caviar," Vadim suggested. "It's delicious."

As Batkin turned to follow his wife, Ryland casually slipped his hand inside his jacket to deposit the drive and retrieve a Cohiba Reserva Selection Especiales 2003. With the USB secured, he would stay an additional thirty minutes, so as not to call attention to himself whilst relishing his aged Cuban cigar on the veranda overlooking the English style gardens. Depending on the target and where he or she might be located would determine his departure flight. He'd always prided himself on a job well done and this one would be no different.

He caught a streak of red in his peripheral vision as he made his way back to the bar. Turning, he sighted her long blonde hair. His chest tightened. Making his way through the throngs of people that were clustered in small groups, he eventually closed the distance. The red silk scarf draped around her neck and down the flesh of her shoulders, seemed to merge with the dress that swathed the curvature of her lower back. She spun on her heel—a stranger.

Ryland veered ever so slightly to his left, following his altered path toward the bar. The veranda could wait. Nodding his head in answer to the bartender when asked if he'd like another, he placed both forearms on the padded leather lining of the counter. The past needed to stay in the past. The amber liquid appeared before him and he relished the spice of the Canadian rye juxtaposed by the sophisticated blend of dried fruits and honey as it made its way down to his stomach. The item in his pocket had his mark's information. He or she was just one of many.

✧   ✧   ✧   ✧

Jax heard her soft footsteps coming down the stairs. Not even the carpet could stop the creaking that the old wooden floors let out with each step. He'd been catching some sleep on the couch when the light noises had reached him. He immediately palmed the weapon lying on his stomach, but then carefully eased it into his shoulder holster, leaving the fastening open.

"Trouble sleeping?" Jax heard the audible gasp and knew that she had stopped a foot from his location. "It's almost three-thirty in the morning. We're secure, if that's what's keeping you awake."

"No, I just needed a drink of water," Emily said. She kept her voice low, almost as if she were afraid speaking too loud in the dark would alert someone or something. "There is another bedroom upstairs, you know."

"I wouldn't be much protection to you if a threat made its way in here, now would I?" Jax tightened his jaw, wishing he had curbed his sarcasm. It wouldn't do to maintain this tension between them. Who knew how long this protection order would drag out and he needed to sustain her trust if the situation became dangerous. "I'm going to need you to be ready to move on my word. Make sure the bag you were given is packed and ready to go."

"What is it that you're not telling me?"

"The Attorney General was killed in an automobile accident yesterday morning," Jax replied, figuring at this point it was useless to keep it from her. She probably would have heard it on the radio last night had she not gone directly to her room after their last row. It'd been for the best, as he wasn't sure how much longer he could keep from touching her. He sat up and placed his boots on the floor, running a hand through his hair. "Connor feels, and I agree, that Alekseev has hired an independent contractor."

"Jax," Emily said, hurrying around the couch to stand in front of him, "has anyone checked in with Schultz? He needs to go into hiding."

Jax didn't answer right away, too drawn to the fact that she was wearing a thin pink T-shirt with a pair of matching sweat pants. Jessie had packed the bag and probably hadn't given a thought to the modest nightwear, but the way Emily was standing in the moonlight had given it a totally different appearance. The swell of her breasts was prominent through the lightweight fabric, although shadows in front of her kept him from seeing if her nipples were hardened. He had no doubt they were, considering how cool the house had gotten at night.

"Jessalyn isn't my concern," Jax replied, knowing that he wasn't going to get any more sleep this night. Morning was right around the corner anyway. He squeezed the bridge of his nose, hoping to erase the exhaustion that was starting to set in. Standing, he walked around the couch and into the kitchen to put on some coffee. "You are. Connor will give us the heads up if we need to leave sooner than planned."

"Schultz is the only other person who has the evidence that I put together."

Jax flipped the switch, bathing the kitchen in light. Emily had followed him into the kitchen. Since there were no stools at the counter as the area was so small, he saw that she leaned her elbows down on the granite as he walked to the cabinets. He went about making the coffee, giving himself something to do besides taking in her appearance. He'd noticed that she'd wrapped her hair in some tie, so that the mass of blonde strands sat atop of her head. She wore not a trace of make-up, which caused her to look years younger, but made the dark smudges underneath her eyes all the more noticeable. It didn't take away from her beauty.

"As I said, Jessalyn is a big boy who can fend for himself. He's got the Secret Service at his disposal." Jax reached for two mugs, turning to see if she wanted coffee as well. "Coffee? Or are you going back to sleep?"

"Coffee," Emily answered, although Jax could tell that she wasn't really with him. Her eyes stared off into the distance, making him wonder exactly what was going on in that cunning little mind of hers. He was about to turn back toward the counter when her gaze came back into focus. "We, uh, might need to go to New York."

"Excuse me?" Jax asked, knowing he had to have heard her wrong. He set the mugs down with a thud and turned around to face her. "I could have sworn you said New York."

"I did." Emily rubbed her face as if that would clear away her fatigue. He could have told her that it wouldn't work, along with whatever suggestion she was about to make. "Even though I handed over the evidence, I wasn't going to take the chance of it disappearing into the wrong hands. There are multiple places where I hid the proof of Alekseev's side deals."

"That's not what the Attorney General was after him for," Jax said, pointing out the obvious. Was she now ready to give up a little more information? "You and Jessalyn made it sound as if the government wanted to take Alekseev in front of the Security Council on the charge of murder."

"They do." Emily paused and Jax waited, not knowing how much she would reveal. She would eventually come to realize that she'd place her future in his hands. Until then, he'd have the patience needed to see this through. It sucked, but that was his fucking plan. "In order to obtain a summit with the Security Council, the Attorney General was going to present to them what I found and then hopefully, plan a hearing in which I would testify."

"So what you're saying is that because the Attorney General was murdered, we have no idea how far along they were in the process." Jax rested his hands on the counter behind him. "It shouldn't matter. Jessalyn wouldn't have just handed over everything on a silver platter. He would have kept his own copies for just this reason. I guarantee this investigation is progressing as planned."

"And if what you're saying is true, Schultz and I have a bounty on our head." Emily pushed off of the island and walked around it, accidentally brushing her hand against his arm as she reached for the coffee pot. If he hadn't been looking close enough, he would have missed the way her lips parted. It wasn't as if he doubted what she felt for him on a physical level, he just wished it mattered enough for her to be truthful. "I know what we have to do."

"What you need to do is let me do my job," Jax said, crossing his arms and steeling himself against whatever concoction she was dreaming up. "You asked for me. You got me."

"I coaxed Schultz into placing my protection under your hands, because no matter what you may think, you're the only one I trust to do so." Emily didn't bother filling up the mugs. She slid the pot back on the burner, tilting her face up at him in determination. He was already shaking his head in dispute, knowing whatever it was she was about to suggest would only put her life in further peril. "We need to go to New York, get the evidence I hid, and take it to the media. I need the international press to run this story and end this cat and mouse crap once and for all."

Chapter Eight

"Y ou're what?" Connor asked, his tone quiet while keeping the intensity of his words. Jax hated when he did that. "Have you lost your fucking mind?"

"What would you have me do, Connor?" Jax asked, taking his free hand and rubbing the back of his neck. This entire situation had been fucked from the beginning, and by that, he meant two years ago. "Even you said it was a matter of time before they find us. She's a sitting duck."

"You take her out in public and you might as well paint a fucking bullseye on her back."

"Has Jessalyn been in touch? Have the investigators ruled the Attorney General's accident a murder? Have Crest's contacts heard any chatter regarding an independent contractor? No? Then as I said, we're sitting on a time bomb."

"I need a few days to get the team together," Connor replied. "You can't do this on your own. I'm pulling Crest in."

"Fine." Jax knew he had no choice at this point. They worked better as a team, but he hoped like hell that Connor took point. This was life or death...Emily's. Connor was the only one who had never let him down. "Twenty-four hours and then we're heading out, with or without the team."

"Taryn says she needs to speak with you immediately, but I keep putting her off and saying that no one has heard from you. She said it was personal."

"Tell her that you'll relay whatever she has," Jax instructed, adrenaline rushing through his body at the thought that Taryn might have found out what Emily had been trying so hard to hide. Knowing she was intentionally keeping something from him was a constant dagger to his side. "I need that information."

"Fine. She'll be more useful to us here at the office, so I'll get in touch with you if it's significant. If you don't hear from me, we'll be set up in and around Cloquet, ready to follow you out. Driving is the safest method, as we don't know what this contractor has at his or her disposal."

"Think the worst, hope for the best," Jax said, disconnecting the call.

"Thank you," Emily said softly, causing him to look toward the doorway. She seemed wary, as if she didn't know how he was going to react. The first emotion he felt was satisfaction that she couldn't get a read on him, but then he felt remorse for having lost the memories that there was one person in this world who had understood him more than anyone on such an intimate level. Now that was gone. Had he really expected anything else? "I know you don't agree with me, but maybe this is what should have happened two years ago. Going public does have its upside."

Jax sat down in the worn leather chair, feeling just as damaged. Over the past few days he couldn't help but wonder how things would have turned out had he handled the initiating situation differently. Hearing her voice on the other end of the phone all that time ago, trying to give him all the facts in a three minute conversation had sent his world reeling.

"I think about it...the choices we made." Jax said, placing his elbow on the armrest and resting his head on two of his fingers. He studied her, sensing an acceptance that hadn't been there before. She'd made a judgment and was at peace with it. Was he? "Every minute that has gone by, I second guess my decision. There were people I knew who could have helped you. I could have figured out a way not to go to Iraq. I let you convince me of the danger and set our lives on a course to be determined by another's sins that have now been resurrected. That made me weak."

"You are the strongest man I know, Jax," Emily said, shaking her head in denial for what he knew was the truth.

"I pushed my limits, Emily. I played in clubs night after night trying to replace your image in my head." Jax closed his eyes, remembering the day he landed back on American soil after his combat tour. He recalled the days and nights leading up to ultimately coming to the realization that she was never coming back. "Months and months went by and even though I had you promise me you wouldn't reach out, it didn't stop me from hoping. And every day after that, little by little the likelihood faded and all I was left with were those memories. I knew it had to be that way and I'd come to accept it."

"Jax—"

Finally looking at her, a certainty descended on him like those inevitable waves washing across the beach covering the sand. When this was over and he'd done his job, he would make sure that she was safely tucked into middle America to live out her life. His fate had been carved out long ago; he just needed to accept it. The words wouldn't stop coming, but he wasn't repentant in any way for sharing them with her.

"I was taking chances that didn't need to be taken. I knew if I'd gone back into the field, I would be putting Connor's life and that of my team at risk. So I took Crest up on the offer of civilian life." Jax shifted in the chair and leaned forward, wanting to stress to her the importance of what he was about to say. "I used to imagine what it would be like if you walked back into my life. This…once in a lifetime reunion. But never in a million years did I think you could stand in front of me with such obvious deceit."

"You need to trust me," Emily said, taking a step into the room but stopped before she came any closer. "Just as I'm trusting you."

"You're not trusting me and I've also already explained my take on that." Jax finally stood, mentally exhausted from exposing himself in such a vulnerable fashion. He wasn't a man who opened up easily. He doubted it would happen again. "You have faith that I can keep you alive physically. The rest is just fucking lies."

Jax was surprised when she quickly closed the distance between them. She came up on her tiptoes and palmed his face. Her blue eyes flickered back and forth on his, as if trying to gauge his sincerity.

"You make it sound as if you're giving up on what we had," Emily whispered. She then leaned in and pressed her warm lips to his. As much as he tried to fight the gentle yet desperate kiss, he found his hands closing around her waist and holding her in position. She was the first to pull away. "I'm doing this to make sure we get what we had back."

"I adjusted to a new way of living. Without you." Jax let his hands fall and then stepped around her. "Your attempt at clinging to something that's no longer there changes nothing."

✧   ✧   ✧   ✧

Emily watched the monitors, catching sight of Jax as he made the rounds outside. His tall frame was easy to follow and she found herself thinking back to their conversation last night. Should she come clean with him now? Would that change things or put him in a more perilous situation? It would probably place her in a more difficult position, but it wasn't like she had anything left to lose…except Jax, of course. She could admit that his threat last night regarding having her tied to the bed at his mercy didn't have some influence over her decision. If anything, it made her want to fess up every detail just to see if he'd carry out his promise. It triggered memories from their time together and Jax's image on the screen faded as it was replaced.

He leaned over her, flashing that devilish smile, and disappearing from view as his lips descended onto her neck. His moist tongue traveled up to her ear.

"There is nothing more arousing than having you at my mercy," Jax whispered, sending shivers across her naked flesh. Her wrists and ankles were bound to her bed, almost creating an X, although her ankles felt farther apart than that. Her bare pussy felt the air as it drifted from his movement. He too was unclothed, yet she couldn't get a good look at his body from the way he was situated above her. "You're vulnerable, exposed, and held still, yearning for my touch. You'll be overloaded with so much pleasure that you'll scream my name over and over."

A beep from the kitchen pulled her back to the present. Emily quickly spun in the chair, facing the doorway. Her hand had gone directly to her hip where she'd gotten used to carrying her service weapon, before she recognized the sound of the coffee maker. She emitted an audible sigh of frustration, grabbing her hair around her face and pulling it back. Twisting it, she fashioned the blonde strands into a loose knot to keep it under control. She grimaced at the color but knew she'd have to wait to turn it back into its natural state.

Emily glanced at the monitor, seeing that Jax was making his way back to the house. Somehow, he must have known she was watching him, for he looked directly at the camera. She had searched the house for any sign of video equipment and hadn't spotted anything to alert a person of surveillance.

Jax had been right. She had no doubt that he was the person who could pull her through this alive. Emily recalled when she had first seen him playing pool with Connor in a bar across from the United Nation's offices. The way his biceps moved upon pulling the pool stick back to the way he methodically took his time before shooting. Hell, she'd been hooked. He and Connor had taken a week off before his next combat tour, having completed several months of mandatory preemptory unit training to visit the various kink clubs in New York for fun. That one kiss had him changing his plans. They'd spent the majority of his leave at her apartment with him teaching her things that had helped keep her sane on those many lonely nights since. Emily had wanted the kiss today to do what it did back then, but now realized how futile that was.

First and foremost, she needed to get a grip. Emotionally, Emily knew that she would have to wait to convince Jax they could continue where they left off until this was all over. She had confidence in her connections that once Alekseev was sent back to his own country and any remaining contracts on her head neutralized, she could live her civilian life out in the open. The same question remained…would Jax want to be a part of it?

Chapter Nine

"I must admit, you and Connor have certainly prepared for any situation," Emily said breathlessly, tossing her bag up and out of the square opening. They'd walked at least a quarter of a mile, maybe more, in an underground tunnel to where a decent sized pole barn was located. Jax had pulled down the wooden ladder and allowed her to throw the backpack up, but made her stay behind as he ascended first. "Is this even on your land?"

"No."

Emily gritted her teeth at his one word answer as she followed behind him on his okay. He'd been like that since yesterday morning, but she refused to let his attitude get to her. There would be a time and place to restart their conversation, although she was positive he would try to evade it. Right now she needed to let him concentrate on getting them out of here in one piece. She had to wonder how much her head was worth and if they'd already been found. Was the person just waiting for them to show their faces?

"Wait in the back until I check the vehicle over."

"Yes, Sir," Emily murmured to keep him from hearing, although she would have loved for him to hear the sarcasm dripping from her words. She shuffled to the rear of the musty building and was glad that she wore a sweatshirt. The temperature was still cool, especially for this time in the morning. "You mentioned that your team was going to be following us to New York. I take it we're meeting up with them?"

"Connor's out there now, waiting for us to exit." Jax replaced the electronic device that he'd used to sweep the vehicle into a second bag that he seemed to have gotten out of thin air. She needed to start paying attention. "The rest of the team will be strategically placed along the routes we will be taking."

Jax opened the passenger side door and for the first time this morning made eye contact with her. The old fashioned gesture reminded her of their past and she couldn't bring herself to move. She found herself wondering what their life would have been like had they met under different circumstances. Would they be married by now? Would he have wanted children? They stood there for a few moments just staring at each other. Emily would have given anything to know what he was thinking.

"We need to go."

Emily leaned down and snatched up her bag, frustrated that he wouldn't even give her an inch. She really shouldn't have expected anything else, but this distance between them was becoming more than she could handle. Besides exposing the rest of her secrets, against Schultz's order, what else could she do or say that would make this situation better?

"Truce?" Emily asked, slowly walking past him. She went even further, needing to feel some semblance of intimacy. "I need you."

Jax didn't move, although his eyes lowered to her lips as she filed past. Again, she wanted to know what he was thinking, but knew he would play his cards close to his chest. Was he remembering all the times she said she needed him during their lovemaking? He'd probably call it out and out sex right now, but not once had he touched her that she felt it wasn't in affection.

"Then do as I say," Jax replied in a stern tone, reminding her far too much of those special nights they'd shared. "Get situated. I want you to pay especially close attention to our surroundings. If we pass a vehicle, I want you to know if you've seen their face before. Regardless if a car or truck passes us...the same requirement applies. If we stop for fuel, you'll continue to scan the area. Are we clear?"

"What makes you think I'm going to know who's taken the contract out on me?" Emily asked, shoving her bag in the back seat of the black SUV that was similar to what they'd driven before. She grasped the small hand bar and hoisted herself up into the seat. "It could be anyone."

Jax didn't immediately shut the door. Instead, he stepped up until his knees hit the running board and brought his face close to hers. Her inhalation immediately stopped, leaving her holding her breath after she'd already caught the scent of his soap.

"You and I both know you're privy to much more training and information than I've given you credit for," Jax murmured, reaching up and tucking a loose strand of her hair behind her ear. It wasn't in affection and she felt a coldness settle over her. Had he figured out her secret? "I'd like to live through this as well, so I'm telling you that if you see or think something that isn't as it should be, announce it."

Emily could only nod her head while biting her lip to keep from blurting out everything. Schultz would have her head, but it would eliminate Jax's hostility. She knew the possibility was nil, so ended up not saying anything. He eventually stepped back, giving her breathing space and shut the door.

"Just get to New York and do what you have to do," Emily told herself, watching him walk to the front doors of the shed and slowly cracking them open, taking care to keep his body shielded. He must have been satisfied with what he saw, as he turned and walked to the driver's side. "Please let this work."

Jax climbed into the vehicle and shoved the keys into the ignition. He put the shift in drive, but didn't pull forward. Emily looked over to find him watching her.

"Connor should be in position when we get to the end of the drive. As I said earlier, he'll pull in behind at a distance, while the rest of the team are ahead of us. This is your last chance to change your mind."

Emily slowly shook her head, ignoring the look of disappointment that shadowed his face. Now that she'd made up her mind to go public, her life would either be given back to her or force the hands of the people trying to kill her. Either way, it had to be done.

"I'm ready."

✧   ✧   ✧   ✧

Three hours had gone by when Jax decided to pull off and top the gas tank with fuel. Using his blinker, he pulled the vehicle into the right hand lane behind a semi-tractor trailer. Emily had been quiet the majority of the time, with the exception of an occasional question regarding their route. He could see that she needed to use the restroom from the way she was fidgeting in her seat, although she hadn't said anything.

"We'll pull off on the next exit," Jax said, rolling his neck to ease the tension. He hadn't relaxed since they'd left the safe house, nor would he until they were out of sight. "Wait until I'm done at the tanks and then I'll walk you into the station to use the restroom."

"I've been meaning to ask you something," Emily said, her voice hesitant, which immediately garnered his attention. If it was one thing she hadn't been since this entire thing started, it was uncertain. He glanced her way and noticed that her arms had folded across her midsection. "Do you have a spare weapon I could carry? I saw you place some ammo within one of the packs. Maybe a carry model that would be easy to conceal?"

"Since when do you know how to use a handgun, let alone know the difference between a carry model and a full frame?" Jax knew he needed to contact Connor, who was keeping pace with them, but was too curious to do so at this moment. "Did you learn to shoot?"

"Yes," Emily answered, shrugging her shoulder, "I did. And I'm good at it, too. I made sure I was always armed, at least until Schultz made me leave everything with his men before we met with Mr. Crest. He said it would be returned to me, but that obviously wasn't the case considering you took me AWOL."

"Did you think I would do anything else?" Jax asked, raising an eyebrow.

"No, I didn't." Emily smiled for the first time since she'd returned and he found that it was like a punch to his gut. He'd forgotten how her face lit up or how her blue eyes sparkled. "You did exactly what I thought you'd do, which was very reassuring."

"Glad something's gone as planned," Jax replied, trying to keep from smirking. For that brief moment, he felt as if they were once again lovers exploring their way through the enjoyable aspects of life. Seeing a sign for the next exit brought reality crashing down. He'd address her carrying a weapon at a later date. "I'm letting Connor know we're pulling off."

Had Jax been making a normal call, he would have used the vehicle's automated mobile feature. As it was, he would utilize the encrypted phone for the remainder of the trip. Hitting a sequence of numbers, he was finally able to get the call to go through.

"Everything okay?"

Connor hadn't bothered to say hello. Jax looked in the rearview mirror, spotting a matching vehicle around ten car lengths behind. The windows were tinted, as well as bullet proof, but that didn't mean damage couldn't be done.

"Yeah, we're just stopping to fuel up."

"You realize that the minute we hit the highway, we were probably tagged," Connor said, reiterating what another voice just said. "There's only so much Taryn can pull off."

"Who's with you?"

"We're broken up into three vehicles. Kevin is with me, keeping tabs with Taryn. She was able to tamper with all but one surveillance video. Ethan and Lach are situated in front, although Kevin will have them slow down while we follow you off the ramp."

"Speaking of Taryn, what did she have to say?" Jax asked, making sure the phone was pressed firmly against his ear. He didn't want Emily to be privy to what he was about to learn.

"Emily Weiss came to be in existence around five years ago just before she became an administrator for the United Nations."

"Isn't that miraculous," Jax replied, tightening his fingers on the steering wheel. He obviously knew that now that Emily had confessed the other night, but had no doubt Taryn had siphoned through numerous databases to locate a woman by a different name. "And beforehand?"

"Taryn back traced her to Grace Emily Weisslich, who seemed to have fallen off the earth right after she left college." It was nothing that Jax hadn't known, but the time frame was certainly off. "Get this. Records have been sealed regarding the particulars having to do with one Grace Emily Weisslich. The years between Grace disappearing and Emily appearing are what's troubling. Taryn's not giving up."

"Interesting." Jax was well aware that Emily's head swiveled in his direction, but that was just too bad. "Sealed by whom?"

"That's part of what she's working on. I'll be honest with you, Jax. Emily's flare of innocence back then had me fooled too. Don't beat yourself up over it."

"When we get there, I want to meet with you in person. Have Kevin cover the restroom when I escort her in. She'll be wearing a pink ball cap over her hair so that the visor hides her face from any security cameras that Taryn can't get to. Hopefully we'll be at the tanks long enough for Kevin to tell her our location and she can get a hit on their surveillance feed." Jax continued when Connor tried to interrupt. "I agree that we might have already been tagged, but why make it easy for them?"

"Fine," Connor said, giving a resigned sigh.

Jax pulled the phone away from his ear before Connor added anything else to the conversation. He knew his partner was concerned and making sure he had Jax's back, but there were sometimes when things just had to maintain their course. He laid the phone in the console between the seats.

"There's a hat in the backseat. Pull your hair up and tuck it in inside the cap."

"If we haven't gotten out of the vehicle yet, no one would know I'm even in here. So why is Connor saying we've already been made?"

"We're talking about the United Nations, our government, our Secret Service, and a contractor who's probably getting paid millions to serve your body up to the Secretary-General," Jax said with a pointed look, stressing the facts. "We have security cameras, drones, satellites...you name it, at the discretion of whoever has the power to use them. Trust me, they probably know exactly where we are. My job right now is just to keep you alive long enough to get this so-called evidence—that from my understanding is based on nothing— and presenting you in front of the camera at an international news agency."

"Well, when you put it like that..."

Chapter Ten

"I want a weapon."

Jax had finished filling the tank of the SUV and had gone around to her side. He watched as Emily tucked the last strand of her blonde hair into her cap. Blonde didn't suit her personality one bit, but it would definitely throw off someone to give him enough time to shoot to kill. It was what he was trained to do and he was damn good at it. Giving her a gun now would only complicate matters until he was sure she knew how to handle one, regardless of her confession of having been taught.

"You'll get one when I say you'll get one." Jax was standing inside the open door, shielding her the best that he could. There was no way he was going to arm her right now. Emily was well covered and until he was certain she spoke the truth in regards to her weapon training, he felt more comfortable being the one equipped. "Right now, I want you in and out as quickly as possible. Kevin has already established the restroom is empty."

"Fine," Emily snapped, shifting her body in a way that caused Jax to back up. She slipped down the side of the leather seat until her feet hit the ground. Peering up at him, her dark lashes gave testament to what her natural color was. Her blue eyes verified her irritation. "But it had better be soon."

Jax bit back a reply, knowing it would only fuel another argument. If they were in any other situation than the one they were in now, he'd have her strapped onto the spanking bench at Masters with a black leather paddle in his hand for copping that attitude. The image made him smile, but this wasn't the time or place, so he shut the door and pressed the button on the key fob to initiate the locks. Scanning the area to make sure it was clear, he kept her by his side until they were through the doors. He then ushered her directly to the back, keeping her on his left side and out of view from the cashier as they passed the counter. Kevin stood nearby looking at the drink selection.

"Go inside and lock the door," Jax ordered, waiting for her to follow his instructions. As she was about to close the door, he said, "Once you're finished, stand by with Kevin and pick something to drink, along with some snacks. We'll stop for food later."

With her nod of acceptance, Jax then waited for her to close the door. Not wanting to waste any more time than necessary, Jax slipped into the men's room and flipped the switch, essentially locking him and Connor inside. Turning, he faced his partner.

"You want to tell me the truth about what happened two years ago?" Connor was leaning against the opposite wall, his arms crossed and his jaw tightened. "I get that you seem to think you are untouchable, but fuck, you can't just go AWOL and put your life on the line for a woman you knew for one damned week, Jax."

Jax mimicked his friend's stance, pressing his back against the tiled wall. He laid his head back against the cold inlay and thought about lying. He really did. But then he knew he couldn't. This man was like his brother. Connor knew him better than anyone.

"I knew then what had really happened," Jax confessed, raising his head and running a hand through his hair. "I helped fake her death and made sure she had enough tools at her disposal to remain hidden for the rest of her life. She apparently didn't want it that way anymore. And here we are."

"I guess I don't have to ask if she's that important, but one week?" Connor rubbed his jaw, as if he were trying to understand Jax's actions.

"At the time, I felt like she was a gift." Jax looked at him directly in the eye, needing him to understand why he'd made the decisions he had. "Why do you think I fought you so hard when you wanted to throw in the towel with Lauren? I told you time doesn't matter, but now that two years have passed and I'm presented with a version of Emily that I don't recognize…maybe time is relevant."

Silence descended over the small enclosed room. It even seemed to echo off the walls as his ears felt a vibration. He told Connor the truth and they didn't have time for the fillers that weren't important.

"I'm not going to question why you didn't ask for my help," Connor said, shaking his head and getting on with the situation at hand. "We can't change the way things went down. What I want to know is how you think it's possible to get her to New York, find this so-called evidence, and have her placed on national television when the people we are dealing with can see our every move."

"I've been thinking about that," Jax replied, about to bounce some ideas off of his partner. He'd missed this lately. "If Schultz had truly wanted her out of the way, it would have been easy to make her disappear. Let's go on the assumption he *is* on our side and wants her kept safe until he has a chance to get her in front of the Security Council. With the Attorney General being dead, the only remaining target is Emily. Granted, Alekseev has access to surveillance, but he's not going to want to draw attention to himself right now."

"So you're assuming the only one we have to worry about is this contractor they've hired." Connor had a far away look in his eyes that he often got when he was contemplating something. "Taryn said the chatter stopped, which could only mean that Alekseev or one of his henchmen have decided who to use."

"I think we should continue on, let Emily play this the way she wants, and then hand her back over to Schultz." Jax tightened his fists as he got the last part of that sentence out. He might as well give Connor a heads up on what came after that as well. "I told Crest I'm walking when this is done."

Connor met his gaze and didn't back down. "I'm going to ignore that last part. You should know by now that Crest makes decisions based on the information at hand. Maybe if you'd been upfront about the choices you made, this would have turned out differently. Shit, if you'd have come to me back then, we certainly wouldn't be here now, would we?"

"I did what was best at the time."

"For a woman who obviously isn't telling you the truth." Connor pushed off the wall and stepped in front of the sink. "This life we live, the credo that we live by, and the duty we serve to our country is what makes us who we are. Truth is everything. You think I don't know that's what made you get into the kink we like? We practice the lifestyle because it gives us comfort in the fact that submissives need to be honest in their needs."

"You think I don't know that?" Jax practically spat out the words as he, too, pushed off the wall. They were now face to face. "Which is why when this is done, she's Schultz's problem. As for Crest, I've paid my debts just as I'm sure the government will pay him for saving the life of an *innocent civilian* caught up in an international incident."

"And me? We have a partnership, Jax. In the real estate that we bought, the club that we purchased together, and the brotherhood that I rely on in my daily life. Are you just going to go AWOL on me?"

"You have Lauren," Jax replied, turning to the sink and placing his hands on the porcelain. He hung his head, feeling plain old tired. "I just need a break, Connor."

"Fuck that." Jax looked up in the mirror to see Connor walk to the door and then turn around. "The last two years have been a break for you. You're just now facing reality from the decisions that you made. Fix them and let's move on with our lives."

Leave it to his partner not to cut him any slack. Jax sighed, wondering if Connor was right and he would feel differently when this was over. He'd never been one to waver over decisions, but maybe he wasn't in the right frame of mind. His thoughts went to the club.

"I could run the club full time."

"And be bored to tears during the day," Connor said, his hand reaching for the doorknob. "Face facts. There is nothing else for men like us. Now get your head out of your ass. We have places to be."

With that, Connor left the restroom. Jax looked at himself in the mirror and almost didn't recognize the man staring back. The anger and resentment that shone through his eyes took him by surprise. His partner was right. It was time to get his shit together.

✧   ✧   ✧   ✧

Emily opened the door a crack and peered out. No one was waiting to use the facilities, for which she was grateful. Kevin was standing three steps away, still perusing the drink selections. When she looked at his reflection in the showcase window, it was only then that she realized he was actually watching her. The color of his grey eyes seemed to glow even in the reflection.

Opening the door wider, she stepped out. Making her way to him, she stood by his side and pretended to be interested in the choices as well. What she really wanted was coffee, but didn't know if she should bring it up. The dislike he apparently felt staring at her right now had made its point.

"Is there a reason you don't like me?" Emily asked softly, although no one was near them.

"I don't dislike you," Kevin said, his large frame moving forward and pulling open one of the glass doors. He chose a bottle of water and stepped back, letting the panel close. "At least not yet."

"And that means?"

Emily was curious now. He didn't intimidate her, although his size alone would do that to many women. There was something in his eyes that screamed compassion though. Not that he had any for her, but she was relatively sure that was due to his friendship with Jax.

"Jax has been known to bend the rules, but he's never out and out broke them." Kevin turned to face her, causing her to do the same. She had to tilt her neck to maintain contact with his penetrating gaze. "Either you're the best thing to ever happen to him or the worst. I'm just reserving judgment."

"That's kind of you," Emily replied sarcastically, although it made her feel a little better to know that Jax had surrounded himself with people who cared for him. He'd shared his history with her and she knew that the death of his parents had left him shattered as a teenager. The service and Connor had given him back what had been taken. She was trying to do the same now, but couldn't let on…at least not yet. "A vehicle just pulled up. Tinted windows."

"I see it," Kevin said, looking over her head. She didn't have to turn to know that another glass-paneled door reflected what was behind him. She involuntarily jerked when he tossed the water bottle past her. "Connor, buy this for me along with a bag of chips. I'll check out the new customer and meet you in the vehicle."

Kevin didn't move like she thought he would, but instead waited for Connor to take his place. She understood that he was shielding her, but did they really think that if this were the man hired to kill her that one body would prevent that? Emily had been so caught up trying to look around Connor to see what was taking place outside that it took her a moment to realize he was staring right at her.

"Connor, it's good to see you again." Emily hadn't meant for her greeting to sound so formal. They'd met a few times back when she and Jax had been enjoying each other's company, but then fate had given her a different path. She knew how much he meant to Jax. It was his opinion most of all that she coveted. "Thank you for helping."

Connor's blue eyes were like ice as he looked her over with contempt. A knot formed in her throat unexpectedly and she tried her best to swallow around it. She knew exactly what he was going to say, but hearing the words still hurt.

"I'm doing my job."

"I—" Emily broke off before she declared her love for Jax. Did she love him? Did a week give a person a true insight into another? Or did she only love what he represented? Security. She needed Connor to know that Jax was the only thing that had gotten her through these last two years. "I'm doing this for Jax."

"Don't kid yourself. You're doing this for you." Connor looked over her head, obviously done with the conversation. It took her a second to realize that Jax was standing behind her. "Kevin's given the all clear, so we're good to go."

"Do you want anything?" Jax asked, coming to stand beside her.

"Coffee."

Emily looked up and saw a completely different man from the one she'd come into the convenience store with. His hazel eyes seemed to have come to life and he flashed her that smile that had kept her warm at night in her dreams. When he placed his hand on her lower back, she knew something had changed drastically in the last ten minutes. Whatever it was seemed to be very misleading and she knew then that she was losing control of whatever thread she'd had left.

Chapter Eleven

Jax looked into the rearview mirror, assuring himself that they had no tail. Honestly, if they were going to be ambushed on the way to New York, it wouldn't come from a vehicle following them. The contractor would think ahead and be stationed, ready to launch some type of attack on their convoy.

"Will we be stopping off for the night?"

Jax glanced at Emily, still sipping on the coffee that she'd gotten at the store. They'd ridden in silence for a good thirty minutes, but now that she'd struck up a conversation he'd take advantage of that.

"No, we'll drive straight through." Jax shifted a bit, trying to prevent the holster from digging into his side. He'd tossed his jacket onto the back seat and adjusted the heat accordingly. He knew that Emily liked the interior on the warm side, so there was no way in hell he'd last long with Ethan's leather jacket. He made a mental note to swap back at the first opportunity. "It's an eighteen hour drive, so I figure we'll pull in the hotel around eleven tonight, although it will probably be more like midnight."

Emily fell silent and looked out the passenger side window. Her index finger was lightly tapping the side of her Styrofoam cup, indicating that she wasn't as relaxed as she wanted him to think. He was about to make things more uncomfortable. He had an idea of what she was withholding, and at this juncture he had to force her hand.

"We have a long drive ahead of us," Jax said, turning the radio down slightly. "How about we play a game?"

He could feel her eyes bore into him and it took everything to keep from smiling. To hell with it. Jax turned and displayed a smirk. Emily's brows furrowed, showing her bewilderment. It felt good to finally have the upper hand. He felt more like his old self.

"What kind of game?" Emily asked warily.

"The one where we get to ask each other questions and the other has to answer honestly." Jax switched on his blinker and carefully drove around a semi. "That is, if you remember how to."

"You can cut out the sarcasm, Jax," Emily snapped and shifted in her seat to face him. "I've already told you that I stashed the evidence. The best thing we can do is take this on the offensive instead of waiting for Schultz to convince the government to act—it's not their asses on the line."

"It's simple. Either you're out or in."

"Fine," Emily replied, placing her coffee in the cup holder. She pulled the band out of her hair and then pulled the strands back again, as if readying herself to do battle. "I go first."

"No. I suggested the game, so I'm up in rotation."

"Fine. Shoot."

"You have an aunt, although you didn't mention her before." Jax could tell by her expression that he'd surprised her by bringing up something other than the case. "Is she your only family?"

"You know that my mom was a single parent up until the day she died," Emily replied, shrugging her shoulders as if to say it wasn't important. Jax knew differently. "During college, I stayed with my aunt. She's like my second mother. I think that was the hardest thing for me when I went into hiding, but revealing that to you would have only held you back from giving me the opportunity I needed."

"You're smart enough to realize that every time you made contact with her, you put her life in danger." Jax couldn't help but chastise her for those actions. He'd made it clear back then that she was to cut all ties with her past. Seeing all the things she *had* done made him realize she ignored each and every directive. "It doesn't matter how careful you were or how ingenious your methods were, you still could have gotten her killed."

"You weren't the one waiting every second of the day to be found out," Emily responded with her voice full of irritation. "Now it's my turn. Did you really expect me to be on the run until the day I died? Let's face it, Jax. While I was doing my damnedest to fix everything that had gone wrong, you were living your life as if I hadn't existed. I'm done with this game. Don't bother replying, because the answer is evident."

Emily quickly faced forward, her anger apparent, and put her head back against the seat. She crossed her arms and closed her eyes. Jax hadn't planned on the made-up pastime going in this direction. His goal had been to get her to reveal more than she'd been. He did feel a twinge of guilt for doing exactly what she'd accused him of. Although there wasn't a day that passed that she hadn't been on his mind, he had moved forward in his own way. Having her back only made him realize how much they had both sacrificed, which is why he was about to throw down the gauntlet.

"We'll come back to that another time," Jax said, turning his focus back on the road. He knew that his words had her attention. It was time to play hardball and he hoped like hell she didn't call his bluff. He was the one responsible for keeping her alive and he would go to any lengths necessary to make that happen—even blackmail. "You have until we reach New York to come clean with me. If not, I'm calling Jessalyn myself and telling him that you're his responsibility or you're on your own. Either way, I'm out."

Emily opened her eyes to reveal the glaring lights of New York City. She used her fingers to massage her eyes, trying to adjust to the harsh illumination. Stifling a yawn, she sat up a little straighter. They'd come to a red light and she glanced around, noticing the sleepless patrons as they roamed the streets. She pretended they held her interest for she refused to glance over at Jax, not wanting to be forced to give in to his ultimatum. At least not yet.

Weighing the pros and cons, Emily's big fear was that Jax would walk away anyway. His expertise and that of CSA in dealing with governments was her best chance of coming out of this alive. Either way, his mind was probably already made up. She just needed to come to terms with it. It wasn't like Schultz was around to tell her this was a mistake.

She pushed aside the thought for now, wondering where Jax and the team had chosen to stay for the evening. Emily wasn't about to suggest the apartment that she still had, for by now the contractor might have already located it. She'd never stayed long in one place and that one had outdone itself a while back.

They'd stopped a couple more times, although not for any length of time. Connor and Kevin were a constant, although she never saw the other members of the team that Jax had said were in on the transport. Would they all stay at the same place or would they separate, giving them better leverage against whoever might be hired to kill her?

"You understand that by doing this, you've just exposed yourself?"

Jax's voice jolted her out of her thoughts. She understood better than he knew, but refrained from saying that. Instead, Emily nodded. The minute they left the safe house, she was well aware that she'd made herself visible. But it had to be done and with his protection, and that of CSA, she was positive this choice held the best chance to get her life back. It was what she was about to reveal that had her questioning the outcome.

"The evidence I have are recordings of Alekseev discussing the murder of Bianchi," Emily said, as if they were engaging in a normal conversation. She kept her face toward the passenger side window, looking out at the random people who were living their life with no thought to international corruption or hits for hire. "Within these series of recordings, Batkin and Alekseev prepared for the murder, executed the murder, and thought they got away with it."

"Recordings?"

Emily could hear the caution within his voice. She was well aware that he probably had just put all the pieces together, but it was best if she spell it out for him. She didn't want him to claim she withheld something after this.

"I'm an agent for the NSA." Emily paused long enough for her admission to really sink home. In her opinion, the NSA was the most dangerous and lethal agency on U.S. soil. "Or I should say *was*. My mission, going undercover as an administrative assistant, was to place listening devices throughout the United Nations' building to garner intelligence on certain foreign missions. I did as I was told and when things turned sour…"

"Fuck me. The National Security Agency used you as a NOC," Jax said in a deadpan kind of way, finishing her sentence. His verbiage stood for *non-official cover*, which meant she was disposable. She could be disavowed if her cover was blown, which she was. The NSA would claim no knowledge of her position within the agency, which they had. He didn't seem shocked, although he did seem to have trouble believing it. She didn't blame him, but there were clear rules about classified information. Would he respect that? "You're about to go on national television to expose a government agency for engaging in illegal activity."

Emily could hear the disbelief in his voice, but needed to make him understand. This went far beyond the NSA listening to private conversations. This had to do with international policies and relationships. The crimes committed on U.S. soil had to be brought to light. It was the only way that she could ensure that she got her life back. Whatever semblance of a life that was left after this.

"No," Emily argued, finally turning to look at him. Even in the dim lighting of the vehicle, she could see the brown in his eyes flashing. "I'm exposing an assassination of an international presence on U.S. soil."

"We'll all be dead before we step foot inside any media outlet. Fuck me," Jax said, repeating his words.

"Crest and your team handle government contracts, Jax. I'm sure they can handle this. Why do you think I made Schultz call in that favor to Crest?" Emily knew they had hurdles, but nothing they couldn't overcome. "This is something I have to do in order to get my life back."

"Is that what Jessalyn promised you?" Jax asked, easing off the brake pedal and following at a decent distance from the vehicle in front of them. Despite his outward appearance of relaxation, she saw his fingers tighten on the steering wheel. "He's lying through his teeth. As an agent, you should know that. The NSA fucked you over the minute you accepted that assignment."

"You don't seem surprised at my occupation," Emily responded warily. Had he known all along? "And Schultz has no clue that I'm about to expose Alekseev on national television. But I'm sure my chosen profession has answered your questions."

"Let's just say I had a gut feeling that you were in way deeper than you originally claimed. But actually hearing those words come out of your mouth...Jesus Christ! As for your profession answering my questions, you mean the fact that you knew who to call when the shit hit the fan back then? With you being an agent for the No Such Agency, why would you have Jessalyn on speed dial? What's the connection?"

"I met him a few times over the years before my last assignment." Emily shrugged, but then realized he was watching the road. "I took a chance calling him, but then changed my mind. I trusted you more."

"Should I be thankful?" Jax asked, finally glancing her way. The icy stare had returned and instantly dashed her hopes of his understanding her predicament back then. "Do you even understand the ramifications of what you've done? You withheld information that would have made me make different choices back then, Emily. I sent you into deep into a forest, right into the path of rabid wolves that would pick their teeth with your bones as if you meant nothing. And it doesn't negate the fact that you contacted Schultz afterward. All it did was put you on the NSA's radar. Is he the one who aided you in digging up more information?"

"I was the only one who knew where the other bugs had been placed within the building. It was my only leverage and I knew it was keeping me alive." Emily resisted the urge to touch him. She thought for sure that she'd made the right call back then, withholding her true identity. If anyone had made a connection between the two of them, it would have been his death on her conscience. And that was something she refused to even consider. "For all I knew, Schultz had contacted the NSA and it was only a matter of time before he took me out. So I made a deal and so far, everything's been running as planned and Schultz hasn't let me down yet."

"Except now you have a bounty on your head, an assassin on your tail, and you've changed courses," Jax replied sarcastically. "I hate to break this to you, but the assassination of the Secretary-General will take a back seat with the public once they hear that the NSA is placing illegal wiretaps within the United Nations. They'll immediately leap to conclusion that the NSA is doing the same with the general public. They're a rogue agency, playing cowboy on the international stage. I'm curious about one thing. Who do you think took the contract out on you? Is it the Secretary-General or your former employer? Let me tell you the real truth—we're fucked either way."

❖ ❖ ❖ ❖

Ryland walked over to the hotel mini-bar in the penthouse that he'd reserved for the week and poured himself his usual whiskey. The clink of the crystal echoed slightly as he slid the top back into the neck of the decanter. Tumbler in hand, he strolled across the living room to the open balcony where the sheer drapes blew in the light breeze. The taste of the vintage liquor he savored calmed his busy mind as he took in the visage before him.

Ryland stood in the middle of the balcony, watching the city come alive as dusk approached. A particularly poignant violin concerto drifted from the speakers, creating a focused ambiance that was highly inductive to his train of thought. The fact that Vivaldi had been a priest worked for his cruel sense of humor. The irony of it twisted a smile onto his lips as he plotted.

He'd spent the last two days communicating with his various contacts to find out more about Grace Emily Weisslich. What he found was astounding and only added to the mystery of this elusive woman. Ryland smiled and then lifted the glass to his lips, allowing the warmth of the liquid to seep into his chest. It was similar to the feeling he acquired when finding out his adversary was more intelligent than the average citizen. It was as if he'd found a worthy opponent, similar to that of a good game of chess. He was coming to really like that analogy.

His target had few choices left to her. Grace Emily had to have heard about the Attorney General's *accident* by now, leaving her to wonder who now had the evidence that she'd turned over to him. Ryland had destroyed all of it as per his instructions. It wasn't his place to be concerned with the reason for their contracts. He was simply hired to clean up a specifically defined mess. Initiative was rarely rewarded in his business. He had a code that defined him and his actions worked toward that objective without error. He did not concern himself with the morality of it all. That was not his job.

Grace Emily apparently had her hands on the original recordings, which he would obtain and subsequently obliterate what remained. It was in the back of his mind that his employers had let this go on far too long before trying to clean up their mess, but far be it of him to criticize. He was just reaping the rewards of their procrastination.

Raising the glass in a toast, Ryland congratulated himself on making the first successful move. The target was flushed from the hide. At the time, he had no idea that taking out the Attorney General had anything to do with this case. He'd done what he was paid to do and then had flown directly into New York for his next mission. Now, given the details, he was well aware of what Grace Emily would do. Unorthodox as it may be, he was able to place himself into the mindset of his target and calculate his or her options. She didn't have many alternative moves left. He just had to wait until she made her contained choice, funneling her toward his sights. He was a very patient man. He had never missed his quarry once he had obtained a sight picture.

Chapter Twelve

"Taryn just informed me that Emily's file has been wiped clean," Crest said, not a hint of exhaustion in his voice. His arms were crossed and he was leaning against the hotel room's wall. Wearing more casual clothes than usual, the brown cashmere pullover was rolled to his elbows. Jax was itching just looking at it. "There is no trace of her employment with any government agency."

"What *has* Taryn been able to pull up?" Jax asked, fiddling with the one-cup coffee maker. They chose a random hotel, nothing too low grade, but not too extravagant. Luckily, the room across the way housed Connor and Kevin, who were monitoring the hallway thanks to specific surveillance equipment Taryn had equipped them with. "She was behind the eight ball from the beginning. We should have known Emily was NSA the minute we took this case."

The shower was still running, indicating that Emily was still busy getting ready for what was going to be a hellish day. The map she had been pouring over most of the morning showed various places throughout New York City in which she'd hidden the recordings of the listening devices. Considering they were running on borrowed time before the contractor tracked them down, Emily wasn't going to be happy with what he and Crest had decided for obtaining them.

"I know you're frustrated, but Taryn's acquired everything that's still available. As I said, anything on Emily has been erased in NSA's system. As far as the world knows, Grace Emily Weisslich disappeared right after college. Although we know that Emily Weiss was created, she ceases to exist other than the fact that she died two years ago." Crest raised an eyebrow at Jax's attempt to jimmy the filter into the cone of the coffee maker. He was ready to throw it out the fucking window. "Taryn did manage to trace and monitor specific areas of the United Nations, thanks to the next agent they had in position. Apparently they have several assets in play during this op."

"They left her to fend for herself, all the while continuing on with whatever the hell it is they're doing?" Jax knew his question was more rhetorical than anything, but it still managed to astonish him how disposable people were for a *greater good*. The water shut off, indicating that Emily would be joining them soon. He had to maintain his distance or he'd never get through this. Having confirmation that she was an agent distorted his thoughts and opinions of their actions so many years ago. He knew he was coming across as a hard ass toward her, but that was the only way he could keep his head on straight. It was his job to keep them both alive. "What did Taryn hear on these listening devices?"

A specific knock sounded on the door, indicating that Connor or Kevin was on the other side. Regardless of them recognizing the explicit thuds, he and Crest had their weapons pulled within seconds. Jax trained his P220 on the door and waited while Crest took lead. After getting an affirmative code word response over the radio he held in his hand, he still looked out the small, magnified circle embedded inside the wood. He gave the all clear with a nod of his head. Jax had already holstered his weapon before Kevin stepped in.

"Lach and Ethan are downstairs in the lobby. The heavy weapons are stowed away in our room," Kevin said, closing the door behind him. Jax tossed the filter in the garbage upon seeing him carrying a take-out tray with four coffees. The only thing better would have been if he'd included breakfast, but Jax wasn't going to quibble. After Kevin took his in hand and passed off the recyclable container, he leaned up against the door, resting the heel of his boot on the lower half before finishing his part of the conversation. "Has Jessie managed to set up the live media bit?"

"Yes," Crest replied, returning his 1911 to the holster attached to his black dress pants. It would be concealed by his dress coat before they left the building. Jax handed him a cup. "But I want to wait until Emily is finished getting ready before explaining how the rest of this mission will be carried out. I don't want to have to repeat myself."

"Getting back to Taryn and this agent they seemed to have replaced Emily with, what chatter is Taryn picking up?" Jax cleared a spot on the side table, placing Emily's coffee down but taking his own. "Anything in regards to the person Alekseev has hired to take out Emily?"

As if right on cue, the door opened and out walked Emily. Her blonde hair was still wet, although she'd pulled it back at the nape of her neck. She was dressed in jeans and a black long-sleeved shirt. There were slight shadows underneath her eyes that gave the appearance that she was tired, but the blue of her eyes were lit with determination. She zeroed in on the coffee and Jax handed his over, since he'd yet to even take off the lid.

"What have I missed?"

"Apparently, Taryn has discovered that another agent took your place. Is there anything specific that the NSA is trying to find?" Jax figured he'd throw that question out, not sure if it really mattered. "What were your original instructions?"

"We aren't told much," Emily admitted, walking to the end of the bed and tucking a leg underneath her as she got comfortable. "We are given instructions and we carry them out."

"You weren't supposed to listen in on these so-called conversations, were you?" Jax asked, not knowing if he could truly believe her. He wanted to, but Emily's track record wasn't winning her any points. It was something he knew that would have to be dealt with on a personal level, but right now, they were just trying to keep her alive. "You know what? Forget I asked. You did and we're here."

"Taryn's narrowed it down to two contractors who might have taken the assignment. Trevor Neonni and a man who only goes by Ryland." Crest lifted the cup and took a drink of the hot liquid. "Both are in town as of yesterday, which can't be a coincidence. We have a location on Neonni, but Ryland fell off the radar the minute his plane touched down in LaGuardia."

"Do you think they're working together?" Jax asked, taking his own coffee and removing the lid. He hated the damn things. "I would think they wouldn't want to split the money. They've got to be offering a massive amount."

"Which is why we're going on the offensive," Crest answered. "Connor's going to pay Neonni a visit while we gather the intel that Emily's hidden. As Kevin said, Lach and Ethan are waiting for their coordinates. You just have to supply them to us, Emily."

"It's not that easy," Emily protested, obviously not wanting to give up the only evidence that seemed to be keeping her alive. "I should—"

"Crest is right," Jax said, leaning a shoulder against the wall opposite of Crest. "The more hands in the pot makes it harder to know which one to burn. If Neonni isn't the man hired to kill you, then the chances are good it's Ryland. And as of right now, we have no clue as to where he is. Once we have the evidence in hand, we'll all meet up at the news station, where Crest will have everything ready to roll. It's not like you have a choice right now, Emily."

Jax could see the confliction within Emily's blue eyes. He understood her need for control, particularly since she'd been on her own for so long. But now wasn't the time to try and do this without help. She needed them and she knew it. Plus, he was finally back in control and had no plans on losing it now.

"Fine," Emily said in more of a sigh than a formulated word. She shifted on the bed and pulled the map of New York City toward her. "I'll mark the places in red, then cut the map into four sections. Mr. Crest can assign three of the areas, although you and I will need to be the ones to go to West 24th Street."

"It's just Crest. No need for formalities."

Jax turned his head to see Crest smirk before taking a drink of his coffee and noticed that he observed every red X that Emily marked on the paper. Only when she was finished and had started to tear the map into sections did Crest meet his gaze. It wasn't in confrontation, although there did seem to be a question in his eyes with regards to Jax's scrutiny. He shrugged it off, knowing that Crest would never needlessly put his team members in harm's way. Jax didn't like his superior's policy when it came to withholding information on a personal level, but that would be discussed at a later date when this case was over and done with. Hell, like he'd told Connor, he might be finished with this life by then as well.

"Any particular reason we need to be the ones in that area?" Jax asked, watching as she started to tear the paper.

He didn't know why, but the sight of her blonde strands that were pulled back at the nape of her neck caught his attention. Although the thickness and shine remained, he preferred her as a brunette. Would he ever get the chance to see her natural coloring again? The question made him ponder why his anger had dissipated. Nothing had really changed, although he had given her fair warning that when he learned the truth and it was something he could forgive, he'd have her at his mercy tied to his bed. Were her lies forgivable? Had he forgiven her?

"Yes," Emily replied to his question, finally standing up and facing them. She then held out three squares of paper toward Crest, causing him to step away from the wall and take them with his free hand. "There's a piece of art being held at a gallery. We need it and the only way to retrieve it is to show up in person."

"The only reason I'm giving the green light for this antic you planned is that Schultz is MIA," Crest said, directing his statement to Emily. "When we do get a hold of him, he takes point. Understand?"

"Understood," Emily said, her chin rising just a bit at Crest's stance on this mission.

Jax downed half his coffee, ready to get this show on the road. There would be time to deal with the personal aspect of what she'd put them through after this ordeal was over. He didn't like his slip up a few moments ago, wanting to see her back to her natural ways. He needed to get his head in the game, but her next words sent his thoughts astray once more. At this rate, his death would likely come before hers.

"So, who's going to give me a weapon?"

Jax had finally been able to switch jackets with Ethan. He felt more like himself and a hell of a lot more comfortable in the worn brown leather. Although it was still March, the weather was on the cold side and wearing the coat concealed his weapon easily. The shining moment of the morning was when Ethan had tossed him his skullcap. Unfortunately, it didn't relieve the tension that had balled up inside the both of them at being so exposed as they walked down 24th Street.

"Are you warm enough?" Jax asked, making sure to keep a hand firmly in place on Emily's lower back. He could feel the pistol in the small of her back, the MOB holster attached to the waistband of her jeans. He wore his sunglasses, allowing him to scout the area for any foreseeable threat. Unfortunately, nothing would be able to stop a sniper, which was why he had her practically attached to his hip. "The hooded sweatshirt should be keeping the wind out of your face."

"I'm okay," Emily said, her words muffled since she hadn't lifted her chin toward him. He was pleased to see her training kick in, although could feel the stress radiating from her body. "It's the art gallery on the far corner."

Jax casually lifted his left hand up to adjust his skullcap, and pressed it more firmly on his head while listening to the conversation that was taking place between his team members in his ear bud. Connor had paid Neonni a friendly visit to find out why he was in New York City. On one hand, Jax was relieved to know that it had nothing to do with Emily. On the other, no one could locate Ryland. He took one last look around before crossing the street and stepping up to the entrance of the gallery.

"Lach has reached his destination and retrieved the first recording," Jax murmured, reaching for the door. "Let's get ours. In and out."

Emily quickly turned to block his way, catching him off guard. It was a good thing he was obstructing her visual from the streets, as she tilted her head back, revealing her blue eyes. The smudges underneath seemed to have darkened in the span of a few hours, indicating her fear of what she about to do. He gave her credit. She hid it well.

"Jax, now that you know the truth, tell me this is something we can get past." She searched his eyes for a response behind the darkness of his glasses and he was relieved she couldn't see them clearly. "Please. Just tell me that you'll have me tied to your bed when this is all over like you said. Tell me you understand that I was just doing my job. You should appreciate that, considering your service to our country."

Jax inhaled deeply, wishing he had a clear-cut answer for her. Her plea gave him an indication of what she'd been fighting for all this time. But the fact was they'd spent seven days together and two years apart. A lot had happened in that time span and truth be told, they really didn't truly know each other. Since that reality was now setting in, he didn't have an answer.

"You're really starting to piss me off, Jax," Emily said, her blue eyes tinting with anger at the fact he'd remained silent. "Just remember, you got to carry on with your life while I was fighting to get back what I'd lost. You don't get to stand there and judge me."

"The only thing I can promise is that I'll do everything in my power to make sure you live through this," Jax said, keeping his voice low. This wasn't the time to hash out their personal demons. "We have no idea what the fallout will be. Let's focus on what we need to do and deal with the rest later."

He could see her accept that was the only answer he could give her. They'd had this conversation too many times to count, but it wouldn't change until the situation altered course. With a slight nod of her head, Emily turned back to the door and waited for him to open it.

Once they were inside, the background music was the only thing that could be heard. The sound was so low that the only sounds Jax could distinguish were melancholy. Emily went to remove her hoodie when he laid a hand on her arm, shaking his head. He'd spotted the surveillance cameras immediately. Taryn was busy covering the area where the news station was located, not the various individual locations. They were easy to notice since the gallery floors and walls were pristine white and the only color that appeared was on the canvases spread far apart from each other.

"May I help you?"

The voice came from a classic elderly woman who had aged with grace and still remained beautiful in her own right. Her reddish blonde hair was sprayed to stay in place, while her make-up had been precisely applied. There was an air of elegance surrounding her, but it seemed to explode upon setting eyes on Emily.

"Oh, my dear," the woman whispered, a manicured hand covering her lips. "You—you're alive."

"What the hell, Emily?" Jax asked in a low voice, although he made sure she knew that he wasn't pleased with this turn of events. "You know her?"

"Ms. Lansing, I'm here to pick up the painting that you've been so kind as to hold for my aunt," Emily said loudly, as if the original exchange hadn't happened. She reached into her pocket and pulled out a receipt, handing it over to the woman. "Would you please wrap it for me?"

Ms. Lansing seemed to pull herself together and she gave a small, if not nervous smile. Her eyes flickered to him, and Jax did his best to flash a grin when all her wanted to do was ask Emily what the hell she thought she was doing. As a former agent, she knew better than to have any contact with anyone she knew. Those kinds of mistakes were what got people killed.

"I met this woman once or twice in my mid-twenties," Emily said. She turned and faced him as Ms. Lansing crossed the sterile showroom and entered a back room. "She's an old friend of my aunt, but the distance is what is relative here. No one would think I would hide evidence within a prominent art gallery in New York City."

Jax removed his sunglasses and pressed his fingers to his eyes, trying to stem off the headache that was forming. He needed more caffeine to deal with her rationalizations. Knowing it made no difference now, Jax situated himself so that he could see the back door and the entrance. He didn't want them to be boxed in should they be approached.

"Taryn just got confirmation that Ryland took the operation." Jax turned his head slightly, not surprised by the information Kevin had relayed, but taken aback that corroboration had come through. Various voices could be heard in his ear, but Kevin's came through loud and clear. "She has video surveillance of Ryland meeting with Alekseev's security chief. Crest, she needs you to look at his photo."

Jax's gut twisted. If Taryn needed Crest to get a visual on this guy, then it wasn't a contractor that made mistakes. This meant they were dealing with one of an elite few when it came to hired assassins. Their time was running out.

Chapter Thirteen

"**C**rest, who is Ryland? I overheard Ethan say that Taryn had a video surveillance picture of him."

As Jax and Crest engaged in a conversation that she partially listened to, Emily's thoughts were running at a thousand miles per second. She tightened her grip on the small USB drive, which contained the digital recordings she was about to air on international television. She glanced toward the entrance of the media station and then in the opposite direction, catching sight of Connor and Kevin walking around the central news desk. The other two men were nowhere to be seen, which made her think that they were watching the outside of the building.

Emily knew she should be worried about Ryland, but right now, her stomach was tied up in knots over the fact she was about to accuse the Secretary-General of murder. Would it backfire, like Jax suggested? Would the public only hear the fact that the NSA was listening to private conversations? Or would the travesty of the crime Alekseev committed take front and center?

"We'll discuss it at a later date," Crest said, his voice consumed with tension, which garnered Emily's attention. "Just know this…he changes his appearance as easily and more often than Jessie does her nail color. We'll never see him coming, so as much as I advocate a strong offense, our defense has to be equally as determined as Bataan."

Emily felt a chill travel down her spine and her fingers itched to hold her weapon in protection against an unforeseen evil. It was hard to defend against an opponent she couldn't see coming. Jax's hand came to rest on her lower back and although it did nothing to relieve the tension, it did give her the strength to start walking toward the heart of the station.

"Place this in your right ear," Jax said, as he walked beside her. He was holding up a small earpiece, similar to the one that he had in his. "Whatever you say, we'll hear. You'll also be able to hear the rest of us. Do not hesitate if I tell you to hit the ground. Understand? If Crest's body language is anything to go by, Ryland is a worthy adversary that we can't underestimate."

Emily's steps faltered a bit as realization sunk in. The team had heard every word she and Jax had exchanged. They'd heard her practically beg him to tie her to his bed and fuck her. Normally, she wasn't the type to care what other people thought, but this situation was a bit extreme. Damn.

"Did you hear me?" Jax asked, a tightness in his voice that indicated he didn't like how this day was going.

"Yes," Emily said and then cleared her throat. She knew that Crest was behind them and decided now was the time to ask for one more favor. Why not? She owed them more than just her life. "Crest, would you please have someone verify that my aunt has left the country? She's always followed my directions, albeit reluctantly, but I need to know she's safe."

"A friend of mine is currently enjoying a break overseas and appreciating the art," Crest replied, giving Emily her answer. She looked over Jax's shoulder and smiled her thanks, hoping it conveyed how much she truly appreciated the extra miles he was putting in. She was now understanding Jax's original anger at her for potentially ruining the life he'd built. "Let's get this over and done with."

Emily was able to really view her surroundings, her vision no longer obscured by the walls of the hallway. There was an upper level with a balcony that circled the middle of the station. She could see people walking around the shadows, but couldn't make much out other than that. The open vulnerability made her uneasy. At the center, the ceiling was vaulted, allowing for metal structures to be the anchor for heavy lighting and camera equipment. Vast amounts of cords dangled and lights flashed from various angles, giving the sense of disorder when it was obvious it was anything but.

"Ms. Jenkins, thank you for allowing our client to use your network for this live press conference." Crest stepped forward, shaking hands with the beautiful anchorwoman. The blonde was meticulous in her appearance, with her classic red suit and high heels. The smile that Emily assumed was usually false shined bright with this woman's eagerness to get the scoop of the year. "We appreciate that your station was willing to work with us on our demands."

"It's our pleasure, Mr.—"

Ms. Jenkins allowed her voice to drop off, hoping that Crest would fill in the blank. Even Emily knew that wasn't going to happen, so when the blonde turned toward Jax with her hand held out, Emily stepped forward.

"Ms. Jenkins, let me reiterate that I am grateful for your time and that of your station. Where would you like me to sit?"

From the slight tightening of Ms. Jenkins' mouth, it was obvious that she wasn't happy she couldn't garner more information. That was just too bad, because this woman was only getting what Emily wanted her to get. She was pointed out the far chair, so she and Jax walked around the V shaped wooden anchor desk. Her position would allow for her to better see Ms. Jenkins and the camera, although the anchor-woman didn't seem to realize this wasn't a question and answer session.

"Let's get you ready," Jax said softly, kneeling down. His action brought him to eye level as she sat straight in the uncomfortable chair given for guests. There was a glass of water to her left, although Emily had no intention of drinking it. "You certainly aren't dressed to go on live television, are you?"

The humor in his voice was a first and her eyes flew to his. Jax's soft lips were curved up at the corner, giving him that boyish charm she remembered. He lifted up the small black mic and carefully attached it to her sweatshirt. She wasn't sure why, but what she was about to do suddenly caved in on her and the feeling of losing control brought a snap of panic that she wasn't used to. She'd become immune to the threatening feeling she'd been living under, but now that it was finally coming to an end, terror balled up in her chest. It would have been better had he remained distant.

"You're not going to panic on me now, are you?"

Emily shook her head, not able to speak past the lump in her throat. He then held up a hand, silently asking her to let go of the small device that she had a death grip on. It was humorous, considering that Kevin now held the rest and would be the one to operate the recorder. She understood she had to release it and trust that it wouldn't end up in the wrong hands, but it was hard to do when she'd only had herself to rely on for so long. She swallowed hard and then cleared her throat. It was time to end this.

"As long as you don't," Emily replied, returning his half smile. She also wanted to make one thing clear. "Next time I'm being broadcast to your entire team, let me know. There's a lot of stuff that they should know about Jax Christensen that they probably don't. With the exception of Connor."

"My earpiece is in and activated." Jax winked and for a brief moment, she felt like they were in the past and nothing had gone wrong to waylay their lives. The spark of merriment disappeared and in its place was a gravity and plea that she listen closely. "This place is crawling with staff, although this was such an abrupt event, everyone who is here should belong here. That doesn't mean something can't go wrong, so you listen closely to my voice. In the meantime, recite what you want to convey the minute Ms. Jenkins gives you the go ahead. Remember, in and out."

Emily gave a nod of her head and forced herself to release the small piece of evidence into his hand. He looked as if he hesitated, but instead of saying anything else, he stood and walked to where the cameraman had positioned a large camera sitting on top of a tripod. He tossed the evidence to Kevin who was only a foot away, standing in front of what looked like a sound machine. She'd lost sight of Connor and Crest.

"May I have some name to introduce you as?" Ms. Jenkins asked as she took the seat on the opposite side of the V. "The audience will relate to you better."

"I don't need them to relate with me." Emily hadn't meant to sound so standoffish, but her nerves were wracked and this wasn't a social call. She reached up and placed the earbud in position. It was eerily quiet. "I just need to give them evidence of a murder that happens to be an international incident."

❖   ❖   ❖   ❖

Ryland smiled at who must be a beautiful intern, as she was walking by with more coffees than she could carry. The place was all hustle and bustle, or at least had been, until his target had walked on the set of the station. Everyone seemed to be glued on the secretive interview that was about to take place. He glanced below, making certain they had yet to roll live. A man was kneeling in front of his target, adjusting her mic. It was obvious that he was helping her in this endeavor, along with the man standing a couple feet away. His smile faded.

From this angle, he couldn't tell if there were any more men or women who'd come with her. Had Ms. Weisslich had the wherewithal to hire bodyguards? Or was there more to them? It was rare that he underestimated anyone. Now that he thought about it, there was only one person who had that honor. He merely brushed her memory aside and concentrated on the task at hand.

Presuming what dear Emily's next move would be hadn't been that hard. She had limited options. Who else besides the Attorney General was she going to give the evidence to? Ryland usually kept his part minimal…doing what he was hired to do. But being given two high paying missions in the same week warranted his interest. He needed to protect himself first and foremost and what intrigued him was the loose string in the name of Schultz Jessalyn. He'd yet to be given Jessalyn as a target.

Given that all he had to do was monitor calls into surrounding media and radio stations, Ryland hadn't even needed to really exert himself. Grace Emily was making this relatively easy, although he did need to get his hands on that evidence that she just presumably handed over to one of the men.

Ryland kept walking around the circular upper half of the station, not stopping even when he reached his destination. Climbing the stairs, he was able to get a better visual and noticed a shadow off of one of the hallways. Still ascending, he came to the rafters where darkness kept his form hidden. Maneuvering carefully, he kept to the outside as he circled the structure. What he found didn't surprise him as much as it peaked his interest. His target had definitely brought assistance and from the way they were stationed, they knew exactly what they were doing.

Well, well…this changed the game. Ryland wouldn't be able to just take her out quickly and be done. No, she had to go and play more than just the pawns in this game of chess. Ryland quickly amended his plans as he saw the exchange of evidence between two of the men, while the cameraman prepared to take Grace Emily live on international television. It was time to play his gambit, but first, he needed a delay.

The back of Jax's neck itched and he quickly glanced around, wondering what caused the intuitive sentiment. It had never failed him in combat, and when he glanced toward Connor, his partner seemed to be searching for something as well. Jax looked to his left, but couldn't spot Crest.

"Eyes on Emily," Crest ordered, his voice coming in loud and clear over the earpiece. Where had he gone? "I brought Lach in. He's up in the rafters. I don't like where the exit door is positioned to the roof."

"We should have cleared the station."

That comment came from Kevin, who was waiting for his cue to play the evidence. Jax was getting antsy himself and he agreed with the response. They should have cleared the station, or better yet, had a remote television van come to the hotel. Unfortunately, they were running out of time now that Ryland was confirmed as the contractor. They had no idea how much of a lead this man had on their whereabouts. It was better to execute this quickly and efficiently.

"No time." Had Crest positioned himself on the second floor? "Jax, move this along."

"We need to go live now," Jax said, as he turned to the cameraman whose name was Steve. "Do what you do and make it happen."

"There's something wrong with our feed," Steve said, shrugging his shoulders as if this happened regularly. Jax wasn't at ease with this in any way. "Our technicians are looking for the short."

"You have a lot more cameras." Jax pointed to the surrounding equipment. "Use one. Now."

"It's not the camera," Steve said, giving him a look that made Jax want to wipe it off immediately. "I'll try and simplify this for you. There seems to be a problem with the feed that transmits to the satellite. That means no camera will work right now."

"Clear out."

Crest's order was instant. Connor pulled his weapon, keeping an eye on the exit behind him down the hallway. Kevin's attention was on the soundboard, hopefully obtaining the thumb drive with the evidence that he'd placed inside the equipment. Jax crossed the distance between him and Emily, whose gaze had never wavered from his. He knew she heard every word that was said, but she hadn't panicked. In fact, she had an obstinate look on her face.

"It's not worth the risk," Jax said, already anticipating her argument. "It's too coincidental. We need to abort."

"No," Emily replied, ignoring Jenkins gasp at what Jax assumed was her reaction to Connor and his weapon. "Have them fix it and let me do this. We're here, for crying out loud."

"I'll have to agree with her," Jenkins said, her hand at her throat as she looked at someone behind him. "Whatever this is will make wonderful news. Steve is right and this happens all the time."

"Ethan is outside with the car," Kevin said, letting Jax know it was his presence that had Jenkins all atwitter. "The natives are getting restless and none of us are comfortable with this."

"Signs of a sniper," Lach said, his voice coming through the earpiece loud and clear. "Get out."

Jax and Kevin had their weapons drawn instantly and unless Crest had some pull with the entire staff of the news station, this incident was bound to make international news. It just wasn't exactly what they'd intended. Jenkins had pushed her chair back as if she thought she might be their target. Emily stood, ripping the mic from her sweatshirt and pulling out her own weapon.

"Kevin, give me the evidence," Emily ordered, holding out her other hand.

Ka-boom!

The entire building shook as if in slow motion. Screams, crashes, and exploding glass from office windows and equipment resounded through the air. Jax forced Emily low to the ground, covering her with his body as one side of the building seemed to collapse. The noise was deafening and Jax couldn't hear the voices in his earpiece. Apparently, neither could Emily or Kevin.

"Stay low and I'll lead," Kevin yelled from his left. Jax tightened his grip on Emily's sweatshirt and pulled her with them. Dust and smoke filled the air as they tried to make their way toward the exit where Connor had last been seen. "Shit. It's blocked. Go back."

Jax immediately turned and headed north, knowing there was an exit on that side. It would make them a target, because it was obvious whoever set the bomb wanted them trapped to the extent that they needed the northern exit. Ryland was earning his paycheck, the cocksucker.

"Emily, stay between me and Kevin." Jax veered around some smashed equipment and stepped around the glass. His boots wouldn't be penetrated, but Emily's tennis shoes would. The fire was spreading behind them and they had no choice but to continue what was most likely an ambush. "Be ready for an attack on our remaining exit. He's funneling us into his kill zone."

"I got a lock. Sniper north side." Lach's voice finally broke through the carnage on the earpiece. "I'm taking a shot."

An exchange of gunfire could be heard and Jax knew they had to exit now while Ryland's attention was diverted. He picked up the pace, making sure he kept his hand in hers. People had come out of nowhere and were running in front of him, helping his case. It would make it harder for Ryland to distinguish between who was who. He tried to blend them in with the crowd.

"I lost visual," Lach yelled. "The smoke is too thick. Crest, he was headed for the second floor."

The mic was silent, so Jax wasn't sure that meant Crest had lost his earpiece in the chaos or he'd been taken out. Not having time to dwell on it, he looked ahead and saw light streaming in from a door that someone was keeping open as they helped people escape. He hoped that Connor had gotten out of that fucking hallway before that half of the building fell. There was no way in hell Jax would go back to Lauren and tell her that Connor had bit the dust over his past indiscretions and bad choices. No way in hell.

Thwack!

"Fuck!" Jax yelled as he yanked Emily to the side away from where the bullets were slamming into the cement. Taking the chance that no innocent bystander was still on the second floor, he raised his gun and returned fire. Kevin did the same. Not giving Emily the chance to raise her weapon, Jax pushed her forward. "Move, move, move!"

Chapter Fourteen

Emily watched the dark scenery whiz by as their SUV finally left the city behind. It was hard to see what was beyond the guardrail of the highway. She really wasn't interested in the landscape anyway, but it was better than addressing her mistake that could have cost people their lives. She wasn't sure it hadn't.

"Do you know if everyone made it out?" Emily asked, rolling her head on the back of the seat so that she could see Jax. He'd taken his jacket off and thrown it in the back, while his holster and weapon remained in place. Her piece was now stored in the glove compartment. Although his jaw was set, he'd remained conspicuously silent since they'd started driving. "Were there any casualties?"

Emily's ears were still adjusting from the resonating sound of the explosion. The silence of the vehicle was almost painful, but hearing him confirm her suspicions would hurt worse. Her head was pounding as a result and she reached up and let her hair down, hoping it would ease the tension. What she really needed was Tylenol, but she wasn't about to ask him to stop. She'd already requested too much.

"Two people perished who were near the end of the building where the bomb was located," Jax said in a low voice, as if to lessen the hurt. She didn't know why he was being kind about it. No matter how it was said, it was still her fault. She hadn't taken his warnings seriously and thought they'd still been able to carry on. She wasted precious seconds arguing with him that cost people their lives. "We've warned Jenkins to not to release any information she may have gotten from us, but we can't gag her either."

"She'll be dead before morning," Emily murmured, knowing that Alekseev wouldn't have a loose string to contend with. Besides her, there actually was one more strand who'd been noticeably absent. "Has anyone heard from Schultz?"

"Crest has." Jax flipped the handle for the wipers, allowing them to clear the raindrops from the windshield. She wished it were that easy to wipe away the stains on her soul after today. "He obviously wasn't happy with your decision to go on international television. He wants us to trust him that he's handling his part."

"He wants us to go underground and wait until Ryland corners us like rats," Emily said with a wry laugh. She wasn't going to allow the innocent people who'd given their lives to die in vain. She had no choice but to atone for her own sins at this point. "Doesn't Schultz realize that Alekseev isn't going to allow him to turn evidence over to anyone else? With the Attorney General out of the picture, we now know how easily they can get to prominent figures. I still say going international is our best bet."

"After what happened today, I agree with Schultz that we need to hit the pause button and take a deep breath. You had a knee jerk reaction to the Attorney General's death and I allowed that to happen. I'm not saying it was wrong, but we rushed it," Jax said, surprising her when he reached across the center console and laid his hand over hers. The warm contact stole her breath for many reasons. "Crest has a friend whose house we're going to borrow for a while. The team is doing everything they can to throw them off of our trail. They'll meet up with us in a few days and we'll figure out a safer way to get your story out there."

"What's made you change your mind in working with them?" Emily asked, almost afraid to shift her hand for fear that he'd cease all contact. It felt more than nice to have his touch and she hadn't realized how much she'd needed it. "You said trust was an illusion and now here you are, letting them take the reins."

"I'll be honest, Emily," Jax said, sparing her a glance before then returning his concentration to the road in front of them. "When I saw you in that office, basically throwing away any chance of survival I had given you, I didn't know what to think. I reacted, just like you did. I'll admit I'm instinctive at times. I can also acknowledge when I'm wrong and in this case my team put their lives on the line for you. I can't ask for more than that, can I?"

Emily knew he wasn't expecting an answer, so she didn't give one. Instead, she leaned back her head and closed her eyes. It was impossible to shut out the images from today. They'd made it outside, breathing much needed oxygen into their lungs. Ethan had been standing by the SUV. Connor rushed by, entering the burning building while Jax had ushered her inside the vehicle. Kevin and Ethan made sure they escaped, before joining the fray. It wasn't until they'd used a secure phone to contact Jax some fifteen minutes later that he received an update. Ryland had somehow escaped, but not before a slight confrontation with Crest. They still didn't know the details, but it really didn't matter. He was still out there, coming for her.

Jax's hand still covered hers. Taking whatever he'd give her at the moment, Emily turned her wrist until their fingers entwined. He gently gave them a squeeze and as if his action were the cause, a tear escaped her eye as she turned her head back to the passenger window. More deaths were now a result of this mess she'd been caught up in. The hope she'd clung to for the last two years had dwindled and she was left with a fear that this wouldn't end the way she'd envisioned it.

Ryland stepped into the shower, letting the hot water run over his body and wipe away the soot and defeat of the day. That's how he viewed it too...a defeat. An unacceptable defeat. He rubbed his face, trying to get rid of the glue around his hairline. The wig and make-up he'd used for today's purpose was of quality substance, but it was hell to get off. He then pressed his palms against the cool tile of the penthouse suite's luxurious bathroom and hung his head, although he could have cared less right now about money. His pride had been given a beating and he didn't take that lightly.

Images of the day sped through his mind. Once Ryland had realized that Grace Emily had help in the form of what appeared to be a tactical team, he'd had no choice but to improvise. He'd made his way quickly to the other side, descending until he'd reached the bottom floor and located an electrical utility room far enough away so that he could create a diversion. He would have blown the damn building with her in it had he'd thought he could make it out before the explosives he'd planted would detonate. This team had the exits covered.

The blast had caused enough disorder and mayhem that he'd been able to return to the rafters relatively easy. Upon exchanging fire with one of the men, Ryland used the smoke and debris to cover his path in order to finish his mission. Unfortunately, the same pandemonium had been the cause of making it so difficult to eliminate his target. Before he'd been able to get a better angle to take the kill shot, he'd encountered someone from his past.

Gavin Crest. A man whose path Ryland had run across only once in the hell that was Iraq. It had been many years ago and he rarely thought of that operation, although it had been successful. It wasn't as if it had been a tough assignment. He finally managed to dredge up enough energy to reach for the soap as his thoughts drifted back to the past.

Ryland had been given the name of a high-ranking official to eliminate and he'd done his job efficiently. He'd been leaving the tent that had been his target's makeshift office when he'd been confronted by Crest, who'd stopped him to ask what Ryland was doing in a restricted area. In preparation of the assignment, he knew every ranking official that had been stationed there from the photographs he'd been provided. The resistance from Crest that Ryland had been facing could have been the catalyst for dire measures had the incoming alarm not gone off to indicate their camp was under rocket attack. Crest had immediately sprung into action, letting go of the fact that Ryland hadn't had the right credentials to be in the controlled space.

He gave little thought to what Crest had done after the raid. Ryland was too preoccupied with exiting as smoothly as he'd entered, which wasn't hard considering the commotion that had been taking place. What did stand out was one adversary recognizing another. And now here they were, on opposite sides once again.

Ryland rinsed off his skin, feeling clean although he hadn't been able to wipe away the day's disappointment. Stepping out of the shower and onto the cream plush mat, he dried himself off and then tossed the towel in the corner for the maid to pick up in the morning. Walking naked across the bathroom and then the bedroom floor, he made his way into the living room. Pouring himself a healthy douse of his favorite brown liquor, he then situated himself at the desk with his laptop.

Ryland knew he'd lost his target, which made this chase only that much more interesting. For the first time in a long time, he felt a sliver of adrenaline rush through his system this evening. He'd almost forgotten what it felt like. What he did know was that there was now a trail that would lead him straight to Grace Emily—Gavin Crest.

✧   ✧   ✧   ✧

"Who is he?"

Jax held the phone to his ear after having entered the code to which made this call encrypted. He looked over at Emily who'd fallen asleep an hour back. She needed it, although he wasn't so sure it was voluntary. Her body seemed to just shut down.

"He has no known last name," Crest said, his voice coming over the speaker loud and clear. "I ran into him once before…years ago. Taryn has found traces of him over the last decade, although he's very good at masking his whereabouts. He appeared in the late nineties as a contractor for hire on the jobs that no one was willing to take and has worked his way up the ladder as an independent contractor. He's never failed to get his target and anyone could have hired him that has enough assets to put into play."

"If that's the case, then I'll have to agree with Emily on the timetable rather than Schultz," Jax said, keeping his tone low. "We don't have time to wait for him to do this with his T's crossed and his I's dotted. I understand how it would be better than causing an international feud between countries, but not if it means Emily's life. Just in case anyone has lost sight of the fact that we really aren't sure who hired this hitter, whether it be Alekseev or the NSA, his intel could be better than we think."

"So does that mean you're over your tantrum?" Crest asked, an edge of slightly dry humor coming through the speaker.

Jax smirked, not willing to verbally admit that he'd acted out of anger. One thing that being a part of this team had taught him was that past transgressions would be forgiven. He wouldn't be handing in his resignation, but he wasn't about to let Crest's bad decision of not disclosing Emily's case to him the moment he had it in hand pass without some recognition at some point in the future.

"Be careful with the fucking *boy* treatment, Crest," Jax replied. "You should have told me. Things could have been handled much differently."

"I did what I thought best and won't apologize for that. Remember, you should have told me first that you were the one to help stage her death," Crest said, returning as good as he got. It did surprise Jax that he knew, but on the other hand, Crest could probably figure out the mystery of the Bermuda triangle during a lunch break. "Then maybe it *would* have been handled differently."

Jax would have told him eventually. He was curious to know how Crest had found out, but not enough to ask outright. He was positive that it wasn't Connor. His partner would never give him up like that, but Taryn on the other hand let her emotions rule her job. If she thought it was for their own good, she'd convey whatever Crest needed to know.

"How safe is this house you're sending us to?" Jax asked, changing the subject. "The address sounds like it's in bum fuck nowhere."

"It is. No worries," Crest said in reassurance. "Taryn worked her magic. She's also following your route, making sure the surveillance cameras don't trace your path. It buys us time to make a plan. Talk it over with Emily, but I think we should give Schultz a couple of days to pull through whatever he's got planned. If nothing happens, I'll arrange for equipment to be brought in so that we can remotely satellite a broadcast signal of Emily's statement."

"Which we should have done to begin with."

Jax checked his rearview mirror, not liking that Connor wasn't back there to cover their ass if needed. He didn't like the sense of vulnerability.

"All that matters right now is that we contained the situation. Now that we know who we're dealing with, we'll be better prepared." Voices were starting to break through the call and Jax recognized Connor's. "If you need anything, let us know.

"Are you heading back to Minneapolis or are you staying in New York?"

"At the airport now. I'm sending Kevin and Ethan your way, so they'll be close by should you need them. Connor is flying back with me and Lach is headed to DC to keep tabs on Schultz."

"That'll be a piece of cake," Jax said sarcastically. He looked at the sign for the next exit and then glanced down at the fuel gauge. He could make it another hour before stopping. "The Secret Service will be everywhere. What the fuck does he think he's going to do?"

"Who the hell knows," Crest said with a short laugh. "He's proving to have more contacts than me and that's saying something. Like I said, sit tight until I contact you and don't either of you do anything foolish."

With that, Crest disconnected. Jax pulled the phone away from his ear and dropped it into the middle console. He caught sight of Emily's hand, which was lying closed in a fist on her thigh. Even though she was asleep, the tension in her body hadn't disappeared. It had been instinct to reach out to her earlier, but he didn't regret it. Time, the truth, and being shot at was making him reconsider things. He reached out once more, covering her hand with his. Her warmth felt right, as if he'd been cold for some time yet hadn't realized it. Jax settled back in his seat, grateful to have this time to think. It was time for a new strategy.

Chapter Fifteen

Emily awoke to the evening sun streaming in the bedroom of a cabin located in the Upper Peninsula of Northern Michigan. She knew it was a mirage though, as the temperature probably hadn't reached forty degrees today. Spring this far north was cold in comparison to the Midwest. They'd arrived at six o'clock in the morning, both of them exhausted. He'd sent her immediately to bed and she didn't argue. It was as if fatigue had taken over to the point of collapsing.

As she lay on the bed in nothing but her bra and panties, she watched the dust swirl in the ray as it drifted down to the hardwood floor. Emily listened to the silence and although Ryland was still out there somewhere, she felt safe with Jax in this secluded cabin. It didn't have the bells and whistles that the previous place contained, but it would do for now. She had no doubt that Jax would come up with some type of home-made security system.

Emily leaned up on her elbows, looking at the nightstand, but didn't see a clock. She'd gotten used to not wearing jewelry, as people had the habit of remembering shiny things. She was good at blending in. Tossing the covers aside, the cool air brushed over her body and she quickly leaned down to pick up the jeans she'd shed before getting into bed. She was sick and tired of wearing the same clothes, but hopefully this place would have a washer and dryer.

Finishing getting dressed, Emily seized her weapon which was still in her MOB holster and then clipped it to her waistband at the small of her back. Walking to the door, she slowly opened it and listened for movement. Hearing nothing, she stepped out into the tiny hallway and looked to her left. A small bathroom was located on the end and directly across from her was another bedroom. Both doors were open, revealing empty spaces. She took advantage of the facilities before making her way into the large living space, which consisted of a living room/kitchen area. Jax was sitting at the table with a cup of coffee.

"Morning," Jax said, a slight grin on his face. She could have sworn there was hint of tenderness within his smile, but thought better. Maybe she needed some caffeine as well. Emily walked over to the coffee maker and poured herself a cup. She'd learned long ago to like it black. "Sleep well?"

"Better than I have in a while, which is odd, considering this Ryland guy is still out there, my plan didn't work, and the United Nations has no idea the lengths Alekseev will go to for his own purposes." Emily carried her mug to the table and sat catty-corner from him. He was studying her like he used to, causing her to want to shift her body, but she refrained. A stirring of anger at his nonchalant attitude started to well up inside of her. He didn't just get to take their relationship back to what it was after taking her up against the wall and then tossing her aside as if she were an inconvenience. "And you?"

"I slept enough."

Emily was reminded of one morning years ago where he'd said the same thing, only he'd been referring to their night of sex and the rest he'd gotten in between. Maybe that was why she felt so off kilter. His mannerisms this morning were reminiscent of their past.

"So what's the plan?" Emily asked. She then took a sip of her coffee, closing her eyes as the warmth invaded her body. "Have you spoken with Crest?"

"No, but I didn't expect to this morning. As I said last night, he wants to give Schultz a couple of days to formulate a plan." Jax rubbed his jawline where a five o'clock shadow had appeared. "As we know, he can't just barge into the United Nations and accuse Alekseev of murder. It's a diplomatic issue and one that needs to be handled properly."

"Alekseev isn't one to be dealt with, Jax," Emily replied, setting her mug on the table. "You mentioned that Crest could set up a remote broadcast. Why not do that now?"

"We all need a couple of days to decompress." Jax pushed the chair back and walked over to the counter. He poured himself another cup, replaced the pot, and then turned to face her. "*You* need a breather. So go take a shower and use the robe that's hanging on the back of the door. I'll throw your clothes in the washer and then make us something to eat. Whoever owns this place keeps it well stocked."

Emily's first instinct was to argue, but the thought of a hot shower and clean clothes was too much of a draw. He didn't get to say what she needed. She'd noticed a shift in his attitude since yesterday but couldn't decipher what it meant. It was making her antsy and some more time alone wasn't such a bad idea. Now that she really looked at Jax, his hair was slightly damp and the basic black T-shirt wasn't one she'd seen before. It would be nice to have clean clothes. She gave a slight shrug in concession and without a word, took her coffee and went to walk out of the kitchen.

"Emily." She stopped abruptly in the doorway, her heart pounding at the tone of his voice. It was the way he'd said her name. She didn't turn around for fear of what she'd see in his eyes. This mild, tender, caring manner of his was injecting hope into her. It made Emily wonder if he thought she was still keeping something from him and this was they way to go about obtaining that information or was he finally understanding why she'd made the decisions she had? "We'll talk after dinner."

✧   ✧   ✧   ✧

Emily was holding court in the living room. Snuggled in her robe with some hot chocolate in hand, she was comfortable on the couch in front of the fire…at least physically. Emotionally was another matter all together. She'd showered, Jax had taken the time to make them grilled cheese sandwiches and chicken noodle soup for dinner, and he'd stayed true to his word and placed all of her clothes in the washer. Considering she'd only had two jeans and three shirts to go with them, it was a small load and they were now in the dryer. Now the tension was thickening and for how long she'd wanted this conversation, she wasn't so sure anymore.

"More hot chocolate? There's more milk in the pan," Jax said, walking back into the living room from the kitchen.

"No, thank you." Emily held up her half-full mug, grateful he'd asked such a mundane question. "This is more than enough. I'll have trouble sleeping tonight as it is, considering we slept all day."

Jax sat in the overstuffed chair and from her angle on the couch, she could see him clearly. As his hazel eyes seemed to drink her in, she felt that familiar feeling start at the base of her spine. Emily held her breath and waited for him to speak. The truth was out there, laid on the line. It was up to him if he could accept the decisions she'd made.

"We really don't know each other, do we?"

The question threw her, for that wasn't how she'd pictured him starting this conversation. She'd rather he go back to talking about hot chocolate. Was this question rhetorical? Did he truly believe that? Notwithstanding of his anger, Emily had put herself out there to reclaim what they had. She'd already admitted to underestimating his initial fury, but if he wanted a literal answer than she would oblige.

"I know you're honorable. I know that you would lay your life down for your country and those you love." Emily lifted the mug to her lips, but instead of drinking from it continued. "You're spontaneous, yet you take responsibility for your actions. You're compassionate and although you have a dominant personality, you genuinely desire to give your lover what she needs."

Jax smiled faintly, but shook his head as if she were wrong. Emily sipped her hot beverage, more to give her something to do than being thirsty. He'd asked a question and she'd answered it. It wasn't her problem if he didn't like the response.

"I was forged by the corps, hammered into the man that I am." Jax hadn't shifted his body at all, remaining in a casual pose with his legs spread out in front of him. His elbow was on the arm of the chair and his fingers were placed against his temple. Yet the disappearance of his smile and the seriousness of his tone resonated his level of intensity. "Honor? I'm doing my job. Spontaneous? I make judgment calls—some good, some bad. I take responsibility for my actions because I'm a man, and that's what a real man does. As for giving a lover what she needs, don't mistake that for generosity. It gives me pleasure, so some might think that selfish."

Emily tilted her head, as if that would get her to understand where this was going. She didn't like the harsh light that he saw himself in, yet understood why he would think that way. Losing parents as young as he had molded the mind to think of yourself in a different manner. What she did like was that they were finally connecting, so maybe this discussion wasn't such a bad thing. She just didn't want to be on the receiving end of more angst. She'd lived with it long enough.

"What are you trying to say, Jax?"

"I want you," Jax said bluntly, with a shrug of his shoulder. It was as if he were just stating a mere fact that had no repercussions to her. Before her mind could follow along with his bizarre roundabout dialogue, he continued. "Time hasn't erased my need to have you, but unfortunately, it has changed us. We're not the same two people we were back then. Hell, let's face it. I didn't even know who you were back then. We took something, an ideal moment that we'd carved out of reality, and made it more than it was. But I'm not ready to let go of that moment though."

Emily finally understood what he was saying and her temper started to simmer. She sat up carefully, reached behind her to set her hot chocolate on the side table, and faced him. His jaw was still covered in stubble, his hazel eyes held an intensity that would only deepen should she decide to accept what he was offering, and his body seemed to be right on the edge of reaching out for her.

"Let me see if I understand this," Emily said carefully, trying to hold her anger in check. "You've decided that the time we spent together wasn't enough time for us to really get to know each other, but you're willing to put aside your hurt feelings to have sex now. What was it that you said? If my reason for coming out of hiding was good enough for you, you were going to have me in your bed and at your mercy. Do I have that right?"

Jax shifted but didn't alter his expression. For someone who was usually adept at reading his women, she was damn sure that he'd read her wrong. Emily stood and tightened the belt on her robe, wishing she could do the same to her emotions.

"You're twisting my words and making it sound like what I'm offering is cold and calculated," Jax said, finally moving and leaning forward on the chair, letting his elbows rest on his knees. "You were the one who said you wanted to pick up where we left off."

"No, I said I wanted back what we had. I didn't say that I would be a fuck partner until this mission was over and you could waltz back to your club." Emily resisted the urge to back away when he stood, which caused her to tilt her head to look up at him. She refused to back down when so much was at stake. "Let me explain this to you in simple terms. I'm submissive only in the bedroom. I'm your equal outside of it. You've been fucking with me since you walked into Crest's office. I've told you countless times that everything I did was for you, you ungrateful son of a bitch."

"You do keep saying that, but I'm not sure I believe you," Jax said through clenched teeth, finally showing emotion. He grabbed her arms and pulled her to her tiptoes. "I'm thinking you used me as an excuse and just wanted your old life back. You can't have it. We've established that. And if you're being truthful for once in your life and you did it for me, than why? I need to know why!"

"I—"

Emily bit off her words. He'd worked her up to the point that she was ready to just lay her heart on the line. Would she regret it?

"Tell me, Emily," Jax ordered, his fingers tightening on her arms. His hazel eyes had become full of gold. "Did you do it because you love me?"

"Yes," Emily said, her voice rising. He wanted her to bare her soul, then fine. She did, but now searched his face for some sign that he would believe her. "Yes, I did it because I love you."

Emily tried to step back, needing time and space to wrap her mind around what she'd just admitted. Jax didn't give her an inch and if anything brought her closer to him. The air around them seemed to be filled with a static charge, as if knowing how important this moment was.

"You thought you loved me," Jax murmured, rewording her declaration. His lips were inches from hers. "It's my turn to share with you now. I thought I loved you back then as well. But with all of the lies that have surrounded us these last few days, you have me wondering if that little time that we carved out of reality was all a lie. I don't think we *know* what we feel. Either way, it doesn't negate that you risked your life based on it. You know what that tells me? That you're not my equal outside of the bedroom, Emily. You're better than me, and I'm humbled. Another thing I know is that you're not a fuck partner."

"Then where does that leave us, Jax?" Emily asked, searching his eyes for some sort of answer.

"I want to get to know you again." Jax loosened his grip, altering his hold from one of intensity and desperation to that of leisured sensuality. The air crackled. "I want to take this slowly and see if we can recognize if there is anything left of what we had."

"Not just recognize, Jax," Emily whispered, shaking her head. She wanted there to be no doubt as to what they were about to embark on. "I want to build on what we had."

"We start now," Jax declared and then claimed her lips. His hands moved up her arms, over her shoulders, and into her hair. The tips of his fingers sent the two pins which had been holding her hair on top her head flying. She vaguely heard them hit the wood floor. Her grip on his shirt tightened when he surprised her by pulling away. Opening her eyes, she stared into his and saw a heat that rivaled the crackling fire in front of them. "On your knees."

Chapter Sixteen

Emily's heart fluttered, her hearing seemed distant, and her vision tunneled slightly at the sound of his words. It had been so long since she'd heard them and no matter how many times she'd fantasized about this exact same scenario, her body only responded like this for Jax's voice. With trembling knees that had nothing to do with nerves and everything to do with arousal, Emily stepped away from him and slowly peeled the robe away from her overheated flesh and let it drop to the floor. The warmth of the fire trailed across her skin. It was not any comparison to the heat Jax now had radiating from within her. Gradually and with measured steps, she stopped in the middle of the throw rug and lowered herself to the floor.

"Do you remember the guidelines that we covered?" Jax asked in a low voice, standing in front of her with his arms crossed.

Emily's breath caught in her throat and she immediately lowered her eyes. Focusing on the black laces of Jax's boots, she recalled the parameters as if the list were written in the leather. Her mouth felt slightly dry as apprehension settled in her shoulders, which straightened involuntarily as she placed her hands behind her back. Swallowing proved difficult as she started to speak.

"Safe, sane, and consensual," Emily murmured, pausing as the rest came into play. Jax had always been upfront with his predilection of living the BDSM lifestyle and the more he explained the ins and outs of such kink, the more she became highly interested. When he actually showed her, she wondered if one could become addicted. "My eyes are to be downcast at all times. My body is yours—"

"Safe, sane, and consensual," Jax replied softly as he walked around her. Emily wanted to watch his progression, but thought better of it. "Those are the three words I live by. That is really all you need to remember. You are right though. I do ask that your eyes be downcast to show me respect. Your body is mine to pleasure as I see fit. And you will *always* accept my touch, whether in pleasure or pain. All discipline and punishment will be discussed. As I said—safe, sane, and consensual. Which brings us to your safeword that you haven't mentioned. Do you remember what that is?"

"Red," Emily answered, her body already on the edge just from being reminded of the rules. Her breasts felt full, while her pussy swelled. She had understood early on that to be a submissive, one had to have the strength to place oneself in the hands of a Dominant. She had no doubt she was submissive. "And I may use *yellow* should I need to discuss something that makes me uncomfortable."

"Respect is important to me—do you remember that, Emily?"

She recalled the conversation as if it was yesterday and even he acknowledged his need for control stemmed from not having any as a teenager. The respect aspect gave him that control and she had relinquished it willingly. He was waiting for it now, for the word signified her reverence. She also knew that would be his cue that she was ready to continue.

"Yes…Sir."

"That is how you will address me." Jax finished circling her, although he had yet to touch her since she'd knelt on the floor. She wanted his touch. Needed it. "From your position, you obviously remember how I like you displayed. I suggest you widen your knees farther apart."

Emily did as instructed, her heart racing. Would he lean down and touch her? Being so open made her feel vulnerable, and his last vow of having her tied to his bed and at his mercy reverberated in her head. What would please him more? Keeping her on edge the entire night or giving her more pleasure beyond her wildest imagination? Not knowing was what would keep her on the edge.

"Are your soft and hard limits the same?" Jax asked, still not moving. It was driving her mad. "I need to know before we continue."

"The same, Sir."

Jax knelt before her, resting his left arm on his knee. She saw clearly from the way her eyes were downcast as his right hand extended toward her pussy and couldn't help but hold her breath as she waited for contact. None came. Eventually, Emily had to exhale for she was feeling a bit lightheaded. It was then that his finger slid between her folds. The brief contact gave her everything, yet nothing at the same time. The room spun and she had to dig her heels into her buttocks to maintain her grounding.

"It pleases me to know that you're ready for me, should I take you this evening." Jax pulled away, and even went so far as to stand again. "There is one rule that you seem to have forgotten."

Emily's mind was trying to keep up with his words, although that proved impossible. Visions of Jax tying her to a bed and having his way with her flashed through her mind. Memories of so long ago barged in, reminding her of how good it was to be restrained by his hand. Would he do that this evening?

"Honesty." The word brought the room to a halt and her eyes focused directly back on his boots. Was he about to cut this scene to a halt? Had nothing she said had an impact on him? Did he not believe that she'd been totally truthful? Were her reasons not valid enough for him? As she felt her anger surge back, he stepped forward. "Look up at me, Emily."

Parting her lips to inhale some much needed oxygen, Emily did as he ordered. Jax must have seen the resentment in her eyes, for he smiled gently, as if in reassurance. Her ire immediately tampered, although irritation remained. He was keeping her off balance and that is something she would never get used to.

"Yes, Sir?"

"From this moment on, dishonesty will end this immediately. Trustworthiness is not like your submissiveness, which runs only in the bedroom. I expect honesty inside and outside of that room. No excuses. If there is anything—and I mean anything at all—that I should know about, now is the time to tell me."

Emily maintained eye contact, wanting him to see all the way through to her soul. She would not apologize for taking the roads she'd used to get here. For whatever reason, fate had dealt them this path. It was up to them to make sure they took it together.

"I've told you everything. I'm yours, Sir."

As if he'd been waiting on those words, Jax lifted his arms over his shoulders and pulled his T-shirt over his head, leaving his blonde hair mussed. Emily would have thought the whiskers on his jaw would have given him a boyish appearance, but it did anything but. He was all male and the contours of his upper body showed that. His chest was broad, with a light dusting of hair that led to a flat, hardened abdomen she would have given anything to touch. To prevent herself from doing so, she tightened her fingers in order to keep them at her lower back. She was just grateful that he hadn't requested she lower her eyes once again.

"As I undress, I want you to pinch your nipples to keep yourself ready for me."

"Sir?" Emily tried to remember a time that he ever had her touch herself and nothing came to mind. He had always been the one to caress or stroke her. In all honesty, she didn't need to touch herself to keep herself aroused. His voice was doing that, all on its own. "I—"

"You were given an order." Jax remained where he was, waiting for her to follow his command. His brows furrowed. "I don't like hesitation, Emily."

She remembered all too well. By the end of their previous time together, he'd trained her body and mind to instantly follow his orders. Jax had told her there was nothing better than to see surprise written on his submissive's face when she immediately followed orders only to find it was something she normally wouldn't do, yet pleasing to her body. He liked to mentally push his subs.

Emily slowly released her fingers from her lower back and brought them to her front. Raising them to her breasts, she knew that he would watch closely enough to see that she was doing as she was told. Having him pinch her nipples was one thing, but to bring herself pain was something she wasn't sure she would enjoy.

"Now," Jax ordered. Emily took both nipples in between her index fingers and thumbs, pressing down and squeezing until she felt the jolts of pleasure connect with her clit. Biting her lip, she continued to manipulate her nipples until she felt herself panting. "I didn't say play with your nipples. I want you to pinch them."

As Emily followed his instructions, she felt her cream leak out of her folds and trail down her inner thigh. A whimper escaped as the erotic pain seemed to encompass her and it almost seemed as if he appeared in a fog. His hands reached for the button of his jeans. As if in slow motion, he slipped the button through the hole and then lowered the zipper. She didn't hear the sound, for the beat of her heart was too loud within her own head. When he didn't proceed to remove the denim, her eyes flew to his face.

"Return your hands behind your back, Emily," Jax said, his voice slowly registering. It was harder to do than she thought it would be, as her nipples now needed stimulation. He was taking it away. She bit her lip harder to keep from crying out as she followed his command. "Good girl."

Emily's breathing had become heavy and all she wanted to do was have him take her, like he had against the wall at the other safe house. She wanted Jax to claim her with the same intensity of that night. She forced her body to loosen its muscles as she watched him finish undressing, convincing herself that he would be within her soon. Those hopes were dashed when he took a seat on the couch, facing her in all of his glory.

"I've always considered myself a fair Dom," Jax said, resting both arms on the back of the couch. The tone of his voice should have been her first warning that she was about to be at his mercy…just as he promised. "In the time we spent together, would you agree?"

"Yes, Sir," Emily whispered, watching him closely. He'd yet to tell her to close her eyes once more.

"As much as I would love to pick up right where we left off, it would be remiss of me not to punish you for your dishonesty." Jax seemed to settle further back into the leather of the couch, indicating they would be in these positions a while longer yet. A light sheen of perspiration coated her skin, though she knew it had little to do with the fire behind her. He'd spoken of punishment and that was something she had yet to receive from him. Emily considered using her safe word, but it was a fleeting thought. She could take whatever chastisement he meted out, for she understood why he needed to. "Twenty-four months, give or take, is the agonizing amount of time that you put me through thinking you were safe from harm whereas all the while you were playing cat and mouse with a murderer. You were mine to protect, which I thought I had done. You *are* mine, considering you are on your knees in front of me, giving me your body. To make certain you understand that, you'll take your punishment and ask for more. Agreed?"

His hardened tone made her breathing shallow in trepidation, while the heat in his eyes continued to arouse her. The dual sensations were opposite, yet kept her right where she knew he wanted her. Did she agree or should she use her safeword? Emily's mind was telling her one thing while her heart told another. Hell, maybe they were expressing the same thing. She had no idea what she felt at the precise moment. She only knew that she wanted him more than life itself. He was a few feet away, arranged in such a way that it would take nothing to climb on top of him and take his cock inside of her. Yet here she was, staying in place.

"Agreed, Sir," Emily whispered, hoping she hadn't taken on more than she could handle. Jax had never placed her in this situation. Actually, it was her actions that brought her here, although her only regret was that she hadn't been truthful with him to begin with. And technically, that was what he was enforcing now. So if she understood that, was it really necessary to continue this chastisement? "Sir—"

"It makes me happy to hear you agree." Jax seemed to get even more comfortable, if that were possible. She would have thought maybe he meant a spanking or something to that effect. He wasn't moving, so her mind ran in a thousand different directions. "Since you've now told me the truth, instead of twenty-four orgasm denials, you'll give me twelve—by your own hand. You'll pleasure yourself until you are on the brink of release. I'll see it in your eyes, as they crinkle at the sides right before you come. Before you go over the edge, you'll stop. That is, until I tell you to start again. Are we clear?"

Orgasm denial? Emily almost laughed out loud. The count seemed to be a bit high, but it was a hell of a lot better than taking some makeshift paddle from the kitchen and having her ass sore for the rest of the night. Her body was already heightened as it was, so getting through twelve would go by fast.

"Yes, Sir," Emily said, her voice loud and clear. His mouth lifted up at the corner, which should have been her warning, yet she brushed it off to amusement. She lowered her eyes to see his cock hard and resting against his abdomen. From the rigidity, he wouldn't want to wait too long either. "And this wipes the slate clean?"

"Yes, as all punishments do. This will cleanse the resentment as well as remind you of what is really important."

"I'm ready, Sir."

"Then using your left hand, spread your folds so that I may watch as your right hand strokes your clit." Emily saw his shaft pulse with the beat of his heart and she smiled as well. "I don't mean caressing, either. I want long hard strokes across your nub."

Emily brought her left hand down to her mound and slowly parted her folds, even raising the skin up a bit to give him a nice view. The action caused her to suck in a deep breath, as the air instantly hit her clit and caused even more swelling, if that were possible. With her right hand, she placed her middle and ring finger onto the engorged flesh, not even needing to dip them in her cream. The entire area was drenched in her arousal.

"Hmmmm," Emily hummed, unable to contain herself. The jolt of pleasure, in addition to having her clit so exposed, immediately affected her ability to keep her knees apart. Seeing his raised eyebrow, she quickly widened them. It had been so long since she'd had an orgasm that a few more strokes were going to send her over. "Sir, I'm ready."

"No, you're not." Jax's tone broke no argument. His own hand was now wrapped around his shaft. "Keep going."

The nerve at her inner thigh started to make itself known, shooting electric currents up through her pussy. There was nothing for her entrance to grab onto and being so open only made it worse. Forcing her fingers to keep rubbing the distended nub yet not cave in to the release was torture. Her breath become shallow and her vision darkened. She was going to come. Now.

"Stop."

Emily cried out, though her fingers instantly pulled away. A throbbing took place of the sharp release that had been on the horizon. Her skin felt like it had been exposed to chemicals, as the heat radiating behind her seemed to singe the light hairs that cover her flesh. Could he not see how badly she needed release?

"Did I tell you to remove your left hand? I want to see how swollen your clit is. Open yourself," Jax demanded. With shaking fingers, Emily did as he instructed. The exposure literally hurt and she wasn't able to contain another plea. "Pink. I want it red. Continue."

Emily felt her breathing stutter as realization came crashing down around her. This punishment wasn't easy. That was one denial. How did he expect her to do eleven more? How had he known she could stroke herself more? How had he known when to tell her to stop? As if they had a mind of their own, the fingers on her right hand returned. The touch was agonizing, yet her body craved more.

"Slower this time. Up and down," Jax said in a throaty voice. "Same pressure."

His direct demands were like knives to her clit. With each directive, they become sharper and her fingers only seemed to drive them home. Emily deliberately moved her fingers up and down, drawing out the pleasure as he led her with his words. The concentrated pleasure blossomed once more, encompassing her entire body and producing a floating sensation. She was on the verge of release, knowing that one more swipe would send her over, when he commanded she stop. It was excruciatingly frustrating and she found herself pleading.

"Please, Sir. I need to come."

"What is one of the most important aspects of a Dominant/submissive relationship?" Jax asked. He started to come back into focus as her body was given a slight reprieve. She didn't remove her left hand, knowing he wanted to see how swollen her clit had become. Emily was too afraid to look down, knowing what she would see. It had never been this engorged and suddenly, she was terrified of what it would feel like to finally splinter. "Emily, I asked you a question."

"Honesty." The word released from her throat with a strangle and she understood his need to continue on with her punishment. Emily didn't know how much her body could take, but she would finish this for him. Had he held something back so vital from her, would she have been angry? Yes. Even as a submissive, she would have been hurt and livid had he lied to her. "I'm ready to finish, Sir."

"Good." Jax slowly pumped his fist over his cock. She wanted what he held and was ready to do what needed to be done. Her nipples still ached from when she'd pinched them, her thighs were drench from her cream, and her pussy had never felt so empty. She needed him like the fire behind her needed oxygen. "I want your clit bright red, Emily. Show me you'll take the punishment I see fit. Continue."

Chapter Seventeen

J ax had never seen anything so beautiful in is life. This woman kneeling in front of him, taking her punishment in grace and almost what he'd call gratitude. His intention was not to force her to twelve orgasm denials, but one or two more wouldn't hurt. That she was willing to go to those lengths to satisfy him spoke volumes.

His cock was like granite in his grip. Jax's flesh was stretched to the breaking point and the more Emily stroked her clit, the more he pumped his shaft. She'd kept herself bare. He'd never seen such a swollen nub, her need for him evident in the distended red flesh. Emily's eyes had glossed over and the corner of her eyes started to crinkle in that endearing way he loved so much.

"Stop."

The guttural groan that escaped her lips caressed his soul in a way that no other submissive's cries ever had. She tilted her head back, peering at him through her lashes. Jax never would have thought lies could hurt as much as the ones she told, for whatever reason she thought was good enough. It wasn't. He knew that she understood that now and from here on out, they had a new beginning. Her resurrection had brought about an elevated level to their connection. Seeing her in this state of arousal, in such abandon, made him realize he couldn't wait any longer to claim her.

"Lay on your back."

Emily's vision cleared. He could see her hands and arms trembling as she comprehended his next instruction. Her flesh glistened as a light perspiration coated her skin. He didn't like the blonde coloring of her hair. In fact, he missed the warm chestnut color that used to glisten in the sun. He studied her face as she started to lie down. Jax didn't perceive the relief he thought she would experience, but instead, a brief moment of terror crossed her stunning features. Jax waited until she was finally on her back before moving from the couch.

"Grab your knees and hold yourself open for me," Jax said, standing above her and waiting for her to comply. It was then that he realized what she feared. Her impending orgasm was going to be intense…earth shattering. And that was how he wanted it. She just didn't know that it was coming sooner rather than later. "I need to taste you."

Jax squeezed the base of his shaft, doing his damnedest to see this scene through to the end. When Emily was in position, with her fingers tightened on her knees and spreading herself open for him, he slowly lowered to the ground. Her lips parted and her chest started to rapidly move.

"I think it's time that I take over and give you a break. Do not come, Emily."

Jax deliberately flattened his tongue against her entrance and slid it through her folds, up to her clit. The ball of flesh was covered in her cream, which he licked clean, enjoying the spice of her flavor. Once he was sure he got every crevice, he sealed his lips over the swollen nub. Emily didn't release her knees, although she did raise her hips. He used his hands to hold her still.

"Sir!" Emily cried out as Jax sucked a little harder. Extracting her clit a little more, he nursed until he felt every muscle in her body tighten. Facing his palm up, he slid his middle finger into her warm entrance. He loved how her moist tunnel tried to grip his digit and keep it inside of her. The spasms were rippling and he could feel her try and ward off the impending release. What she didn't understand was that the more she tried to relax her muscles, the more accepting her body became to surrendering. "I…I'm—"

"Come for me," Jax murmured against her mound, knowing the exact moment that her body relinquished itself into his care. A surge of dominance swept over him, hardening his dick to extreme proportions. He needed inside of her. Now. He got to his knees and looked down at the beauty beneath him. "Keep yourself just like that. Open. Accepting."

If anything, Emily widened her knees even more. In one thrust, Jax thrust himself balls deep inside her hot core. Closing his eyes, he gasped for air. Nothing had ever felt so…right. Not moving, giving himself time to gather his bearings, he placed his arms on either side of her shoulders. It gave him leverage as he drove his cock into her as if it were the last time he would ever have the privilege. He opened his eyes and made sure to watch her face as she once again reached release, catapulting his. Seeing those pretty crinkles made everything right again.

With the strength he had left, Jax lowered himself to her side, holding her close. Never again would he be separated from this beautiful creature. Not by an assassin, nor a government official, and certainly not by an international organization. She was his.

✧ ✧ ✧ ✧

Ryland took his drink and snack from the flight attendant and dismissed her with a glance. He wasn't in the mood for toying with the woman and giving her what she obviously wanted. He had more pressing matters at hand and anticipated he would get what he wanted in a matter of days. Patience was one of his fortes and he needed to rely on that now.

He'd removed his jacket the moment the plane took off for Paris. Ryland would use the eleven-hour flight to do additional research on Crest and this agency he'd started. Ryland found it odd that he couldn't find a picture of one of Crest's agents. It should have been easily accessible. He placed his drink and the small bag of pretzels on the other tray, grateful to have found that the other seat in first class would go unoccupied. Unbuttoning the cuffs of his white dress shirt, he went over what he already knew.

Finding the information on Grace Emily and her only living relative had been easy, although they were making him work for his money by flying across the globe. According to Beatrice Weisslich's neighbors, she had grieved deeply when her niece had perished in a convenience store robbery. Ryland had no doubt that Beatrice knew Grace Emily was alive and well. Women were ruled by their emotions. His target would not allow her elderly aunt to believe she'd lost her last relative. It wasn't a coincidence that Beatrice jetted off to Paris either. Once he located her, it should be effortless to bring his target out of hiding and put an end to this assignment.

"Aren't you going to eat those?"

Ryland turned his head to the other side of the aisle. He'd noticed the boy earlier, but hoped that he would keep to himself. It was obvious the child was traveling on his own. Ryland spared a glance down the passageway and saw that the flight attendant was busy with some mundane task. He sighed and reached for the snack.

"They're all yours." Ryland tossed the bag over, watching with interest as the child opened it and pulled out a pretzel. He didn't look like he was malnourished, but maybe he'd skipped dinner. The boy was no more than five feet tall but had an average build. His dark hair was longer than Ryland would have thought a parent would allow. It was obvious that he had music on his phone, as ear buds hung around his neck. "You know, they serve us two meals during the flight."

"My mom says I'm going through a growth spurt." The boy took a drink of his soda and then studied Ryland with dark inquisitive eyes. "Thanks for the pretzels. I'm Matt. What's your name?"

"How old are you, Matt?" Ryland asked, diverting the conversation back to him. His name wasn't something he shared with children. "Ten?"

"Twelve," Matt replied. He pulled another pretzel out of the bag without looking away from Ryland. "I'm going to see my dad. He lives in Paris. Do you?"

"No."

Ryland pulled out his cell phone with every intention of doing the research he needed. He located the email from a contact who'd promised to deliver him the information. The man wasn't cheap either, but well worth every penny.

"Is that a new model or something?" Matt asked, pulling back Ryland's attention. The boy was looking at Ryland's phone like he viewed a target through the lens of his Leupold Mark 4 scope. "It's cool."

"Something like that," Ryland responded, keeping his answer vague. Were all kids this inquisitive? "It's more like a prototype."

"You must have a great job. What do you do?"

Ryland could button a man's breast pocket at a thousand yards, yet somehow managed to walk right into the kid's snare. That fact was astonishing.

"I'm…a messenger," Ryland replied, smiling to himself at the comparison.

"Oh, you're a minister or something," Matt said with a nod, as if it all made sense to him. "You'd need a good phone for your people to reach you."

"You could say I lead people to their final resting place." Ryland was amused by this conversation. Had he ever been so innocent? Memories of his childhood surfaced, answering him instantly. "Enjoy your pretzels."

Matt smiled, plugged in his ear buds, and then sat back in his seat. Ryland stared at the kid a little longer, thinking of the purity that would eventually be taken away. It astounded him that society brought into the world such goodness, knowing it would be tarnished by reality. People thought he was evil for doing a job quickly and efficiently. They did it slowly and painfully…for recreation. He could only shake his head at the hypocrisy of it all. He took his drink and swallowed the only single malt brand they had on board. Holding it up, he indicated to the flight attendant that he'd like another. It was going to be a longer flight than he thought.

Chapter Eighteen

Jax had an arm overtop of his eyes while holding Emily close with the other. They'd spent the night on the couch in front of the fire. He'd cleaned her up with a warm cloth after their scene, but neither had addressed the fact that he hadn't used a condom. He wasn't ready for it now either, for it would mean questioning why he'd done it. He would have to say something to let her know it was the first time he'd ever gone without protection. Jax would never put her health at risk.

The shift in Emily's breathing told him she was awake. He leisurely caressed the silky flesh of her arm, his lips curving into a smile as she seemed to melt into him a little more. This peace that had settled over them was a nice change from the tension and anger that had become a staple since her return. Again, Jax ignored the niggling worry of the potential consequences of his actions.

"Does it always feel like this?" Emily murmured again his chest.

"What's that?" Jax lifted his arm and glanced down at her. Some blonde strands had made their way onto her cheek and he brushed them aside.

"A...well, a scene." Her voice was low and Jax could see the faint blush that colored her cheeks. He was glad he'd repositioned her hair behind her ear. "Okay, a punishment."

Jax chuckled at her attempt to correct herself. He knew exactly what she meant, but he also knew that having her know the difference was essential. He loved the dynamics of her personality. She could blush, yet not hesitate to hand her body over to him. Her disposition was one of strength and she gave her all once she put her mind to something. However, the air of innocence still remained.

"Yes." Jax knew she understood the meaning of it, but wanted to make it clear. "There's a tranquility that overcomes both a Dom and sub after a punishment. It's as if it's a new beginning. A cleansing, so to speak."

"I like it," Emily whispered, taking her hand and placing it on his chest. "Not that I want another one anytime soon."

Jax remained silent, leaning down to kiss the top of her head and inhaling her scent. He could still smell the shampoo she'd used from last night. It wasn't her usual scent, but it was pleasant. He couldn't wait until she returned to her natural chestnut color.

"Talk to me," Emily requested, seeming very comfortable and in no hurry to move. She didn't have to worry. He was very content as well. "Tell me about the last two years."

"Well, I already told you how Connor and I came back from Iraq and took Crest up on his offer to work at the agency." Jax thought over the past and realized every day had relatively been the same. "A couple government contracts a year to keep us sharp, and the normal cases at home kept me busy."

"You still played?"

Jax knew she meant at the clubs, but didn't hear reproach in her voice. He was grateful. He wouldn't lie to her, and technically she already knew. They'd spoken of it back at the other safe house. Honestly, playing at the clubs was the one thing that kept him from tracking her down and placing her in danger.

"Yes." Jax waited for the stiffening of her body, but she remained at ease. They'd spent the night in a scene driving home the point of honesty and he would give no less. "Nothing serious, but it almost kept me from thinking of you. I did push my limits though. I'd lost the feeling of control and it wasn't until Connor mentioned something a few months ago that I'd realized I'd probably gone too far."

Emily tilted her head up, her blue eyes focusing on his. There was no judgment, only understanding. He did see a trace of pain, which tugged at his heart. Her fingers started to trace figure eights in the middle of his chest, trying to pull his attention away from the conversation. It was too soon to commence with another scene, as she had to be sore from last night. He could wait a while longer. He was actually enjoying this reconnection, though he wasn't used to revealing so much of himself.

"What limits did you push?"

"Edge play," Jax answered honestly, searching her face for condemnation. "Don't get me wrong, I found the control I was looking for, but that's not how I wanted it. I can see in your eyes that this conversation is—"

"I'm not angry, Jax," Emily said, raising her hand and placing her palm on his cheek. "That doesn't mean hearing about it doesn't hurt me. We'd gone our separate ways and I understood the chance I was taking by walking away and going into hiding. But last night—this moment—erases our past. Wouldn't you agree?"

Jax felt his chest swell with an emotion he wouldn't put a name to. He gently kissed her, wanting to thank her and show her how he felt at the same time. Had they fallen in love back then? Maybe. But two years had changed them both. They needed time to get to know one another again. Pulling away, he tapped her nose with a finger and flashed her a smile.

"I do agree," Jax answered, lifting her until she was laying flat on top of him. Her warm mound fit right over hardening cock. He closed his eyes for a moment to appreciate the sensation. "To keep me from taking you right this second, tell me about you. Why didn't you mention you had an aunt when we were together before?"

"And what's keeping you from taking me right this second? Oh, wait," Emily exclaimed, resting her chin on the back of her hands. "Is that your punishment for playing in the clubs?"

Jax immediately reached for her sides, tickling her until she couldn't draw air. Laughing with her, he finally relented and let her shift back into position. He brushed her hair behind her ears once more, taking in her radiating smile. Emily's blue eyes sparkled with merriment and he fought the urge to call Crest and tell him to delay the inevitable as long as possible.

"You have to be sore," Jax said, stroking her back. "It's not my intention to cause you pain…at least, not right this moment."

Another laugh escaped her lips. "There are many things I'm interested to try that I've placed on my soft limits list. But until you feel up to it, I'll talk about Aunt Beatrice."

Jax pretended to go for her sides once more and she immediately reacted by rolling into the couch with a giggle. Feeling the cool air drift over his front, he reached for the throw and tossed it over the both of them. Emily seemed to be pushing him a little, testing the waters as to how far she could control their sexual scenes. She couldn't. Deep down she knew that and wanted to play. He felt the same, but it was also his responsibility to take care of her. Right now, her body needed a few more hours reprieve.

"Continue," Jax instructed, settling back and enjoying this newfound intimacy. Emily sighed, giving in.

"She was my father's sister and when my parents passed, she took care of me. We only had each other." Emily went back to making figure eights on his chest. "That week was such a whirlwind and when it came to a close, the shit hit the fan."

"That's an understatement." Jax chuckled when she lightly tapped his chest. "Where does she live?"

"Long Island. I'm grateful that Crest sent someone to watch over her. I know she's in Paris, but now that Ryland has my information, I have no doubt he'll go for her."

"Crest wouldn't hire anyone he didn't trust or who couldn't handle the job." Jax thought about their current situation and what he would do if he were in Ryland's shoes. "If he's desperate with no leads as to our whereabouts, he'll go for her. The only other person you were connected to before your disappearance was me and I doubt he'd be able to garner that information. It was a week."

"It felt like longer."

Jax held her tighter against him. "You're right. It did."

A vibration came from his jeans, which were lying a few feet away. Leaning over the edge without letting her go, Jax snatched up one of the legs and dragged the denim their way. Using his one free hand, he managed to get the small device out of the pocket.

"Yeah," Jax said into the phone as he settled back onto the couch. Emily rose up enough to replace her chin on his chest. In a lower voice, he said, "Speak of the devil."

"I'm worse than the devil," Crest countered, all business. "Listen up. Schultz wants us to hang tight. He's maneuvering the evidence around to various people within the United Nations, taking advantage of Alekseev's attention on Emily. Right now, too many people are getting wind of this now for Alekseev to be able to sweep it under the rug. Apparently, it's a shitstorm in DC and New York right now. If we can just keep Emily hidden and away from Ryland until a hearing is scheduled before the Security Council, he should be able to contain this himself with the next couple of days."

"We're at our destination," Jax answered, sitting up a bit. Emily remained where she was, but placed her chin on his stomach. He smiled when her brows furrowed. She wanted to know what Crest saying, but his voice was too low. "Are Kevin and Ethan in place?"

"Yes. If you leave there for any reason, make sure they know. Kevin's got one of the mobiles that's programmed into the one you have." There was a pause, causing Jax to be on alert. Whenever Crest took time to formulate words, people paid attention. "After this is said and done, she'll have to deal with the NSA."

"They used her as a NOC, Crest." Emily stiffened beside him, but before she could sit up, Jax grabbed a hold of her hair that was lying over her shoulder. She remained in place, with her chin on his abdomen. "She's given two years of her life to do the right thing, not to mention being targeted for murder. I'm sure Schultz can pull a few strings."

"Let's hope you're right," Crest said, his voice wary. "He's pulling in every favor he can to make sure this information gets into the hands of the Security Council without losing any more people. Alekseev needs to be sent packing as soon as possible."

"Agreed." Jax sunk his fingers into Emily's hair and found that the urge to claim her once more was becoming overwhelming. What she needed was a hot bath to take away the sore muscles and raw clit. Then they could have some fun. "We'll remain in place unless we hear otherwise or I feel a threat is imminent. Keep in touch."

"Something change that I should know about?" Crest asked before Jax could disconnect the call.

"Meaning?"

"Just remember the case comes first. I realize that Emily is one and the same, but making decisions based on emotion is not how we complete a mission."

"As you said, it shouldn't matter," Jax answered, his voice hardening. He respected Crest and although they didn't always see things eye to eye, he wasn't one to be micromanaged. "Contact us when Schultz has things ready to go and I'll have her back in New York for the hearing."

Jax pulled the phone away from his ear and then severed the call. It wasn't until Emily lifted her head and laid her palm against his face that he realized how tightly he was clenching his jaw.

"What's going on?" Emily asked, the softness in her face from this morning disappearing. Was this how he was? Were his team members the same when switching their thought process from their personal life to a case? "Has Crest been in touch with Schultz?"

"Yes," Jax answered, rubbing a hand down his face. He needed to shave and shower. Now was the perfect time to do that, since he wanted her to take a hot bath. "Schultz has put things in motion and will contact us when you need to be at the United Nations in New York to give your statement to the Security Council. In the meantime, we have the original tapes should we need a back-up plan. We sit tight and wait for things to play out."

Jax could see it took a moment for her to digest everything. She didn't relax her muscles right away, but eventually, she lay back down on his chest. He hadn't mentioned Ryland, for there was no need. They had no idea where he was or what he was planning.

"Up you go, my little spy," Jax said, nudging her until she let the blanket fall off of them and stood. He took a moment to appreciate her body. She was lovely, with her curves and ample breasts. Having this view to look at while he shaved might cause a few nicks, but it would be well worth it. "Let's get you in a hot bath and then put food in our stomachs. Let's just say we're going to need the stamina."

Chapter Nineteen

J ax walked the perimeter of the house, making sure the handcrafted security system was still in place. It was difficult in the dark, but it had to be done before they retired for the night. The air coming off the lake was downright cold and it didn't help that the wind had picked up. He rubbed his hands together in order to keep them warm, blowing hot air into them as he walked. Spending the day with Emily had given him a glimpse of what they could have and he found himself having those same feelings as when he'd first met her. Time had changed nothing.

Walking to the far edge of the property next to the border of the long drive, Jax carefully studied the area. There were three places that Kevin or Ethan would be staked out, but the dark prevented him from seeing too much. He whistled, knowing that if they were there, they would return the sound. Sure enough, the mimicked echo broke through the still of the night. Jax headed that way.

He was no more than twenty yards in when Kevin's dark form appeared before him. "You want to hand us over to Ryland on a silver platter?"

"Ryland arrived in Paris this morning," Jax informed his teammate. "I just spoke with Crest and Taryn seems to have found her magic fingers once more. Obviously he used an alias, but she was able to obtain CCTV footage from De Gaulle."

"She said she was working on some facial recognition program," Kevin said, nodding his head in approval. "Unless he changed his bone structure, regardless of make-up or wigs the database will vet him out. Unfortunately, that doesn't help us. He's going after Emily's aunt. Does she know this?"

Jax shook his head. "Not yet. Crest's man that he's using in France has been able to make contact with Beatrice. He's taken her to an undisclosed location until Connor can get his ass to Paris and take this fucker out."

"Think he'll stay there long enough for that to happen? If Beatrice isn't easily accessible, Ryland will just come back to the States and pick up where he left off."

"He's scrambling and you know it," Jax said, shoving his hands in his pockets. He'd left his gloves in the SUV. "Ryland has no bead on our location and the only string available was Emily's aunt. Take that away and what's left?"

"A desperate man," Kevin said, shifting back on the heels of his boots.

"He doesn't strike me as the type to ever be desperate, but he will be pissed." Jax had been given time to process the information and he was relatively sure he knew how this would play out. "Crest tell you that Schultz has things in motion? I figure we'll get a reprieve until we have to get Emily back to New York. The Security Council will want to hear from her exactly what went down, regardless of the physical evidence they are presented with. We're talking about sending a Russian diplomat back to his country for crimes against the international community, not to mention his security detail. Ryland will be given instructions to take her out before she enters that room."

Kevin didn't reply, but instead swept the area with his eyes. Regardless of their views on how this might play out, he and his team would still do their job. Their safeguards wouldn't be let down and they would remain in position, just in case.

"Have you spoken to Elle?"

The question threw Jax for a moment. Yes, Kevin had assisted Elle in getting off the streets, but to Jax's knowledge, they had a somewhat tremulous relationship. Elle had worked the streets for a while before trying to get her life together and Kevin worked for a security agency that took private cases and government contracts. The two didn't exactly mesh and in all honesty, she seemed wary of his forthright nature. She didn't come across that leery of Jax or the other men, but then again, they hadn't witnessed her at such a low point in her life the way Kevin had. Jax understood about pride.

"Not since this started," Jax said, raising an eyebrow. Was there something he should know? "I trust her to take care of things at the club. Elle's good at her job."

"One of my contacts called the office," Kevin said. His steel gray eyes came back to focus on Jax. "Jessie mentioned that one of his girls has been missing for a few days and wanted me to check it out."

Jax put two and two together and he nodded in under-standing. As much as Elle was turning her life around, she still kept in touch with some of the girls still working the streets. It was as if she felt a responsibility to save the other women. Kevin's tone indicated that his contact had to be the scumbag who Elle used to work for.

"Why don't you call her or have Jessie stop by the club?" Jax asked, wondering why he was the one suggesting it. Kevin was an intelligent man and didn't need his hand held on common sense shit. "Hell, ever since Connor and I took over, it seems to have become the hangout for our fellow team-mates."

"Elle and I…let's just say I don't think she'd appreciate me checking up on her," Kevin said, his stance shifting as if he were uncomfortable. Jax stared a little longer, thinking maybe the dark was playing tricks on him. "I'll do that though. Call Jessie, that is."

It was like looking in the fucking mirror. Jax just barely contained his laugh, covering it up with a cough. Shit, he'd seen the same expression when he'd been shaving this morning. Kevin had a thing for Elle. There were a million things that he could say sitting on the edge of his tongue, but he held them back. His friend looked absolutely miserable.

"Jessie will check on her for you." Jax nodded, as if were an everyday occurrence. A thought struck him. "You don't think the missing prostitute is related to your case, do you?"

"I don't know the details. Crest is dealing with the family that hired us. You know, the ones whose daughter was the first one to be raped? She was a runaway who'd ended up on the street. Anyway, he has one of the detectives in Hennepin County working some angles while I'm away. He's a solid guy."

There were times when a major assignment similar to Emily's took the attention of the entire team. Jax knew it wouldn't be long before Kevin was ensconced back in Minneapolis, working the case for this family whose daughter had been the victim of a rapist. This girl's family had money and wanted someone private to look into their daughter's rape case.

"It shouldn't be too long before this is over." Jax looked to his left, seeing the soft glow from one of the windows. He made a mental note to make sure the curtains were closed, not that anyone could get near the place without him knowing. "I need to get back."

Kevin smiled for the first time since they'd started talking and Jax knew the shit was coming. Now that he was loaded as well, Jax slowly returned the smile and waited for the first missile to fire. Kevin's lips gradually fell when he realized it too. Jax laughed and slapped him on the shoulder, before turning to head back to the cabin.

"Dropping like fucking flies," Kevin muttered under his breath as he turned to go.

Jax didn't argue. Hell, who was he to say anything? He'd had sex with Emily last night without protection. Had he done it subconsciously? Did he want a family of his own so bad? Maybe it was time for Crest to hire a profiler. They all needed their fucking heads examined.

Emily waited patiently while Jax was outside, making certain the area was secure. This cabin didn't have the security system the previous safe house did, but since it was out in the middle of nowhere, she felt relatively safe. She was back on the couch wearing one of Jax's black T-shirts with nothing underneath and her weapon by her side. She had a feeling she wouldn't have it on for long once he came back in.

The day had passed by in a blur, yet had given them time to get to know one another again. As she'd soaked in the bubble bath after having found the foaming liquid in a bottle underneath the sink, Emily was mesmerized by the vision of Jax shaving. His movements were erotic, to say the least. He had leaned against the sink wearing nothing but his jeans. With each graceful scrape of his face, the muscles on his chest would move in sync. The cords of his neck were the most interesting part, as she wanted to run her tongue alongside the indention of his warm skin.

Jax spoke the entire time, telling her of cases they'd worked on and the latest having been one that had Connor falling in love. He talked of his team members, telling her about their quirks and personalities, causing her to laugh at some of their antics. By the time he was done and in the shower, she'd been surprised to find that he liked to sing. His lower register seemed to have strummed something inside of her and by the time he'd dried off, she'd joined him in hopes of continuing where they'd left off. It was just as he'd said yesterday…they needed to get to know one another again. Emily was sure the reason for her amazement was the fact that this was actually happening. She'd dreamt of it for so long that it seemed surreal. Maybe that was why she hadn't brought up the fact that he hadn't used a condom the night before, because she hadn't wanted this to end.

Jax was taking longer than Emily thought he would, so she stood up from the couch and walked over to the window with her gun in hand. Looking out, night had fallen to the point of pitch-black darkness, with cloudy skies covering whatever moonlight that would have been available. She couldn't see a foot away from the house. Where was he? And why *hadn't* he mentioned what had happened?

Emily placed a hand to her stomach, wondering what it would be like if she were with his child. Reality was setting in though and she knew it would have to be addressed. She'd been honest with her feelings about him playing in the clubs, but the one thing she wouldn't sacrifice was her health. When she'd located the bubble bath underneath the sink, there had also been a box of condoms. They would be used and no more chances taken.

The rest of the day had been spent much of the same, although in front of the fire. He'd made them breakfast and dinner, while she made them sandwiches for lunch. When she'd asked whose place this was, Jax had shrugged, saying that Crest had things covered. Conversation had switched back to their childhood and he'd entertained her with stories from his youth. She was finding that under his carefree attitude, he had a philosophical way of looking at life.

The door sprung open, causing Emily to pull up her weapon. The reaction was instant, but the second she zeroed in on her target, her arms relaxed. Damn it! She could have shot him. Jax closed the door, his cheeks rouge from the cold night air and gave a small smirk at her stance.

"Do you really think Ryland is getting through me?"

"You're not infallible, Jax," Emily snapped at his cavalier attitude that he was better than this trained assassin who was after her. He held up his hands as if in surrender, which in a better frame of mind she would have found slightly humorous. "Not funny."

"I should rephrase my question into a statement then," Jax said, shrugging out of his jacket and then tossing it over the coat rack by the door. He walked toward her, his skullcap still in place. "Ryland's not getting through the make-shift system I've put into place without us hearing it and giving fair warning. I've been at this a long time, Emily. On top of that, I guarantee that Kevin and Ethan are taking turns staking the place out. We'll see him well before he sees us."

"Just as you've been having sex for a long time, but that didn't stop you from forgetting to use a condom last night." Emily closed her eyes in irritation, not meaning for it to come out like that. Damn it. She turned before he reached her and walked back to the couch. She carefully placed her gun on the side table before facing him. "That came out wrong. It wasn't how I wanted this conversation to start."

"I don't think it really matters how it starts," Jax said, his tone indicating things had just turned serious. He swiped the skullcap off his head. His blonde hair was mussed, but it only added to his charm and further frustrated her that all of a sudden she was having trouble concentrating. She was better than that. "I have no excuses. It happened, but I need you to know that I have never done that before. Ever. And yes, I should have told you that last night to ease your worries. The team also gets tested once a year for every damn thing the human body could obtain, due to our overseas trips. Mine was done not more than three months ago."

Emily felt a little of her anger dissipate. It wasn't as if she hadn't been there. She'd been the other participant and could have said something. The truth was she hadn't wanted to.

"I, um, haven't been with anyone since you," Emily said, meeting his gaze head on. The brown flecks of his eyes started to shimmer at her words, but there was also a hint of sadness. He felt guilty for playing at the clubs during their time apart and that wasn't what she'd been aiming for. They were in the here and now. "I think we'll be fine, since it's a week after that, uh, window. We should use the condoms that were found under the sink though."

"Agreed," Jax said, tossing his skullcap on the floor. He then proceeded to take off his shirt, which joined his hat. Emily felt her body responding, regardless that they just had an important conversation that seemed pretty damn vital to her. Granted, there wasn't much left to say, but it felt so monumental. She was surprised when he walked over to the fire, holding out his hands and then starting an entirely different conversation. "I spoke with Crest. There's something you need to know."

Emily's heart started to race, a thousand things running through her mind of what could possibly have happened. Had Ryland gotten to Schultz? It was a possibility, considering the Attorney General had met his demise. Or maybe Schultz had finally turned over the evidence to the appropriate people in the Security Council and this entire mess was over. Knowing that wasn't it because she would have been brought in immediately, Emily tried to tamp down her patience as she watched Jax turn around and cross his arms, allowing his back to receive the kiss of the heat.

"Taryn found a way to trace Ryland, at least temporarily. He was in range of closed-circuit security cameras in which she was able to get a facial recognition." Jax paused, as if studying her...and not in the good way. Her stomach seized and she knew what he was going to say before he spit out the words. "He's in Paris."

Emily let it sink in, struggling with the first thing they needed to do. She was grateful that Jax stayed where he was, for as strong as she thought of herself, if anything were to happen to Aunt Beatrice she'd break down.

"We're staying right here," Jax said, as if he knew what she was thinking, which was impossible. "She's not the one he wants and you know it. Crest's man has Beatrice and she's safely ensconced at a secure location. Either way, Ryland will be on the next flight back."

"Why fly all that way only to turn back around?" Emily asked, moving one leg and then another, giving herself something to do. She paced back and forth twice before continuing. "This Ryland character doesn't strike me as the type to give up. He wants her for leverage and he'd be right in assuming I won't let him hurt her."

"He's not giving up so much as probably being told exactly when and where you'll be within three or four days. Schultz was able to pull it together. When we're given the word, I need to have you in New York at the United Nations to present the evidence."

"So that's it?" Emily asked incredulity. She stopped pacing to face him. "We go and hope like hell he doesn't pick me off? That's—"

"Have a little faith, huh?" Jax said, finally closing the distance between them. He'd given her the time she needed to adjust to this new piece of information and was now grateful when his now warm hands clasped her arms. "Connor's on the flight to Paris now. We're hoping he gets close enough to bring Ryland down. If something goes wrong, we'll have back-up plans in check. You know this and are familiar with how it works."

Emily stepped into him, resting her cheek against his chest. She took comfort from the heat from his skin, which kept the chill of what the future held in store at bay. It didn't stem the tide of reality. Aunt Beatrice was in danger, although safe and sound for the moment. How long would that last? Emily hoped extensive enough until either Ryland came back for her or Connor was able to stop him. This was her responsibility, not Aunt Beatrice's. She didn't deserve to have her life threatened.

"There is nothing that we can do for her right now. Your aunt is safe. You're safe. We stay."

His words made sense, but that didn't mean they weren't hard to come to terms with. Emily was here with Jax in a bubble of security and swore to take advantage of the time they had left. She also refused to contemplate what would happen should Connor not be able to carry out his mission. Right now, she just wanted to wrap herself around this man who'd become her reason for living.

"As long as she's safe, I'd like to take advantage of the time I have with you," Emily murmured against his chest. "I'm not ready to face reality yet. I want you."

"This is reality, but *want* is not good enough," Jax said, kissing the top of her head while holding her close. She moaned a little when he stepped away. "You have to need me like the air you breathe."

Chapter Twenty

Jax had used the time he searched the cabin for the items he needed in order to let the embers of the fire die down. He wanted just enough heat coming from the fireplace to give Emily the sensations needed for the scene they were about to start, but would never place her in danger of getting burned.

Stopping for a moment, he admired her beauty. Currently, Emily was spread eagle against the wooden mantle and the brick hearth that jutted out a good foot and a half. He'd used the sashes on the terry cloth robes to fasten her wrists to the hooks that must have been left over from Christmas stockings. He'd smiled at their convenience.

Jax had also taken a towel and cut wide strips of the material to do the same with her ankles, using the edges of the brick hearth for leverage. The rest of the fabric was used as a makeshift blindfold to enhance the various stimulations he was about to bestow upon her. He'd made sure to use specific knots that wouldn't pull against her skin should she struggle against her restraints.

"I can see your pussy glistening from here," Jax murmured, as he set the bowl of ice down on the floor. He knew that most would melt before he was able to use it, but didn't want to have to halt the scene to run into the kitchen. Prepping for a scene was most vital. "Bondage agrees with you, as does your anticipation."

Jax took in the sight of her lovely body, appreciating the way her ample breasts swelled at the sides. She was a C cup, just perfect for his large palms. Her areolas were no bigger than quarters and her nipples the ideal size to nibble. Not too big and not too small. Most important, he knew how sensitive the hardened peaks were.

"Your breasts are lovely." Jax ran a finger down one side, making sure to stay far away from her nipples. "I think they need a little color though, wouldn't you agree?"

He waited patiently to hear her answer, knowing her body was waiting for her mind to catch up. Jax glanced over at the thin bamboo fly rod section that he'd found in the closet. He'd removed the eyes, making sure that the wood was smooth and free of the bindings that had tied the eyes to its length. This was for her pleasure and nothing more. He'd introduced her to flogging way back, but now it was time to familiarize her with a type of cane that would only enhance her longing and desire. He loved that she had no hesitation in her soft limits. She was willing to try anything once and he was more than willing to be the one to do it. The only one.

"Yes, Sir," Emily answered softly. She didn't waver, but her voice did shake with anticipation.

Jax took a step back, assuring himself that everything was in place and all the items he'd chosen were at hand. He reached over and picked up the thin bamboo rod, giving it a few practice swings in the air. The sound that it made was unmistakable. He smiled when he heard her swift intake of air.

Anticipation was a beautiful reaction and one that he would never get enough of.

"Take what I give you and accept it into yourself," Jax said as a reminder, stepping closer. The rod was long enough that her ass was easily in reach. He lightly started to tap the generous flesh. Instinct had her pulling forward. "You know how I like to warm you up. Relax into it."

Jax could see Emily forcing her muscles to obey one by one. Her lips remained parted as the bamboo patted her skin lightly, awakening the sleeping nerves. A fly rod is actually constructed of multiple thin reeds of bamboo cut and reassembled in such a way as to increase the action of the flexibility and gain strength from the way the grain is plied. It made for the perfect lightweight cane. Once he was done with one thigh, he moved to the other. It was once he started on the inside of her legs that he noticed her breathing getting a little more shallow. From the swelling of her clit, which was easily seen through her folds, Emily was partial to the light stings.

Jax purposefully didn't go near her clit, but instead transferred the tapping to her breasts. Her audible gasp was like music to his ears. Keeping a rhythm, he danced the bamboo underneath her ample flesh, maintaining a light impact. Her pale skin started to take on a healthy glow.

"If only I had my bag," Jax said, keeping his eyes on her face to make certain she was reacting in the manner he wanted. "Imagine what it would feel like to have your breasts peppered with stings while wearing nipple clamps. The vibrations would cause a pulling that would make you feel as if your nipples were connected to your clit."

"Hmmmm." Emily's head tilted back slightly, giving him a glance of her elegant neck and the way her cords sensually pulled against her muscles. The small fire gave the scene an intimate ambiance, although she was unaware of what he was seeing. What she was feeling was more significant and as much as he admired the golden hue surrounding her body, that was beyond essential. "More, Sir."

Jax immediately stopped and stepped forward. Leaning down, but without sucking her nipple into his mouth, he bared his teeth and bit the nub lightly. She cried out but had nowhere to move. He waited patiently until she stopped struggling and then laved the smarting away with his tongue. His dick was throbbing at hearing the sweet mewling sounds fall off her lips.

"Do you get to ask for more?"

"No, Sir," Emily said breathlessly. "I just—"

"Whose body is this to pleasure?"

"Yours, Sir."

Emily bit her lip when he didn't move, do, or say anything else. Jax wanted her kept off guard, not knowing if or when he would touch her again. The more he elevated her senses, the more enjoyment she would have at the end. The build-up was the most pleasurable part, although he was sure she would disagree at the moment. He waited until she was cocking her head, straining to hear any sound that he might make.

"Let's continue then."

Three rounds later and her skin was just the right amount of pink that he liked to see. Knowing she was now used to the pattern, Jax started once more, only to bring the bamboo up at an angle to tap her directly on her engorged clit. Emily cried out and from the way her thigh muscles flexed, tried to bring her legs together.

"More?"

"Yes, please," Emily pleaded, the air whooshing out of her lungs. "Sir."

Moving to the side, he angled the rod and let it snap direct-ly over her left nipple. Emily's short wail sounded strangled and then her head leaned back. Jax doubted she was even aware, but she was pushing her hips out. In quick succession, he worked both breasts, including her engorged nipples. With one more smack to her clit, he stopped completely.

Jax could only imagine the endorphins flying through her body right now, but that was about to be elevated. He'd given the back of her body enough time to be well acquainted with the heat of the fire. It was time to cool her down.

"Your cream is dripping down the inside of your thigh, Emily," Jax said, tossing the bamboo rod on the floor. He then picked up the bowl of ice and took one out that was already half melted. "I'm surprised it's not boiling, as your body seems to be on fire. Would you like for me to quench your thirst?"

"Yes, Sir," Emily said, nodding her head quickly.

Jax ran the cube across her pink lips and then traced the outline of her mouth. Her lips parted immediately and he was pleased to see her tongue peek out to capture the cool liquid. He allowed her to lick and suck until she was satisfied and then continued on his journey.

"I want to know every nuance of your skin." Jax studied her expressions as he glided what was left of the chipped ice over her jawline and down her neck. Again, he found himself fascinated by her graceful cords and the way they blended into her shoulders. "What your likes and dislikes are. Every stroke and caress that sexually arouses you. I want to be in your head, Emily."

"Oh!" Emily exclaimed as the rest of the ice in his hand melted against her nipple. Goosebumps broke out across her stomach as beads of water made a path directly to her clit. "Sir, I can't—"

"You can, Emily," Jax murmured, reaching for another cube. "And you will."

✧   ✧   ✧

Emily's teeth chattered and she sucked in her lower lip to stop the reaction. The heat at her back seemed to intensify the moment Jax had placed the ice cube on her mouth. The dual sensations were almost too much, yet it only seemed to fuel her arousal even more so. This was the reality that he spoke. This was the reality that she didn't want to leave behind.

She felt more than heard Jax drop to his knees in front of her as the air caressed her wet skin from his movements. Emily knew what was coming but still couldn't contain a moan when he took another chip of ice and made a circle around her belly button. He then proceeded to trace the outline of her hips. She could feel the drops of water trailing down her body and following the contours of her mound. The water wasn't cool by the time it reached her clit, but the awareness of the liquid was enough to bring her further to that out of reach precipice. How much longer was he going to do this?

"Does your clit need a little relief?" Jax asked, his voice warning her that he didn't mean it the way she was taking it. She instinctively tried to shift her legs closed, but the loose strips of material made it impossible. She groaned in frustration, yet anticipation, for she knew what he had in mind. "Or someplace else a little more heated by the fire?"

Another ice chip made its way to her lower back, but as something lightly brushed her clit, it dawned on Emily that he'd reached underneath her. It was his arm that she felt grazing her pussy. Before she could clench her cheeks together, Jax slid the melting cube through her crevice. She hadn't realized exactly how hot the fire had heated her skin. It wasn't refreshing and oddly, the shocking cold didn't diminish her need to come. It only made it worse.

"Sir," Emily pleaded, trying her damnedest to push her hips out hoping his arm stroked her clit once more, "please."

"That's what I'm doing," Jax said, his tone low and sensual. He wasn't pleasing her, couldn't he see that? How much more of this torturous overload of stimulation was he going to make her take? "I'm pleasing your body and I think your thanks should be warranted for what I'm about to give it."

Emily struggled to comprehend what he meant as her body was still distinguishing between the stimulus it was receiving and the release that it wasn't. Her eyes flew open behind the material that she wore over the bridge of her nose as his finger pushed what was left of the ice cube into her anus.

"Oh!"

"More?"

Before Emily could reply or even accustom her body to the foreign sensation, Jax once again slid a chip of ice through her crevice. Not giving this one a chance to melt, he used his finger to push it through her tight muscle. It wasn't as if she could say her body didn't like what he was doing, for the next one he slid into her, her pussy gushed more cream.

"I see something else would like the attention your ass is getting," Jax murmured, his breath caressing her clit. Just how close was he? As if she'd asked that question out loud, she felt the tip of his tongue lick the swollen nub. She whimpered when he pulled away. "I want to hear you ask me for it. It's similar to the scene we had last night, in that you're honest with me. This time, be honest with yourself. As much as it is a shock to your body, you and I both know your pussy is craving what I just gave your ass. You know that it will only heighten your experience. So ask."

"Please, Sir," Emily said, not knowing if she could really ask him. There were some things better left unsaid, for the vulnerability was almost too much for the mind to take. Especially hers. "Please."

Jax had taken another ice cube and ran it around her ankle and up the inside of her leg. Her pussy clenched at the thought of what was to come, but instead of following through, he skipped to the other leg and ran the frozen water down until he reached her other ankle.

"Unless you ask me, your clit and pussy will remain untouched."

Emily knew by his tone that he wasn't bluffing. He would leave her this abandoned unless she spoke the truth. Even she knew what she wanted, but found it hard to articulate it into words. Exposure came in various ways…words just seemed so final. It would be admitting that she loved the sinful things he did to her body.

"P-please put an ice c-cube inside my pussy, Sir," Emily whispered, feeling the weight of the words yet also the freedom they stood for. "I-I want whatever you'll give me."

Jax expressed his appreciation for her honesty through his actions. What felt like a larger ice cube began the journey up her leg and didn't stop until he'd slid it through her folds and directly into her pussy. Not stopping, he used his finger to push it farther up inside of her while suctioning her clit through his lips. The heat of his mouth rivaled that of the fire behind her.

Pushing out her hips as far as they would go, Emily let the back of her head rest against the mantle as he continued to thrust his finger in and out, all the while nibbling her clit and sending higher and higher. Just when she thought she was going to come, Jax pulled away.

"Sir!"

In answer, she felt him tug at the ties around her ankles. In an instant they were undone. He must have stood, for she felt him do the same to her wrists and immediately she was spun around.

"Hands on the mantle in front of you and don't let go," Jax ordered in raspy tone that made her knees quiver.

As she tightened her fingers on the old wood, she listened closely to the sounds around her. He was tearing a condom wrapper and rolling the latex over his cock. She didn't have to be told to spread her legs.

"You're mine, Emily," Jax exclaimed as he grabbed her hips and in one thrust was balls deep into her cunt. Her sheath expanded and accepted his width and length. "Say it."

"I'm yours, Sir," Emily whispered, giving him the words he so desperately wanted to hear. They exposed her just as her pleas had earlier, but she had no regret. Her soul was his to explore and that was what tonight seemed to be. Her body had just been a vessel. "I'm yours."

Jax pulled out slowly, returning inside of her the same way. He kept her hanging on by a thread, continuing at that speed. It wasn't until one hand crept up and grabbed ahold of her hair that she instantly teetered on that precipice. What was it about that action that sent her spinning out of control?

"You feel so fucking good." Jax's warm lips were against her neck. "When this is all said and done and we're back home, I'm going to take you to my club and strap you down to the spanking bench. I'll flip up the short ruffled skirt you'll be wearing, baring your ass for all to see. They'll understand who you belong to by the time I'm done."

The second Jax tugged a little more on her hair, giving him full access to her neck, he bit her skin and pushed her over the edge. Emily was unsure if that was the action that sent her over or his words which created a vivid image in her mind. She would accept the scene he'd described because not only would it show every Dominant that she was his, but it would also be inked into every submissive's mind as well. Jax was hers.

With each thrust her pussy clenched his cock, trying to keep him inside of her. Her orgasm seemed never ending and she cried out with every spasm. Over and over, he thrust until she felt his shaft expand and knew his seed was now filling the reservoir on the tip of the condom. The other reality that she didn't want to face was now impending on her mind and she did everything to shut it out. That was, until Jax's phone rang.

Chapter Twenty-One

Ryland stretched his fingers several times, using the action to calm the irritation that was flowing through his system. Beatrice Weisslich had been checked into this very hotel but now seemed to be missing. No one on the staff knew a thing about it either, although they willingly shared the places she liked to tour and dine. Five hours into his search, he was relatively sure that Crest or someone working for him had scooped her up.

He bumped his shoulder into a random tourist on the street, not bothering to apologize as he made his way to the taxi. The driver had already taken his overnight bag and stowed it in the trunk. Once situated in the back seat, he placed his elbow near the side window and contemplated his next move.

Someone had to know something. For such an easy mission, this was turning into a cluster fuck that he was wasting too much time on. He ran a hand over his mouth, easing the tension from his jaw. Ryland felt as if this assignment was going awry. It was a foreign feeling and one that he could do without.

The vibration of his pocket alerted him to an incoming message. Not bothering to look out at the city as they drove toward the airport, Ryland reached inside his suit jacket and pulled out his phone. He opened the email and read the contents, disbelief coursing through him.

"Stop," Ryland demanded, tapping on the front seat. "Pull over."

"But sir—"

"Now!" Ryland shook his head at the useless man, not able to take orders. With his hand already on the handle, he swung the door open the instant the car had pulled next to the curb. "Stay here."

Ryland didn't look back to make certain the driver listened. Walking into the first shop he saw, he let the door close behind him as the smell of rich coffee surrounded him. It was a café, which was perfect for what he intended to do. He strode to the counter, speaking fluent French as he asked to use their telephone. Once the landline phone was in hand, he dialed a contact of his at the embassy and called in a favor.

"Transfer me to this number," Ryland said in a rather low tone, not wanting to draw attention. He rattled off Vadim Batkin's number. He knew the call into the security member of the Security Council would be incoming from the embassy located here and would not seem suspicious in nature. "You'll be handsomely paid for your service."

The man on the other end stuttered his appreciation, which caused Ryland to tighten his fingers on the phone. He loathed people who weren't secure in their lot in life. That thought had him turning toward the window, looking out at the taxi driver as he waited to be connected.

Something caught his eye a few vehicles back. Another taxi, although this one with a passenger in the back. The sun glinted off of the windshield, making it hard to see who was within, but the hairs on the back of his neck stood on end. Ryland always trusted his instinct.

"Hello?"

"As you are obviously aware, I need more time. It seems you neglected to inform me that my target has qualified protection. The risks are more profound now, wouldn't you agree?" Ryland casually stepped back to the counter, although never once turned his back against the open windowpanes. He calculated his options as he continued speaking. "You should know that while I am usually given a target's name, relevant information is vital to my delivery."

"You cannot call me here," Batkin whispered harshly, indicating he was near people. Ryland wasn't worried and remained silent, not bothering to ease the man's mind of how the routing of this call would show if someone were to trace it. He waited for Batkin to take the bait. "All hell has broken loose. All you have to know is where she'll be in order to facilitate your end. I've given you that, along with another name. They will both be in the same location."

Ryland remained silent for a moment longer, contemplating how problematic this assignment had become. He recognized the symptoms of a racing heart and tight chest as one of prey and found himself enjoying this feeling that he'd been given. Was one of Crest's men in that car outside of the café? Had they decided to hunt him instead? He would have taken this second target on for free, but that would ruin his reputation.

"I take it the money has been delivered into my account?"

"Yes," Batkin responded, his voice still low. "Just see that it is done."

"My pleasure." Ryland disconnected the call and turned back to the young barista. She blushed when their fingers brushed against each other and he paused long enough to give her a small smile. The petite brunette wasn't his usual type, but there was something about her innocence that made him want to claim it. "Thank you very much, Miss. I'll remember your hospitality on my return trip."

Having mulled over what he was going to do with the possible visitor in the other cab, Ryland walked to the door and stepped outside into the street as if nothing was amiss. Walking directly to the taxi, he opened the door and situated himself in the seat before having the driver take him to the airport terminal. He sat back, getting comfortable for a ride that would ultimately lead him toward a potential confrontation.

Jax listened to Emily's even breathing as they lay in bed. The sun was shining through a window that overlooked the lake, allowing the reflection to dance along the rose colored walls of the bedroom. He didn't want to move, for his left arm was tucked in somewhat uncomfortably under her head. He smiled when a little snort came from her pert little nose. If she knew that, she would be mortified.

He turned his head, leisurely watching the spring birds fly by on their way to the fresh cool morning water. The freedom for which they spread their wings was a fascinating sight as their graceful movements cut through the air. The carefree way they glided toward their destination caused an envious feeling that he normally didn't feel. They trusted one another to guide each other during their route. It wasn't as if he didn't have the same thing with each team member of CSA, but he'd told

Emily that he thought trust was an illusion. It wasn't. Sometimes he took things for granted.

Trusting Emily and then finding out his decisions had been based on a lie was what had been an illusion. If he were to examine the situation a little closer, she'd been doing her job and then had made choices based on the path she'd been given. Just like those birds outside of the window, acting in accordance with what nature threw their way. She'd given herself to him twice in two days...her mind, body, and soul. That in itself was what trust was all about.

Jax had his shortcomings and one of those happened to be the fear of losing the people he cared about. If he were honest with himself, that was why it had been so easy to help Emily create a new life. He was able to control when she left versus having fate take her away from him at a later time when losing her would completely devastate him. He understood her need to avoid the reality of the situation, for he'd been doing it for years. He'd be a hypocrite to ask something of her that he hadn't been able to do.

"Morning," Emily murmured against his arm. She slid a hand around his chest and managed to scoot closer, if that was possible. He brought his arm down around her back as she shifted her head to his shoulder. "Hmmm...how long have you been awake?"

"Around an hour. Your snoring kept me awake," Jax softly answered, smirking as he stroked her warm skin in reassurance. "Kevin gave his SITREP and everything is clear right now."

"Crest's phone call last night wasn't very optimistic. And I don't believe for a moment I snore." Emily started to trace the figure eights she seemed partial to on his abdomen. "Are you sure we're safe staying in place?"

"Crest gave us the facts, that's all." Jax kissed the top of her head. "If Ryland manages to slip by Connor, getting you into New York City and then to the United Nations for that hearing won't be easy. Crest's motto is plan for the worst, hope for the best. Well, at least one of them. I swear he has a new motto every day."

"Is it possible for me to talk to Aunt Beatrice without giving our location away? I know you have the capability, but does the man who is keeping her safe have the same technology?"

"No," Jax replied, leveling with her. "It's just a friend helping out. Crest pulled in one of his favors. It was an impromptu situation, but be assured she's safe."

They lay quiet for a while with the only interruption being when Emily used the bathroom. There were a lot of unthreaded strings dangling in front of them, what with Ryland still on the loose, the hearing coming up, and undoubtedly the NSA. Would they allow her to walk away without penance once this was over? He wasn't sure what the protocol was with that particular agency. Right now, they were given a reprieve and he wanted to make the most of it.

"I want your mouth on my cock," Jax murmured against her forehead. He smiled when he felt a shiver go through her body. He remembered as if it were yesterday her drive to succeed at taking him down her throat. "Practice until you can take me down your throat, sweet spy of mine. If you make me come any other way, we'll do this all afternoon until you get it right."

Emily lifted her head, her blue eyes shining with determination. Her mouth pursed as if she couldn't believe he would question her ability, but he remembered the last blowjob she'd given him vividly. Not that Jax liked to admit it, but she had him coming under two minutes with just her tongue and hand. His smile grew, which he knew would urge her downward.

"Yes, Sir," Emily said, her voice still raspy from sleep, although the way her eyes lit up made him well aware she was wide awake. She gracefully slid down his body, pulling the sheet with her, and situated herself in between his legs. "May I?"

Emily was holding up her hands and wiggling her fingers, her question in reference to using them. Pride shot through him that she remembered to ask for permission to touch him with her hands. He roamed his gaze down her body, taking in the ample swell of her breasts to the fluid flare of her hips, which led to her bare pussy. He recalled the time when her hands were bound behind her and she had only been allowed to use her mouth. He hadn't lasted long then either. She had a way about her that no other submissive came close to touching.

"Yes, you may," Jax replied, shifting the pillow behind his head so that he had full view of what she was about to do. There was something sensual about watching a woman take him in her mouth...especially this woman. His cock was already hard, if not past that point. "Slowly, Emily."

She leaned down on her knees, her hair draping to the side. Jax reached out to brush the remaining hair around her ear, so as not to block the view of her tongue reaching out and swiping the tip of his dick. He wasn't ready for the heat that her moisture created, causing his balls to immediately draw up. His intake of air echoed throughout the room.

"You taste good, Sir," Emily said, her breath heating the slit that she'd just licked, making it feel as if his dick had caught fire.

Before Jax could reply, she covered his tip and sucked him into her mouth until he felt the back of her throat. It was then that she eased back up, using her tongue to stroke the underside of his shaft. Emily's long fingers wrapped around the base of his cock and held him upright to continue the on-slaught of pleasure.

Letting Emily have her way for now, Jax settled back on the pillow and enjoyed watching as much as receiving. She didn't miss one inch of his dick, using her tongue, lips, and fingers. She worked him from top to bottom, while her other hand massaged his balls and inner thighs. Small spasms were occurring, producing pre-cum that she managed to lap up as fast as it appeared.

"Deeper. Swallow me," Jax instructed, his voice dropping an octave.

Emily bent over him, getting a better angle as she took him back to her throat. He heard her stop breathing as she tried to take him farther in, but eventually pulled away. Her fingers slipped up and over his shaft, curling around his tip and causing a jolt of electricity to shoot through his balls. She tried to take him deeper once more, halting at the same time.

Jax allowed her to continue on the same path and it ended up being the swirl of her tongue around the tip of his cock that sent him over. To her credit, she greedily sucked him down, draining him until the last ripple of pleasure tore through his lower back and into his sac. Not that he would let her know it, but having her do this again so quickly was going to be the death of him. The issue at hand was he'd thrown down a challenge and would see it through.

"Again," Jax murmured, gritting his teeth as the tortured ecstasy flowed through him as she continued to lick and nibble on his dick. "I want you to take me down your throat, Emily."

Her hand continued to pump his still hardened cock, twirling her hand up, over, and around the tip. Over and over, she manipulated his shaft with her fingers and mouth until he was once again on the verge of having another release. She used her other hand to massage his sac, as she knew he liked the feel of it.

"Will you help me, Sir?"

Emily lifted her head and looked at him with those beautiful blue eyes of hers. They sparkled with something he couldn't put a name on, but knew he wanted it to be there for as long as they drew air. That should have scared the shit out of him, but instead, it made him want to give her whatever she may need for the rest of her life. Jax groaned and wrapped his right hand into her hair, pulling it tightly so she felt the pressure on her scalp. Her head tilted with the action and her lips parted, taking his cock into her mouth as if she was sucking the juice out of a ripe strawberry. That alone almost sent him over the edge once more.

"Relax your throat," Jax said in a strangled voice. "Breath through your nose."

His fingers were now tangled in her mass of blonde hair. To give herself leverage, Emily placed both hands on either side of his legs, which in turn gave him the leeway he needed without interference. Pushing her head lower, Jax felt the back of her throat. She instinctively tried to pull back, but he held tight, watching closely for signs that she couldn't do this. It was the guttural moan that signified her desire for more and he slowly angled her mouth to accept all of him.

His eyes rolled, although he did his damnedest to keep her in focus, as he was the one to maneuver her mouth and lips up and down over his cock. The vision before him faded into a bright light as he felt the raptured pressure explode. Her throat muscles continued to work their magic and his yell echoed throughout the room one more time as she swallowed his cum.

"Thank you, Sir," Emily said with what sounded like a smile in her voice.

He struggled to open his eyes and looked down the length of him to see her blue eyes sparkling with confidence as well as gratification. He knew the look well, as he felt it every time a scene was successful. It wouldn't do for her to feel she could top from the bottom, so keeping his hold on her hair, he dragged her up his body and claimed her lips. Her knees were now on either side of his waist and he could feel the heat of her pussy on his abdomen. It was only when they needed oxygen did he let her pull back, gasps falling from both of them.

"Very good, little spy of mine," Jax murmured, finally having found some ground on which to stand. She had an effect on him like no other woman. "I think it's time for your bubble bath."

"But—" Emily's lips went into a cute little pout.

Jax laughed, knowing his little vixen knew how close she was to breaking him down with that beautiful face. He was also aware that he wouldn't be the Dom she needed should he cave every time that she felt she needed something. He was well educated and experienced in reading her tells and right now, Emily needed some down time. A bubble bath would do wonders for her body, as well as her mind.

"It's my job to make sure you're safe," Jax said, rolling over on top of her and stealing one more kiss. "I'll check in with Kevin one more time and then walk the perimeter. We can never be too sure. Then we'll make breakfast and go over more of your soft limits and see if we can find something that you really enjoy. I'm thinking there's different uses for the spatula that I saw in the drawer."

✧   ✧   ✧   ✧

Ryland knew what had to be done and was well aware of the consequences should he carry it out. The driver pulled the cab to the curb at the drop off area underneath the sign of the correct airline. He'd used the drive to contemplate how Crest had located him and didn't like the answers he was coming up with.

He happened to see the passenger using the side mirror on the taxi when they had turned at one of the city intersections. A man with short black hair and aviator glasses, maybe of Cuban descent, was comfortably ensconced in the backseat of the car and talking on his phone. Ryland recognized him immediately as one of Crest's team members. Connor Ortega was his name, if memory served him right from the military files he'd accessed on the flight here.

He'd only met a worthy opponent once in his life and to this day, she remained on his mind periodically. He now reserved that spot for only her and damned if Crest or one of his men got to join her ranks.

"Don't get out," Ryland said to the driver, keeping his tone casual so not to alarm the man. "We'll be heading to the train station momentarily. I just need to have a discussion with someone before we change our route."

Ryland had given enough time for the other man's taxi to pull up behind him. He wasn't too worried that Crest's man would take him out immediately. According to his research, they liked to follow rules within the law. That was their first mistake. Their second was thinking he would follow suit. He glided his hand under his suit jacket, palming the Walter PPK.

It was a throwaway that he would have tossed before security, but it would execute the job he needed it to do.

He pulled on the handle and swung the door open, taking his time unfolding his lean frame out of the vehicle. Timing it right, Ryland was no more than five feet from where Mr. Ortega now stood. They had similar poses, with their hand tucked into their jackets. Ortega wasn't as well dressed as he was, what with wearing denim and a leather jacket, but it didn't matter to him what the man wore to his death. But before that were to happen, this was the perfect opportunity to garner information.

"Mr. Ortega, it seems that you haven't had time to tour the City of Love," Ryland said, tsking at the end of his statement. "I assure you that I am not as fascinating as the history of this wondrous place."

"Cut the shit, Ryland," Ortega said, not wavering his gaze. Ryland saw that he'd removed his sunglasses, which was to his disadvantage. Didn't the man know that the eyes were the window to the soul? Ryland made sure to see as much as he could. "I'm taking you into custody for the murder of Lieutenant Colonel Samuel Hendersen, Sergeant Major Chad Pierce, the General Counsel to the Director of the CIA, and most recently, the Attorney General. I'm sure the list will continue to grow, but you do leave a specific mark with these murders. Lay your weapon on the ground and kick it toward me."

Ryland made sure that his facial expression didn't change, although anger boiled in his bloodstream. Those men had been his marks and he'd done his job, but over his fucking dead body had he left evidence behind that he was the one responsible for executing them. The crime scenes had been clean and for this scumbag of a man to suggest otherwise was repulsive. Ortega was bluffing.

"I'm very interested as to what evidence you think you have that would tie me to those unfortunate events," Ryland said, cocking his head to the side as if he were studying a cockroach. This man didn't deserve to be on the sole of his shoe. "I guess that will give me something to ponder as I go on my way. Alas, it seems as if we've run out of time. A shame, considering I had so many more questions for you."

Ryland knew how this would play out and although he'd spoken the truth about regretting how short their conversation had been, he needed to use the current situation to his advantage—and that would be the businesswoman walking up to him. It also helped that disposing of Ortega would be one less minion he'd have to worry about. After all, Crest seemed to have a handful at his disposal should this one not return. It niggled in the back of his mind that he still hadn't located the picture of the female agent and wondered if he was about to be played. Seeing the opportunity present itself, he knew he'd have to take his chances.

"I take it you're arriving?" the woman said, a black leather briefcase in her hand, gesturing toward the cab. "I'll—"

In an instant, Ryland had the woman against his chest and his weapon drawn. As with all adrenaline-pumping occurrences, Ryland allowed his hearing to fade and his vision to lock in on said target. Unfortunately, it seemed as if Ortega had foreseen his swift actions, for the man dodged to his right before the snap shot Ryland had gotten off had a chance to catch up to him. It would seem fate had other plans for Mr. Ortega.

Ryland disregarded the screams and shouts of the people surrounding them, hysterics having no place in this situation.

Baggage was abandoned as people tried to escape the unknown. It was easy to spot the security officers and police as they seemed to come out of nowhere. Seeing as he had a woman's life in his arms, Ryland knew they wouldn't shoot. They didn't have what it took to make life-altering decisions. He didn't have that problem.

"It seems as if our time has run out, Ortega." Ryland calculated his angle and knew his next shot wouldn't come close to his target, though it would deter him from making any rash movements. He paused and waited for the right moment. "Please congratulate your lovely new woman on her upcoming nuptials. I assume you'll make an honest woman out of her."

With that last statement, Ryland rounded off a shot near Ortega's location the exact moment he shoved the woman away from him. Swinging his weapon to bring her in sight, he drew the trigger back and fired a round. The impact on her inside left thigh had her stumble a few steps back, but he was already in the cab before the police could bring their guns to bear. Placing the barrel to the driver's head, the man didn't need to be told what to do. Ryland kept his head low, knowing Ortega wouldn't fire at the vehicle where an innocent man might take a hit.

The breakaway was clean. Within a few miles, Ryland had the driver stop the cab. The man was obviously terrified and in any other situation, Ryland would have disposed of him. As it was, he needed this man to tell the authorities that Ryland was heading for the train station. That would buy Ryland the time he needed to make other arrangements. Knowing there was nothing in his overnight bag that wasn't replaceable, he let himself be drawn into a group of tourists and swept along the city street.

He ran a thumb across his index finger, rubbing the smooth skin. Ortega would no doubt confiscate the luggage, but there would be no fingerprints. As for knowing how he was in Paris, Ryland could only fathom they had used facial recognition software on the airport's closed circuit system. In which case, no amount of make-up could hide him from the cameras. It was time to go old school.

Chapter Twenty-Two

"It's been six days," Emily said, shoving the coffee pot back onto the burner. Grabbing both cups, she turned toward the living room where Jax was putting on his jacket. As much as she'd loved this time with Jax, she wanted more than days in a cabin. She wanted more and the only way to obtain that was to expedite the situation. "What are we waiting for? Ryland could be anywhere, Aunt Beatrice has got to be going out of her mind, and Schultz has again gone MIA. For all we know, they've hired another assassin who we don't even know! I say we stick with our original plan and broadcast this on international television."

"No." Jax seized one of the mugs and took a healthy swallow. His clear and concise answer raised her hackles. Now that he knew the truth and knew what her abilities were, he should be willing to listen to her opinions. "We wait."

"For what, Jax?" Emily asked, her voice rising. Didn't he see that they had been in one spot for too long? A couple days was one thing...almost a week was another. "For you to make another sweep of the property? For Ryland to show up and do what he's been paid for? For the NSA to get their hand in this little cat and mouse game? Let's face it, there's enough people who know who could have ratted me out to my superiors. For all we know, they've hired someone of their own to track me down. You said it yourself. It's only a matter of time before—"

"Do you remember what you said to me the first night we arrived here?" Jax asked, raising an eyebrow in question. He took another drink of coffee, like they weren't having an argument over whether she lived or died. His calm demeanor was infuriating. "You said you'd be my submissive in the bedroom, but you were my equal outside of it. Now I'm not going to stand here and tell you how important it is for us to rely on my team, who has been out there every day and night trying to find the location of Ryland. I realize that you're used to working on your own, but now is the time to take the advantage of what you worked so hard to have…and that's me and my team having your back."

Emily gritted her teeth and turned back around, taking a sip of her own coffee to calm her nerves. Today was different than the others and she knew why. They'd gotten into a routine in the mornings with Jax creating a scene and keeping her attention on him. But he'd gotten a call an hour ago from Kevin that said Crest was flying to Washington DC this morning and that it would be an additional three to four days before she and Jax were to head that way. She didn't know if she was angry at the pause in the momentum of events or the fact that she'd been relying on Jax every morning to take her mind off of reality. For some reason, that smacked of weakness.

"Emily," Jax said, his hands landing on her shoulders and tenderly squeezing. He slowly turned her so that their faces were inches apart, his features softening and the brown flecks of his eyes seemingly reaching for her and caressing her cheek.

"I know it seems as if you've been running on adrenaline for the last two years, but it's okay to take a mental break. That's what we're doing, but that doesn't lessen the importance of what's going on outside of our bubble."

"A woman was shot for being in the wrong place and the wrong time. She's alive, but she will never again be the same. And Connor almost died," Emily whispered, searching his gaze for any resentment that she was the cause of that. "He's like your brother, Jax. I know how important he is to you. I understand that he's your family. It all seemed like protocol the day I walked into the CSA offices. But now…"

"It is protocol," Jax replied, lifting a hand and brushing away a loose strand that escaped the hair tie at the back of her neck. "Nothing has changed that you didn't know would happen. Anything to do with the United Nations is paramount to being in the middle of the desert with mortars falling and making contact with the ground. The stakes are high. I know it, Connor knows it, and my team knows it. Was Ryland making comments about Lauren to try and show us he can reach anyone? Or was it a serious threat? We don't know, but we'll take every precaution to make sure our loved ones are safe."

Emily dropped her forehead against Jax's chest, careful to hold tight to her coffee. She closed her eyes and took the comfort he offered by stroking her hair. She remembered coming out of college and the excitement of being recruited by the NSA. If only she knew then what she knew now.

"Word has got to have reached Alekseev that the Security Council is convening for a hearing." Emily lifted her head and met his gaze. "If we thought it was dangerous before, there will be no stopping him now. I have the evidence that Kevin grabbed from the news station. There are other routes I can take, Jax, besides putting everyone else at risk. The risk has risen to a level that supersedes what I originally thought would happen."

"Equals, right?" Jax asked, taking her chin in hand. She rolled her eyes and took a deep breath, letting him know that she would listen but thought it ridiculous that he wasn't even willing to really hear what she had to say. "You were paid to do a job, which you did. I'm being paid right now to do mine. Let me do it. And if I see you roll your eyes at me again, little spy, I'll have you over my knee before those long lashes of yours covers those pretty blues."

"I don't see a bed," Emily quipped as he stepped away to zip up his jacket. He was right in the way of the best course of action was to wait for word on when they should head out to New York. It just wasn't what she wanted to hear. But retiring back to bed for the rest of the day would pass the time. Maybe she could convince herself that an innocent woman being shot didn't affect her and the decisions that would have to be made going forward. "Which means rolling of the eyes is permitted."

Jax raised an eyebrow once more, a caution that she was crossing the line. If her emotions weren't in such a turmoil and so divided, she would have pushed a little farther in hopes to keep him inside the cabin with her. As it stood, Emily brought the coffee cup to her lips and took a sip, giving him a wink. He laughed and then kissed her on the cheek, taking advantage of their close contact and connecting his palm with her ass. Taking his skullcap out of his pocket, he situated it over his blonde hair and walked out the door.

Emily slowly made her way back to the kitchen, draining the rest of her coffee before she even reached the counter. Refilling her mug, she turned back around and leaned against the marble. Her MOB holster dug into her back, so she turned slightly and rested against her hip. She should have joined him on the walk around the perimeter, but knew he would have said no, regardless that she was armed.

She took another small sip of coffee, hoping that the caffeine would help with the small headache that was starting to form in her temples. Emily remembered that the medicine cabinet located in the bathroom only had ibuprofen, which she was allergic too. What she needed was acetaminophen. She wondered if Kevin would be able to stop at the pharmacy in the closest town or have Ethan bring it when they switched shifts.

Knowing there had to be a junk drawer somewhere, Emily placed her coffee on the counter and started to open all of the drawers in the kitchen. The one drawer off to the side in almost every small kitchen she'd been in that didn't fit the normal sized silverware had what she was looking for. Pulling out the small tablet and pen, she wrote down a couple of things that she would like in preparation of their trip back to New York.

Placing the back end of the pen against her lips, she contemplated writing down condoms. She decided against it, thinking that Jax could be the one to ask for them. So that just left the acetaminophen, hair color with the appropriate brand and shade, and a box of tampons. It wasn't something that she would have put down if it weren't essential and hoped Kevin or Ethan were the kind of men who weren't squeamish about that kind of thing.

Emily's time of the month had to be coming up. Things had been in such turmoil that she couldn't remember the date, so she grabbed the tablet and her coffee as she crossed the area to the couch. Picking up Jax's watch that he'd left on the side table, she looked at the two little white squares within the dial which displayed what day it was. Calculating the weeks, she frowned when it didn't add up.

She set down her coffee, counting again. She came up with the same date…two days prior. Emily's heart started to palpitate and her hands trembled. No. She was wrong. She tried to steady her breathing and slowly started from the beginning. Marking the days off on the paper, below her list, she stared at the evidence in front of her.

Emily hadn't lied to Jax when she said they shouldn't have had anything to worry about when they hadn't used protection. She'd passed her ovulation cycle and had been coming up on the last week of her period. It shouldn't have been a problem. It wasn't a problem. She tried to rationalize the situation. This last month had been very stressful and hard on her body. She'd started to have sexual relations again, which also had to contribute. Right?

Emily snatched her mug and took a drink of coffee, only to spit it back in the mug. What if she was pregnant? Drinking caffeine wasn't a good idea. But she wasn't pregnant. She wasn't.

✧ ✧ ✧

After spending every second of every minute of every day for the past two weeks in Emily's presence, Jax was relatively sure that he was in tune with her mental health. When he'd left her this morning, she'd been riddled with anxiety over what had transpired in Paris, as well as the instructions from Crest that they stay in place a while longer. By nightfall, it was like she was off in a different world all her own.

"Emily."

"Yeah?"

Emily gave the right response and even managed to stop staring at the fire he'd just started. He placed the poker back into the stand but stayed sitting on the hearth. He rested his elbows on his knees, wanting to give her the space she obviously needed. But they'd agreed that they were in this together and she didn't get the right to shut him out. That was one of his hard limits.

"Talk to me. If this is about that woman, she's fine," Jax said, wanting to reassure her that Crest was going above and beyond in paying for anything the woman might need. "She's back home and—"

"I had a headache this morning and realized we didn't have any acetaminophen. I thought maybe we could give a list to Kevin or Ethan, so I wrote one up. I needed tampons."

Jax waited for her to continue and when she didn't, he stared at her for a moment longer. She'd spoken past tense, but maybe he was mistaken. A mixed set of emotions started to boil up inside of him, bringing him to his feet. His mind struggled to comprehend then and now.

"You said—"

"I know what I said, Jax," Emily said, the frustration evident in her voice. He didn't want her upset, but he did need to verify whether or not she really was...fuck. He ran a hand through his hair as he thought of the implications. Emily tossed the blanket aside and sat forward on the couch. "I don't know that I'm pregnant. I knew I was close to my time of the month, so the window of that happening should have passed. I was due two days ago, but in all reality I'm late because of stress."

Jax zeroed in the on the word *pregnant*. Regardless of the timing, whether it made sense or not, a shot of joy ran through his system. It was similar to the adrenaline rush he got when going on an overseas mission, knowing that his life could change at the toss of a dime. He was honest enough with himself to know that he longed for the family he never had, yet was also aware that he was delving into deep waters that he had no idea how to navigate. The conflicting feelings were hard to undertake and while he normally would have called Connor immediately, he knew this was something he would have to deal with on his own. Jax looked at Emily as she stood in front of him…really looked at her. He wasn't alone anymore, was he?

"We'll, um, I'll have Kevin or Ethan make a run into town," Jax said, knowing the words sounded disjointed. He still needed time to let this soak in. "I'll put on my jacket, check out the perimeter again, and then talk to Ethan and have him radio it in. They'll pick up whatever you need and drop it off at shift change."

Jax smiled at her, hoping it didn't come across as fake. Another thought resurfaced from a week ago, when he recognized that the reason he'd made love to her without a condom was because maybe he wanted fate to take over. Had he? Jax started for the door and had even managed to pick up his jacket before she spoke.

"I said this once before, but don't you dare walk out that fucking door, Jax Christensen," Emily whispered, her voice unsteady. For how low her tone was, it still seemed to echo throughout the room. The fear in her voice was evident and squeezed his heart as if it were in a vise. He'd told her just last week that they needed to start fresh, get to know one another again, and take things slow. This was the polar opposite and faster than his preferred round of .45 caliber ACP 230 grain hydra-shock when he pulled the trigger. "I'm scared and have dealt with too much on my own. I need you with me on this."

Jax looked down at the jacket in his hand, shaking his head at how easily she was now sharing her feelings with him. Wasn't this what he wanted? Hadn't their first scene been to drive home how vital honesty was in a relationship? Hell, add on the Dominant/submissive part of the relationship and it became even more essential. He slowly hung his jacket back on the coat rack and then turned to face her.

"You're not alone, Emily." Jax walked towards her, connecting his gaze with hers. He needed for her to see that he could bare his soul as well, regardless of the terror it put into his being. He finally reached her and placed his palms on her cheeks, wanting her to truly hear what he was about to say. "The truth is I'm scared shitless. Do not take that to mean I would walk away from you. I wouldn't. If you are pregnant, that complicates things from my perspective because I cannot let anything happen to you or our baby. The very thought that something could happen to either one of you makes me want to leave this place and go hunting. My kind of hunting that the Marines taught me. That's a part of me that I never want you to see. It's ugly, but I will do what I need to do to ensure the both of you are safe."

"Jax—"

"I told you just this morning that Connor and the rest of the team knows the dangers of our occupation. Lauren and their families…they understand the risks as well," Jax said, not wanting her to speak until he was done having his say. She needed to hear this. "To be honest, I don't know what the hell I told myself to actually believe that. Maybe it's because I've only ever had myself to think about when situations go awry. Now there's this possibility that you are the mother of my child. A child that I would be honored to have with you, Emily. I am not unhappy about this, but I do need to come to terms with the possibility. This will not just change us, but it will alter the man I am."

"Thank you." Emily had rested her fingers over his wrists while he laid his soul bare for her. "Thank you for not making light of this or—"

"Never. What you and I have, what we could have, signifies the dreams that have haunted me since the day my family was taken from me. I admit, it's fun to play around in others' lives," Jax said, flashing a real smile now, thinking of the shit that he'd pulled to get Connor and Lauren together, "but not with you, Emily. Not with you. This isn't a game to me. This is our future. This—"

Bam! Bam! Bam!

Both Jax and Emily had their weapons drawn in seconds, pointed at the door. He would have laughed had he had the time in regards that his adrenaline rush didn't alter in the slightest from their previous conversation to now. Although it hit him in that moment as she stood side by side with him, that he would have to find a way to convince her to stay behind him from this point on. This wasn't going to work and it would be over his dead body before Emily had to protect herself and now maybe their unborn child.

"Jax!" Kevin's deep voice vibrated the wooden door. "Pack up. We're heading out in the morning."

Chapter Twenty-Three

J ax leaned against the wall in the convenience store next to the bathroom and crossed his arms, trying to remain calm. He'd made sure to wear his jacket inside to cover up his holster, but all it did was make him overheated. How long did it take to pee on a damn stick?

"Here," Kevin said, shoving a large cup of coffee into Jax's hands. "It's six o'clock in the damned morning and after what I just saw, you need the caffeine."

Jax resisted the urge to wipe the smirk off of Kevin's face and took the proffered drink. His nerves were stretched thin as it was. Kevin and Ethan had arrived at the house at five o'clock sharp, ready to follow him and Emily back to New York. The plan was to make it just outside of the city, stay at a random hotel, and have Crest and the rest of the team members meet them there. Taryn and Jessie were still back in Minneapolis as far as Jax knew. Unfortunately, having Ethan stay in the SUV to keep watch outside allowed Kevin to come into the gas station with them, thus seeing Emily buy the pregnancy test. It had been unavoidable, since he and Emily didn't want to wait to find out. They needed to know, especially before entering into Ryland's territory.

"I just bought a club," Jax said, after having taken a drink of the hot liquid that he seemed to be living on lately. "Seriously, I just bought a kink club. If that stick turns purple—"

"Blue."

"Whatever the fuck color it turns," Jax replied, irritated that Kevin thought this was funny, "my life changes."

"It's changed regardless if she's pregnant," Kevin said, as if his words made sense. They didn't. Why wasn't he seeing this as clear as Jax? "Having a relationship is a hell of a lot different than playing the field."

"I know that, farm boy." Jax thought maybe it was a little leftover redneck shit that was skewing with Kevin's head that he didn't see the picture that Jax was painting. "I think about what I did to Connor. I mean, I practically forced him and Lauren together. Now, she's been threatened by this fucking killer that's disappeared into thin air. His life was fine beforehand, when it was only himself that he needed to worry about."

"Well, you do have a tendency to do that," Kevin said with a shrug of his shoulder, as if they'd come to expect something from him.

"What fucking tendency?"

"To meddle in other people's lives." Kevin had that crooked ass grin on his face and somehow it stayed through a drink of his own coffee. "Let's just say that karma can be a bitch sometimes."

The bathroom door opened and Jax would have sworn the earth's axis tipped. He turned so fast, the coffee splashed out of the hole in the top of the cup. He didn't feel it though. He didn't feel anything other than his heart racing and then the uninvited joy that sped through his veins at her tremulous smile. Fuck. It must have been purple. He was going to be a father.

❖ ❖ ❖ ❖

"This changes everything, you know that," Jax stated, his fingers tightening on the steering wheel. He glanced in the rearview mirror, seeing Ethan and Kevin securely sitting behind them two car lengths back. "The stakes are higher and when we get to the hotel, we'll come up with a new plan."

"Jax, my pregnancy changes nothing." Emily said one thing, but the protective way her arm was wrapped around her stomach said another. "I have to be at that hearing. Alekseev needs to be sent back to his own country and I need to deal with the NSA if I want a normal life. We stick with the original plan."

This equal shit out of the bedroom was getting old. Jax didn't say anything for a minute, trying to formulate the words to get her to understand why they couldn't just waltz her into the United Nations buildings.

"When I spoke with Crest, he informed me that Schultz was going to have Secret Service crawling all over a two mile radius. The buildings themselves are already secure. With the added manpower, Schultz is banking on being able to get you inside."

"Then I don't see a problem if—"

"We've finally agreed that Schultz is on our side, because if he wasn't, we know that you would already be dead." Jax glanced over at her in time to see her wince. Saying those words tore him up, but she had to understand this wasn't some walk in the park on a sunny fucking day. "You said yourself that you wanted me to see you through this. And you, of all people, should be aware of what information the government has and how they get it. We can kid ourselves, but don't think that Schultz hasn't known our whereabouts this entire time. Which is why we came to the conclusion that Ryland is working on his own. But this man, this killer, has more accuracy than any sharpshooter that Crest has ever seen. Which means I don't want to take a chance with you or our child's life if this murderer can take you out in as much as a little past two miles."

"I'll be surrounded. I'll be wearing a vest." Emily rested her head back against the seat, as if she didn't want to talk anymore. Tough shit. He'd speak the entire trip until he got through to her. "And you'll be by my side."

Jax fisted one hand, placing it on his thigh to prevent him from punching the dashboard. What if he wasn't good enough? Had she ever thought of that? The pressure inside the vehicle was enough to make him roll down the windows, but he couldn't even do that. He would never place her in danger. That didn't stop his chest from tightening at the thought of losing control of the situation and having her die in his arms.

✧   ✧   ✧   ✧

Emily closed her eyes, hoping that Jax would just drive and give her a moment to gather her thoughts. She understood what he was doing and why, but nothing he said would change the route they needed to take. Regardless of anything monumental happening, Emily would be standing in front of the Security Council tomorrow morning at nine o'clock sharp.

She'd already given herself time to come to terms with carrying Jax's child while she'd been in the restroom of the convenience store. That wasn't the most ideal place to confirm a pregnancy, but considering the situation they were in, at least she was alive to do so.

A child. Jax's child. Their child. Was it a boy? A girl? A thousand more questions ran through her mind, but Emily knew that the answers wouldn't be there. Hell, she might not be here tomorrow. She felt her eyes burn with tears, which truly shocked her. Emily turned her head to the right, so that it seemed as if she were looking out the window. She didn't want Jax to see her in this state when it was obvious he was just as worried about the outcome as she. She wasn't a woman prone to crying, but life wouldn't be so cruel as to give her such a precious gift and then take it away, would it?

How could the one word that appeared in the small window of the pee stick change her outlook on life? It was as if looking at the word *pregnant* was a magic spell that cast visions of the future. Emily swore she actually saw Jax appear in the mirror that had been before her, his large finger captured in the tiny hand of a newborn baby girl with beautiful blonde curls. The image had faded, bringing to life Jax wearing his skullcap and leather jacket in the snow, while pulling a small boy behind him on a sled with matching flashing smiles.

It wasn't as if opening that bathroom door was going to reveal rabid wolves or really irritated lions, but there had still been a niggling of doubt as to what Jax's reaction would be. He'd said all the right words the night before, but had morning brought more clarity as to what this would mean? When he'd mumbled something about the color being purple, Emily had just held up the digitalized stick. Her heart had flipped at seeing the goofy smile on his face and somehow, she knew that everything would be okay. At least, she'd hoped.

"Had you ever thought of yourself as a father?" Emily asked, rolling her head in his direction so that she could see his reaction. He had reminded her often that they had to get to know one another again…take their time in reconnecting. Some might say it was impossible, but she knew the moment she'd set eyes on him that he was the one. She'd yet to say those words to him. Maybe it was a deep-seated fear of exposing what was left of her soul. She'd already given him everything else. "I mean was it something that you would have wanted eventually?"

"Losing my parents and then becoming a Marine, only to see good, honest men die makes a man want a family more than anything." Jax paused, as if trying to come up with the right words. She glanced down to see his hand fisted against his thigh. She covered his hand with hers, wanting to ease his tension. "Wanting and actually having are two separate things, Emily. I feel…fuck. I feel helpless right now. As if it could all be taken away from me with a pull of a trigger. It can, and that's what makes me—"

He'd broken off the rest of his sentence, but Emily waited, hoping that he would eventually continue. Hearing his insecurities made her feel as if she wasn't alone in hers. As much as she needed to take control of her body, her emotional state needed to feel connected to his. Was it the pregnancy hormones or was she now ready to admit to him how she felt?

"I'm being given everything I want on a silver platter, Emily, and we all know that doesn't just happen." Jax's voice was low and seemed to vibrate the seats. He lifted her hand and gently kissed the back of it. "Get some sleep. We have a long drive."

Emily didn't want the conversation to end, but knew that was all Jax was going to say. His change of tone was obvious. They were both still adjusting to the news and with all the unanswered questions of what was going to happen tomorrow, it was probably pointless to continue talking about it anyway. That didn't stop Emily from caressing her stomach and mentally reassuring this baby snuggled deep within her that she would do everything in her power to make sure they came through this in one piece.

Chapter Twenty-Four

The hotel room fell silent after Jax's announcement. It was five in the morning and Emily watched tiredly as various expressions crossed the team's face and she was baffled by most of them. No matter how well she felt she knew Jax on an intimate and personal level, it was clearly obvious his friends knew him better on another.

Connor had outright laughed to the point of holding the side of his stomach, while Kevin continued to smile. She didn't see what was so humorous about her being pregnant with Jax's child. Ethan looked bemused, while Crest looked a tad bit shocked, although he'd recovered quickly enough. She would have thought they would have been either angry that they allowed this to happen at such a critical time, or maybe just be angry with her.

Lach was apparently left behind in Minneapolis to cover the security details on extended family. From what Crest had said, he'd recruited various men and women to help Lach in that endeavor while they handled things in New York. Taryn also stayed in Minneapolis, apparently feeling more comfortable with her equipment at the office than anything she would have in such a remote area. Jessie was apparently holding down the fort.

"Is anyone going to say anything?" Emily said, looking around the room at the men who seemed to have turned into boys.

Emily took that thought back. Not all of them appeared that way. Crest was dressed in a pair of khaki pants and matching sweater, with a dress shirt underneath. It confused her a little, considering the task they were undertaking this morning, but then understood why. He was going to go inside the hearing with her as she testified in front of the Security Council.

"They've said it all," Jax said wryly, his low chuckle comforting her that he hadn't taken offense to their reactions. He turned his attention back to the men standing around the room. Crest had taken a seat at the small table, a cup of coffee in front of him. "Is there anything that we haven't covered?"

"Nothing." Crest calmly took a drink of the liquid that Emily would have lunged for had Jax not made her a cup of herbal tea. Until she saw a doctor, they were being cautious about what she ate and drank. She briefly wondered if all newly pregnant women were neurotic, but discarded that thought. She had more pressing worries at hand and she made herself focus on Crest's words. "Schultz has the two mile radius covered with Secret Service men. Everyone is on the lookout for Ryland, although we know that he will most likely have changed his appearance. Taryn is monitoring the area through the street security cameras and scanning for facial recognition. Schultz will meet us at the United Nations and we'll escort Emily inside to give her testimony."

"I'm not leaving her side," Jax said, his steel voice implying that his decision was final. She knew it was and felt relief run through her. It wasn't that she didn't trust Crest, but she needed and wanted Jax with her at all times.

"Which is why Schultz obtained clearance for you." Crest looked around the room, as if taking in his team and reassuring himself that this mission was possible. "There is something that all of you need to be aware of. I've seen Ryland's handiwork up close. Once I viewed the photo that Taryn lifted from Ryland's contact with Batkin, I knew exactly who he was. After Connor's run-in with him in Paris, it's easy to conclude he's done his homework on me and all of you. He's taken this personally, which means it's not just Emily who's the target now, but all of us. Jax and I, along with several of Schultz's men, will escort Emily inside. The rest of you will come in from different angles. I want that room well guarded until they make their decision on the fate of Alekseev and Batkin. Once it's done, we'll take the route that's been mapped out and follow Schultz to the meeting with the NSA at an undisclosed location. After that, we'll reevaluate Emily's situation."

The room fell quiet and the commitment and sacrifice that these men were willing to take in order to make sure she and her baby came out of this alive was overwhelming. Emily hadn't realized that Jax had been watching her until she felt his hand on her knee. Meeting his gaze, she gave what she hoped appeared to be a confident smile. The last thing he needed was for her to think she doubted this could be done.

The next thirty minutes was spent discussing various ways this day could go wrong, ratcheting up the already high stress level that simmered below the surface. Once everyone seemed confident that they had everything covered, the men then concentrated on the weapons that were strapped to their bodies and easily accessible should they be needed. Jax had changed into black pants and matching dress shirt that Kevin had handed him in a clothes bag. He slid his arms into the jacket, making sure it covered his weapon. She'd used the bathroom to change into the black pantsuit that they'd also provided and she didn't bother to ask how they knew her size. Jax had probably given them her measurements. What did surprise her was when they were about to leave, Crest had laid a hand gently on her arm.

"We'll do everything in our power to give you your life back, Emily. I see the way Jax looks at you." Crest glanced over at Jax who was talking with Kevin, not yet looking their way. "It seems as if all his previous anger has turned into one of determination to see this through. It's his life as well and the team knows it. We take care of our own."

Jax wasn't the only one that longed for a family and while Aunt Beatrice was her only living relative, it was astounding to know that family didn't always mean blood. These men loved Jax like a brother and now, because of Jax's feelings for her, they'd accepted her like a sister. She blamed the watering of her eyes on the hormones that were obviously racing through her system. Not able to speak, she nodded her head in acceptance. If she managed to live through this, life promised her and Jax what they both longed for.

Ryland forcibly relaxed his muscles as he studied the front of the building which housed the United Nations. From his view, he could easily see the flags that stood tall lining the road, the slight wind coming off of the East River causing the fabrics to dance in the air. The building was magnificent, with the black wrought iron fence surrounding portions of the grounds, while the landscape could take one's breath away. His only focus at the moment was the black vehicles descending upon the entrance.

He'd used the time from Paris back to the States to think on this assignment, as well as what it could to do his reputation. There was also the part where it had turned personal for him and he understood that the stakes had been raised. Crest and this team of well put together military men and women had been a thorn in his side from the start. Had he known all the specifics going into this operation, he might have been able to neutralize the agency. As it was, Ryland now needed to send a clear message to his future business partners. He didn't view the people who paid him for murder to be his employers, but in essence, his associates.

One after the other, the black SUVs and town cars slowly came to a standstill. No one got out, assuring him that they were checking in with the Secret Service and others to assure that he was nowhere to be found or that another threat hadn't materialized. If he were in charge of her detail team, Grace Emily would be safely ensconced in the third vehicle. He zeroed in with his scope, patiently waiting for what he knew was to come.

"Come out and play with me, Crest."

Emily felt nauseous and would have given anything to stay in the back of this vehicle inside Jax's secure embrace. Unfortunately, that rational part of her brain knew that she had no choice but to expose herself to whatever may happen in the next hour, provided she lived for the next two minutes before even entering the building. His fingers were massaging her shoulder close to her neck where the vest rested, but his warm touch did nothing to ward off the cold that she knew was coming.

"Look at me."

The stern tone of his voice surprised Emily and her gaze swung to his. Jax's hazel eyes were gleaming with those radiant brown flecks and he seemed more alive right now than he had since their scenes at the cabin. Why it felt like it had been months instead of just two days ago was incomprehensible to her right now. Mentally she knew what he was trying to do, but her emotional and mental state seemed to need it, for she felt a little like her old self.

"You will do as I say, you will follow my lead, and you will make it through this alive with our child, do you understand me?"

"Just so long as you understand I will do whatever it takes and if that means disobeying you, then so be it," Emily stated with a small smile, feeling more confident than before. "Feel free to punish me afterwards."

"You have no idea the scenarios that are running through my mind right now," Jax whispered in her ear, even though Crest had already opened the door and was preparing to exit the vehicle, "because if you don't do exactly as I say, there will be hell to pay that won't even come close to what you experienced before."

Emily's fear didn't dissipate, but his attempt at easing it did help her transition into what needed to be done. Crest leaned forward, holding his hand out for her to take. She took it, sliding across the seat and feeling Jax do the same. She had no doubt that he would be by her side the entire way.

Several men appeared to surround the door of the SUV the second she stepped out. Crest brought her closer to him, giving Jax the time needed to unfold his large frame and stand beside her. Flanking her, they started to walk. Although she kept her head down, Emily managed to peek to the sides and catch glimpses of the morning light and the area surrounding them.

"Three o'clock." Jax was the one to speak and she tensed at the hardness in his voice. "Four men approaching."

"If I tell you to break off, do it." Crest pulled his weapon and Emily placed a hand on the one in her holster. She knew their loaded arms would have to be handed over upon entering the security station inside the building, but she was damn glad they had access to them now. "Keep on course."

Shouts and cries could be heard and everyone reacted at once. Panic filled her senses, but Emily had the wherewithal to know what was coming and relaxed her body, although she managed to keep her right arm over her abdomen to protect their child. She hit the ground, Jax and Crest doing their best to cushion her fall. She frantically tried to turn and see if anyone had been shot when each man took her by the arm and struggled to get themselves into a standing position.

"Move, move, move!"

Breathlessly, Emily did as instructed, as well as the men still surrounding her. They managed to get inside while police, Secret Service, and the security for the United Nations rushed out the doors. Emily was confused as to what happened, but didn't have time to ask before the men in front of her parted and there stood Schultz Jessalyn, looking concerned and angry.

"Looks like you weren't the only target," Schultz stated. Emily knew then that someone had died outside of the United Nations. She felt immediate remorse for the person who'd been executed, but couldn't help but question as to why it wasn't her. "Let's see if we can get through the rest of the day without casualties."

Chapter Twenty-Five

J ax didn't like to be without his weapon. Connor stood by the far door, which led out toward the public area. Kevin and Ethan had stationed themselves near the interior door, which was where Emily would enter for her testimony. According to Schultz, they were now listening to the recordings she'd managed to confiscate two years prior. A high-ranking official with the NSA was apparently in the room as well. Emily had lost a little bit of her color upon hearing that, but she still managed to straighten her back and be prepared for when they called her in. Jax was wondering if the NSA was purposely making this more difficult by requesting a meeting offsite when they were already here.

"Water?" Crest stood before them with a glass of water for Emily. She gave a small smile in thanks and took the glass, though Jax could see the slight tremor of the liquid as she lifted it to her mouth. "Vadim Batkin was identified as the man who was killed outside."

"How is it possible that someone would take him out and Ryland not try to do the same with me?" Emily asked, holding the glass with both hands as she rested it on her lap. "And why?"

"In my opinion," Crest said, lowering his voice, "I think it *was* Ryland. I don't claim to know what that man is thinking, but I have no doubt he did it. How is another question. Schultz has men scouring the area where the bullet came from and we'll hopefully know something soon."

"Any way Schultz has the connections to have Emily meet with the NSA here after this hearing?" Jax didn't like going to a blind location.

"I highly doubt it." Crest shoved his hands in his pocket. "It obviously makes things difficult with Ryland still out there and I agree with you that we need to expedite this, but we stick to the plan for now. To answer your other question, Emily, Ryland could have several reasons for targeting Batkin. Considering we have video feed of them meeting at a fundraiser, Ryland might feel that's enough evidence to connect them. Or Alekseev hired another assassin to take Batkin out."

"It could be that Ryland is toying with us, sending a message that he can get to you regardless of the manpower that we have at our disposal," Jax said, rubbing a hand down her back to ease the weight of his words. "You testifying could put an end to the job he was hired to do."

"Emily?" Schultz's voice came from the door where Kevin and Ethan stood guard. Everyone tensed and Jax stood, holding out his hand for Emily's water. Once she handed it over, he then waited as she took a deep breath and stood beside him. "They're ready."

They all knew Alekseev would be inside that room, listening to every damning piece of evidence that Emily had been able to produce. The only saving grace for the Secretary-General was that he would be untouchable, for if Jax had been able to reach him, they wouldn't need to be having this hearing. Alekseev wanted more power and he had ultimately received it through murder. The blood money he made from selling WMDs to other mid-eastern countries would do nothing for him now.

"Let's get this over with, little spy," Jax murmured, hoping the determination in his voice set her at ease for what she was about to do. He was truly in awe of her dedication to her country and to their relationship, and if the NSA didn't realize what a gem they had on their hands, then that was their loss. "Show them what being a true American means."

Ryland twirled his preferred drink in a rocks glass minus the ice, loving the way the various shades of gold changed as the liquid spun around the tumbler. He brought the crystal to his lips and closed his eyes when the singular essence hit his tongue. He relished the success of the day and contemplated actually calling one of the escort services that he frequently used when visiting New York.

He walked across the penthouse, watching the scene unfold on his computer as the Secret Service found his remote controlled firing platform located just shy of the two-mile marker from the United Nations. In order to hit his target, he had to strategically place a Polish-made ZSU-33 14.5mm heavy machine gun on a remote controlled firing platform at a higher level so that the shot was clean. He had gotten the idea from an old movie and thought Crest would appreciate the irony. The Secret Service had scoured the vacant buildings using heat-sensing devices, not detecting the highly expensive, yet exclusive equipment. It was well worth every penny. The damage a single 14.5mm shell could do to a human being was incredible to behold. They'd have to mop up Batkin's remains with a wet-vac.

When the laptop screen went blank, Ryland casually leaned forward and closed the lid. Taking a seat on the luxurious cream couch, he made himself comfortable as he contemplated his next move.

Taking out Batkin in a very messy way was well thought out and necessary to send the message he desired to future business associates. If Ryland felt that he was compromised in any way, there would be retribution in the form of death. While normally he was given a name and the contract carried out, if there was pertinent information kept from him that would expose him to greater forces, that person would be held responsible.

As for letting Grace Emily continue into the building where the fate of Alekseev would be sealed and his being sent back to Russia, that was to give her comfort in knowing she was safe for the time being. Ryland was sure that Crest would connect the dots soon enough, but he would be smart enough to know that Ryland would not let sleeping dogs lie.

Just as with the first message, another needed to be relayed. No one was permitted to get in the way of Ryland doing what he'd been hired to do. Emily would face her death, just as fate had declared from the beginning and it would be his hand that delivered it. Eliminating Crest and his band of followers at his leisure was just a present to himself for a job well done.

Emily had never felt so tired in her life. Seven hours of testimony, some of that having to defend herself from the questions thrown her way from the NSA official present, and she was finally back in the room where Kevin, Ethan, and

Connor had been subjected to wait. Only Crest and Jax had been allowed in and only then due to Schultz pulling in favors and stressing the importance of Emily having her own security detail. Having endured countless questions, the malicious looks Alekseev had thrown her way, and the thorough interrogations by several members of the Security Council, the hearing had finally come to a close. Now they would await the outcome.

"I am so proud of you," Jax whispered, holding her close. "No one could have held their composure like you did."

"I want to go home," Emily said, moving her lips against his neck.

The warmth of his skin soaked into hers, making her feel one step closer to ending this debacle. She wasn't sure how he would take her request, as she wasn't sure exactly what she meant either. Had she meant Aunt Beatrice's house? Her abandoned apartment in New York City that was leased under a different name? The cabin on Lake Michigan where she'd given him her heart? Or had she meant his home in Minneapolis?

"Soon," Jax promised, slowly releasing her. The door opened behind them and she twisted in his arms to see who it was. Schultz came through the archway, but he wasn't alone. Jax tightened his fingers on her waist and stood beside her, giving the appearance of a united front. Only it wasn't just a façade and she straightened her back once more for the next battle. "NSA."

"Emily, you answered his questions and deflected his accusations like that of a seasoned agent," Schultz said, expressing his displeasure to the man beside him, "but let me formally introduce you. This is Special Agent Neil Harris."

No one offered to shake hands and Emily knew it wasn't needed. This meeting was supposed to have taken place somewhere else and she wasn't sure if it was good or bad that it had changed. Had her testimony altered what the NSA felt they were compelled to do with a NOC agent who refused to lie down and be eliminated? She knew that they had been secretly hoping that Ryland would dispose of her, for that would limit the damage this would do to the NSA in the eyes of the public, regardless that their actions had just rid this country of a cold-blooded killer.

"Agent Harris, is there anything else you'd like to know about the two years that I was left to my own devices?" Emily asked, squeezing Jax's hand that was on her waist to let him know that she could handle this. "Or are you here to give me a promotion?"

Coughs could be heard around the room, which everyone knew to be covers for the laughs that the men had let escape. Schultz himself appeared to be amused at her offensive take on the situation, but she hadn't done it to make light of the position she was in. She was just nervous as shit that there was a possibility they could throw her ass in jail for going against orders.

"I'm here to sever ties, Ms. Weiss." Special Agent Harris was an older gentleman, likely in his late fifties, with white hair and deep groves in his face. It was obvious that the stress of the job had taken its toll. "I'm sure we can both agree that it would be best for you to go your way while we go ours. After this misfortune, I'm sure you see it in both of our interests to part ways."

"Let me clarify, so that there are no misunderstandings," Emily said, holding her head high. She knew what this man and his agency were capable of and didn't want it to come back to haunt her in later years. "My name will be kept out of the press to protect my privacy. I have obviously been wiped from the system, so no trace of my relationship with NSA will plague me in the future, and any possible charges that could have been brought against me will evaporate. In exchange, I will be given a new identity with a clean slate...one that has never had contact with any federal agency."

"Agreed," Special Agent Harris growled, dismissing her with the turn of his body. "Jessalyn, you'll be delivered her new papers. See that she gets them and her two years back pay, provided she signs the standard NDA and all the requisite addendums."

The door slammed shut, leaving Emily slightly breathless that it was all over. She took advantage of Jax's hold and felt herself sink further into his body. To his credit, he never released her. Two years of hell, of being on her own, of never knowing what was going to be around the next corner, and all the fear and helplessness was gone in a blink of an eye. Emily knew she should feel relief, but her emotions were a little backlogged at the moment.

"You did well, Agent Weiss," Schultz said, holding out a hand. "That is, if we disregard your attempt at going international with a story that would have compromised a lot of agencies. Regardless, I'm sure the hearing will end with Alekseev being sent back to Russia, with the evidence that he'd sold WMDs to the Middle East. You and I both know that some story will be fabricated as to why the Secretary-General has given up his post and he will never truly pay for the murder of Amato Bianchi. Just as the public will never know the service and sacrifice that you have provided your country."

"And what of the NSA? The Security Council cannot be happy that listening devices have been planted throughout these offices. You and I know they replaced me the instant I went off the grid."

"Again, that's not our concern," Schultz said, giving her a half smile. "You have your life back, Emily. Enjoy it."

"And what of Ryland?" Jax asked, directing his question to both Schultz and Crest. She noticed that Crest had taken a phone call the minute they'd entered the room. Had it been in regards to Ryland or had he just been checking into the office? "Yes, Emily saw this through to the end, but Ryland is still out there."

"He has no reason to continue his pursuit of Emily," Schultz said, shrugging his shoulder. "The hearing happened and the outcome is inevitable."

"I disagree," Crest said, coming to stand beside them. "From our run-ins with him, it's obvious he's taken this personally. I've returned your favor tenfold, Schultz. I expect help should we need it."

Schultz nodded slowly, as if letting that demand set with him. Holding out his arm, he shook everyone's hand and then exited through the door that would lead him to the outside world. Emily looked around, waiting for someone to follow so that they too could leave. No one moved, and all looked toward Crest as if waiting for his dismissal.

"They located a remote controlled firing platform that Ryland had somehow managed to situate in an abandoned building. And yes, the area had been cleared by the Secret Service. It happens." Crest held up his phone. "I just spoke with Taryn, though. She's miraculously dug up information on Ryland, which she'll send to each of us. Study it. Memorize it. Use it when needed. It's the only arsenal we have against this man. In the meantime, we'll separate into two groups and drive back to Minneapolis. I don't want to take any public transportation when we're unsure of what he'll do next."

Emily was listening to every word, but the exhaustion must have been getting to her, due to the fact that she felt weightless. Jax must have sensed it, for he kissed the top of her head. She trusted that he would get her somewhere where she could sit and get some sustenance.

"It's been a long day," Jax said, running his hand up and down her back. "Let's circle around the other way and find some dive to hole up in until, say, two o'clock in the morning. It's better to make the trip back home at night."

Crest nodded his agreement and then once again assigned Kevin and Ethan to tag along with them. Connor and Crest would leave now, getting a jump on the drive and scouring the area for anything that seemed out of the ordinary. Emily didn't really care what route or what time everyone decided on; she just knew that it was over. Let Ryland do his best. She'd spent two years trying to prove the guilt of one man and going against three different agencies to make that happen. She could handle whatever came next.

Chapter Twenty-Six

Emily eyes were glued on the sliver of moonlight that had found the slit in the drapes of the hotel room. It wasn't a dive, as Jax had hinted upon when leaving the United Nations, and she was grateful. She'd spent enough time in places like that and she wouldn't mind never seeing one again. For how exhausted she was, sleep just wouldn't come and the events of the day kept replaying in her mind.

"It's midnight," Jax said, his chest rumbling underneath her hand. "We leave in two hours and you haven't slept."

"For you to know that, that means you haven't either," Emily replied softly.

"It's going to be an adjustment for you." Jax kissed her forehead and she briefly closed her eyes, relishing his tenderness. There was something so comforting about that gentle act that it would never get old. "Starting a new life, adjusting to a new name, and living in another city. We'll figure out a way to incorporate your aunt back into your life. No one will be watching her that close, although she'll have to come to you."

She had spoken to Aunt Beatrice the moment they'd gotten into the vehicle. The older woman had still been in Paris and much to Emily's amusement seemed to be enjoying her time with the man that was watching over her. After a much longer conversation than what was originally planned, Jax had finally spoken to Roger Dallen and made arrangements for them to stay in France a while longer. Emily knew then that he was being cautious until they were certain Ryland would no longer be a problem.

"We haven't really discussed my…living arrangements." Emily traced figure eights on his chest, liking how his warmth soaked into her fingertips. He spoke as if it were a forgone conclusion she would join him in Minneapolis, but was that what he really wanted? "We just keep moving forward, not really examining the reasons why."

"Do we need to examine them?" Jax asked, his voice a tad bit cautious. "Emily, we've had a lot of things thrown our way. We need time to digest the fact that both of our lives are going to change. Hell, we need time to come to terms with the fact that we can now live a normal life. But the fact remains, Ryland is still out there and until we can permanently dismiss him as a threat, can we just take things day by day?"

She instantly understood what he was really saying, although to call him out on it would only put further distance between them. He was afraid that she and the baby would be torn from him as his parents had. He'd said as much. Emily knew that fear was valid, but she refused to bend to it. He was clear in his need for honesty from her and by damn he'd get it.

"What I'm going to say is something you need to hear," Emily said softly, sitting up and untangling herself from his arms. The covers slipped from her upper body, revealing her breasts and there was enough moonlight to see the shift of his eyes. She waited patiently until they traveled back up to meet with hers. "I don't want a reply. I don't want to discuss it. I just want it known."

"Emily—"

"Regardless of my being pregnant, what I feel for you is real." Jax shifted into a sitting position against the headboard and reached for her. Emily pulled slightly away, needing to finish what she was saying. "If Ryland were to walk through that door right now and finish what he's been paid to do, I would want to die knowing that there wasn't one thing you didn't know about me. So here it is. My favorite color is pink. I don't have a preferred flower or song…I love them all. My favorite food is Aunt Beatrice's fried chicken. The best movie ever made is the *Wizard of Oz*, the old one. My most desired place to be is kneeling at your feet and wondering what you could possibly do to make the scene better than the one before. My biggest fear changed from not seeing you again to being afraid that I won't get the chance to grow old with you. I love you, Jax Christensen."

With those final words, Emily removed herself from the bed with one last look at Jax's surprised face and lightly padded her feet across the carpet and into the bathroom. Quietly closing the door, she then flipped on the light and squinted when the brightness lit up the small room. Waiting until her pupils adjusted to the harshness, Emily then looked at herself in the mirror. Relief was evident in her own blue eyes and for the first time in her life, there were no more secrets.

Unfortunately, she couldn't say the same for the threat on her life. Until Ryland was eliminated, they were all in danger. Emily placed a hand on her stomach and swore that her greatest fear would not come true.

✧ ✧ ✧ ✧

Jax watched the highway in front of him as the headlights cut through the dark. Emily's words resonated through his head and seemed to be on permanent repeat. As her words haunted him, he glanced over to where she lay sleeping, astounded that she seemed so at peace. Did she really not know the turmoil she'd placed him in?

Before he'd been able to react to everything Emily had said, she'd turned on the shower in the bathroom, leaving him lying in bed and trying to digest her words. She made it sound so simple, yet he knew it wasn't. Weren't they just tempting fate by saying those three words? It was as if they were taunting fate with those types of declarations and he'd be damned if he was ready to face that bitch again.

Reaching for the knob off to the right of the steering wheel, Jax adjusted the heat so that Emily would stay warm. She'd fallen asleep within the first half hour on the road, her body overtaking her obviously busy mind. Thinking of how sincerely she'd declared her love was awe-inspiring and her point of being honest hit home, as well as her fear. It was understandable that she would want to express her feelings.

Jax wasn't saying he didn't feel the same, but was grateful that Emily hadn't pushed him. What he really wanted to do was alleviate her fear that Ryland would come back for her, but he couldn't do that unless he was given proof. Until then he would see to it that she felt safe, regardless that it was obvious she could take care of herself. Emily had training and knew what to do in a crisis, but they all knew that Ryland wouldn't confront her one on one. He'd most likely take the shot from a mile away. That wasn't comforting to know, but he needed to figure out a way to protect her without smothering her. That wouldn't go over well.

Schultz had given them her meager belongings and two years pay at a GS-14 equivalent plus per-diem. The check was from a temp agency based in DC. Her physical possessions all fit into one suitcase. All of it was now in the back of the SUV, along with the backpack she'd been carrying this entire time. He'd open up about his feelings when Emily was finally situated at his place, Ryland a thing of their past, and they'd settled into a new routine. He didn't consider himself a superstitious man, but damn if he was going to tempt fate now.

Chapter Twenty-Seven

One month later, Emily was standing in Jax's bathroom using a warm washcloth to wipe her mouth. She was finally feeling somewhat normal this morning after her bout of morning sickness. It had to be a man who came up with that term, for a woman would have been more upfront. It didn't matter what time of the day it was, if a smell or a taste didn't settle well with J.J., then whatever was in her stomach was coming up. Morning, noon, or night. Jax Jr. was very particular about his wants and desires...similar to his daddy.

"If you aren't a boy, I'll eat—"

Before Emily could finish that sentence, the doorbell rang. She looked towards the bathroom door and then down at her gray sweats and white T-shirt that she'd taken to wearing lately. Shrugging in defeat, she knew that Jax had someone watching the house, which meant they recognized whoever was ringing the door. Emily didn't kid herself that Ryland would be gentleman enough to knock before shooting her. This waiting would kill her first, she was sure.

Relieved that she was feeling better, Emily tossed the cloth in the sink and then walked through the bedroom and down the stairs to the front door. Knowing that she could never be too cautious, she had picked up her piece before heading downstairs. She carefully looked through the peephole that Jax had installed the day after they'd arrived. Lauren Bailey stood on the other side with her auburn hair blowing in the spring wind. Switching the lock on the deadbolt, Emily opened the door with a smile.

"Hi," Emily said in greeting, grateful for the interruption. "Come on in."

"Sweats? Again?" Lauren shook her head, but made up for her words by holding out a red slushy from the gas station on the corner. "You look like you need this."

"You are a lifesaver," Emily crooned, taking the drink with her free hand and immediately sipping the cherry flavored ice. Connor Ortega had done well when he'd chosen Lauren. She was a keeper. "Hmmmm. How can I repay you?"

"By getting dressed." Lauren stepped inside and then closed the door behind her. "You cannot stay cooped up in here day in and day out. You've been given a new identity, Nora Emily Rowland. We might as well use one of her credit cards."

"Jax hasn't handled this morning sickness thing so well," Emily replied with a shrug, grateful that it wasn't really a lie. She was relatively sure that was part of it, but she was also certain it had to do with more. She took her slushy and her gun with her as she headed for the living room. The old style Victorian house had been renovated into a duplex. Jax lived on one side and Connor lived on the other. Emily knew why she still considered it Jax's place and not theirs, but now wasn't the time to dwell on it. She focused on the conversation at hand.

"Add on top of that we haven't located Ryland, he's more comfortable if I stay inside."

"And how's that going for you?" Lauren asked with a small laugh. She followed Emily into the living room and sat down next to her on the couch. Emily placed her weapon on the side table. "I didn't take you for following orders so easily."

"Depends on the order." Emily winked and smiled, but her lips didn't lift too far. Lauren was right and each day seemed to put more distance between her and Jax. She didn't have to wonder if it was her declaration of love that had put it there. She wanted what they had back at the cabin. The only thing that kept her from going insane was her newfound friendship with Lauren. "I do appreciate your friendship, Lauren. I missed out on a lot these past two years and having a friend to share things with is one of them."

"I was getting surrounded by too much testosterone anyway, so the added estrogen is a nice change." Lauren tucked one of her red curls behind her ear and studied Emily with those emerald green eyes of hers. "Have you spoken to him?"

"He's been coming home late." Emily fiddled with the straw, knowing what she just said was an excuse. She just didn't want to admit out loud that she was afraid of rocking what seemed to be an already unstable boat. "You should know that. You're practically living with Connor now."

"Speaking of which, we're thinking of having just one place," Lauren replied, nodding her agreement. "It would be easier and more cost efficient. But that's just my analytical mind at work. I like it here. It's a lot more peaceful than my apartment in the city, but there is this one neighbor I would worry about if I moved out."

"You're in the city almost every day," Emily pointed out, knowing that Lauren had a physical shop in which she sold bejeweled fetish implements. "You could check on your neighbor a few times a week."

"True." Lauren took a sip of her coffee that she'd brought inside with her. "Which is partly why I'm here. Want to come to the shop with me today? We both still have tails on us, courtesy of our men, so there's no reason not to pool together our resources. And it will get you out of the house. If you want, we can even hit one of the salons and check to see if they have some type of hair dye that wouldn't hurt the baby. I know you want to go back to your natural color."

Emily looked back down at what she was wearing. Even on those days when she had been on the run, hiding out from those that wanted to hurt her, she had never stooped to this level of not caring what she looked like. Whether it was the aftermath of what she'd gone through, the pregnancy, or Jax treating her more like a roommate, she didn't know. An idea started to form and suddenly, Emily knew what she needed to do. She just needed Lauren on board for this to be successful.

"Afterwards, will you take me to Jax and Connor's club?"

❖   ❖   ❖   ❖

Jax leaned back in his chair, twirling his skullcap around on a finger. He stared at the computer screen in front of him, trying to decipher the message that Taryn had sent him. It was a bunch of columns with mixed dates and times for what apparently was Ryland's whereabouts during the last ten years. Some didn't appear to be possible, but Taryn was slowly weeding them out and looking for some sort of pattern that might lead them to him.

"Isn't it time to retire that thing?" Kevin said, nodding toward the skullcap and leaning against Jax's cubicle. "The end of April is here and I'm pretty damn sure the weather is too warm for that shit."

"Did you see this?" Jax asked, ignoring Kevin's remark. He nodded towards his computer screen. "If Taryn's right, then Ryland hits New York once a year around Christmas time. How was she able to pinpoint this when he's technically what we'd consider a ghost?"

"Because I'm good," Taryn quipped, her voice carrying over the cubicles. God only knew where she was to have overheard them. By the time they'd made it back from New York, Taryn had taken up the conference room as her office. No one was upset, since there was a table situated right outside the cubicle area they could use to convene around. For how much equipment she'd acquired lately, it was for the better. "I'll show you how good once I decrypt his various aliases, although I'm sure he changes them like a politician's promise."

"Speaking of Ryland, the guys and I are getting a little worried about you," Kevin said, keeping his voice low. Jax tensed, already having heard this speech from Connor not three days prior. "You've been coming in at the crack of dawn and not leaving until well after eight at night. You've been working on the weekends and Elle has been basically running the club on her own."

"I've been checking in with her." Jax tossed his skullcap on the desk and leaned forward, wanting to end this conversation before it continued to the minefield he knew was being laid. "As for Emily, she needs her rest and me being at the house just doesn't help."

"Interesting you would say that," Connor said, brushing past Kevin's large frame and sitting in his seat, letting it roll him around. Jax refused to turn around and face his partner.

He had work to do and didn't want to mollify whatever point they were trying to make. "Emily's not at home."

That had Jax spinning his chair around and leveling his best friend a disbelieving look. Of course Emily was home. He would have gotten a—

Son of a bitch. His cell vibrated against the laminate of the desk. Jax quickly reached for it and scanned the message that stated Emily and Lauren had left his residence and were heading into downtown. What the hell did she think she was doing? He had no doubt this was Emily's idea, for Lauren tended to listen to Connor for the most part. Well, at least when she wasn't being stubborn about something.

"Didn't you tell Lauren that she was to just go to her shop and then home, without any stops in between?" Jax asked, reassuring himself that was the case. "Did you speak with her personally and ask what the hell they think they are doing?"

"I told you three days ago that if you didn't do something to change the way things are between you and Emily, that I would have to stoop to your level," Connor stated matter-of-factly. Jax gritted his teeth, not having time for this petty retribution. "Lauren is having Emily tag along with her for the day. There's nothing to worry about."

"Nothing to worry about?" Jax stared at Connor, trying to comprehend the words coming out of his smart assed mouth. "Is this the same man who drove to the hospital when Lauren was mugged and then spent the night with her, only to have her followed the majority of the last case to ensure her safety?"

"I'm not saying I don't understand where you're coming from," Connor replied, sharing a look with Kevin that Jax didn't even want to contemplate the meaning of. "But I didn't tell her that she was under house arrest either."

"Let's face it, Jax, we don't know if we'll ever apprehend Ryland," Kevin said, crossing his arms. "You've got to at least allow Emily to have a normal routine. The last time I was over at your place, she even mentioned that she would love to teach. Let her go apply for jobs and see where that takes her."

Jax leaned back in his chair, placed an elbow on the arm and ran a hand down his face. They just didn't get it, did they? He rested his head on his index finger and thumb, wishing he were any place but here. He contemplated getting up and heading into Crest's office, for he would rather deal with him than this fucking group.

"Lauren, well, she said that Emily's been feeling...you know, lonely." Connor interlaced his fingers behind his head and leaned back in his chair as if he hadn't just announced that Jax and Emily hadn't been having sex. "For how much you used to play at the club, I don't see why you—"

"For fuck's sake, she's sick almost every hour," Jax snapped, sitting up a little straighter in his chair and ignoring the small ping that called him out as a liar. He hated being a hypocrite. This is what his teammates had reduced him to. "We went to the doctor's office and everything looks good and apparently this amount of sickness is normal, but do you really think she feels up to—I can't believe we're even having this discussion."

Jax spun around and escaped from the document that he'd had up on his computer. He could look at it later. He'd head down to the first floor and grab a bite to eat in the sports bar. By the time he got back, maybe these assholes would have cleared out for whatever assignments Crest had them working on.

"Did Emily say she didn't want to have sex?" Jessie quipped, coming to stand next to Kevin.

"Fuck me," Jax murmured, continuing to power down his computer. "Jessie, go back up front. Doesn't Crest have you working on something mind numbing?"

"Hey, I'm just trying to help here." Jessie's bubbly personality was the polar opposite of the team. Normally, on a good day Jax appreciated the upbeat and fresh attitude that she brought to the table, but today wasn't one of those days. "My sister said throughout the majority of her pregnancy she couldn't get enough sex. When they throw up, that's pretty much it. They go right back to feeling normal. Really, you should talk to her more about it, unless that's not the reason you're not having sex with her."

"I'm not discussing this," Jax snapped, spinning back around and facing all of them. To make his point, he continued, "Connor, that implement that Lauren liked, did you ever—"

"I get it," Connor said with his hands up in the air, indicating his surrender. There was a major different between watching some scenes at the club and discussing one's personal sex life. It demeaned it and it wasn't what they stood for. "I do. But we all know it's not about sex. We're just worried because it seems that now that you finally got what you wanted, you're going to throw it away by being a douchebag."

"Are you fucking kidding me?" Jax asked, his temper ready to boil over. Standing, he let the steam out. "You and I both know where we've been and the shit we've seen. I can handle it with the best of them. When it's my shot that takes someone out, I take responsibility for that and know that eventually I will come face to face with my Maker and have to own up. That I can live with. But every time I hear her over the toilet, it's like my heart is ripping out of my chest. Do you know what it does to my insides to know that it's my fault she's in this position? And that's not to mention this day-to-day routine shit that I don't know how to handle. I have no fucking control and that's the one thing I've depended on my whole life. And just like that, it's ripped from my fingers."

"Um, you know, a little bit of advice here," Jessie said, holding her hand up as if they were in a classroom. Jax stared at her, wondering if she was just damn naïve or just plain stupid to interrupt one of them when they were on a roll. He shared a look with Connor and Kevin, just in case he'd missed something. No wonder Crest tried to stay out of her youthful grasp. He'd likely have a heart attack trying to rein her in. "Emily didn't *get* that way because of you. It took two. As for the day-to-day stuff you're referring to, she just wants you to be there for her. It doesn't take a dominant man to do that, just a decent one. Women are not that complicated."

"Really?" Connor asked, sarcasm dripping from his voice. He stared at her in disbelief.

"Just go with it," Jessie said, giving Connor an irritated look. "We know the facts, but that's not what he needs to know right now."

"It was supposed to be you," Jax said, throwing his hand out to reference Connor. He finally sat back down, feeling deflated. "You and Lauren are supposed to get married, have a couple of kids while I looked on and enjoyed the view from the outside. I was supposed to be the best damn honorary uncle in the Midwest, not a father who doesn't know shit about babies. Instead Emily and I are living together before you had the guts to move Lauren in and now you get to be the fun uncle. That is fucking wrong."

"Kevin. Jessie. Would you give us a moment?" Connor asked, leaning forward in his chair.

Jax felt a twinge of guilt. He knew they were worried about him, but there was nothing they could do that would give him back control of his life. Kevin just nodded, knowing that enough had been said and walked back to his cubicle. Jessie twisted one of her brown curls, as if contemplating leaving them to themselves. Eventually, she blew at her bangs and spun on her heel, heading back to the front of the office. Jax once again ran a hand down his face feeling exhaustion set in. He momentarily wondered what it would feel like when he had less sleep due to getting up for middle of the night feedings. It amazed him how life could change on a dime.

"Jax, do you love her?"

It was such a simple question and one Jax knew the answer to. But didn't Connor know that loving Emily didn't fix the current problems? His feelings only exacerbated them.

"You love Lauren, right?" Jax threw the question back at his friend. He waited for Connor to nod in answer. "I know that Ryland mentioned her name in Paris, but really stop to think what it would be like to have him target her and not know when, how, or where he would try to take her from your life. Then on top of it all, discover that she's pregnant and throwing up morning, noon, and night. And there is nothing you can do about any of it. You can't make it better, you can't make it go away, you only get to stand back and watch it all fucking unfold."

"Would you rather not have the chance?" Connor said, his words meant to put things in perspective, but they were like fucking nails on a chalkboard.

"I get it. I do." Jax leaned his head back against the leather of his chair and stared at the ceiling. "I'll talk with Emily tonight, but you know that I've never been good at that sort of thing."

"What? Like I'm a poster boy for that myself?" Connor asked, obviously taking offense. But then his voice softened, imparting how much he truly loved Lauren. "I get that you feel vulnerable, man. Emily is your Achilles heel and if there is anyone in this world that could get you to beg for mercy, it's her. Be glad that she wants it the other way around. So be the man she needs right now."

"I take it you spoke with Lauren?" Jax asked, bringing his gaze back down and zeroing in on Connor. He felt a little like his old self and the need to go home and be there for Emily. Connor was right and it was time that he stepped up to the plate. Maybe he wouldn't wait for tonight. "Do you know what their plans are for this morning?"

The way Connor just shook his head and shrugged gave Jax the indication that he didn't want to know. But now his curiosity was spiked and he turned in his chair, deciding to call her himself. They had made an agreement that they would always answer each other's calls, specifically due to Ryland still being out there. He pressed the speed dial and listened to the ringing on the other end.

Emily didn't pick up. Fear, angst, and irritation all came together as a ball in his chest and he quickly disconnected as he heard her voicemail initiate. Speed dialing one of the numbers he'd placed in his phone after being given it by Emily's detail, the phone was answered on the first ring.

"Chuck, where is she?" Jax asked, leaning back in his chair and crossing his one arm across his chest. He resisted the urge to tap his foot, just in case Connor was still watching.

"They're in some hair salon." A slight muffling sound came from Chuck's end of the line, indicating that he was outside on the street. He must be facing the wind. Jax wanted to turn and ask Connor what he thought he knew about the girls' afternoon, but didn't want to cave in and give him the satisfaction. "They're both getting their hair and nails done. Lionel went into the alley, covering the back entrance."

"Let me know when she heads home," Jax instructed, hanging up and dropping his cell on the desk.

"I'm heading out," Connor said from behind Jax. "Kevin needs help on that case involving the professional girls on the street corner."

That grabbed Jax's attention and he looked over his shoulder. "Did the police find that girl?"

"Yeah," Connor said, sorrow lacing his tone. They dealt better with government contracts than the cases that hit so close to home. "It's now ruled a homicide."

Jax nodded, unhappy with how this was going to affect Elle. It was actually her that had urged the parents of one of the rape victims to contact CSA. Kevin was just the likely agent to take the case since he worked the streets and had the snitches on speed dial. This just upped the ante and he knew that Kevin wouldn't rest until this killer was brought to justice.

"Let me know if you guys need any help." Jax waved a hand toward his monitor. "I'll just be here trying to make sense of all the data that Taryn's burying me with."

Connor slapped him on the shoulder and then took his leave. He could hear Kevin and Connor talking on their way out and wondered if he should give Elle a call now. Thinking better of it, knowing she was probably just getting up for the day, Jax would wait until this evening. She was a night owl and with her added insomnia, the more sleep she was able to get the better.

Jax spent the afternoon sifting through data and sitting with Taryn as she'd enter the information into some program that was supposed to make any connections should they be there. The only link they had so far was Ryland's time in New York around Christmas, but Jax wasn't comfortable waiting that long to try and nab the son of a bitch. He honestly didn't think Ryland would wait that long to come after Emily anyway.

"Ryland is good," Taryn said, sipping on some tea that she'd gotten addicted to lately. She set her cup back down on a heating tray that she had set up by her various monitors. "I've been thinking it over and I cannot for the life of me figure out why he would attend a public function to get the hit information on Emily. It doesn't make sense. He is so smooth and polished when it comes to these things."

"What if those were his instructions?" Jax asked, playing devil's advocate. Taryn was smart and once she got a whiff of something, it was like a dog in search of his bone. She wouldn't let go until she'd figured it out. He would just try to guide her to finding the bone they needed. "What if in order for him to get that business, that's how he had to get it?"

"He doesn't need business." Taryn picked up one of the many pencils lying around and tapped it against the desk. "Ryland doesn't need anything. There has got to be a reason he went there, risking exposure."

"Someone on the guest list?" Jax asked, throwing it out there. "You say he doesn't have any close connections with anyone, but what if he did in his former life?"

Taryn shoved the pencil behind her ear and Jax was amazed that the action didn't move a strand out of place. Her spikey blonde hair was set with some type of gel and he eyed it warily, wondering if the shit was made of super glue. Her fingers flew over the keyboard as her glasses slid down her nose.

"What are you doing?"

"Going through the guest list." Taryn pointed to one of the screens, which now had three hundred names listed in front of them. "No crumb is going to be left on the ground by the time we are done. If we can't investigate Ryland, then we investigate them."

"Three hundred people?" Jax asked, raising an eyebrow. He thought about Emily and if he hadn't just had a come to Jesus meeting with Connor, then he would have offered to pull an all-nighter. As it was, he was anxious to get home to her…if she ever showed up. He glanced at his watch. "All right. Print the list off and I'll start looking into them tomorrow."

"I'll do it," Taryn replied, shaking her head. She hit the print button and rolled her chair to the side, waiting for the paper to slide out of the printer. "Go home to Emily."

"What?" Jax shot her a look. "Did everyone hear our conversation?"

"You have to ask?"

Jax laughed, knowing that private conversations didn't take place in this office. He stood up, watching Taryn as she started to dive into the potentially vital information. They were assuming much…that Ryland had any sort of life before becoming a contractor, but it was better than nothing. He did look at Taryn a little quizzically, not liking how much time she'd been putting in at the office. He'd been working twelve hours a day but she'd been putting in more. It was like she'd developed a fascination with Ryland.

"Split the list," Jax instructed, walking to the door. Her office, which had once been the conference room, was straight across from Crest's. His desk sat empty, but Jax made a mental note to speak with him tomorrow to ask if he'd heard from Schultz lately. Maybe that was an avenue they could tap should the well dry up here. "I'll see you tomorrow. Don't stay late."

Jax looked over his shoulder one last time to catch Taryn's dismissive wave, already caught up in her research. Again he got a strange feeling that didn't settle well over him. He'd start checking in with her more often, making sure she was leaving at a decent time in the evenings. Walking towards his cubicle, he felt his cell phone vibrate in the front of his jeans. Pulling it out of his pocket, he saw that it was Chuck.

"Hey, everything all right?" Jax looked down at his watch, seeing that it read four in the afternoon. "The women done with their spa day?"

"Um, about that," Chuck said hesitantly, causing Jax to be instantly on alert. "They're entering your club…now."

Jax had to have heard wrong. "I'm sorry. I thought you said they were going into Masters."

"That is what I said."

Jax stood there, staring at his monitor as if he could visualize Emily and Lauren outside of the club. It would be locked up tight. Elle didn't open the doors until eight o'clock at night, although sometimes six o'clock depending if they were having a social hour for the public. There shouldn't be anything to worry about, although he did have to wonder why Lauren would have even have taken Emily there to begin with.

"The place isn't open," Jax said with reassurance, dropping back into his chair. He might as well finish up some loose ends until he knew that Emily was home. "When they head back to our place, let me know."

"I said they were walking in, not standing outside of it," Chuck said, very specifically. "Your pretty manager lady let them in already."

Jax shot out of the chair, grabbing his keys and skullcap. Son of a bitch. What the hell did they think they were doing? Emily was pregnant, for God's sake. If she'd wanted a tour, why didn't she just fucking ask for it? He winced, reality hitting him that she probably had and he'd swept her request under a rug.

"I'll be there in ten minutes," Jax said, walking through the expansive area and into the foyer of their offices. "Keep them there until I arrive."

Chapter Twenty-Eight

"It's nice to meet you," Emily said, smiling at Elle. She'd heard so much about this woman from Jax, Connor, and Lauren that Emily felt as if she already knew her. What she hadn't expected was for Elle to be so svelte and tall. "A little birdie told me this place wouldn't run without you."

A light laugh escaped Elle and the smile radiated her face as she shared a look with Lauren. "I think that's an exaggeration, but I appreciate the sentiment. It's nice to meet you as well. When Lauren called, I was surprised you wanted to stop by. Nothing happens until eight at night."

Emily looked around the entry hall, although her eyes had to adjust to the dimness of the room. The lighting was more golden, casting sensual shadows among the walls. A hostess stand was situated before a door, its cherry wood color seeming alive with the swirls of reds and browns. The area gave off such an erotic vibe she couldn't wait to actually see the inside.

"I just wanted to see what it looked like," Emily said, her smile falling just a bit. She didn't want to reveal too much of what she and Jax were going through right now. Looking at Lauren and the box that she held in her hands, Emily grabbed onto the other excuse as well. "Plus, Lauren had to drop off some new implements that Connor had ordered for the club."

Elle nodded her head in acceptance. "Yes, he mentioned something about that. Let me give you the tour while Lauren goes and hangs up what she brought."

With that said, Elle leaned over the hostess stand and must have pressed a button, for a slight buzzing noise could be heard along with the clicking of a latch being released. Elle walked to the door and swung it open, revealing an entirely different world to Emily. She felt like she was stepping into Wonderland.

The walls were made of dark English walnut. A specific fragrance hung in their air and it took a moment for Emily to figure out it was an orange scent mixed with leather. Not wanting to miss a thing, she slowly followed behind Elle. A bar lined up the left side of the area, with mirrors and lighting set up behind the counter. Black leather stools were situated in front and the brass of their footstools glinted in the spotlights that were glowing down from the ceiling. It had somewhat of a nightclub feel to it, although Emily had a feeling it wouldn't seem like that during actual play.

Her eyes followed along the path of what seemed to be a line of seating areas, separated with palms and ferns. The plants acted as a screening and created an aura of privacy. Emily kept perusing the room and finally halted when her eyes landed on the right side of the room. Red velvet ropes attached to brass poles cordoned off the play areas. The gold stands gave off an antique appearance and somehow softened what she imagined actually took place behind them.

"I can see from your expression that this is not what you thought the club would look like," Elle said, amusement lacing her tone. "If you think it's interesting now, wait until you see the action at night. Your eyes will be glued to the stations."

Emily gave her a smile, not wanting to really reply and not needing to, since she wasn't asked a question. Searching for Lauren, Emily saw that she had walked straight to the far wall and placed down the box. The hooks held various implements which had obviously been adorned with gems by Lauren. The array of items was fascinating, but Emily wanted to peruse the stations first. As if sensing Emily didn't want to get caught in too much of a personal conversation with Elle, Lauren walked back to them.

"Elle, can I have your help in arranging the new items?" Lauren asked, stopping in front of them. "I also want to wipe them down one more time. Do you have extra cleaning solution or should I use what's over there?"

"I'll grab another bottle from the back," Elle replied, starting to walk towards a small room that was situated by the bar. "Do either of you want something to drink?"

They declined and both watched Elle walk across the room. "Thank you," Emily said. "She doesn't know who I really am and I really didn't want to explain that Jax and I haven't played in a club together. All she knows is that I'm Jax's girlfriend. It might instigate her to ask more questions had I gone into detail and you know I can't tell her."

"I understand," Lauren replied, placing a hand on Emily's shoulder and giving her a squeeze. "Explore. Honestly, I'd be surprised if Jax didn't arrive within a half hour. You know that Chuck called him."

"Good old Chuck." Emily shook her head, knowing the guy was just doing his job, but having him hang outside the salon doors was not a convenient thing for her. "On the bright side, I was able to get my hair dyed back to my natural color. Who knew that hair dyes weren't dangerous to J.J."

"You crack me up. Even Connor's taken to calling your baby J.J." Lauren looked up, causing Emily to do the same. Elle was walking back toward them with a spritz bottle and a blue rag. She lowered her voice. "I personally think it's a girl. Now go see what you can before Jax comes and drags you away. By the way, your hair looks fantastic! Seeing you like this will certainly give Jax the kick in the ass he needs."

Emily waited until the two women were back over to the far wall and pulling things out of the box. Turning toward the play stations, her eyes zeroed in on the spanking bench. She'd only ever seen one on the Internet and found the piece of BDSM furniture fascinating. She and Jax had only ever played privately; those first seven days they were together was more of an introduction into a lifestyle he loved. Since they'd been home, Jax hadn't mentioned the club in relation to them and she hadn't pushed. After seeing this and recalling what he said outside of the United Nations' buildings, maybe it was time to do so.

Closing the distance, Emily couldn't prevent herself from reaching out and touching the black leather that encased the bench. It tilted slightly downward, with four shelves that had straps, which she knew to be for the arms and legs. A shiver of excitement ran through her at the thought of Jax placing her on such a device, not allowing her to move and being at his mercy. So many things had changed since their time at the cabin in Lake Michigan and she wanted what they had back.

The hanging X in the corner garnered Emily's attention and she walked over to it, following the chains with her eyes as they went up and up, finding that they were attached to hooks in the ceiling. It looked like a St. Andrew's cross, only horizontal. This section was larger than some of the others, giving a wide berth in which the Dom could play. From what she gathered, the submissive would be lying on either side, wrists and ankles strapped to each end, keeping them spread eagle. Emily had never given Jax the slightest hint that she wouldn't want to play at a club and felt irritation start to flow through her at his obvious assumption.

The banging of the door had her drawing her weapon and facing the door within seconds. Jax stood there, the brown of his hazel eyes seemingly flashing even at this distance. Elle's gasp was audible and Emily winced, wondering how she was going to explain why she was carrying a weapon, let alone her actions. Shit.

"Elle," Jax called out, his voice carrying across the room. He never removed his gaze from Emily and she just knew that something was different now. It seemed as if the old Jax was back and she would freely admit that her body responded in kind. "Could I speak with you a minute?"

"Of course."

Elle gracefully walked across the room, warily looking at Emily now. The last thing she had wanted was to alarm Elle. Emily quietly replaced her handgun in her holster, sensing Lauren coming her way. He had told Emily some of Elle's background and what the woman had gone through was something Emily wouldn't wish on her worst enemy. When the tall raven haired woman finally reached Jax, they spoke in hushed tones.

"Don't worry," Lauren said, finally standing beside her. "Jax will come up with a good cover story."

"It's hard," Emily said, watching Elle as she listened intently to what Jax was saying. "Remembering a past that doesn't belong to me."

"At least you are still Emily. That's got to count for something, right?"

Emily nodded, knowing she had a lot to be grateful for. "Why don't you head on home? I'm sure Connor is waiting for you and I've had you running around all day."

"I kidnapped you, remember?" Lauren bumped shoulders with her and got the laugh she'd obviously been hoping for. "Besides, I had fun. Be safe."

"You, too."

Emily watched her friend cross the room and say goodbye to Jax and Elle. Emily would really like it if she and Elle could be friends as well, but would wait to hear what Jax said to her before attempting another conversation. They all needed to be on the same page.

Another few minutes of conversation and Elle didn't look too happy. Emily tensed, thinking it had to do with whatever story Jax came up with in regards to her pulling her weapon. Her mind changed when Kevin walked in behind them. Elle's body language immediately altered. Emily debated on whether she should cross the room and join in on the conversation, when Jax started speaking with both of them. Within a minute, both Kevin and Elle were walking back out the door, although Elle didn't look too pleased with the situation. Emily wasn't so sure what she felt at the precise moment. Jax turned around, faced her, and then flashed that smile that she'd come to love but hadn't seen in weeks. This was her Jax and for the first time since they'd arrived in Minneapolis, Emily felt like she'd just been welcomed home.

❖ ❖ ❖ ❖

Jax waited until Kevin and Elle had left the main room of the club before facing the most beautiful woman he'd ever set eyes on. Emily stood there, her newly chestnut colored hair shimmering underneath the spotlight above her, with a similar twinkle in her blue eyes. Her pink lips were parted with a natural sheen on the plush flesh and her cheekbones were flush with color. There was a radiance about her that called to every dominant gene inside of him and he wanted nothing more than to personally give her a tour of this place that he loved.

"Before I give you the personal tour, would you like to tell me why the hell you didn't answer your phone like promised?"

"Lauren took me out for the day. We had fun, and for the first time I feel somewhat normal." Emily gave a little toss of her hair and the long natural waves fell behind her back. "I must have been sitting under the dryer because I didn't hear your call. I never even thought to check it when we decided to walk over here. I'm sorry."

Jax fisted his hands to prevent him from lecturing her and ruining what stood to be a promising evening. Walking the city streets? Did she want to go around with a target taped to her back? With the uncertainty of Ryland's actions, they couldn't be too careful. On the other hand, he understood Connor's sentiment that they still needed to live their lives. It was such a fucking catch twenty-two.

"No morning sickness today?" Jax asked, focusing on her statement of feeling back to normal. "Do you think it's past?"

"I wouldn't say that," Emily replied with a half smile. She still stood next to some of the play stations, so he started to walk slowly toward her. "This morning wasn't so good, but I've been doing okay this afternoon. You know that the doctor said it would probably last throughout the first trimester."

"I can keep hoping it doesn't," Jax said, returning her smile. He stopped when he was a foot away. Staring at her beauty made it hard for him to formulate the words, but he needed to wipe the slate clean. "If it feels like I haven't been here for you, I apologize."

Emily's blue eyes widened in surprise and if he'd felt like a heel before, he felt like one now. Jax never meant to give her the impression that he wasn't man enough to face his mistakes. He was dominant by nature, but that didn't mean he didn't own up to his responsibilities.

"I could give you reasons, like seeing you sick day in and day out literally kills me on the inside." Jax was grateful she remained silent while he got this off of his chest. He wanted her aware of how every little thing she felt affected him. "I'm helpless. There is nothing I can do to make it better and being the man I am, I want to be able to do that. I want to be your savior."

"I just need you with me," Emily whispered, taking a step closer to him. "I want you by my side. I don't want to feel like we're roommates."

"Is that how I made you feel?" Jax felt his chest tighten, hoping that he could fix the damage he'd caused. He closed the distance between them and captured her sweet face in the palms of his hands. "God, Emily, I never intended for you to feel like that. I've been going into work early and staying late, doing everything in my power to track down Ryland. It's all a vicious cycle. I can't locate him, we don't know if he's moved on, I can't help you when you're sick, and I feel completely helpless all around. This is fucking with my brain and I feel like I'm out of options."

Jax slid his right hand through her hair, feeling the silkiness surround his fingers. It made him think that's what her soul would feel like should it wrap around his. It was his fault that their connection was disheveled and he would be the one to mend it.

"I'm your option, Jax," Emily murmured, leaning up on her tiptoes and brushing her lips against his. "Me. Be with me, and stop treating me with kid gloves. Make love to me like you did at the cabin. I miss our scenes. Being pregnant doesn't hinder my submissive side. I can't tell you what it does to me not to be able to kneel in front of you, have your stroke my hair, and have your presence make me feel secure."

Jax leaned his forehead against hers, closing his eyes for just a moment and savoring the warmth she was emitting. Not from her body, but the love she was radiating from within. It enveloped him and he didn't want their physical link severed quite yet.

"Emily, as much as I want your submissiveness, you're pregnant." Jax sealed her lips with a quick kiss, not wanting her to interrupt him. "I don't feel comfortable with impact play and I'm relatively sure that you're not ready to play in public."

"You mentioned that you had started to lean towards more edge play to feel more alive," Emily said, searching his eyes. "Will you still enjoy the scenes if they're light? This is about the two of us."

"Ah, my sweet little spy." Jax needed to make sure she understood where his heart was in this matter. "You are all I need. Scene or no scene, being with you and making you happy have come to mean more to me than you'll ever know. It's your response that gives me happiness, Emily, not the scene itself. When you hand your pleasure over to me, that gives me my pleasure."

Jax brought both hands down to grasp her shoulders, maintaining contact. They had always played privately and it was a big step to take those scenes out of the privacy of their bedroom and into the public eye. There was a different level of sensuality, more like being vulnerable to perfect strangers that he didn't feel she was ready to experience. But he did know what he could do to make certain their mental and physical beings received what they needed.

"We'll ease back into this and I know just how to do that with both of us feeling comfortable that our baby is safe and sound," Jax said, stepping away and really taking his time to look at her. He needed to assure himself that she was up for a light non-impact scene. "How do you truly feel? Any nausea?"

"No," Emily replied, shaking her head. He loved the way her brunette strands bounced around her shoulders and her blue eyes sparkled. This was the Emily he met and fell for. "I feel great. What do you have in mind?"

Jax smiled at the enthusiasm in her voice and then laughed when she threw up her hands at his silence. Some scenes were better staged and set into motion without the sub knowing and now was one of those times. He'd neglected this part of himself and her for way too long and he looked forward to obtaining that connection again.

"Undress."

"What?" Emily looked toward the door where Kevin and Elle had exited. "But what about—"

"Did I not just promise a private scene?" Jax asked, raising his eyebrow in question. "And in case you missed the cue, the scene is now in progress."

He could see her restraint in not rolling her eyes, but to her credit she trusted him and reached for the hem of her long sleeved cotton shirt. Pulling it over her head, she let it drop to the ground. She'd been wearing a pink lace bra with what looked like glitter around the edges. Jax had not seen it before, but he did appreciate the way the material cupped her breasts. Lowering his gaze, he liked how the waist of her jeans dipped low enough to expose her belly button. She wasn't showing yet, but there was something inside of him that wanted her to be. He had no doubt she would be glorious with the swell of her stomach.

"Bra."

"Yes, Sir," Emily replied, her tone slightly lower and breathless. Hearing the underlying carnal tenor had his cock hardening.

She reached behind her, unsnapping the pink material. The cups fell off of her breasts, revealing slightly swollen flesh. They'd gotten larger since she'd become pregnant and he couldn't wait to see if the sensitivity was heightened as well. A sense of urgency to have her bound and at his mercy surged through his bloodstream.

"Finish undressing and go lay down on the bondage table," Jax instructed, walking away while he still could.

Crossing to the door, he made sure it was locked. The other door at the other end of the club locked automatically from the inside, so he didn't have to worry about anyone entering from the parking garage. They only released the mechanism during club hours. Jax went about collecting the items he needed, having no doubt that Emily was following his instructions.

Within five minutes Jax was walking over to the station which housed the bondage table. He saw her clothes lying in a heap, although her weapon had been set on the spanking bench. His steps faltered at seeing Emily lying on top of the padded black leather with her eyes glued to his movements. She was radiantly beautiful and having her here in his club, at his mercy, took his breath away.

"Your body responded so well to sensation play that I thought we would continue that route," Jax explained, walking around to the backside of the table. "As before, you'll be blindfolded. We'll partake in wax play today, slowly getting your mindset back to where you feel as if you are floating in my hands and in my care."

"I'd like that, Sir," Emily replied, her blue eyes softening until he felt as if he were looking down into the depths of a clear sea.

"Know that I will not allow you to be burned or harmed in any way." Anytime a Dom played with wax or fire, it was important to know the safety behind the scene. As a precaution, the club had a fire extinguisher at several locations around the club, specifically at the bondage table. "I'll be using paraffin wax, which burns at a lower temperature. I will test it on myself before you and you should know that your safewords remain the same. I know some Doms prefer to use oils, but I don't. If you're a good girl and don't come until I tell you to, I'll let you stay for the first hour of public play, watching from the bar so that you can see what really takes place after the lights go down."

The slow smile that spread across her face told him he'd made her happy. She wouldn't be that way for long, considering that he might not let her come at all while they were at the club. Jax wanted her aroused while she witnessed other submissives bound within their stations, but that didn't mean he wouldn't change his mind. Sometimes too much planning ruined a scene. He would see how she reacted and take his cues from her body language.

"Are you ready?"

Chapter Twenty-Nine

"Yes, Sir."

Emily looked at the items in Jax's hands and felt her body instantly respond. A black leather blindfold was kept, while the other things were placed on a small stand beside him. She concentrated on it, not wanting to think about the lighter and candles. There also seemed to be a wet cloth of some sort, but she didn't want to crowd her mind with anything other than what he was about to do.

"Close your eyes," Jax ordered in a stern tone that sent shivers over her skin. Her flesh seemed to be in total awareness of what was coming and was just preparing itself. Her eyelashes fluttered and eventually, she caved in to her basic instinct to hand over control to this man. He slipped the blindfold over her eyes and made sure it sat comfortably across the bridge of her nose. "Keep your arms down by your side, leaving maybe an inch from your body. Your legs are to be spread wide...and I mean wide. I want you to experience what it is to have wax dripped onto your pussy."

As if he were already doing so, Emily's clit throbbed in response. It didn't help that as she spread her legs as he'd ordered, the air brushed across the sensitive tissue of her inner thigh. Her cream must have coated the area, for the coolness was evident.

"Wider."

"Hmmmm," Emily hummed, loving the touch of his rough fingers as they firmly fastened her ankles inside fur lined cuffs. He then did the same to her wrists. What surprised her was when he secured a strap across her abdomen. "Sir?"

"I don't want you to accidentally pull up if I have the flame close to you." Jax's voice sounded like honey and rich vibrations rumbling across her skin gave an indication of what was to come. "I'll usually have it high enough that is shouldn't be a problem, but there will be times when I think you can handle a hotter sensation."

Emily nodded, wanting it now. Just this pre-preparation had her wanting more and she'd yet to even experience the hot wax. Her nipples felt pinched, the light hair on her arms stood at attention, her clit was swollen, and her pussy felt empty. As if he were reading her mind, she suddenly felt a different vibration that wasn't from the tone of his voice.

"Sir," Emily said, although not sure why. Jax was running something hard through her folds and whatever the toy was, it was pulsating. As he slowly started to insert it into her entrance, her sheath gradually stretched to accommodate what must be a large vibrator. It felt wickedly good and she wanted to lift herself up to receive more, but the strap held her in place. "I need more."

Immediately, the vibrator was gone, leaving her body only remnants of the pulses through the slight spasms her pussy was still experiencing. Emily realized her mistake and bit her lip, not knowing if he would put it back or not. A rush of heat stole through her and she literally felt a drop of cream leak out of her folds. Jax knew what she needed and she would gladly accept what he gave her.

"I want you to feel the different sensations of what I have planned, but you don't get to tell me when and how to do them." Emily hissed when she dragged in air through her teeth upon his fingers closing around her nipple. The already hardened pebble felt like it was being shocked with how he was rubbing it between his calluses. It felt so good, yet the sharp pain she experienced when he pulled shot through her belly and to her aching pussy. "I remember you liking nipple clamps. Do these feel good?"

Before his words registered, Emily felt the sting of the pressure from the pads of the clamp as they closed over the receptive ball of nerves. Her pregnancy had definitely had a hand in the different level of sensitivity and she didn't know whether to laugh or cry it was so overwhelming.

"I asked a question."

Emily struggled to remember, but it slammed into her when he tugged on the clamp. "Yes, Sir, I like the feel of nipple clamps."

"Now, where were we?"

She felt something slide through her folds once more and this time when he pushed it inside of her, Emily breathed through the overpowering length and width of the toy. He must have the vibration set on low, for slow pulses were being sent into the walls of her pussy and keeping her right on the edge. Not too much, but not enough. It was maddening, just as it was exasperating that only one nipple had a clamp. What about the other? It was the one that she felt the most, which was frustrating to say the least.

"Perfect," Jax murmured. She felt him play with her hair and understood that he was moving it out of the way. "Just perfect."

He finally pulled away and while she could hear him moving about, her focus was on her body. Ever so slightly, Emily could feel her muscles relaxing and accepting the intruder in her pussy and the vise that was around her right nipple. The more she accepted the sensations, the more she could feel herself start to float.

"A feather. Nothing more, nothing less."

That was all Jax said as she felt the light caress of the tip fall against her cheek. Down and over her chin, Jax brought it up the other side, around the top of her eyebrow, down the bridge of her nose and over her parted lips. There wasn't a place on her face that he missed before starting a slow path to her neck. It was there that he brought it up and down, over and over, until every square inch above her shoulders was caressed in someway.

"Feel the difference and let it overwhelm your senses."

He had pulled away for a moment and within seconds; she felt something soft against her shoulder. It was some sort of pelt, yet it felt quite large. It took a moment to register that Jax was using some sort of mitt with fur. Down her arm and then across her abdomen, the velvety fleece was then brought up her other arm. By the time he brought it around each breast, her breathing had become shallow. He ignored her nipples, leaving them wanting more. By not touching the hardened peaks, she was all the more aware of them.

"Shall we try something different?"

Emily inhaled, waiting for the wax to strike her skin, not knowing where or when. It was then she realized she hadn't heard a match light or a lighter being flicked. Jax didn't seem ready for that and her thoughts were confirmed when she felt something prickly being rolled down her leg. The small pierces weren't painful and if anything, the sensation was almost too lenient. As he brought it back up on the inside of her thigh, Emily instantly tried to move her leg when it tickled an underlying nerve. Instead of stopping near her pussy, he ran it over the inside of that sensitive flesh, up and over her hip. She bit her lip once more, knowing where he was going and wanting it more than her next breath. Even with anticipating the tiny pricks, she couldn't contain her cry when the device ran over her nipple.

"Is something feeling neglected?"

This was a question Emily knew he wanted her to answer, so after hissing in some oxygen, she formulated the correct response. "Yes, Sir."

"Very well," Jax replied, although his voice still seemed far away. "Your clit seem rather swollen, so I think I'll open you wider so that you get the full on impression of how much a little stinging pain can impart."

He parted her folds and even went so far as to pull up, exposing her engorged clit. As if answering in kind, Emily felt cream leak out of her pussy. Her face flushed as she knew he couldn't have missed it. Expecting Jax to roll the wheel back down her stomach, she cried out when he stroked it directly down her clit. How it was even possible that she could want an orgasm so fast when they hadn't been at this for too long was beyond her comprehension. She had a feeling that Jax could make her come from just staring at her.

"Sir, Sir, Sir," Emily panted, moving her head back and forth to prevent herself from begging.

Jax's hands pulled away and Emily felt as if she were now floating on air. She was sure there hadn't been a spot on her body that he hadn't touched, yet it felt as if he really hadn't caressed, stroked, or rubbed her at all. She could hear him moving about, but amazingly the time he spent getting things ready, the more her body seemed to prepare for it.

"Emily, I've tested the wax on my arm," Jax murmured, coming closer to her. "I want this to make you feel good…not hurt you in any way. If you feel the intensity of the temperature is too much, I want you to be truthful, do you understand?"

"Yes, Sir," Emily replied and then held her breath.

She didn't know where the wax would land and was a little hesitant to experience it. It felt as if some great unknown was about to happen and on one hand, it could turn out to be the most exhilarating occurrence or on the other, it would douse the flames that he'd lit within her.

A splash of hot liquid fell on her shin and Emily jerked, not expecting it to happen on such a non-erogenous area. It didn't burn and within seconds cooled almost immediately. It hardened, tightening her skin and by the next line he spilled on her, it felt as if her skin was being massaged.

Jax remained silent as he continued to work on her leg, and it wasn't until she felt her nipple clamp being pulled that she comprehended her body was now on a different plane. This plateau was diverse, but no less exciting. She then experienced a dash on the other leg and as she relaxed every muscle, now knowing what to expect, he changed it up.

Hotter wax fell on her left arm, which had her pulling at her restraint. She hissed, but the warmth soaked into her bicep and it had her anticipating another. Why did the rest of her body feel so cool? It was her middle core that needed attention and apparently, as she felt a long line over her other arm, she wasn't going to get it. Maybe she needed to ask.

"Sir, would you please—"

Searing wax doused her nipple and had Emily screaming his name. Her back immediately tried to arch, but the strap across her lower abdomen kept her in place. As she evened out her breathing, she grasped that the temperature of the wax was no stronger than what he'd used on her arm. The clamp on her other nipple was tugged, sending different signals of sensations running to her brain. Instead of gathering there, they all balled up in her clit and she felt ready to explode. Emily had no doubt if that wax touched her clit, she would fall off of that precipice he had her clinging to.

"Now imagine," Jax murmured, as a line was dribbled right underneath her breasts, "that this room is full of strangers and watching as I decorate your body with wax."

It was then that Emily felt a hesitation. Would she want that? Would she want people to see her in this state? She wasn't sure and that made her even more grateful that Jax had nixed the idea early on. She tended to jump into things with both feet. It was a nice change to know that he would always be there, holding her hand and making sure she didn't drown.

"You. Only you, Sir," Emily whispered, managing to formulate the words.

As he had spoken and she had answered, Jax hadn't stopped covering her with what felt like trails of fire. It felt as if he was everywhere and her sensitized flesh responded in kind. There wasn't an inch of her that hadn't been touched in some way and it wasn't just the outside of her body. Her heart and soul felt the flames as well, sparks and flares igniting a love that had never died.

"There will come a time that I will share this beauty," Jax said, the richness of his voice an added sensation, "but as of right now, this view is only for me."

Suddenly, the heated lines of wax stopped. The hardening of the smooth liquid had finally settled over her and for the first time, Emily was able to take in a deep breath. She listened, waiting for him to remove the blindfold and wanting eagerly to see these designs that he spoke of.

"Hmmm, it seems as if I have forgotten something."

Not having expected such a blaze to light up her clit, Emily screamed his name when a scorching silky fire smothered her clit. Jax added more and she felt it dribble down the inside of her thighs. It felt as if he held the candle directly above her pussy and let the wax just drip, drip, drip to surround the base of the vibrator. The most unusual, yet arousing trails traveled down to her anus, hardening on the way. Her pussy clenched against the large phallus, the slight pulses not enough.

"Very nice." Jax, once again, pulled away although there was something in his tone that made it appear softer. It didn't stop Emily from remaining slightly tense, not knowing if he'd changed his mind or would follow through and allow her to see what he created. "I want you to stay that way for just a few minutes while I take care of some things."

Why was lying here causing her to be more aroused? Had Jax done this on purpose, to make her more aware of how the hardened wax tugged on her skin? It somehow felt as if her pussy and anus were initiated with a homemade chastity belt. Unless the wax was removed, nothing else was entering her. That thought made her want him even more.

"Deep breath." Emily automatically did as he asked, but mentally wondered why. It was only when the sharp, heated jolt of pain flowed through her right breast, that she comprehended Jax had removed the clamp. When his mouth covered the oversensitive nub, she moaned in pleasure. His tongue lathed the sting away, but all he did was make her want him more. "Good girl."

Jax pulled away once more and with her blindfold still in place, she strained to hear what he was doing. It was useless as the minute he touched the vibrator and set it to a higher setting all she heard was her shallow breathing and racing heartbeat. There was no slow build up, as that's what he'd been doing to her body all along. In a matter of seconds, the strong vibrations traveled through her clit in such rapid succession that the intensity of her orgasm ripped through her body.

Emily was grateful for the restraints that bound her to the table, as her body arched into the contractions that seemed to saturate her and cause each muscle to tighten in rapture. The hardened wax around her anus cracked, as the contractions were so strong. She had no idea how long the orgasm lasted and it wasn't until he removed the vibrator did she start the slow descent back to reality.

"That was a wonderful sight. The way you tried to arch into your orgasm, with your pretty pink lips parted in a silent cry, and your matching nails being drawn into your palms was breathtaking. You are truly magnificent."

Emily had no energy to reply as her muscles loosened one by one. She was slack by the time he reached for the restraints. Her body temperature was cooling at a fast rate and she felt a shiver go through her. What she wanted more than anything was for him to hold her.

"I'm releasing your wrists and ankles. Once you feel as if you can stand, I want you to remove yourself from the table. Do not take off your blindfold. There is one thing left to do before we retire to the couch."

"Yes, Sir," Emily murmured, all the while wondering why he'd given her those instructions. Why couldn't they just go to the couch now? Somewhere in the back of her mind, a thought drifted through that he'd wanted her to see what he'd designed. The wrist and ankle cuffs were detached and true to his word, he gave her time to recover and sit up. Doing so, she felt dizziness swarm through her, making her feel as if the table wasn't stabilized by legs. Giving herself a few moments, she took a deep breath and nodded her head. "I'm ready, Sir."

As Jax helped her off of the table, she felt the wax crack in certain areas all of her body. Had there been any inch of her skin that he hadn't covered? Emily was finally standing and it was when he pulled her forward that she felt the wax pull against her pussy and anus. She was honestly surprised there was any wax left back there, considering she felt the fracture of the hardened liquid.

"Keep your eyes closed as I remove your blindfold."

It wasn't an option, not unless she wanted to receive an orgasm denial punishment. That wasn't impact play and she had no doubt that Jax would do it should she not follow orders. Emily had every intention of coming again tonight…it was just a matter of when. And damn, she wished that he would hurry and allow her to do so now. The blindfold fell away from her face.

"Open your eyes," Jax said softly, his warm breath brushing against her ear. For just a moment, she savored the closeness of his body as his heat soaked into the back of her. She then let her lashes flutter open, adjusting to the dim lighting of the room. A mirror stood before her and what she saw would forever remain etched into her memory. "If I were able to tattoo every line of that into your body so that you never doubt me, I would."

Written in red on every inch of her skin was *I Love You*, with an intimate white heart over her pussy. Some of the words were cursive, some were print, some were large, and some were small. But each one of them stood out against her porcelain skin. The words felt like they were heating against her flesh as her eyes caressed each and every one. When Emily told him that she loved him and that she hadn't expected the words in return, she'd been telling him the truth. His actions throughout her ordeal had been enough, but this...this was of his own free will and the meaning was not lost on her.

"You *are* my family, Emily." Jax's voice broke on her name, bringing tears to her eyes. Here she stood, naked and vulnerable, but that wasn't how she felt inside. Her heart was cushioned and secure within his love and she noticed that his eyes did not leave hers. Her gaze latched onto his and the brown flecks in his hazel eyes seemed to melt into warm brown wax that coated her soul. "*We* are a family. I love you, Emily Christensen."

Emily turned in his arms and stared up at him with what she knew had to be surprise. Did she just hear him right? A bubbling laugh started to erupt from her chest. She really was going to have to talk to him about his timing.

"You've had enough name changes that I think a permanent one is in order," Jax softly said, searching her eyes as if he couldn't already see her answer. She could only imagine how she looked right this minute. "Will you marry me, Emily? We'll create our own family, our own traditions with a love that is obviously too strong to die. We'll nourish it every damn day of our lives. Will you do that with me?"

"Yes," Emily whispered in reply, "I will marry you. I'd like to be Emily Christensen for the rest of my life, but will you promise me one thing?"

"Anything within my means." Jax's arms were around her waist and holding her up. Her strength seemed to have evaporated, but she was determined to relish in this moment. He brought her closer into his body. "What do you need me to promise, little spy?"

"I want your promise that you'll do this exact scene on our wedding night and on every anniversary there after." Emily brought one hand up and traced his lips, wanting to hear him say again that he loved her. "Promise me and then say I love you again."

"I will promise, but the scene will be done my way. One proposal and you think you can top from the bottom?"

Emily laughed and laced her hands around his neck. "Nothing wrong with seeing how far I can push, is there?"

"Not at all." Jax raised his eyebrow and slowly smiled. Her heart lurched and she had no doubt that when they were eighty, that brilliant smile of his would still excite her. She had a feeling that her words would get her in trouble, but wasn't it her job to keep him on his toes? "It's best for you to know that there will be a chart for every infraction during your pregnancy—"

"Let's be clear," Emily said, interrupting to make sure they were on the same page. When his smile became infectious, she had no doubt he knew where she was going with this. "Infractions in the bedroom or within a scene."

"…that will result in your first scene on the spanking bench for when you are cleared to resume to such activities," Jax finished saying in that stern voice that set the butterflies free within her stomach. "Whether you can sit down afterward is up to you, but it does give you something to look forward to, now doesn't it?"

Emily's face flushed, although she wasn't sure why. Admitting she craved such a scene was very exhilarating in its exposure and she had a feeling that her next eight months of pregnancy was going to be very long. To stop his chuckling, she in turn raised her eyebrow and waited for her second request.

"I love you, little spy." With those words, he swept her into his arms and proceeded to the couch. "Rest with me for a bit and then we'll get you cleaned up. One hour to watch the patrons afterward and then we're heading home. I have additional plans that I think you'll enjoy. It seems I'll have to be a little more creative for a while to tide us over until J.J. arrives."

Jax sat on the couch, draping her over him and covering her with a blanket that had been folded on the end. She rested her head on his chest and placed a hand over her stomach. J.J. She even had Jax calling him that now and wondered what he would do if they were to have a girl. Such a dominant and overprotective man would be a bear of a father, but Emily wasn't worried. It was those types of men that little girls tended to have wrapped around their little fingers. Hearing his steady heartbeat settled hers and as his arms enveloped her she had no doubt they could face whatever came their way together.

Emily tried not to let reality intrude as she soaked up his warmth, but ended up losing. The threat of Ryland would always be there unless they made the first move. She had no doubt that CSA was working on it, but vowed to herself that even Ryland wouldn't take away this newfound happiness. The future was theirs and no one would take that away from the three of them.

Chapter Thirty

A few days later, Jax walked into Taryn's new office digs. She was sitting behind her desk and was fiercely concentrating on one of the screens in front of her. Her staple of the pencil behind the ear was securely in place, as well as the spikes of her blonde hair. He couldn't say the same for the slight bags underneath her eyes, which were visible behind her black-rimmed glasses. Those blemishes were new. After conversing with the guys, he found out that he wasn't the only one getting worried about her. He needed to speak with Crest about her long work hours, although Jax was relatively sure the boss man already knew.

"Anything interesting?"

Taryn didn't even bother glancing up as she shook her head. "No, but do you know if there are any donuts left?"

"You realize it's lunch time, right?" Jax pulled out a seat and plopped into the black leather. A squeak sounded from the wheels due to his weight, although was deafened by the printer that suddenly decided to churn out paper. "You want to grab a bite to eat?"

"No, thanks." Taryn sat back in her chair and waved a hand toward her monitor. "Did you know that there were three people on that guest list where Ryland met with Batkin whose pasts are basically nonexistent? Their names appeared out of nowhere, with no pasts. I've started another program to try and locate the specific years they appeared with those that disappeared."

Jax was torn between asking more questions about her theory and doing what he'd set out to do. Taryn needed time away from the office and he truly thought she and Emily might hit it off and form a friendship. He was hoping she'd join them for dinner and get her mind off of work. As it was, he and Taryn were still investigating ten hours a day into Ryland's case. The man had to be somewhere.

As for Emily, Jax still felt that fear of having her and their future ripped from his arms, but he was now able to substitute his feeling of dread for one of consumption. He consumed her every night and left both of them so satisfied that they were both able to sleep through the night. Except for last night, when she'd gotten up twice to pee. That was new.

"Taryn, you're putting in longer hours than me," Jax said, ignoring the questions that were rambling through his brain about why Ryland would have put himself into a position to be seen on video surveillance with one of his employers. "Have dinner with Emily and me. It'll be a nice change. She's only really formed a friendship with Lauren. I'd like to see her fit in with the rest of the group."

Taryn finally focused on him and he knew her answer before she actually said it. "I appreciate the offer, but now that we've found a potential lead, I'm going to see it through. If it doesn't pan out, how about we get together over the week-end?"

Jax could tell by the way her chin was set that she wasn't going to budge. He only nodded, having definitely made up his mind to speak with Crest. Something was going on with Taryn and if anyone would know what it was, it was Top. He might as well ask about the connection she thought she'd found.

"Is there a specific person out of the three that you think has ties to Ryland?"

"A woman," Taryn said, a smile forming on her lips. "Isn't it always?"

Jax laughed out loud, finally seeing a glimpse of the old Taryn. "Let's just say they can be a man's Achilles heel. I was told that lately. I take it you already started investigating said woman?"

"Like I said, her existence just came to be around ten years ago." Tarn leaned forward to grab a piece of paper. "Yvette Capre. She's in her mid thirties. There is absolutely no past known, although I did locate a Swiss bank account in her name."

"Do you have a picture?" Taryn handed over one taken from a newspaper clipping. The woman had long blonde hair and was simply striking. He looked a little closer. "Wow. That's interesting."

"What?"

"She kind of looks like you," Jax said, his other hand hitting the paper. "If this Yvette had short hair, the two of you might be interchangeable."

When Jax looked back up and across the desk, Taryn shifted uncomfortably and scrunched her nose. "I noticed that, but she's a lot taller than me and seems to have green eyes. And I certainly don't have as much fucking money as she does."

"How much?" Jax asked, interested more so now. Maybe they were looking at this wrong and Ryland had actually taken two jobs that day. Had Yvette paid him to murder someone? "And are there any discrepancies in her accounts?"

Taryn was already shaking her head. "I know where you're going with this and the answer is no. Her account actually hasn't been touched in the last two weeks."

"What does that mean?" Jax asked, tossing the news clipping back on her desk.

Before Taryn could reply, an annoying beeping sound came from a monitor at the end of the table. She stood, pushing the chair back with her legs and walked over to the screen.

"Well, fuck me," Taryn whispered, as if she'd forgotten he was in the room.

Jax stood as well and walked down to that end of the room. "What? I hate when you find shit and then don't share."

"I always share," Taryn shot back. She was leaning down and resting her hands on the edge of the desk, but she did look his way. The shock was evident. "Yvette Capre was just identified as the body of a Jane Doe. A purse was just turned in with identification. The policeman who found the body happened to be on duty and put two and two together. I wonder what her real name is."

"Ryland killed her?" Jax tried to fit the puzzles together, but it was like forcing oil and water to mix. He felt frustration well up inside of him at the roadblocks that kept getting thrown in their way. "It doesn't make sense."

Taryn was shaking her head and grabbed a folder off to the side. Placing it on the table between them, she quickly shuffled through the papers until she found the one she was looking for. She slid it his way.

"She wasn't killed by Ryland. This is the mark of Trevor Neonni. He was who we thought might have initially been hired to kill Emily. Connor said the man has no humanity left after his little visit to him in New York. Neonni kills by strangulation because he likes the up close and personal feel of it. As far as I can tell, Ryland keeps things impersonal."

"We should have had Connor take out Neonni when he had the chance." Jax looked down at the information she'd provided him. It looked to be a list of names and dates of Neonni's hit list. How the hell had she figured this shit out? "Do you have one of these on Ryland?"

"No. If I did, you'd have had it long ago." Taryn stood there staring at Neonni's victims, her brows pinched together. "Other than the few casualties I attributed to Ryland from years prior to the specific bomb he liked to use, I lost his trail when he changed up his style. Apparently he's partial to a scope nowadays."

"Was Neonni at the same function as Ryland?"

"No." Taryn pulled the pencil out from behind her ear and placed the eraser end in between her teeth. She had the bad habit of chewing on the metal piece and he winced when she started. He was glad when she pulled it out and started talking again. "Do you think Ryland could have been there, hoping to get a second contract? I wonder who wanted Yvette dead and what they paid for it."

"Unless he was there to try and warn her?"

"Too many questions with no answers. It only leads to more questions. We don't even know who she is." Taryn snatched up the paper, placed the pencil back behind her ear, and walked to her chair. Plopping into it, she rolled herself in front of another monitor. "I did find a list of old aliases that Ryland used to go under when he traveled back then. Let me see if I can connect Yvette to Ryland that way. It's just too coincidental that she and Ryland were at the same function and then she ends up dead by his competition a couple months later. If the morgue in New York has her body, then they should have her prints. Maybe I can trace her that way."

Jax knew he lost her by the time her fingers started flying over the keys. He left her to her own devices and walked out of her office. Looking into Crest's, Jax saw the room empty. He'd been absent a lot lately, but Jax had no doubt that he was doing some digging of his own. When Crest had figured out that Ryland was the man who assassinated the Lieutenant Colonel, it had made this case a little more personal for him.

Jax continued to his cubicle, knowing the office would remain quiet and that he would take advantage of it. Sitting down, he powered up his computer. Connor and Kevin were out on another murder that could be in relation to Kevin's case, Lach was home packing for what was that government contract that was to make up for the one they'd passed on a couple of months ago, and Ethan and Jessie had each gone to lunch. It was the perfect time to dig in deep and see what else Taryn's information had yielded.

Chapter Thirty-One

Emily smiled as she looked in the box that Lauren had given her earlier this morning. A set of nipple clamps and a clit clamp adorned in blue sapphires and white diamonds to go with her wedding dress lay on an inlay of lace. She would wear it underneath her dress and reveal it to Jax on their wedding night. Putting the lid back on, she hid it in the closet.

Lauren had asked if she wanted to grab a bite to eat but Emily had declined, wanting to surprise Jax at the office. There were some minor details of their ceremony that she wanted to go over with him before she confirmed with the Justice of the Peace. The wedding would be small and intimate, with only the team and her Aunt Beatrice. Her aunt was being flown in discreetly by Crest next month. By then, Emily was hoping for a bit of reprieve from the morning sickness. The medicine that the doctor had given her had made it manageable, but she still couldn't wait for a day to come where the nausea didn't. At least Jax was handling it better.

Putting on her running shoes, Emily then proceeded down the stairs and snatched up her purse and keys. She'd walk across the street to where Chuck was situated for the afternoon. He seemed to like the day shift, while some guy by the name of David took the midnight shift. She figured they'd be with them for quite a while since Ryland had yet to show his face. Maybe she'd order a sandwich to go and give it to Chuck after her lunch with Jax.

Walking out, she closed the door behind her. She slipped the key into the hole and turned until the deadbolt clicked into place. Emily walked off the porch and took a deep breath of the warm air. It was a nice change of pace from how cold spring had started out. The temperature had to at least be in the high sixties and she knew from the radio this morning that it actually might hit seventy degrees today. The jeans and lightweight pink shirt she wore was perfect for such a sunny day.

"See J.J.?" Emily asked, placing her hand on her stomach. "By this time next year, I can take you for walks and we can enjoy the sun together."

She and Jax had agreed to hold off her getting a job until J.J. had arrived and they'd gotten into the swing of things. Emily was very content to do that, as it gave her time to adjust to having a normal life. She'd even suggested that maybe she should wait until J.J. was in school, so if she did pursue her desire of teaching, it would give her the summers off. Jax had looked at her with a serious expression and had asked what she'd do when their second child came along. If Emily remembered correctly, she'd ended up over the toilet before she could answer.

Emily looked both ways as she started to walk across the street. The vehicle was black with dark tinted windows, preventing anyone from seeing inside. It was a good choice, as they didn't want the neighbors to become uneasy with someone sitting outside their house day in and day out. He was facing towards the right, so she crossed behind the vehicle and walked up to the window. When Chuck didn't immediately roll it down like usual, she rapped her knuckles on the glasses.

"C'mon, Chuck. I'm hungry."

When nothing happened, a shiver of unease went through her. Emily carefully looked around the area. The street was quiet and nothing seemed out of the ordinary. Why, then, did a chill sweep over the back of her neck where the sun had been moments before?

Shoving her right hand into her purse, Emily closed her fingers around her weapon, resting her finger along the barrel. She mentally tried to rationalize that if Ryland was out there, he'd have taken the shot already and she would most likely be dead. Somehow, that didn't cause her to feel any better about what she was about to find. Using her left hand, she slowly reached for the handle, all along praying that Chuck had just fallen asleep. It happened, right? Men who were on the details like this had to get fatigued. She also knew that Crest and Jax would never have hired someone like that, which totally negated any prayers she might have been sending upward.

Emily pulled on the handle, finding that it was unlocked and easily popped open. Edging the door wider, she blinked a few times to make certain that what she was seeing was real. Fuck. Her vision tunneled and her stomach revolted when the coppery odor wafted out from the vehicle. Her fingers slipped from the handle and she struggled to breathe, the oxygen not making its way into her lungs.

Chuck's head was tilted at an odd angle and the bullet hole located at his temple was smaller than what the average person would have anticipated. The trails of blood had stopped, but even she could recognize the glistening liquid as still being somewhat fresh. Despite her trembling hands, Emily kept enough composure to lean forward and place a finger to his carotid artery. Fuck. Tears sprang up in her eyes, causing the vision of his dead body to swim. Fuck. Fuck. Fuck.

Emily's survival instinct kicked in and although she knew it had to be done, pulling his body out of the car seemed too sacrilegious. Unfortunately, there was no way she had the strength to push his dead weight across to the passenger seat and time was of the essence. Releasing her weapon, she pulled on Chuck's arm until his own weight had him falling out of the vehicle. Not wasting time, she climbed over his body and inside the driver's seat, slamming the door. Thank God the keys were in the ignition, for she turned the engine over and instantly slammed the gear in drive and gunned the accelerator.

It took a moment for the car to catch up with the how fast her heart was beating, but eventually, Emily managed to get the speed up and drove like hell into downtown. Looking in the rearview mirror, she didn't notice anyone following her. Then again, it would be hard to distinguish with all the traffic. Frantically, she reached into her purse and rummaged around until she located her cell. Pulling it out, she brought it to the steering wheel, trying to drive while hitting the right button. A sob rose up when she saw that blood was on the fingers of her left hand.

"J.J., mama needs some help," Emily whispered, trying to stop her body from shaking. "You need to help me stay calm and remember my training. Think you can do that for me?"

Rationally, she knew that the baby couldn't help her in any way, but hearing the words out loud somehow helped. It wasn't just her life at stake anymore. Taking a few deep breaths, Emily was able to speed dial Jax. Bringing the phone up to her ear, she also managed to swerve out of the way of a car turning left a little too abruptly.

"Hey, little spy. I was just thinking about you."

"Jax, he's here," Emily choked out as another sob escaped. Hearing his voice seemed to open the floodgates. "He's here."

Ryland released the curtain that he'd parted with the barrel of his weapon and let it fall back into place. He shook his head and gave a small smile at the fact that little Miss Emily had enough balls to leave a dead man lying on a sidewalk in the middle of a family dominated neighborhood. It seemed as if the NSA had certainly underestimated their NOC agent who they let so easily slip through their fingers. Their loss, but it wasn't like she would be around for very long anyway.

He slowly looked around the living room, noticing the little touches that she had obviously mixed with that of her future husband. Ryland hadn't missed the bridal magazines and brochures lying on the coffee table. He would have saved Jax Christensen the headache of going through with the wedding, had Emily only reacted like that of every other woman when presented with a dead body. He'd expected her to run back inside and lock herself in until Jax came to the rescue.

"What to do?" Ryland asked aloud, continuing to walk around the quaint Victorian house. It wasn't his style, but to each their own. "What to do?"

He'd deliberately bided his time, wanting to play with Emily and the members of CSA a while longer. Ryland had taken a quick and easy assignment over in Bali of all places, but the weather had been spectacular. He'd even taken time for some pleasure, knowing that business would roll around soon enough. He'd come back to the States upon hearing that Yvette

Capre had been missing for some time. He did find irony in his situation, so much like Jax Christensen's.

Unfortunately his stop into Minneapolis did not go as planned, but he wouldn't let that deter him. Shrugging, he holstered his weapon. Maybe it best to wait until they'd settled into a new routine. A year wouldn't hurt and it would certainly get Crest to lay off of his contacts within the government. He was making some people uneasy and it wouldn't surprise Ryland if Crest's name didn't come across as one of his targets. How fun would that be if his execution came through Ryland's vocation? He thought maybe it would be more exciting should it remain personal.

No, it was better if he left and continued on to New York. Yvette had to still be there, for her target was still alive. He was well aware she'd been given the contract on a high-ranking official. The man was still alive, as Ryland had just seen him give an interview on national television. There were rumblings that she was losing her edge. That was just something Ryland couldn't see, but he couldn't resist finding out what game she was playing.

"We'll meet again, Miss Emily."

Ryland walked through the kitchen, already anticipating the year ahead. He could always return around the holidays to deliver his present. Crest would have to see the humor in that, just as he had to be fully aware that Ryland always finished a job. Emily was his contract and he would follow through, despite that it no longer mattered. Batkin was dead, the message that he wanted delivered to future dealers conveyed, and Alekseev had been sent back to his country. It was more an ego thing, which Ryland would fully admit. He appreciated a clean resume.

As he reached for the doorknob, his cell phone vibrated. Pausing long enough to see if he had a new assignment coming in, Ryland stopped short and stared at the image in front of him. The photo of Yvette Capre took up the screen. It was obvious she was lying in a morgue and from the ligature marks around her neck, how she'd died. He made himself continue to stare at it, gathering as much information as he could before sliding the screen to the accompanied message. It was from a contact that he'd had in place should anything happen to Yvette. Ryland would see that he was paid his due.

Ryland felt a slight twinge in his heart for a colleague that had garnered his respect. It was unfortunate that this had come to an end though. He felt as if the one time in his life that he'd been outsmarted couldn't be undone. He would never find retribution. It did pique his curiosity though as to who would want her killed. Not enough to continue on to New York, but enough that he'd make use of old favors. Neonni could be paid easily for that information. It was his honor to make certain that the one person who had taken his retaliation from his fingers be dealt his or her own payback.

Letting himself out of the house through the back door, Ryland crossed through the yard and waved to the little girl swinging on her set. Her sweet smile reminded him of Yvette, which he found odd. He wasn't prone to such endearments. Ignoring such platitudes, he continued on his way. He had things to do and places to be. Emily and CSA would be here when the time was right.

Chapter Thirty-Two

Jax had never felt such rage, contempt, and helplessness overtake his senses like he had upon hearing the strangled words crossing Emily's lips. He had no idea how he'd gotten to the attached garage in their building, but he'd stood waiting for her to pull up. He'd made her continue talking so that he knew exactly where she was and that she was okay. It wasn't until he saw the car pull in next to Connor's Jeep that he actually been able to breath.

"Are you sure that someone went to get—"

"Yes," Jax answered, still holding onto her a little more tightly than necessary, but he didn't give a shit. When he'd yanked the door open, he all but pulled her out and plastered her against his body. All he could think to himself was that she was safe. Alive. Now, the entire team was congregated in the large area outside of the cubicles with the exception of Jessie and Connor. The round table easily accommodated them. "Lach alerted the police and they're on the scene."

"Thank you," Emily murmured, glancing over at Lach who nodded his acknowledgement. Lach didn't speak much, only when needed. She'd overheard Jax say he'd flown back into the country the day before last. "I know this is asking a lot, but do you think you could drive over there and make sure they're treating him okay?"

Everyone at the table knew that she was referring to Chuck's body and it didn't surprise Jax in the least when Lach stood and told her not to worry, that he would see to it that Chuck was taken care of. Crest had already been standing and talking into the phone when he stopped Lach with a hand to his arm. Jax knew that Crest was asking that he case the scene and report back, with the added warning to watch his back.

"Jax, what are we going to do? He's a ghost. He comes and goes. No one knows where he's been and no one knows where he's going. We can't live like this."

"We're doing everything we can, Emily," Crest said, rejoining them at the table. "Connor is bringing Lauren in right this moment. It's paramount that the team is safe first. We just needed to make sure everyone was accounted for."

"What about Jessie?" Ethan asked, sitting on the opposite side of the table. "She said something about dropping some files off at the courthouse."

"I was able to get in touch with her and told her to head back to the courthouse and stay there. She's safer inside that building than she is walking the streets to return here." Crest leaned down and placed his palms on the table. He'd rolled up his sleeves in his usual habit when things became tense. "Kevin, once we brainstorm and think of the possible areas Ryland might be holed up in, I want you to retrieve Jessie and bring her back here."

"In the meantime?" Jax asked, trying unsuccessfully to relax his grasp of Emily's chair. She was sitting back, whereas he was leaning forward on his, with his knees touching hers. He held both her hands in his left one and was resting his right forearm on the arm of her chair. "We all knew he'd show up again. That it was only a matter of time. We should have prepared better for this. Now we're fucking sitting ducks."

"We did prepare for it, which is possibly what saved Emily." Crest stood and cross his arms. "I'm not claiming to know what Ryland is thinking, but he took the time to take out Emily's detail before continuing on with his intended target."

"What if he didn't intend to actually kill Emily?" Kevin asked, putting in his two cents. "What if Ryland is just toying with her? Psychopaths enjoy shit like that."

"Ryland might be a psychopath, but he's got his own set of rules that he never breaks." Crest ran his fingers down the side of his face, the toll that they were all feeling evident. "If he returned, it was to kill her."

"What'd we miss?" Connor asked, entering the room with Lauren in tow. She immediately released his hand and walked around the table to where Emily was sitting. Jax refused to go of Emily while Lauren leaned down to hug her friend. "And where's Jessie?"

"At the courthouse. Kevin's going to retrieve her later in the day." Crest motioned for Connor and Lauren to take seats. "Taryn's bringing out layouts of the city. She's in her office now printing them off. I've called Schultz and he'll be here within the next three hours. Depending on what he can access, along with Taryn, we'll run scans to see if he shows up in any place public."

"And if he doesn't?" Jax asked, the urge to do something right now becoming overwhelming. "We all know the fucker can disappear into thin air."

A shriek came from inside Taryn's office and they all turned to see her running out, papers in hand. Her expression said it all and for the first time since Emily had arrived, he was able to let go of her hand and stand. Squid had managed to locate Ryland and Jax wanted the information instantly so that he could end this once and for all.

"He's at the train station, Midway in St. Paul," Taryn said breathlessly. "My facial recognition program got a hit when he bought the ticket a few minutes ago. He must think he's in the clear as he didn't even bother to disguise himself. He's leaving on the four o'clock train to Ontario."

"He's crossing the border," Crest said, his voice booming. He circled a hand in the air. "Round up. It seems as if Schultz will miss this bust, but we're sure as hell not. Once everyone's loaded up, meet back at the table. I'll have the scenario in place with a couple of back-up plans. Taryn, that means you too. We need everyone we can get."

Jax had initially thought that Taryn would be left behind, but drew a deep breath and knew that Emily could cover herself and Lauren. Especially if Taryn was able to take a remote laptop and assure everyone that Ryland was still inside the Midway Station in St. Paul. He felt Emily's cold hand slip into his and looked down.

"You need to end this for us," Emily said. He pulled her up and wrapped his arms around her, breathing in her scent. Her arms wound around his waist and she clung to him. "If I wasn't pregnant, I would be right by your side, but I know where our priorities are. What I will do is make sure Lauren and I remain inside the office. We won't go anywhere. I promise."

"I'll keep in contact."

Jax claimed one more kiss from Emily before following his other team members into Crest's office. There was a discreet closet complete with inserts and drawers where additional weapons and ammo were kept for emergencies such as these.

The team was anything if not efficient, prepared, and properly armed.

It was Ethan who chose a Remington 700 variant with a Nikon scope. He would be stationed outside of the station up on the opposing building, should Crest and the team not be able to take him into custody. Jax and the others already had their weapons holstered, but he did add a few additional clips. It was better to be prepared, especially since there would be civilians in the surrounding area and Ryland had already made it known that he didn't have an issue taking their lives. That included his own. Jax had a feeling that Ryland wasn't the type to be taken and would either have an escape plan already laid out or he'd take himself out before spending the rest of his life in prison.

"I meant what I said out there," Crest said, walking up beside him as he chambered a round and holstered his weapon. "We need everyone on this team if we're to bring him in. But if his actions have clouded your judgment and there's a shred of doubt that you can't do your job, tell me now."

Crest was asking if Jax had plans to kill Ryland on sight. If it came down to a life for a life, Jax wouldn't hesitate to kill. Jax had at times been ruthless in his duty for his country, but he'd never crossed that moral boundary and murdered for the sake of murder. He didn't intend to start today.

"I'm good." Jax secured the extra clips in a magazine pouch attached to his belt and then met Crest's gaze head-on. Finally being able to have a chance to end this had calmed his heartbeat and a peace had enveloped him, such was the case when he'd been in combat. It wasn't that he didn't feel fear— he did. This was Emily, their baby, and their future he was fighting for. He just knew how to use his fear in order to get the job done. "No worries. I'm not saying I don't want to see the man dead at my feet for what he's put Emily through. But if there's a chance that he can suffer in solitary for the rest of his life, that's where I'll put him."

Crest studied him for another three seconds before nodding his head in acceptance. As everyone started to head back to the designated meeting spot, Jax spotted Taryn slipping on her red blazer that would cover the holster form-fitted to her body. He also spotted a small knife that was attached to the waistband of the jeans she wore. It was rare that he got to see her in action, although she'd gone on government contracts for Crest in the past. It just seemed as of late that Taryn had become their resident tech guru.

"Squid, you ready?"

Taryn looked his way and her brown eyes met his, giving him a glimpse as to why Crest had hired her. The set of her jaw, the straightening of her shoulders, and the way her eyes shined with readiness to do battle was a sight to see. Their office geek had transformed before his eyes. If it weren't for the pull at the edge of her mouth, he would have bought the entire package. Something was off.

"I'm ready." Taryn gave a small smile, erasing the tell he'd caught sight of.

She was out the door before Jax could question it. He had no doubt that Taryn would do her job, but again, her fascination of this gun for hire seemed to have taken over her waking hours. Was it something more than wanting justice? Did it matter if in the end the team acquired their target?

"Jax?"

His eyes went straight to Emily. He saw the protective way she covered their baby with her hand and that same surge washed over him. Jax pulled her close as Crest took the pictures of Midway Station that Taryn had just handed him and laid them out on the table. He didn't let her go until every detail was covered and even then, not until they were at the door.

Today was the day when the sins of others were eradicated from their lives.

Chapter Thirty-Three

They'd arrived in several vehicles and waited to enter on Taryn's signal. She'd brought a remote system that connected through the station's security surveillance video feed, continually monitoring Ryland. He'd moved several times, knowing exactly when to turn his head from the cameras. It was only when two overlapped that his features were caught on film.

Jax had no doubt that Ryland knew each and every one of them, from their physical appearance to their favorite fucking color. He thought that he had the advantage, but Ryland would be surprised at how much they knew regarding his career and past as well. Take for instance Ryland's connection with the bombs from specific hits. He'd used the same bomb maker before switching to his preferred method of using a FN FAL 7.62mm assault rifle with a Leupold Mark 4 scope. No one was perfect.

Jax was wearing a light black jacket to cover his weapon so as not to alarm the passengers. As he and Connor entered through the doors, he immediately went to the left while his partner blended in with crowd on the right. Smiling at an elderly woman passing by, he continued through the rows of seats. The last information that Taryn had provided them before leaving the vehicles was that Ryland was located directly in the center of the station. Crest and Taryn were coming in from the opposite direction. Lach and Kevin were to enter through the employee doors, while Ethan remained outside with his scope at the ready.

Catching sight of Kevin and the signal that all was clear so far, he continued through the throngs of people. An announcement came over the loud speaker, broadcasting the boarding of the next train. Jax glanced up at the red digital clock, seeing that they had one hour before Ryland's departure. Within two minutes, he spotted their target.

The loud chatter of the station dimmed as blood rushed through Jax's ears. As if in slow motion, the people milling about kept crossing his line of sight, their hands gesturing in conversation as if nothing extraordinary was about to happen. Their worlds were carrying on with laughter and animation, while his only focus was the man sitting in the middle of the row, reading a newspaper. He'd be lucky to have such enjoyments where Jax intended for him to spend the rest of his God-given days.

Crest had gotten permission for his agency to use government identification cards for just this reason. Not wanting to alarm the other passengers, Jax held up a finger to his lips and lifted the right side of his jacket so that they could see his ID. The rows of chairs were back to back and Jax needed the one facing him to clear out. The last thing they needed was another civilian hurt in attempting to apprehend this son of a bitch.

Connor must have crossed back over Jax's way, for he was standing to Jax's right side. Quickly scanning the area, he saw that Kevin and Lach had each taken up positions farther down each corridor. Crest and Taryn were approaching from a connecting hallway directly in front of Ryland. The man had positioned himself well, but not good enough. Jax focused on Ryland's fingers and saw the slight tightening of the paper, indicating his awareness like that of prey.

Not losing this chance, Jax withdrew his weapon and had it against the back of Ryland's skull before the man could twitch. Jax knew that Connor would have his back and continue to clear the area while he focused on his one and only target. His partner was also aware that Jax was the one who needed to be the first to speak.

"Don't move an inch." Jax held his weapon steady, making sure the barrel rested snugged against his target's head. He ignored the gasps from the crowd. "It's over, Ryland."

"I must say, this is quite a surprise."

Jax compressed his lips, hating the smug way Ryland said those words. The way he spoke gave the indication that he was from money, which was surprising. The wealth he made from his contracts couldn't instill that type of condescension. A person was born into it. The man thought he was above all this. A piece of the unsolved puzzle fell into place. It still wasn't enough information.

"Let me guess," Jax said, seeing that Crest was now almost upon them. He also spotted security guards out of his peripheral vision running towards them. Kevin and Lach would take care of them, making certain they stayed out of the way. "That's two in one day. Did you think Emily would go back into the house? Did you want to end this contract on a more personal note?"

The way Ryland's shoulders tensed for a fraction of a second told Jax he'd been right. He'd thought about it while the team had driven to the station and the only possible conclusion for Ryland not taking Emily out while he had her in his sights was that he wanted to make a personal statement to Crest and the agency. Crest had been right in the fact that Ryland would have bided his time longer, but he'd have returned to make his claim.

"I admit that your Emily is quite special. She certainly made this an entertaining adventure. Enjoy her."

Jax could hear the unspoken words *while you can* and resisted the urge to butt his weapon against the back of Ryland's head. It was as if he still thought there was a way out of this. Jax refused to let doubt creep into his thoughts.

Crest had timed it well and was now standing in front of Ryland, studying him like one would a bug under a microscope. Jax kept his weapon pressed against Ryland's head, unwilling to give him an inch of freedom.

"It's been a long time, Ryland."

Crest didn't waver in his stance and kept his arms by his sides. It gave him easier access to his weapon. At this point, there was no need to have it drawn and risk upsetting an already distressed crowd.

"Crest, I must say, you're becoming a thorn in my side."

Ryland slowly folded the newspaper and set it next to him on the empty seat. Jax didn't like his nonchalant attitude, but trusted the team to keep their eyes peeled for another player in the mix. It wasn't like Ryland was getting out of this himself. He wasn't that good.

"I think it best we discuss the rest of this in private."

"You and I know that's not going to happen." Ryland casually glanced around, taking in the scenery. As his eyes came to rest on Taryn a few feet away, stillness overcame him in a way that engulfed the atmosphere with uneasiness. Jax didn't hesitate to tighten his finger on the trigger. "I'm not the type of person to be kept behind bars."

"Then you should have picked a different career."

Jax took a moment to look at Taryn. She'd lost color in her face upon Ryland's observation, but that didn't appear to affect her sense of duty. Her hand was resting inside her jacket, ready to draw if necessary. It wasn't lost on him that the picture Taryn had of Yvette was positively linked to Ryland. His slight reaction to Taryn's likeness to the dead woman was apparent, although he wondered why Ryland didn't make the connection during his research. Another piece of the puzzle fit, but still not enough to unravel the entire picture.

"It appears that we're at a standoff." Ryland kept his hands on the armrests, but that didn't give Jax any respite. "You and I both know how this is going to end. You can simply tell your team to let me go or I take you out before they succeed in doing the same to me. See, I'm prepared to die, although hadn't thought it would happen in this manner. Are you ready to die, Crest?"

"You're lying," Taryn said, her voice carrying across the distance. Jax could see Crest tense, not liking that such a well-trained agent was veering off course. What the hell was she doing? "You have unfinished business, Ryland. You're not concerned that Yvette Capre died, but you want to find out who killed her."

Fuck. Was she trying to antagonize him? Jax readied himself for what he had to do. This man was being taken into custody, regardless if he was dead or alive.

"Taryn Emmeline Sisal." Ryland's fingers twisted underneath the arms of his seat, indicating that Taryn's words had got to him. "It's not in my nature to worry, but I must admit, you have me intrigued. And now the question that begs to be answered is why Crest would go to such lengths he has to wipe out your photo on every agency database in existence."

Jax wanted badly to look at Crest to see if that were true, but now wasn't the time. He remained focused on his sights, waiting for any indication that Ryland was going to make a move.

"No one is dying here today," Crest responded, cutting off their exchange. There was a surety in his voice that superseded anything Ryland had said. "Government officials are meeting us to place you under arrest. You'll be tried for the murders of several high-ranking officials. So I'll make this simple. Slowly open your jacket with the thumb and forefinger of each hand. Move slow enough for Jax to count the hairs on each of your hands."

"I do feel sadness that you and I will not get to continue our conversation, Taryn." Ryland shifted ever so slightly. "Unfortunately, fate deals us our hands and we must accept it."

In that moment, Jax knew the inevitable was about to happen. Ryland was going to make a move on Crest, taking both their lives. There was no way this fucker was getting off so easy. Right when Ryland shifted his body to launch himself at Crest, Jax was left with no other choice and brought his weapon up, slamming it hard at the base of Ryland's skull. The blow was hard enough knock him unconscious. His body fell to the side from the impact.

The team moved in, although Taryn remained a few feet away. She had to know a lecture from Crest was unavoidable. Jax hadn't like her fascination with Ryland from the start and this only confirmed that she'd let it get out of hand. The question was why?

"Secure him," Crest said, reaching into his suit jacket for his phone. "I'll contact Schultz. He can take it from here."

Kevin stepped in front of Crest and leaned down to frisk Ryland. Pulling a Walter PPK from the shoulder holster, Kevin held it up for Jax. He seized the handgun and only then realized there was a slight tremor in his hands. This could have gone down a dozen ways, but the relief traveling through his blood stream was proof that they got the son of a bitch. A hand slapped Jax's back and he knew Connor had come to stand by him as they watched Kevin use a very thick double zip tie cuff to secure Ryland's hands.

"Call Emily." Connor's fingers tightened on Jax's shoulders before releasing him. "Let her know it's over."

"Is it?" Jax could feel the solid ball of uncertainty fill his chest cavity. With Emily in his life, and that of their child, would he ever feel they were safe enough? "This man has more contacts than we know about. He'll be kept in a federal prison, but those walls have leaks. You know it and I know it."

"For the time being, we'll take what we can get," Connor said, his voice flat and accepting of what this life that they'd chosen gave them. "I'd rather be on the front lines, doing something to secure our families, than I would have my head buried in the sand."

"Aren't we the ones responsible for bringing this to our doorsteps?"

"Don't kid yourself. This shit would find us no matter where we went."

Connor stepped away, walking around to where he was needed. Jax agreed that this was where they needed to be. Whether it was a local case or an international one, it was their duty to follow through in maintaining the peace. He wouldn't change who he was, but he would see to it that additional safety protocols were put into place.

Jax looked over at Crest, who was talking into the phone, and their eyes connected. He nodded his head at a job well done and that did get Jax to smirk. It wasn't the ideal way to take down one of the most elite assassins. It certainly lacked finesse, but he'd take the tag anyway he could get it.

He distanced himself so that he could speak with Emily in private. God only knew how long it would be before he saw her, especially with Schultz and his team coming in. They were going to want SITREPS, with every T crossed and I dotted. He fucking hated that part, but when Emily's hopeful voice sang across his speaker, it more than made up for it.

"We did it."

✧   ✧   ✧   ✧

Jax lifted his hand to wave goodnight to Connor as they both let themselves into their own half of the house. A quick look across the street where Chuck's body had been recovered weighed heavily on his mind. The entire team had stopped by his residence to speak with the man's wife. He knew that condolences weren't enough, but Crest would see to it that all the details of his funeral were taken care of and then some. Unfortunately, it would never make up for the loss of her husband.

"Are you okay?"

Emily's voice traveled through the air like an anchor and he shut the door, wishing it was just as easy to lock out the memories of those hurt by their need to survive. Turning, she stood there with her halo of brunette hair and warm blue eyes to welcome him home.

"I am now."

"I'm thinking maybe after J.J. is born, I should come work with you. This waiting is for the birds."

"Not on your fucking life, little spy. You finally convinced me being a teacher was a safe occupation. Let's just stick with that."

Jax opened his arms and as she stepped into them, he sent a prayer to whoever was listening. Burying his nose in her hair, he felt his muscles finally start to relax. Exhaustion started to settle in, but he knew that she would want every detail. He'd rather get it out of the way, so that tomorrow started off as a day of hope. Pulling away, he looked down and took a moment to count his blessings.

"How about some hot chocolate?"

"For me too?" Emily asked, her voice full of anticipation.

"You can have a sip of mine, but I think J.J. should have regular milk." Jax laughed when she scrunched her nose and loved her even more for trying to make this homecoming as normal as she could. "I'll warm it for you. How's that?"

Taking her hand, Jax led her into the kitchen. Sitting her at the table, he started to prepare their drinks. Emily remained quiet, as if she knew he needed to gather his thoughts about all that went on today.

"Ryland was taken to the hospital to be checked out," Jax said, offering up the first round of information. There was a lot to get through that had happened after he'd spoken to her on the phone. "Schultz eventually arrived, but it seems I hit Ryland a little harder than necessary. He was out for a while, which all things considering, wasn't a bad thing."

"Were you there when he regained consciousness?"

When Jax looked over his shoulder, he saw that Emily had pulled her feet up into the chair and crossed them. He smiled softly, wondering how much longer she'd be able to do that. She wasn't showing yet, but it was just a matter of time. He was looking forward to seeing her belly grow with their child.

"No, but Crest was. He didn't share the details of their conversation, but from what I can gather, Ryland's not saying much." Jax stirred the milk, watching the white liquid as it heated. "I doubt he'll offer up anything. A lawyer appeared before they escorted both of them to the Stillwater prison by Schultz. It has a supermax facility, although as soon as transport can be arranged Ryland will be taken to the only supermax prison left in the United States. ADX Florence, located in Florence, Colorado."

"How's the rest of the team doing?"

"Fine," Jax answered, knowing that every one of them had their own way of coping when it came to big cases like these. Hell, even he used to hit the club pretty hard before the little spy behind him came back into his life. Kevin and Ethan had been making their way to Masters when he'd left their offices. The milk was heated, so he reached for two mugs. "Taryn pulled something stupid tonight though. I'm sure she's getting a lecture by Crest as we speak."

"Taryn?" Emily appeared by his side, having opened up the cupboard to his left and grabbed the marshmallows. "What happened to her? You didn't mention that she got hurt."

"She didn't, but when Crest was trying to talk Ryland into turning himself in, she interrupted and basically told Ryland he was a liar." Jax glanced at her hopeful face when he started to mix in the chocolate. It was his heart that melted as he then did the same to hers. The way her blue eye sparkled was all he needed. She added the marshmallows until both cups were overflowing. "I've had this gut feeling that she was getting too involved in the case, but who am I to talk? It's consumed my every waking hour."

"Too involved how?" Emily followed him back to the table and pulled both feet up onto the chair. It was then that he noticed she didn't have any socks on. Setting both mugs on the table, he pulled out his chair catty-corner from her and drew her feet into his lap. She moaned when he started to massage her inner arch. "You better answer quick. I don't know how long I'll be awake if you keep doing that."

Jax smiled, but kept rubbing. "She was putting in longer hours than me. Taryn seemed to have almost become fixated on him and the weird part of it all was that she connected him to this woman named Yvette Capre. They look almost exactly alike."

Emily's eyes had drifted closed but shot open when he revealed that piece of information. "What do you mean, they look alike?"

"Their facial features were almost the same," Jax replied, taking each tiny toe and rolling them between his fingers. "Ryland noticed it too, but didn't comment on it. There's no connection between the two women, but I'm sure Crest is going to want answers as to why she interrupted them at the train station."

"What do you mean were?" Emily reached for her mug and sipped the hot chocolate. A little melted marshmallow was left on her upper lip and he watched her tongue peek out and lick it off. After such an adrenaline filled day, even he was surprised when his dick stirred to life. "Did something happen to the other woman?"

"Apparently she was strangled to death. I'll fill you in on the details later, but Taryn seemed to not want Ryland to make a move that would end his life. She practically baited him."

"Did you ask her about it?"

"I didn't have time to talk with her," Jax replied, keeping one hand on her foot while reaching for his mug with the other. "By the time Schultz arrived, his men zeroed in on us.

We gave our SITREPs and spent the rest of the night typing them up. The government doesn't want a loophole in this case that might be a potential danger and neither do we."

"So that's it?" Emily asked, seemingly a little more awake now. She nudged his crotch when he didn't immediately put down his cup and rub her foot. He arched a brow at her assertiveness, knowing she would comment that they weren't in the bedroom. He liked her spunk, but the way his cock was responding to her strokes, they were technically already there. "Lauren and I spent the evening together discussing how it doesn't seem real that it's over."

"It'll take time, but I don't ever want you to lose your awareness." Jax lowered his mug and then reached for the rung of her chair, dragging it across the floor. She must not have been aware of it, but when she'd had her legs crisscrossed earlier, he'd seen a small hole in the seam. Reaching for it now, he used two fingers and ripped them in two. He smiled in satisfaction that she'd followed his order regarding no panties in the house. Her bare pussy was a sight to behold. "What I would like is for you to sink that sweet pussy over my cock."

Emily's blue eyes sparkled as she set down her hot chocolate. "I like that idea. What I'd like better is to coat your cock with marshmallow and lick it off of you."

"Stand up."

He hid a grin as her startled look met his. Emily's eyes deepened into a dark blue, the way they got upon entering a true scene. She liked to push, to see how far she could go, but he would always be there to ensure their roles stayed in place. This no impact thing was a little harder than he'd anticipated, but that didn't mean there weren't ways to keep her in the submissive mindset she craved.

Emily stood and he motioned with his hand that he wanted her to remove her top. Doing so, she stood naked in front of him. Her breasts had definitely gotten fuller. Since she was standing in between his legs, all Jax had to do was lean forward and her nipple would be in his mouth. But that's not what he wanted. He'd been too lenient since she'd become pregnant. Maybe it was time to change things up.

"Pinch your nipples for me until they're swollen."

Emily's breath hitched and her hands came up to cup her breasts. With each thumb and index finger, she took each nipple and slowly started to manipulate them. She'd told him time and again how sensitive they were with her pregnancy. She was about to find out how much more so they could be.

"Did I say softly? Pinch them." Jax sat back, drinking his hot chocolate.

"Yes, Sir," Emily replied, a little breathless. Her cheeks were starting to flush that nice shade of pink that matched her lip gloss.

Jax watched as she pinched and rolled the nubs in between her fingers. Their coloring started to deepen, but not enough to his satisfaction. He wanted them engorged so that one swipe of his tongue would set her on edge.

"Pull on them."

"Sir," Emily breathed, her intake of air shallow. "I—"

"Would you like to stop and go to bed?" Jax asked, raising an eyebrow.

"No, Sir." She'd answered quickly, while at the same time, pulling and distending her nipples. A nice shade of plum red was starting to appear. But he still wanted more and remained silent as she continued to pinch, tug, pull, and all but twist the now swollen nubs. "Please, Sir."

"Please?" Jax rested his mug on the table. "Let's gauge if it's been long enough. Spread your legs wide."

Jax slowly reached forward with his hand as she got into position. Emily watched it the entire time, until he'd reached her pussy. Using one finger, he slid it through her folds and collected her cream. She was drenched, but he wanted it pouring down the inside of her thighs.

"More," Jax instructed, sitting back in his chair. He picked up his hot chocolate. "You're to stand there, pinching and twisting your nipples until I finish my drink. Then maybe it'll have been long enough."

Emily wasn't the type of woman who whimpered, but that's exactly what emitted past her parted lips. The beautiful sound had the zipper of his jeans digging into his cock. He took his time and when he was through, went about taking off his shoulder holster. Her eyes had started to glaze over and her breath was now coming out in pants. As he laid his weapon on the table, he caught wind of her sweet fragrance.

"When you slide down on top of me, you are not to stop playing with your nipples." Jax unbuttoned his jeans and then slid the zipper down. His eyes almost rolled in the back of his head at the sweet relief that it had provided. "I've got to say I'm enjoying you pregnant, as we can make love with nothing between us."

Jax wasn't sure she even heard him. She'd gotten into the manipulation of her nipples and was in a world all her own. He lightly tapped her pussy with his fingers.

"Oh!"

"Attention on me, little spy," Jax murmured, motioning to her that she straddle him. "Slide down my cock and don't stop until I'm fully inside of you."

He praised her when she didn't remove her hands from her breasts as she lowered herself over him. Jax kept a hold of his cock at the base. The minute her warmth surrounded him, he couldn't contain the guttural grown that erupted from his chest. She was so goddamn perfect and fit him like a glove to the point of pain. As instructed, Emily took him inside of her until there was no more to take.

"Fuck me."

On her tiptoes, Emily started to push up and then let her body weight carry her down. Jax released the base of his shaft, no longer needing to hold it. She had a pretty damn good grip on it.

"If I see you loosen your hold on those nipples, you won't be getting your nightly orgasm," Jax warned, mesmerized by the twists she was incorporating in her manipulations. It was downright beautiful. "That's right. Those sensitive nubs have been neglected a little too long. Maybe I'll order some nipple clamps from Lauren. Would you like that?"

Emily moaned something incoherent, her lashes fluttering over her flushed cheeks. She didn't stop her gyrating or the pushes from the tiptoes. It was as if her body was on autopilot, doing exactly as he instructed. Jax felt a little pressure build in his lower back. His balls began to tighten into his body.

"I'm thinking clover clamps, since you seem to like the pressure." Jax slipped a hand in between them and placed his thumb and index finger alongside her swollen clit. "Your clit has been ignored today, although that's usually not the case. We'll get a clit clamp to go along with the nipples ones. Would you like to know how it would feel?"

Emily's whimpers had effectively driven him to the brink. As he felt his awareness start to slip, he wanted more than anything for them to find release simultaneously. He pinched her clit just in time as his cum shot out of his cock and into the depths of her pussy. The spasms her sheath was creating were gripping and milking him like nothing he'd ever experienced. By the time they'd each drew air into their lungs, Jax realized she'd yet to let go of her nipples.

"Arms around my neck," Jax instructed.

He wasn't surprised that she didn't say anything as the day's events had obviously caught up with her. He didn't regret what just happened, as they both needed the relief. As Emily wrapped them around and clasped her hands behind his neck, her head rested against his shoulder. Jax stood. With her pussy still cradling his cock, he walked them through the kitchen and into the living room. Taking the steps, he proceeded into the bedroom and didn't release her until they'd reached their bed. Pulling out of her warmth was hell.

Helping her undress, Jax then did the same and went into the bathroom for a warm cloth. After cleaning her up, he tossed the washcloth across the room and pulled the covers over them. Fatigue was washing over him and he pulled her close. Jax thought about how he'd used to burn off steam after a case, but nothing compared to what he held in his arms. Emily had filled his home with love and family, the two most important things life had to offer.

"I love you, Jax," Emily whispered.

He'd never get tired of her saying that. Tucking her closer, Jax spooned her body and placed his hand on her warm belly. J.J. was safely ensconced within his mama's belly. Emily was safe in his arms. Jax would move heaven and earth to keep them that way.

"I love you, too, my little spy."

Chapter Thirty-Four

Emily waited for Lauren to put the finishing touches to the bottom of her wedding dress. Aunt Beatrice, Lauren, and Taryn wouldn't allow her to turn around and face the mirror otherwise. She shared a tender look with her aunt, who already had tears in her eyes. The woman had been a mother and father figure for the majority of Emily's life. Jax had managed to envelop her into their lives despite the arguments the NSA had given. What they had to say was valid, but if it was one thing that she and Jax had learned, was that life was too short not to take the chance and lose those important in their lives.

"You look absolutely beautiful," Aunt Beatrice whispered, lifting a white handkerchief to her eye. "I cannot wait to paint you onto canvas."

"Thank you, Aunt Beatrice," Emily said, smiling. "I'm glad we postponed the wedding until the end of June. The weather is much warmer and the sunset will be absolutely perfect for the ceremony. Plus, your new beau was able to attend. He seems to fit right in with the crew out there."

Aunt Beatrice's cheeks flushed at the mention of Roger Dallen, the man who had watched over her in Paris. Crest had called in a favor with the retired Army Sergeant Major, who had been visiting his granddaughter in France. While Emily and Jax had been taking care of business at home, it seemed that Aunt Beatrice had been taking care of another.

"Well, it was nice that he could attend," Aunt Beatrice replied, suddenly seeming more interested in the lace of her dress.

"Chartering a boat on Lake Minnetonka was a great idea," Taryn said, giving Aunt Beatrice a reprieve. Emily winked at her and when Taryn returned the smile, her lips didn't quite meet her eyes. Emily studied her, noticing the slight shadows underneath her eyes that she tried to unsuccessfully hide with makeup. Jax mentioned that whatever Taryn and Crest had spoken about remained between them and it was obvious that she didn't want to talk about it. "Add on top a wedding at sunset, and it couldn't be more romantic. I hope you have lots of taxis waiting for when we dock though. This group won't be in any condition to drive."

"Isn't that the truth," Lauren mumbled between pins that she held between her lips. She was currently on her knees, regardless that she was wearing a pink bridesmaid dress. "Turn slightly."

It sounded like *urn ity*, but Emily got the gist. Adjusting her low heels an inch to the right, Lauren continued to fix whatever she felt was wrong with the dress. It had something to do with the blue sapphires that were sewn into the bottom. Emily had asked Lauren to do so after she saw the gems she'd adorned in the nipple and clit clamps that Emily now wore underneath the dress. Those cruel devices made Emily want the ceremony over with so that she and Jax could enjoy their honeymoon. They'd chartered a separate yacht which would be waiting upon their return to the dock for just that reason.

"Knock-knock."

Emily looked up to see Elle step into the small room which had been designated as the bride's changing room. It was small, but when Aunt Beatrice excused herself to check on Roger, Elle slipped right in and joined the fray.

"Oh, Emily, you look beautiful!"

"That's what Aunt Beatrice said, but this one won't let me see," Emily replied wryly, patting Lauren's head. She mumbled something but didn't look up. "And look who's talking. That green dress is stunning!"

Elle waved away the compliment. Emily noticed that she was quite good at that, but her defenses weren't going to mean a thing if Kevin decided he really wanted her. Jax had mentioned just the other day that when the two of them were in the same room he could cut the tension with a knife. When Emily had mentioned they should have both of them over for dinner, Jax fanatically shook his head and mumbled that it wouldn't be such a good idea. She could have sworn he mentioned something about paybacks being a bitch, but he'd already switched topics.

"I just wanted you to know that everyone is ready. So the minute you open this door, I'll have the music start."

"I appreciate your help, Elle." It was Jax who suggested asking Elle to help with the wedding details, especially when the medicine for the morning sickness had stopped doing its job. Fortunately, she was now in her second trimester and her body seemed to have adjusted to having J.J. around. "I wouldn't have been able to pull this off without you."

"My pleasure," Elle replied, giving her a real smile. With another wave she was gone.

"That's my cue to grab my seat." Taryn stepped forward, giving Emily a light hug. "Ethan mentioned he snuck in popcorn. No worries. I see the horror on your face. I promise that he'll put it away before you walk down the aisle, but I'm not missing the look on Jax's face when he sees Ethan kicked back and enjoying the show."

Emily was aghast that Ethan would try to push Jax's buttons on his wedding day, but then had she really expected anything different? Separately, they came across as serious men and each had their own unique personalities. Put them together and they became frat boys. She had no idea how Taryn put up with them. Lauren spit out the pins that were in her mouth in a coughing fit from what Emily assumed had started in laughter.

"I don't know what you're laughing at," Emily said, a teasing smile on her lips. "Weren't you the center of attention the other night?"

Lauren's cheeks got as red as her hair and had she not had a twinkle in her green eyes, Emily would have felt bad about ribbing her on her first scene at the club. It was actually beautiful to watch and from what Jax explained, very cathartic for the two of them. Connor had her situated on the St. Andrew's cross and had executed a light flogging scene. Lauren had shared with Emily her deep-seated fear regarding bondage and how Connor was helping her deal with her phobia.

Jax and Emily had decided to hold off playing at the club until after the baby was born. A couple reasons went into that decision. One, she wasn't sure she was ready, although would leave that choice in Jax's hands. He knew her mind and body better than she did. He had been letting her watch from the bar area and she was getting used to the atmosphere. It was a hell of a lot different than their scening in private. Two, her morning sickness had taken over and Emily really didn't want to throw up in front of a room full of people.

"You're just jealous," Lauren quipped, picking up the fallen pins and then standing up on her high heels. "Taryn, what do you think of the finished project?"

"I've never seen a more beautiful bride."

"I concur," Crest said, having walked into the room. "Taryn, can you go swipe the popcorn bowl that Ethan brought? Jax looks ready to shove the kernels down his throat."

"On it."

With that, Taryn left the room. Lauren leaned in and kissed Emily on the cheek, whispering her the best of luck. Before Emily could turn and look at herself, Lauren whisked past Crest and was out the door. Taking in a deep stutter of air, she turned and faced the mirror. The woman standing before her was a woman in love.

Baby's breath was entwined like a halo into her hair, which was up on the sides and wrapped around in a stylish flair that Lauren had fashioned. The rest of her hair draped down her back. Emily's cheeks shimmered from a glow that only Jax could acquire, while her blue eyes sparkled with life. The form-fitting gown glittered with gems that Lauren had sewn on in various places, although Emily's favorite were the sapphires at the bottom of her dress that matched her nipple and clit clamps she was wearing underneath.

"They're waiting, Emily."

Tearing her eyes away from the mirror, Emily turned back around. She wondered why Crest was still in the room. All she needed to do was grab the red rose she would carry with her upon her walk to where Jax waited along the bow of the boat.

As she thought of why Crest was still in front of her, a cold feeling swarmed her.

"Did Ryland—"

"No, no," Crest replied, holding both palms up to her as if to ward off any omen she may have put forth bringing up his name. "I'm sorry. I didn't even stop to think what my presence might mean to you. I was just going to offer to walk you down the aisle."

Emily couldn't contain the shock that must have crossed her face. Crest was a hard man to read and she wasn't sure what he thought of her and Jax getting married. Crest hadn't said much during their time in New York and he'd been so preoccupied with other cases since things had returned to normal that they hadn't really had time to sit down and get to know one another.

"I realize that I'm not exactly a father figure, and please, whatever you do, don't look toward me as one either," Crest said with a half smile. "But as I've told the team numerous times, we are a family. A dysfunctional one, but one nonetheless. I'd be honored to be the one to give Jax his future wife."

"I'd like that," Emily said, feeling tears sting her eyes. They were a family and J.J. would have the best uncles and aunts a child could ask for. "As would Jax."

"Then let's not keep him waiting."

Crest reached over to the small table that contained her rose and picked it up, holding it out for her. Gently taking it from his hands, Emily placed her hand in the crook of his arm. Just as Elle promised, the moment the door opened, soft music started. Crest escorted her to where a red runner led the way to her future husband. It lay between the white wooden chairs where their family sat to watch her and Jax exchange their vows.

Jessie caught her eye and the vivacious brunette seemed to have trouble taking her eyes off of Crest. When she saw that Emily was looking, she quickly looked away. It was a shocking revelation that Jessie obviously didn't view Crest as a father figure, when in fact the difference in years could very well make that case. Did Jax know this?

All thought fled of everyone and everything the moment she laid eyes on Jax. He stood at the bow of the boat in a tuxedo that seemed tailor made just for him. The way his broad shoulders looked as the jacket molded to his upper body was beyond compare to what she just saw in the mirror. His blonde hair was trimmed, but there was more than enough for her fingers to grab hold if needed. As gorgeous as the man appeared, it was his eyes that stole her breath. Even from here, the brown flecks shimmered brighter than the sun that was setting behind him and glinting off of the water.

"He's waiting."

Emily absently nodded, knowing Crest was right, but wanting to embed this image in her brain. The past two and half years faded and all that mattered was what was standing before her. If someone came and told her now that she would have to do it all over again in order to be with Jax, Emily wouldn't hesitate. Their love, their life, and their family had been well worth it. This was the life she was meant to have.

Ryland lay on the cot he'd been given, resting his hands on his stomach. The time had arrived that the transfer of another prisoner would take place. He found it comical that these federal employees thought their facility was impervious from escape. He'd had strategies in place for this exact scenario. Those people involved knew what to do and it was only a matter of time before it was him in that armored truck, driving to an awaiting plane. He'd spent many years cultivating the right contacts should he need them. The time spent was well worth it.

He started to hum the Vivaldi concerto that had been recurrent in his thoughts. The music reminded him of Crest, although there was no need to dwell on things that couldn't be changed. The notes lingered in the air as if they were soaring in the air. Ryland felt more relaxed now that things were about to be set in motion.

Anger was a wasted emotion. Crest and his team had made a strategic move on the board, and although they thought the game had come to an end, it was far from over. He appreciated a good opponent and would bide his time for when it was time to enter the match. He had many things to accomplish and didn't want to waste anymore time.

Money was the source of all evil, and in this case, it had bought his freedom. It did give credence to the old saying, but he looked upon freedom as a gift. It just happened to be the one thing he never took for granted. One just had to have money to keep it. It was a good thing he had it in spades.

Ryland opened his eyes, but instead of the ceiling, he saw the beautiful face of Taryn Emmeline Sisal. He wondered what her thoughts on freedom were.

✧　✧　✧　✧

"You nervous?"

"No," Jax answered Connor's question, shaking his head. "Not a bit. Look at her. She's so goddamned radiant, she's like a beacon."

The soft music drifted through the speakers as the boat sailed through the still waters. Jax knew the sunset was behind him, but he only had eyes for Emily. She'd picked out a lovely gown, but it in no way compared to her beauty. The sapphires adorning her dress didn't come close to rivaling the vivaciousness that shone in her eyes. He would forever remember this moment and couldn't wait to share it with their son or daughter. He or she deserved to know how strong of a woman his or her mother was in her quest to assure them this moment.

"I've heard all pregnant women get that glow." Connor shrugged his shoulders beside him and Jax resisted the urge to shove him overboard. Jax knew it was his partner's way of lessening his nerves, but he didn't need to. Jax hadn't lied. There was nothing more right than what was about to happen. "You know—"

"Boyo, if you don't want to end up in that water…"

Connor chuckled, but remained silent as Jax returned to admiring the view before him. Crest slowly walked Emily down the red runner, each step bringing her closer to him. He made a mental note to thank Crest for taking the initiative so that she hadn't had to make the walk by herself. Hell, he needed to thank every one of his friends for even making this possible.

"Did you set up everything I need on the yacht we'll be taking out for the weekend?" Jax asked, wanting to assure himself that all was completed to his specifications.

"Yes," Connor replied in a low tone as Crest and Emily were almost upon them. "Although the person you rented it from thinks you're going to burn his boat down. I had to up your deposit."

"I'll repay the favor when you and Lauren decide to take the plunge." Jax held out his hand, loving the feel of Emily's warm fingers slipping into his.

"I wouldn't have it any other way."

If the Justice of the Peace thought that Jax could wait until the end of the ceremony to claim those perfect pink lips, he could join Connor overboard. Dipping her at the waist, he caught her cry of surprise and took his fill. She was fucking delicious.

Neither one of them heard the hoots and hollers from their family.

Epilogue

Crest stood on the stern, watching the moonlight dance off of the wake of the boat. Placing the fat cap of the Gurkha His Majesty's Reserve into his mouth, he drew on the tobacco until his mouth was full of the spiced cognac flavor. Savoring it for a moment, he parted his lips and released the smoke. It was a picturesque way to end the evening.

The elite team that he'd handpicked had survived an assignment that could have easily destroyed them. They'd overcome not only emotional hurdles but the life threatening ones as well. Life was particular in the challenges that it put in their paths. The one thing they needed to take from this was that they worked better as a team than they did separately. Crest had a feeling that they were going to need that solidarity in the future.

"That was a very sweet gesture," Jessie said, her soft voice carrying on the wind.

Crest knew that she was referring to walking Emily down the aisle, but he didn't want to make a fuss about something that had just been common courtesy. Unfortunately, he didn't know what else to discuss with Jessie unless it was in regards to work and that shouldn't intrude on such a night.

"The boat should be pulling into the dock at any moment." Crest didn't bother to turn around to see if he was right. The moons location told him all he needed to know. "Until I'm satisfied that we've mastered every last piece of this assignment, I'd like you to remain cautious."

"Does that mean going with the group to Masters?"

Crest heard the challenge in her voice but refused to rise to the level in which it was thrown. She'd lose. Jessie was too young to understand what kind of man he was and what made him who he was. She should have the chance to maintain her innocence and he wouldn't be the one to take it.

"If that's what you want to do." Crest made sure his voice didn't falter. He paused long enough to take another draw on his cigar. He should have had that scotch he'd been offered earlier. "Just be safe, sane, and consensual."

Crest's warning was three-fold. Yes, he wanted her to be careful in her personal safety, but she also needed to know what she was getting into. He was well aware that she was playing in the club and had no doubt she originally did it to get a reaction out of him. He declined to be drawn into her little games. If she kept pushing him, he might be tempted to show her that it wasn't a game to him. That would be bad for both of them.

"Goodnight, Gavin."

Crest refused to place an emotion to the softness of her voice. She was too young to know what she was feeling. He felt the boat pulling into the dock. Jessie walked away without waiting for a reply, joining in with Ethan and Kevin as they made their way to the wooden pier. He let himself turn and watch her graceful figure step over the side. It surprised him that she didn't turn back to look his way, but then again, wasn't that what he wanted?

The vibration of Crest's phone kept him from exiting with the group. Holding the cigar with his lips, he reached into the jacket of his suit and retrieved his cell. Entering the proper code, he waited for the message to appear in the display. Taking the cigar and placing it between his fingers, he read the words. Kevin's latest case had just taken a turn.

Hearing laughter drifting down from the marina, Crest slowly followed suit. Tonight was a night for celebration. He wouldn't take that away from any of them. Tomorrow could wait.

~ THE END ~

Continue reading for special bonus content...

Cowboy Command

Cowboy Justice Association, Book One

The waitress refilled their coffees and bustled away. Seth looked around the diner and then leaned forward in his chair. "That was Evan on the phone."

Her body stiffened in response. She'd almost forgotten why she was in this town. It was easy to forget as she became more involved in her new life and less enmeshed in the old. Tampa seemed very far away at the moment.

"What did he want?" She waited for the answer. Just when she thought her life was her own again, something came along to disabuse that notion.

"He said they're ready to convene the Grand Jury. They're ready to indict Simon. They need your testimony."

This was why they were protecting her. She'd always known that fact. She sipped her coffee and tried to appear nonchalant. "When and where?"

Seth was gazing at her, his eyebrows raised. It was clear he wasn't convinced she was as calm as she looked.

"Tampa Federal Courthouse. December tenth. He gave me the name of a hotel for us that will have their protection. We can fly you in and out quickly."

She nodded. "They get what they want and I get my life back. It's a fair trade."

Seth fiddled with his spoon. "Evan didn't say anything about you being released from protection."

"Did you ask?"

"No," Seth admitted. "I was busy getting the logistics for getting you in and out of Tampa."

"Out? Evan said back out then?"

"He did." Seth nodded. "I can call him back for you if you like." She shook her head, holding her coffee cup with both hands and letting the warmth of the ceramic seep into her cold fingers. "There's no need. It sounds like he made things clear. It appears the plan is for me to come back here, at least for a little while. I just want to get this over with. I'm not sure I know anything that's going to help them."

Disappointment at having to come back to Harper warred with happiness at getting more time with Seth. When the time came, she had to admit she would miss him. She genuinely liked him and there weren't many men she could say that about.

Seth sipped his coffee. "Did you see anything that made you wonder what was going on? Anything at all?"

Presley felt a flash of annoyance. If she said no, she was an oblivious idiot and if she said yes, it made her look foolish and weak. It was a stupid, no-win question and she didn't like it at all.

"How do you want me to answer that, Seth? Would it be better if I was totally ignorant or if I suspected something but did nothing? Which is better to you?"

Seth scraped his hand down his face. "I'm not accusing you of anything, honey. It was just a question."

"It was a trick question. Like if I asked you if my butt looked big in these jeans. If you say yes, well, then I have an oversized load and you won't get sex for the foreseeable future. If you say no, well, do I have a big, fat ass and it just looks small in these particular jeans or do I not have a big butt? Either way? You're not getting laid."

That got a peek of a smile out of Seth. "I promise no matter which way you answer, I'll have sex with you."

She thought about kicking him in the shin but she wasn't the violent type. "I don't think I know anything. I clearly remember the invoices and emails, but I never saw anything that looked out of place. I'm going out on a limb here as I'm not a criminal, but I doubt they'd leave a paper trail of their illegal activities."

Seth nodded. "I've found that criminals are rarely very bright but I've never dealt with something like selling arms to terrorists. How does one even do that?"

Presley shrugged. "I have no idea. Nothing I saw in email or paper even hinted at something like that."

Seth stroked his chin. "I bet there were a lot of emails, though. It would be hard, if not impossible, to remember details like that months later."

Presley pushed away her empty coffee cup. "I have a good memory, Seth. I didn't see anything that raised any flags. Besides, the longer I worked there, the more Randall had me working on personal things. He was having his house renovated and he asked me to manage the project. It was practically a full time job. I wasn't in the office much the last four months."

She'd only worked for him for six. The fact was she hadn't spent much time at all in the office learning the business.

Seth picked up his hat. "My job is to make sure you get to Tampa safe and sound, not to try and figure out this case. That's Evan's job, thankfully. Are you ready?"

Presley pulled on her coat and gloves. "Where are we going?"

"To the store to buy a turkey, then to Mom's to tell her why we bought her a turkey."

Presley felt her face get warm. "Why don't you let me buy the turkey since it's my fault and all?"

"No way, honey." Seth laughed. "It wasn't your fault. It was mine. I should have known better."

He was taking the whole turkey hunting thing much better than earlier. "I still think you should let me buy the turkey."

"I have another way you can pay."

She heard the promise in his words and felt her body get very warm indeed. "Oh yeah? What did you have in mind?"

Seth leaned down and whisper raunchy, filthy suggestions in her ear. "Do we have time before your shift?" she asked.

He glanced at his watch. "If we buy a turkey, and visit with Mom for a little while, I'm thinking we'll have the entire afternoon to explore those ideas."

Presley grinned. "Let's get this show on the road, Sheriff."

She let Seth lead the way and watched the sway of his very fine ass in front of her. The day was turning out much better than it had started.

About the Author

First and foremost, I love life. I love that I'm a wife, mother, daughter, sister…and a writer.

I am one of the lucky women in this world who gets to do what makes them happy. As long as I have a cup of coffee (maybe two or three) and my laptop, the stories evolve themselves and I try to do them justice. I draw my inspiration from a retired Marine Master Sergeant that swept me off of my feet and has drawn me into a world that fulfills all of my deepest and darkest desires. Erotic romance, military men, intrigue, with a little bit of kinky chili pepper (his recipe), fill my head and there is nothing more satisfying than making the hero and heroine fulfill their destinies.

Thank you for having joined me on their journeys…

Email:
kennedylayneauthor@gmail.com

Facebook:
https://www.facebook.com/kennedy.layne.94

Twitter:
https://twitter.com/KennedyL_Author

Website:
www.kennedylayne.com

Newsletter:
http://www.kennedylayne.com/newsletter.html

Books by
Kennedy Layne

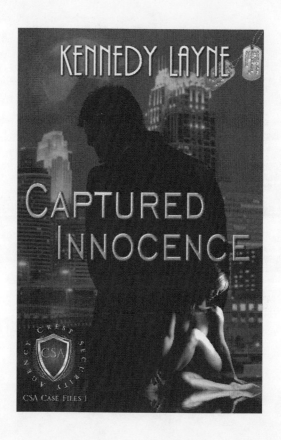

KENNEDY LAYNE

CAPTURED
INNOCENCE

CSA
CREST SECURITY AGENCY

CSA Case Files 1

Captured Innocence
(CSA Case Files 1)

When former Marine, Connor Ortega, was ordered into the offices of Crest Security Agency on a Saturday morning, he didn't expect the latest case to hit so close to home. A submissive has been murdered in a particularly vicious manner and to bring her killer to justice, he must go undercover. Not hard to do considering he's already part of the BDSM lifestyle.

Lauren Bailey, a local vendor of bejeweled erotic implements, lives vicariously through her clients due to her fear of bondage. When Connor's dominant side can't resist trying to ease her anxieties, she accepts his proposal and agrees to his one stipulation…keep things casual.

When the killer sets his sights on Lauren, Connor is forced to rethink their relationship. He has the training it takes to catch a murderer, but does he have the courage to escape his inner demons and capture Lauren's heart?

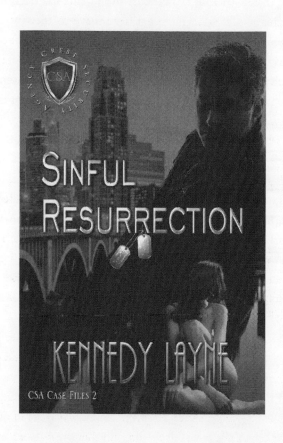

SINFUL
RESURRECTION

KENNEDY LAYNE

CSA CASE FILES 2

Sinful Resurrection
(CSA Case Files 2)

Sins of the past have been resurrected, predetermining their path to love. Can they overcome the treacherous obstacles set before them?

Jax Christensen likes his life just the way it is. He has his work, his club, and the occasional naked submissive to take his mind off everything else. He doesn't talk about the past, as there is no point in reminiscing about things that cannot be altered. His chest has an empty hole where his heart used to be, but he's grown accustomed to the constant pain. It's become the only thing that reminds Jax that he's alive.

Emily Weiss has never forgotten the one and only man she's ever loved. She's hidden for two long years in an attempt to protect Jax and herself, desperate to try and stay one step ahead of those who want her dead. She has information that could destroy the United Nations. Unfortunately, they want to eliminate her first. Emily's exhausted and wants more than anything to feel safe once more. That was how she felt in Jax's strong arms and she longs to be there again.

When Jax sees that Emily has risen from the grave, his heart and soul are full of anger and regret. He'll never forgive her lies and deception. He will, however, keep her safe. He hates her for what she's done, but he doesn't want her death on his conscience. He'll protect her and then walk away.

Secrets are revealed and the danger is more sinister and deadly than anyone could have guessed. Jax and Emily are forced on the run and the passion they once felt for one another burns even hotter and brighter the second time around. Jax doesn't know how he'll walk away this time or if he even wants to. Emily is determined to expose a high-level official within the United Nations and walk away unscathed. She wants a second chance with her first love—even if it kills her.

29940752R00221

Made in the USA
Lexington, KY
12 February 2014